Additional Acclaim for *Fixer Chao*

"*Fixer Chao* is . . . an original and perversely entertaining creation: a luminous picaresque with a distinctive mixture of farce and savagery." —*Kirkus Reviews* (starred review)

"This superb and scathingly satirical first novel paints a fiercely condemning portrait of a shallow and overprivileged upper class. Highly recommended." —*Library Journal* (starred review)

"Ong sets his hook early, a mix of striking language and provocative despair that—as in Denis Johnson's best work—compels the adventurous reader to follow. . . . *Fixer Chao* is a powerful satire." —Stewart O'Nan, *The Hartford Courant*

"[An] unforgettable debut novel . . . Ong's brilliant dissection of spiritual shopping and class difference and racism is breathtaking. Every page offers food for thought. . . . By turns insightfully brilliant and laugh-out-loud hilarious." —Susan Larson, *New Orleans Times-Picayune*

"A wickedly knowing satire . . . By turns funny and dark, *Fixer Chao* should make Ong a fixture on many urban bookshelves." —Colin Covert, *Minneapolis Star Tribune*

"[An] assured first novel . . . mordantly funny." —Kera Bolonik, *The New York Times Book Review*

"Skewers the so-called Beautiful People in New York City with laser-sharp accuracy." —*People* Magazine

"Stylish and wickedly wrought." —*Elle*

"Appealingly skewed . . . clever." —*W* Magazine

"Bitingly funny . . . A fast-paced send-up of Manhattan's trend-obsessed culture."
—*Time Out New York*

"Written with acidic wit, Ong's novel is sharp and savvy, smashing sacred cows casually but forcefully. . . . [It] paints painfully contrasting pictures of privileged society and New York's underbelly, of which Ong offers an invigoratingly clearheaded view."
—*Publishers Weekly*

"Casting a cool, satirical eye on the herd movement and exotic fetishism of the tastemaker class, this first novel is equally sensitive to Chao's ambivalent seduction by the new world he inhabits."
—*The New Yorker*

"Definitely a sit up and take notice book on the literary scene."
—Susan Farrington, *The Sanford Herald*

"A deliciously mean send-up . . . [a] sharp debut novel . . . Ong is a writer of great style."
—Erica Saunders, *Newsday*

"A brisk, glitter-studded catalog of the ways people deceive and are deceived, over and again."
—Paul Maliszewski, *The Review of Contemporary Fiction*

"An extremely satisfying and even moving novel . . . [it] confirms that [Ong's] fierce, edgy prose translates beautifully to the written page. The result is an unrelenting aria of high bitchiness and scathing satire."
—Amy Benfer, Salon.com

Fixer
Chao

Fixer
Chao

* * *

HAN ONG

Picador USA
Farrar, Straus and Giroux
New York

Picador® is a U.S. registered trademark and is used by Farrar, Straus and
Giroux under license from Pan Books Limited.

For information on Picador USA Reading Group Guides, as well as
ordering, please contact the Trade Marketing department at
St. Martin's Press.
Phone: 1-800-221-7945 extension 763
Fax: 212-677-7456
E-mail: trademarketing@stmartins.com

Library of Congress Cataloging-in-Publication Data
Ong, Han.
    Fixer Chao: a novel / Han Ong.—1st Picador USA ed.
        p. cm.
    ISBN 0-312-42053-6
    1. Swindlers and swindling—Fiction. 2. Asian Americans—Fiction.
3. New York (N.Y.)—Fiction. 4. Rich people—Fiction. 5. Feng
shui—Fiction. 6. Authors—Fiction. I. Title.

PS3565.N58 F5 2002
813'.6—dc21   2001051010

First published in the United States by Farrar, Straus and Giroux

First Picador USA Edition: April 2002

10 9 8 7 6 5 4 3 2 1

PART 1

* * *

Beware the life you earn.

Most days I can't take a drink quick enough. Then I wait for that moment. A square of pure light to open up in my head. I peer inside, looking at the many things that I could, if I wanted to, still be. Time being elastic during these moments, it seems like my entire youth is still before me, instead of already half over.

I could be a writer . . . I'd been saying this for years, but the furthest I'd gotten was only to try out sentences in my head like a radio broadcast formulated to pass terse comment on my life and on others', but which I never bothered to write down to see if I had any of the essential ingredients: clarity, focus, insight, concision, the ownership of something to say. I needed to muster a continuous sobriety, instead of the intermittent bouts—full of great, promising starts that go on to crash with a condemnation best described as orchestral— that kept passing through my life like a tease of the worst sort. A writer, hmmm, a writer. I knew how to type, that was one thing. My mother put me in secretary school to get me out of her hair one sum-mer. My fingers danced on a keyboard, revealing their autonomy from the rest of my body. For several years that was how I supported myself. I worked typing up the awful, turgid manuscripts of wan-nabe writers—I charged seventy-five cents a page, undercutting the going rate of a dollar a page. Looking back on it, I realize that that was a stupid thing to do. This was before the predominance of the personal computer when every white-out-covered mistake stood out on the page like a signal flare. My typing was immaculate. That alone would have recommended me, guaranteed that I got more work. Why did I have to continually undercut myself, filled with the pathetic belief that I was a loser with a target on the forehead? Well OK, I *am* a loser, but hey, my typing speed: it was in the range of 120 words a minute. And the mistakes, no one could find any.

For a while I answered phones at an employment agency, a job re-quiring a good voice—which I had—and only light typing skills. But that didn't last long because I soon discovered that I resented having to speak to people. My hands were all I was willing to give. Take my hands, but leave the rest of me alone. And also, it required me to ap-pear presentable, and I was still young enough not to see that getting out of bed and going straight to work bringing the face that I had ac-quired during the night was far from socially acceptable.

Today, it takes me about forty minutes to an hour of reviewing myself in front of a mirror before I'll step out. I want to minimize the chance of anyone pointing to me on the streets and laughing, echo-ing my thoughts. This is my routine: I wash my face to get rid of ex-cess oil, put Chap Stick on my thick lips to replenish the moisture that washing accidentally takes out, and then comb my hair and set it in place with hair spray that I choose for the ability to hold but not stiffen. By the time I get out the door, I'm about as human as I'll ever be.

Then I was a mail clerk for the city's Workers' Compensation claims department. I pushed a metal cart that was a bulkier version of a supermarket cart up and down three floors, distributing mail that I had previously sorted and then rubber-banded together. I would leave these packets at the desks of the lawyers' secretaries, whom I didn't get to know beyond their bright, sunshiny names: Mary, Violet, Clarita, Sara, Jamina.

Later, I worked as a data entry clerk for Arco, the big oil company notorious for owning the tanker that spilled millions of gallons of crude oil into the waters surrounding some part of Alaska. My stint there was postdisaster, but it didn't seem to have bothered me one bit. This is what I'm trying to grow out of: the unwillingness to see that I am connected, even if by the thinnest of threads, to everything else. I remember only that I sat on a stiff chair that had wheels which I couldn't resist sliding back and forth, back and forth, to alleviate the soul-destroying repetitiveness of my task. I stared into a green screen; that at least was helpful. My favorite color, the color of trees, of grass, of certain kinds of ice cream that tickle the tongue, ice cream with names that seem like nothing remotely sugary could be extracted from them: avocado, green tea, pistachio. The screen was green, and the cursor blinking to be filled in like an outstanding debt was a lighter-shaded green, psychedelic in its insistent winking. I keyed code numbers into the boxes that asked for project headings. What these "projects" were I was never quite sure of. I typed names of employees, their titles and designations, locations pertinent to these reports, comments. Comments written by whom? Come to think of it, I wasn't sure of anything that I was typing. It all became abstract: merely speed and touch; keystrokes like paddling in water until I could get to the first fifteen-minute break.

I was supervised in this job by a kindly black woman who looked like a newscaster with her helmet of stiff hair and her repertoire of suits and skirts that always made her look older than she was. Whom did she go home to at the end of each day? It made me sad to think of her unlocking the door to an empty place. A pet—a cat perhaps—the sole witness to her life. But how come that sadness never touched my own thoughts about myself, when the same scenario—minus the cat—was the exact one I lived through? Well, for starters, the word "bachelor" seemed fine, unlimned by bad vibes, unlike "spinster," a word conjuring a winter tree, spindly branches reaching upward in torment.

And then through referral from a friend, I went to work for an old Jewish woman, a survivor of the camps who paid me to type up her memoirs, which she dictated on the spot. The job was frustrating because it required me to supress my natural instinct to improve on another's words. Her grammar slipped in and out, in a touching v.ay that I've only seen white people pull off. Have a colored person speak the same way and immediately you'd yell: English only! And also, her locution was disastrous, sentences that snaked back and forth and then back again until you weren't sure how everything had begun and where you were in relation to two beats ago, in a way that I'm sure would've sent James Joyce into fits of epileptic jealousy. A joke about Irish writers, somewhat applicable to this Jewish woman: Get to the verb!

Here is a sample sentence:

Nowadays walking these ugly gray streets called New York City and seeing American friends going from shopping back to house and we stop on the streets and say many things, saying hi, things like that, also we ask each other about so-and-so, how is so-and-so we ask, and usually so-and-so, for example Mrs. Heifetz from originally Kraków, is fine, always fine, maybe a little under the weather, maybe suffering from like King Lear where the ingratitude of children is sharper than a serpent's tooth, but always, still, fine, and then one day I will hear that so-and-so is dead, and of course immediately I think when will be my time, but after that, I always think, my God, Mrs. Heifetz the Nazis did not succeed in killing, but eventually she is gone to pneumonia, or high blood pressure, or arterial blocking, you know what that is, that is thickness of the blood in the heart or somewhere that blocks the blood from getting to your parts, but that is not a feeling that's so bad because eventually we all have to go, but what is worse is this other feeling, this experience of walking the streets one day and you see a revelation, my God right there half a block away from me, standing at the corner of Eightieth and Broadway near Zabar's, my God isn't that Mrs. Heifetz and you go running, screaming all the time, Mrs. Heifetz Mrs. Heifetz! and you look closer and it's not Mrs. Heifetz at all but someone with the exact same face but a different name, and you become ashamed of making such an unnecessary farce, I mean fuss, and after shame comes such a sadness, big big kind of sadness, like you realize the streets are full of ghosts now, more ghosts than living kind of people, and the way someone stands, something very simple like that, or the way the sun happens to be hitting someone's face or their clothes, will bring back for a very brief moment, your entire life of friends and acquaintances, and yes, even enemies who are now all dead and who you wish they were alive today so you could forgive them, and yes, be forgiven by them, be-cause life, yes life is so precious.

How did I know that that was one sentence? Well, the woman spoke so fast that the comma seemed the only response, like those notations comic-book writers would put at the heels of superheroes to indicate flight, or departure, which was exactly the way she spoke.

She called me *boychik*, her voice going up and down, and it made me afraid because I thought this meant she saw through what I con-cealed from her: that I was a big fag: *chick boy*. But seeing my face seize, she explained: It's the word for young boy in Yiddish.

But all these were things I had been.

What would I be?

This was exactly my frame of mind when, sitting at a bar in the Times Square area called the Savoy, a place frequented by hustlers and transvestite hookers way past their prime and by junkies who resembled stick figures and moved as if struggling underwater—a bar I went to because I liked its sad, defeated air, and because it helped remind me of everything I was afraid of becoming—it was while sitting in there, nursing the first of what would be a million shots of cheap tequila, that Shem C walked into my life.

hem C was a Jew. His eyes sloped up at the sides, giving him a Far Eastern look, but his pupils were the cool gray of steel. His name was given to him by his father. He told me it was the Yiddish word for name. I told him I knew another Yiddish word: *boychik*. OK, he said, I can see we'll get along. Where did his father get the name? From Joyce, Shem replied, and then proceeded to recite a passage from *Ulysses* with the word "shem" in it. Oh wow, was all I could think to say.

But first we had to slog through an opener like this:

Are you a Chink? Shem asked, sidling up to me at the bar. Up until then he had been just another silhouette with red eyes glowing in the dark, the kind of thing that made you think, and nine times out of ten you'd be right, forewarned: Out for meat!

What? I turned to him, surprised out of my stupor. What had I been thinking about before he'd disturbed me? Oh right: What would I be . . . And I was right in that quicksand place when . . .

You a Chink? Shem repeated.

It took me only a few seconds to regain my composure. Flip, I replied.

Flip? What's that?

Filipino.

What's that?

(Is this guy kidding?) Philippines, man.

Philippines, he pronounced, making it sound fictional. That a place?

Country.

Wow.

Well I wouldn't go that far.

You being sarcastic?

Duh.

Listen. Don't make fun of me. His tone was hurt.

No one's making fun of no one. Relax.

Can I buy you a drink? he asked.

What for?

What do you mean what for? This is a bar. You buy people drinks.

I considered for a moment. OK. Sure.

What're you having?

Tequila, I replied. And tell them not to water it down.

He motioned for the bartender, Barney, a thin bookish type who looked wrong in a place like this, like Jesus in the midst of lepers. But when he fixed your drinks, turning everything into rainwater, you realized he was just as snaky as the rest. Another tequila for this young gentleman right here, Shem told Barney, indicating my nodding figure.

Barney laughed, replying, He ain't no gentleman.

He put a shot glass in front of me. I raised it in front of Shem's face to let him see what he was paying for, said, Cheers, then knocked it back in one try.

An expert, Shem declared approvingly.

Then he whispered: The guy over there said you suck cock.

Excuse me?

You heard me.

What guy? I asked.

Over there. He pointed to a mummy figure whom even a six-year-old would know not to trust.

Well, I replied, he's got a big mouth, maybe you should be interviewing him for the job.

Oh no no no. I wanna be clear. I'm not looking to get my cock sucked.

Why did you ask then? I replied in a tone of great indignation.

I just wanted to know how low you could go.

What's that mean, how low can you go?

Limbo. You know the limbo? How low can you go?

I'm in this bar, ain't I?

My point exactly.

So why do you even have to ask?

Just want to double-check. So talk to me. I told you my name. Now tell me something about you. He took a millisecond pause, and then: Besides the fact that you suck cock.

Fuck you. I moved several barstools down from this Shem who should've been called Sham instead.

He came over to me and apologized. His face was crooked, suggesting how rarely the word "sorry" ever crossed his lips, and because of this I thought it would be ungracious not to accept.

Another drink? he asked.

Sure.

Bartender, another—Shem looked at me and asked, Tequila? I nodded. Bartender, another tequila for this young man. And one for me too.

Barney slithered over with two shot glasses, pounding the counter in front of us. He was eyeing Shem with a look of: Is this guy gonna stiff me?

What's wrong with you? I asked.

Barney looked straight between my eyebrows, as if at a third eye. What's wrong with *you*?

I showed him my throat as I chugged down the drink.

Shem, on the other hand, took a faggy sip. Ow, he said, like being burned.

Whatsa matter? I asked.

Do you know, he asked me, that tequila's the hardest form of liquor for the liver to process?

What's that mean?

It destroys the liver over the long haul.

Good, I replied, I can't wait to die. I blinked. Then looked away. My God, why did I say stupid things like that?

Barney eyed the scene to our right with a laconic distaste. People were singing along to the jukebox or talking to themselves. Also, they rubbed their bodies against the vinyl of the small booths, making what sounded like kissy-smoochy sounds. Barney looked away. Everything he did was filled with an implication of wearing a space suit. Why work in a place like this and act like a messenger from God?

He was standing in the center of a clock that radiated sunbeams made of tinfoil. The clock said one o'clock. Two of the sunbeams gave the illusion of being horns on Barney's head. I laughed. Barney moved away. Picking up a comic book from underneath the far end of the bar, he started to read, his sullen expression glued on.

Shem said, Wait a minute wait a minute.

I waited a minute.

Shem continued, OK, I remember what I wanted to say.

I waited another minute. My throat was scratchy but I didn't want to involve Barney again.

Shem spoke as if coming back from a trance. I approached you— God! He stopped suddenly. This tequila's not agreeing with me.

Are you kidding? I asked him. That's not even one hundred percent. It's one third water.

Still my stomach's not— Anyway.

Right, anyway.

Are you being sarcastic again?

Listen. You're not going to ask me to suck your cock, are you?

No.

Good. Cause I don't do that anymore.

Anymore, he repeated, italicizing.

We all get desperate sometimes you know, I told him.

I certainly do.

On his wrist was a fancy-looking watch. Looking at it, I dismissed that this man ever knew what desperation meant. But if that was so, what was he doing in this place that made everyone who walked through its doors partake of its cheapness and sorrow? Maybe like some drunks who wouldn't otherwise have the conviction of their drunkardness, he needed a place ugly enough to loosen his inhibitions.

Oh for heaven's sake, look at him, he's no drunk: one sip of diluted tequila and he's clutching his stomach!

Are you OK?

Fine. And to prove his point, he sat bolt upright. It's one o'clock, he said.

One-fifteen, I corrected.

It's one-fifteen.

I have to go, I told him. I was feeling sleepy. Ever since I turned thirty . . . My God the things I used to be able to do. It's true, I used to suck cocks. In fact, right outside this bar, not half a block away, was my former headquarters, the Port Authority Bus Terminal, where I had to compete with frisky Puerto Ricans and athletic black boys for a cut of the overweight white businessman business.

Cut a montage this way: Bathroom stall door in the men's room of the Port Authority Bus Terminal. Let it be a plain door, black or some blacklike color with the nickmarks of time cut into it. Door opens, a portly white gentleman, with a bald spot in the middle of his head, walks out. A sliver flashes between his exiting figure and the slowly closing door to reveal a young boy of twenty-one, -two, wearing a tight white T-shirt and black painter's pants. That's me! Jump cuts like a staccato radio beat: again and again the door opens to reveal yet another version of the first guy; they all make quick exits, adjust their zippers on the way out, heads bowed down, the better to showcase the tops of their heads. With few exceptions they are all bald or balding. They are on their way home to the suburbs. They've had disastrous days and want to take out their frustration on someone. I'm perfect, a skinny colored kid, almost like the ones they see a lot of nowadays on TV, except shabbier. They're witnessing their time in the spotlight stolen by a whole crew of new, mystifying faces. Or so they think. And they want somebody to pay, be humiliated, physically put under them like restoring their natural position in the world.

Another montage: a love chorus. Though one long sentence, attribute each segment to a separate talking head, forming a comic chain: Yeah suck that dick, come on fuckhead, that's it, take daddy's juicy dick in your hot mouth, isn't daddy's dick juicy, come on, yeah yeah yeah.

Sometimes the montage is interrupted by an errant scene, but whatever its nature, make sure to always run comedy through it.

Say someone comes in who really needs to shit, and seeing that all three stalls are taken up by two pairs of feet, he'll bang on the stall doors and yell: Hey, give it up, someone really needs to use the john and I don't mean you fatsos who can't get a decent date even if you had to pay for it!

Or say a policeman does a random sweep. When we open the doors, the johns sheepish and the boys roguish, think of the one-liners we've had to come up with: Sorry, Officer, I was just performing some Extreme Spunk—I mean, Extreme Unction.

Also cut in a brief scene at the sink. Stand the young boy there, washing his mouth out, gurgling discreetly as if the locale had shifted to some high-class place. He looks up and though he doesn't mean for it to happen, there he is staring back at himself in the scraped-into mirror. Quick, frightened look away. Then look back, curiosity getting the better of him. Quick cut to close-up: face bleached by the lights. Stay on the mirror as he turns his back, and as a retreating figure shrinks.

A second later, the mood turns. He's smiling, bounding up steps and counting his money. You only have to realize: one day this boy will be a typist. He will live in an apartment, paying rent on time. Money no longer the monstrous, lurking thing it used to be.

But back to Shem at the Savoy:

Can you come with me? he asked.

Where? I heard myself asking.

I'm staying at a hotel.

I told you—

And I told you. No sex. I'm straight. I don't want what you got to offer.

I ain't offering.

Well if you did—

Well I'm not.

Just come to my hotel. It'd be more conducive to conversation.

Which hotel? I asked.

The New Yorker.

This was a hotel near Madison Square Garden that I had always passed by but never, in the course of my ho'ing career, entered. It seemed to speak well for Shem C, but my head was like a quickly closing bloom, so I said: I'll take a rain check.

You sure?

I need to be asleep right now, I said.

You sure? he repeated.

Damn sure. (Though, of course, I felt the exact opposite . . . What would I be? What was that corner to be turned? And was it Shem who would show me the way?)

You be here tomorrow. He turned to motion to Barney. He laid down two tens and a five, which Barney retrieved with a small bow and took to the register.

What's tomorrow?

I didn't get a chance to talk.

About what?

Plans. Listen, I didn't approach you just to tell you the origins of my name, OK? For your information I got a plan. A plan that involves you.

A plan that involves me? I don't think so.

What're you afraid of? He reached into his pocket and produced a twenty. Here, he said, pushing it toward me on the bar. A sign of good faith. From me.

I don't want it, I said, although you could tell I was riveted.

Take it.

What for?

Cause I have it and you need it.

Smooth lines like that were a dead giveaway of something bad, but still I couldn't take my eyes off the twenty. I don't want it, I repeated.

He took the twenty between two fingers, did an origami move turning it into a cocaine pipe thing, and proceeded to shove it into my shirt pocket, which I didn't even recall being there. Be here tomorrow, he said.

I staggered home with the twenty next to my chest like a gift of plutonium. And the lights on the street, even when pushed to the outer edges of my vision, seemed to foretell one last fling with black things before I could pull myself up and write all about it later like looking back from a car speeding quickly away.

3

My good deed of the last few months was one that was easy, like breathing. It was to take care of someone whom I loved, Preciosa X. She lived downstairs from me and was in dire need of a new hip. She was biding her time, hoping for some last-minute miracle—a gift from God to reward her for her vestigial Catholicism—until she could no longer endure her situation, and then she would get herself an operation, which would set her back in the vicinity of fifteen thousand, a figure I couldn't even begin to wrap my brain around.

Preciosa, too, had come from the Philippines, preceding me by decades. She'd been in New York close to twenty years, and she, more than anyone I knew, had seen it change from one sure thing to another. Times Square, for instance. She remembered its seedy heyday, something I could only imagine, and in this imagining, build up into something unreachable and glamorous and sad as if history had passed me by.

I never thought I'd say this—she confessed one day—but when I find myself missing something about New York, something from the old days, I think about the smell of come.

The front door to our building also served as the front door to a joint called Peep Corner. The two words were done in neon with an eye blinking in between. It was a place where for twenty-five cents men could make wooden panels go up and view naked women dancing behind glass partitions. Twenty-five cents bought you exactly ninety seconds.

The joint was managed by two Indian brothers, Veejay and Sanjay, who wore serious expressions on their faces—as if they were sniffing some awful scent but couldn't locate its source—which made them look like deeply religious men inexplicably caught in hell, which, I suppose, was exactly what they intended. If they had wives, or girlfriends, they never allowed those women to come close to our building.

Veejay, the older one, worked in front, behind a glass counter that displayed sex goods. While Sanjay, the younger, sadder one, stood at the back, monitoring the entrance to the viewing booths. No one could go past without having bought at least five dollars' worth of tokens from Veejay up front, and Sanjay made sure of this, checking every man's palm as he entered. It was a job he didn't care for because he wasn't protected from what he saw as the contamination of the men by anything like Veejay's glass counter.

Inside stood another family member, a distant cousin named Neil, who did odd jobs, like replacing lightbulbs or like mopping the floors inside the booths in between customers. His sense of smell had been dulled by the Lysol he'd had to use, and as a consequence, he could no longer distinguish one type of cheese from another, a fact he bemoaned because more than anything else in the world it was cheese that he lived for. It was he whom I befriended and who filled me in on this and that while drinking at the Savoy. The girls, he told me, came in through an entrance in an alley at the back and had their own bosses they had to be accountable to, men no better than pimps who kept them on a tight schedule of appearances from one place to the next. The girls often ended their nights—if they were away from the camouflage of the red lights of such joints, none figured—sleeping with the johns who had spent the whole night watching and fantasizing about them. There was an entire operation—dressing rooms and shit, in Neil's words—right next door that Neil and his cousins were only the curtain holders for.

At the end of the vestibule that connected the main door to the two inner doors—one to Peep Corner, the other to the apartments—a camera connected to video screens hung from the ceiling and played behind the counter where Veejay stood. When they closed Peep Corner, they took everything down, but kept the camera where it was, its eye collecting dust.

I bought Preciosa's groceries, using food stamps she got twice a month in the mail. I picked up her mail in a box she rented in the main post office across from Madison Square Garden. Sometimes there'd be letters from the Philippines. At the corners of these envelopes would be blue-white stamps showing rural scenes, and a postal mark reading *Pilipinas*, with a date arranged inside a circle. Looking at them made me sad, knowing that a whole part of my life was over and that I didn't miss it one bit.

I went to the library to check out books and movies for her, using her library card and a letter she signed to explain what I was doing in her place.

My duties for Preciosa made me feel, in a rare instance, connected to everyone else in the city: put-upon citizens on the subway with their air of being mysteriously afflicted I now recognized as fellow errand-runners, all of us grimly determined to beat the city's million hindrances to get our days behind us.

In her apartment, I fed her pet goldfish, Divina Valencia, named after a famous Filipino movie star she liked and who was almost always cast as a haughty villainess: roles Preciosa herself, with her high, regal cheekbones and her aloof stare, would've been perfect for. I helped do her laundry, hand washing in a plastic bucket and then hanging the items to dry on her shower curtain rod. Once a week, I did light dusting, which was actually heavy dusting, because grime and grease from a burger joint half a block away managed to find its way into her apartment through windows in the back.

I read her stories from the *New York Post*, a paper we both enjoyed because it affirmed our view of the world as being filled with tawdry people who saw others as rabbits while regarding themselves as lions blessed with superior speed, skill, and readiness. It was a place, in fact, very much like the Savoy.

In particular, we liked stories involving bodies found in different areas around the city because, first, death was something abstract and pleasurable to us, never having experienced it outside of the movies, and, second, because these stories set our minds spinning in ways to which the closest we otherwise came was having to take drugs: Sparks flew, each one a tantalizing question mark: Who were these people? And who the culprits? Why had they been killed? And why were the corpses found where they were? Was sex involved? Drugs? What were the instruments used? Were the bodies intact? Or did they come in two, three, or more pieces: head, torso, legs, etc.? Was each section found in a different spot? Or all together, dumped next to one another? What were the conjectures of the police? Would the perpetrators ever be apprehended? In life, how did these bodies move, what clothes did they like to wear, what food did they like to eat?—ordinary things whose beauty death, having ended them forever, accidentally revealed. Were these people like us, uselessly vigilant? These were the same seductions that made me buy mystery paperback after mystery paperback, trying to get at the thing that had no name but which I would know once I saw it, and which, when provided in the final pages, was always a letdown, an approximation of a dream of an idea.

I was massaging Preciosa's hips. The look of agony on her face as I did this told me I should stop. But against my better judgment and because of my belief—inherited from my mother—that skin needed to be touched once in a while or it would go dead, I continued. During these sessions, Preciosa would usually tell me a few things about her life, but never much, as if she trusted me to figure out the rest for myself.

Most likely she'd mention jobs she'd taken in New York: a model, a dancer, a salesgirl at Saks. This last job had exposed her to perfumes sprayed liberally to bait passing customers, and soon, just like Neil's, her nose had turned into a useless piece of shit.

There were jobs she didn't mention, only hinting at "dark times." Things she'd had to do just to make ends meet. She intimated connections to shady figures. All small-time hustlers who peddled on the streets, nothing organized and labyrinthine, headquartered in dark, velvet-lined places. Was this how she would get her hands on fifteen thousand?

Looking at Preciosa's beautiful but tired face as I massaged her—the days of my volunteer work piling up around us—I wondered whether I was anywhere close to softening her up so she could reveal to me the things which I didn't have the courage (or was it the imagination?) to fill in.

＊ 4 ＊

The New Yorker Hotel sat on a particularly drab stretch of
Eighth Avenue, surrounded by several storefronts that
were no more than doorways, inside of which cheap
plastic goods manufactured in Taiwan and places like Taiwan were
sold by—and to—those who had recently arrived in this country
and who spoke several foreign tongues plus a new kind of molting,
transformed English. Across from it was a bright McDonald's that
seemed as if it had come down from outer space and simply taken up
root in the middle of the block just to spite the colorless neighborhood.

Inside the hotel, I encountered a group of European tourists
dressed in jeans and sweatshirts which bore the names and insignia
of American things which were "hot" a decade ago—rock bands, actors, movies, TV shows, perfumes—and the effect that these costumes gave off was one of cheap, hopeful participation. The carpet
had on it one large flower and across this flower were several zigzag
indentations left by the wheels of suitcases.

The elevators were right next to the check-in desk, an unmanned ghost station. It took me a while to realize that the check-in person was the short, balding Mediterranean who was helping to facilitate the arrival or departure of the European contingent. I walked past everyone and into an awaiting elevator.

More flowers, smaller versions of the arrangement downstairs, greeted me on the fourth floor. Wall sconces glowed dimly, giving the hallway the feel of a grotto. I took out the piece of paper Shem had left for me at the Savoy. Room 4C. I knocked.

There he was, looking happy to see me. He took my hand and shook it warmly.

I knew you'd come, he said to me. I had a feeling about you. Come in come in.

He put a whole arm around my shoulders and gently influenced me through the door.

Shem's room was taken up by a large, ugly double bed. The bed-spread, again, had flowers all over it, and it was lying on the floor, where Shem's feet must have kicked it. The white sheets were bunched up to one side. On the opposite side was an indentation on the mattress. The bed faced a TV set, which was dead, and which the hotel bolted onto a sideboard to prevent theft. The sideboard was made of compressed particle board and had elaborate whorls and striations mimicking the texture of wood. Shem pushed me into a chair.

You want something to drink? he asked. He reached for a brown paper bag underneath the bedspread. From it he produced a bottle of liquor, with the liquor at the low end of the bottle. Ever tried scotch? he asked me.

No, thanks, I replied.

Go ahead. You should try it. Make a man out of you.

No, thanks, I repeated.

Suit yourself, he said, then uncapped the bottle and took a long, satisfying swig. The way he drank, you'd think it was only water. When he was done, he threw the bottle on the bed, and sat himself down. Facing me, he smiled a frightening smile.

But he was only getting ready to tell a story. The night before, he had introduced the origin of his name. Tonight he was going to start

on the origin of his face, how it got so sad-looking. This was to prepare me for his offer, for me to see exactly where he was coming
from, so that his plans would seem less malignant, or better yet, to
give the malignancy of his plans a personal, a human dimension—
the rush of events capped by our fateful meeting at the Savoy. And
his logic was this: Understanding him, I would have no other choice
but to agree to be his accomplice.

Shem's wife had kicked him out two weeks ago. (He told his story
in a way that made him look like the victim of a conspiracy.) They
had a baby daughter together. She was four and a half. Never cried.
Was in perfect health. The apple of her father's eye. He had to admit
that he'd dreaded the onset of fatherhood. He'd felt in danger of being written over, of having his plans pushed aside. He and his wife
hadn't talked, planned, prepared. They had been married for six
years and it seemed to be part of what would happen next, the big
project it was assumed they shared with everyone. All their friends
. . . children here and there . . . longing in his wife . . . the way her
eyes would look after a gathering where the children of friends and
of family would roost at her feet, a look that was part hope, part re-
proach . . . But he hadn't been asked what his opinions on the matter were because if he had been he'd have told them that for him—
He had just— How could he say this— OK, he had just gotten over
the loss of, not the loss but rather incursion, yes, he'd just gotten
over the incursion into his character which marriage represented,
and didn't want to have to deal with a new incursion—that of fatherhood—so soon after. He wanted time so he could plan out his
future, not have it decided for him.

His character had taken him a long time to construct: an independent man finally deciding for himself the outline of a day, and
telescoping that, the outline of a life, something his wife, it seemed,
had begun to take away from him piece by piece from the first day of
their marriage.

She was kind, understanding, and didn't complain, but that was
precisely it, she didn't need to say a word, it was all clear from the
way she looked at him. Jewish women, he said, disgust in his voice,
have perfected the art of complaint by transforming it into a nonver-
bal, all-bases-covered thing that burrowed inside your spirit and
took root with the virulent industry of a cancer.

More about his character: For starters, he'd had to break free from a father who threatened disinheritance if he continued to pursue his dream of becoming a writer. A useless thing, his father had declared. Financially insecure. But Shem's love for words, for writing—which you'd think a father with enough of a touch of poetry in him to name a child after a passage in Joyce would share—would not be put off, and secretly, maybe, his father's disapproval had sealed it for Shem: He realized that this was exactly what he needed to establish an identity separate from his family's—his would be a bigger life of more ambition and, consequently, more rewards.

So he went to college, learned his trade, got connections, and started freelancing. He wrote for celebrity magazines; wrote book reviews in the daily and weekly papers and in places like *The New York Times Book Review*. He was well thought of in his profession, or professions, but did not have the necessary immune system to mingle with "the right people," and thus never advanced beyond a certain level of keeping up. Still, he was happy. Hadn't he proven his father wrong, gone on after college to make a living from writing?

By this time he was married. And his father, affected by the spectacular rightness of this marriage, soon relented. The family inheritance was once more his. A considerable sum. It was a marriage nobody could improve upon. This sparkling Jewess with a lineage you couldn't invent: the daughter of the acclaimed Jewish novelist Bill Hood. Bill, he paused, just like you.

No, I told Shem. William.

I'm sorry.

Go on.

What a socially formidable family! Think of my own father's joy at being connected in one fell swoop to class and influence! Have you read any of his books? They're on every college syllabus in the United States.

Here I had to confess that I never went to college. Then I admitted that yes, occasionally, I did read books. But none of them were Bill Hood's.

What books? he asked.

You'll think they're trash, I replied, and said we ought to move on. Truth be told, I was getting impatient with his story. At the

Savoy, I would at least have the compensation of some shots of tequila. Or I could be making some cash if this was dictation.

He took a deep breath and continued. His Jewess, the novelist's daughter. Her name was Marianna. He repeated that name several times. Everything was so perfect, but of a kind that was like suffocation. And then without warning, and seeming to arrive like another cell door closing: his daughter. Beulah. That was her name. After his wife's grandmother. The novelist's mother. Now even the dead were closing in on him . . . After her birth, he had visited his bachelor friends and had envied them their small studio apartments where they were free to come and go as they pleased. As for himself, he felt stifled in a prison of somebody else's making: the good son, the good husband, and now, the good father. Was it any wonder he started having difficulty breathing? . . . After Beulah's birth, he had begun to see his career in a different light: bypassable bylines and second-string assignments that never seemed to end and yet all added up to nothing. It had taken his daughter to expose to him his great inadequacy. And to top it off, he was struck with writer's block, frozen at his desk! How could he go on, losing the one thing that was still his, that marked him as separate from his family? This was when they decided to sink their teeth further in. His father-in-law, the novelist, a filthy, social-climbing human being if ever there was one—a man whose two or three good books were thought to be such contributions to American letters that they shielded the rest of his weak, watery (needlessly mournful) work from critical reproof—suggested pulling a few strings. And why not, the sonofabitch had connections up the wazoo. You should see him at a party, his natural environment. A lizard slithering, that was it, no more fitting description: long tongue licking its own lips in a ritual of self-satisfaction; frightening eyes magnified by psychotic black-framed glasses, always on the lookout for the next piece of ass; and finding which, he would use his marquee value to oh so gently steer it toward his bed.

This man casually dropped names while at the dinner table and made sure to surround himself with companions who would remember and then quote back to him either lines from his own works or lines from the critics in praise of those very lines. All the while he conducted himself in public with the air of an ascetic, unsullied by the tactics being used by the new generation, who of course needed them because they were far less gifted: powermongering, self-advertisement, and such. What a performance! This man suggested pulling strings for his beloved son-in-law, husband of the sparkling Jew princess. Why not let him arrange a book contract for Shem with his, Bill Hood's, publishers? They owed him more than a few favors for remaining with them when he could so easily have accepted the far more lucrative offers of other publishers. What did he think? Should he go ahead and arrange a meeting for Shem with one of the senior editors? What would he like to write about? Fiction? Nonfiction? Anything his little heart desired. It was as good as done. How could Shem refuse? It would have been as good as a slap to his father-in-law's face. So he met with an editor who never hid the fact that this had all been cooked up to please Mr. Hood, no matter that the writing samples Mr. Hood had sent along of Shem's work were none too shabby, still Shem without Bill Hood would've been no different from the million faceless people clogging up the city for a chance at the big time, wasn't it lucky Shem had made the tactical move of marrying Bill Hood's daughter . . . In truth, that kind of humiliation was nothing to him next to the money, his promised advance. Six figures, said Shem as if speaking of some repulsive thing. In summary, it had crushed his writing. It represented everything he did not want to become, everything he didn't know he was dreading, until it happened.

Day after day he sat at his computer, stricken with panic and unable to string together the simplest of sentences. The proposal was something he didn't even put too much thought into. He'd approached them with some ridiculous notion about Oriental motifs in recent American literature, an arcane—and what's more, untrue—thing with no possible commercial appeal and which he knew would end any talk of a book contract right there and then, but the senior editor had come back all smiles, saying that the board had approved the idea, and what's more, they couldn't wait for Shem's manuscript! The sheer hypocrisy of the bunch, it was enough to make you want to puke!

The money had come in. The first part of it, at least. He still couldn't write. So he tried to read, get his mind attuned to the rhythm of prose, but his reading soon began feeling like an obligation. It took him the longest time just to finish a dozen pages. Even the clearest of sentences he'd have to read over and over just to grasp its meaning. Meanwhile, his wife had begun to buy things with the money, things which she started to pile around the house as a display of improvement but which, when he looked at them, revealed their unfriendly motives, animated by Bill Hood's spirit. He couldn't look at the new furniture, the new clothes, the new dishes, the baby's things without hearing Bill Hood's voice behind them, taunting, and pretty soon, he found that all of his energy went into trying to avoid his house . . . What could he do, condemned by circumstances and, even more unbearably, by his own actions, to suffer this joke of privilege transformed into hell? Seeing the three of them— his own father, his wife, and her father—huddled together like bowling pins at the far end of his reach: this image had galvanized him. They had to be dealt with, their plans of dealing him a death by turning him into someone else, crushed . . . There were so many women passing by on the sidewalk as he sat at a cafe, women in bookstores, in restaurants. He even started noticing them in the dark of movie houses . . . God only knows it was some fault inside him, some defect, that would not allow him to sit quietly by, as most men would, and simply enjoy his situation. He had to go somewhere, defile things. From where had he inherited this trait? There was talk of an uncle, a malcontent who abandoned his family and was discovered years later in some flophouse, a suicide. Perhaps it ran in the family. But his, he argued, was only temporary, just to rebel one last time before he was too old, he never meant for it to last and therefore reasoned that the punishment he received was outsize, to him it was only like taking a long last gasp of air before plunging beneath icy waters. About the woman he eventually ended up with he didn't say anything specific. Mainly he cursed a lot, invective after boiling invective. It was because of her that his life was ruined . . . worse than a whore, than catching gonorrhea from a whore . . . his life in tatters . . . It turned out that this whore knew his father-in-law. A small world. They'd been lovers once, those two, but the affair—as was typical of his father-in-law—was not publicly acknowledged: she'd only been one in a great store of sideline pussy he'd had while married to his three wives. Out of some residual loyalty and perversely thinking that Bill Hood would take her back, she'd snitched to him, revealed everything between Shem and herself, and Bill Hood in turn had revealed everything to his uncomprehending daughter . . . And here he was, turned out of the family, without even a fraction of the six figures that he now looked back on with a hopeless nostalgia.

What he wanted, he put very simply, was one word, simplicity itself: Revenge. About that there could be no confusion. And he would need my help. What would he want to take of theirs? Not their life, not their health, but something more simple, more powerful: their pride. Life had now aligned him with people like me, he said, using me—mistakenly, I thought at the time—as a sample citizen of the underground. And now he would vindicate that decision. He would turn bad. Real bad. As he said this, I started an organ playing in my head. To me, that was how light and unserious everything was.

* 5 *

Devo lived in the East Village. He was a layabout who occasionally got work styling models and actors for photo shoots. Walking with him in his neighborhood was much like listening to the woman who dictated her memoirs. *My God*, he'd say, *I can remember when this block used to be . . .* Or he'd point at some forlorn-looking window, blacked out and behind which rats scurried—he'd point and say, *So-and-so used to live there, my God those were the days, we'd go down to Tompkins Square Park and get some choice pot, then we'd go up to his living room, my God you should've seen the size of that place, for a while the people who took over turned it into a roller-skating rink before the downstairs neighbors complained and got the landlord to evict, oh God, those were the days, we'd get pot and go there and just sit for days doing nothing but we'd always have a great time, and always people would drop in, and they'd bring their own pot with them, or mescaline, or whatever, and we'd have equipment lying around to shoot it up with, and weeks would go by, I swear to you, weeks, and before anyone knew it, it'd be the New Year, God those were the days.*

Devo hated being called Devo, but what was he to do, it was his name, given to him by parents he proudly hailed "white trash." Always, after introducing himself, someone would ask him, Oh, Devo —are you named after the rock band? And Devo would say, very simply, No.

My God all these people with their funky names like Devo and Shem, and me stuck with William. Oh well, there's always something to be grateful for: No leeway for jokes. Except of course Willie, to which I'd reply, No, William.

Devo was forty and was one of the few older people I knew who did not speak of the younger bunch—the next generation, and the generations after that—with a steely rancor like refusing to surrender the baton. In the streets of the East Village, these young people were everywhere around us, spilling outside the open doors of ramshackle cafes and refurbished cafes, pizza joints, secondhand clothing stores, and record shops, all the while talking and shrieking in party tones whose meanings eluded us and made us feel like tourists from a depressed country. Still, Devo would look at them and smile, though he would never say anything about them, about having to put up with the traffic they caused in what had been his neighborhood for the last twenty years.

I first met Devo at a party given by a mutual friend who was now dead from drugs and drink. This friend went to sleep on the floor of a nightclub one night and never woke up. At the party, Devo had come up to me, presuming that I had interesting things to say. At the time I was probably spending my days at the Port Authority rest rooms, and of course was at the height of my stupidity, a stupidity which, looking back on it now, I recognize as a thing adopted for survival. But Devo didn't know a thing. Or maybe he did, but took the chance anyway. He asked me questions and seemed genuinely interested in my replies. He didn't, like most people I spoke with, glance around the room with a distracted air of wanting to be rescued after only a few minutes. He asked and I obliged, answering. That had been the pattern of our friendship ever since. Now it was my turn to ask him a question.

Devo? I began as we walked down First Avenue. We were heading toward Chinatown for a cheap meal on Mott Street.

Uh-huh?

When you— I paused. When you do something bad, well not bad, but not exactly good either, something not good, when you do that to someone, even though it's your full intention to be a better human being— I paused again. I guess what I'm asking is, can I, does it make sense to you if I say I want to be better than what I am now but that I have to put it aside for just a little bit so I can make some money, but as soon as I have the money, I'll resume my plan of being good?

When I'd eventually confessed about my Port Authority gig, Devo hadn't acted outraged or shocked. I'd been more shocked than he. For him it was just another piece of information. This kind of imperturbability suggested that Devo had a low opinion of human nature and that a list was merely being checked off inside his brain. What would you have to do for the money? he asked.

I'm not sure, I replied.

What do you mean?

I told Devo about Shem. About being enlisted to help him in his plan. I mentioned the word "revenge," but said that I had verified that injury to life or property would not be involved.

What does that leave? asked Devo.

Shem, eventually made useless by drink, had stopped just short of outlining his plans. I'm not sure, I repeated.

Theft? Devo asked.

Maybe.

Devo was quiet.

The air was brisk for late April, with an occasional chill, like being licked by an invisible tongue. The trees were greening once more. I had to stop every once in a while to admire a certain tree, remembering how it had hung limp and frightened during the winter, mirroring the postures of everyone. But it seemed that I was the only one doing this, the young people around us were busy ignoring everything natural, and seeing this made me realize that I had indeed walked over a line which demarcated not-youth from youth, and I realized further that I was not sad about this, perhaps being with Devo had that effect on me.

Devo? I asked again. But he continued to remain silent. Which unnerved me into declaring: I want to be good, I really do, badly do—a statement which, coming from me, definitely needed the conviction-lending strategy of repetition. I added: But I'm broke. And I should've added: And I'm good for nothing else. But I knew he would only have argued otherwise.

And then what would I have said? Probably, I'd amend my statement to: I'm good for nothing else *for now.*

By this time, we'd crossed into Chinatown, where the vegetable and meat markets began. We had to slink past throngs of aggressive shoppers carrying heavy loads in both arms. Their knees, reacting to this weight, buckled and bowed, giving them the walk of chickens. There were a million of these funny-limbed creatures. They were barking questions at the shopkeepers and, when the prices quoted didn't suit them, they started to haggle, their voices going up and up.

On the sidewalk sat plastic bins inside which flopped dark-colored fish with their green gills, turtles climbing on top of one another, eels thrashing their tails, a thousand tiny crabs clacking their claws. Inside the storefronts, there were low counters stuffed with ice on which were arranged various bloody meats and fish. Different dead, dulled eyes stared out at us. The stench caused more than a few passersby to twist their faces but to me it was strangely reassuring, reminding me of my childhood in Manila.

Finally, Devo said, Well, I think— I think you have to know what you're getting yourself into before you agree. You haven't agreed to anything yet, have you?

No.

Well, know what you're taking on.

I will, I replied, eager to please.

You met this guy at the Savoy?

I nodded.

Devo didn't say anything, but the look on his face said it for him: Meeting someone at the Savoy was fair enough warning.

We crossed the busy intersection at Canal and Mott. There was an old man being carefully guided across by a young girl, and they both looked mysteriously perturbed, as if they were fleeing the scene of an accident in which they had been involved. Two women, whose knockoff fashions and thick movie-star makeup spoke of

Hong Kong origins, were distracted by a billboard touting a discounted overseas calling plan. The newspapers hanging in the street kiosks were filled with jiggling script that looked as if somebody had shaken out the contents of their bags. So many things emphasized a sense of being at a remove, of being in America and not in America at the same time, that I could have sworn I was dreaming and that this was the same place I visited every night—not-Manila and not–New York, not-past and not-present. Stuck in limbo. Between departure and arrival. A place like the future, thought of and imagined in ways that barely touched the circumference of its incomprehensibility.

The Hong Kong women's red mouths were wide open, like children's, and their eyes were squinting as they looked up. Predictably, they bumped into two housewives, from whose tight embraces across their chests spilled cans and boxes and plastic packages onto the crosswalk. The two Hong Kong women moved along briskly, unmindful of the accusing stares of the crowd. Nobody helped the housewives, but it was just as well, because they had everything back in their arms in no time. They gave indications of having had to do this kind of thing all their lives.

Behind the windows at Big Wong hung pieces of meat dripping juices onto a metal trough, like some primitive timekeeping device, each ping on the stainless-steel surface one second—my whole life the same way, I thought, dribbling away. Inside, a long, scattered line. Chinese families out for a Sunday meal waited next to curious-haired tourists attracted by the crowds. In front of us, college students conversed in a slangy English, sentences full of joyous "dude"s and "come on"s. Devo stepped out to smoke a cigarette. When he came back, he had a magazine tucked under one arm. In a few minutes we were seated.

We placed our orders with a Chinese man who could've been my father. He looked at Devo, and then at me, donning a disturbed question mark of puzzling over our relationship, but this expression didn't last. Soon he had it tucked behind a poker stare, a commonplace Chinese expression, and he didn't let a second pass between finishing with our table and sliding to the next to push menus in front of barely seated customers.

Devo opened his magazine, and while waiting for our orders, we looked at a layout on which he had worked. Models frolicked and cavorted in a variety of settings, regarding one another with the thinnest of interests. Devo pointed to one model and said that to get her to even look half that good had taken some doing, and even then, the photograph had had to be retouched before publication. He pointed to the flat tummy of a young man in another photograph and said that some flab at his sides had been carefully concealed by expert lighting. He lovingly, painstakingly revealed every aspect that was wrong in the pictures and that had needed his hand or the hand of a retoucher. And suddenly it occurred to me that this was exactly why our friendship had endured: because once more I made sure to surround myself with someone who would instinctively tear down the carefully built facade of the world until all that was left standing in its place was something thin and ragged and shivery. Something, in other words, very much like myself.

6

The mystery section took up a dozen or so large shelves placed next to the cookbooks, for no reason that I could discern. I must have unconsciously spoken my thoughts out loud, because suddenly a clerk was at my side explaining to me that yes, indeed, the mystery section was the most popular section in the entire place. This seemed like a pretext to engage me in personal conversation, as Shem had done. One Shem was enough for me, and so I thanked him and inched away. I took out an Agatha Christie I was sure I hadn't read before and fled.

From other Agatha Christie books in my boyhood I had cobbled together an extensive vocabulary that allowed me—when I needed to—to obfuscate my having been a high school dropout: obfuscate, obstinate, obstreperous, obsequious, ostentatious, oracular . . .

To the library at Lincoln Center, where, of the few remaining titles left on the shelves, I was able to rescue two that I thought Preciosa wouldn't mind seeing or—as was usually the case—reseeing: *The Little Foxes*, with a nasty Bette Davis; and *Double Indemnity*, with a nasty Barbara Stanwyck.

As I was about to leave, I saw someone who looked like an old acquaintance, a hustler from Rhode Island nicknamed Jokey. This person was a few yards in front of me, unzipping his bag for the guard to check. He lifted his head ever so slightly from the bag to look at some nuns walking in through the revolving doors, and suddenly, with the light hitting him in a new way—a light that seemed to have appeared with the nuns—he turned out not to be Jokey at all. My heart sank. My eyes were still on him as I moved toward the guard, and all of a sudden he was Jokey once more, I was sure of it. After being passed through, I quickened my steps to make up the distance between us. How was Jokey doing? I didn't know he was still in New York. And then suddenly this person turned to look back at me, as if I had again spoken my thoughts out loud. It was obvious from his face that the same cycle of emotions that passed through me earlier was passing through him. Up until then a million things could've happened. And then a million things fizzled into one. I heard him say my name. And then he smiled. I felt my mouth go dry but somehow I still managed to say Hello. Or maybe I said Hell, unintentionally dropping the *o*. He looked well. The years—how many had passed? six? seven?—had been good to him. He said the same about me, but I knew he was lying. He shook my hand vigorously. He had on a light shirt with the top two buttons opened. He'd been working out, and immediately I wondered how he'd gotten the money for a gym membership, which would cost how much? Three, four, five hundred dollars? He told me he was at the library to return a few videos he'd checked out for research. What research? Oh, he'd been cast in a movie. Not the lead, but a sizable supporting part. Shooting would begin in New York in two weeks. I listened to his words accompanied by a loud buzzing that I couldn't identify at first, but slowly it dawned on me that it was my heart accelerating. He invited me for coffee. His treat because he was doing so well. My brain was so fogged with shock that I couldn't think of an excuse to ditch him fast enough. He led me across the street to a bistro. Needless to say, he fit in and I stood out. The waiters were deferential to Jokey, who I realized didn't want to be called Jokey anymore, but for the life of me I couldn't remember what his real name was, so I refrained from calling him anything at all. The coffee burned my tongue. I put some milk in, but the concoction was so black it hardly turned, reflecting my mood.

Jokey had been dissatisfied with life in New York for a long time. He didn't mention our having been colleagues at the Port Authority, or our having rubbed elbows at various pit stops of the underground gay circuit: making our living from the standard need of older men to be within squeezing distance of young things. He merely used the term "dead end."

He had saved enough money for a one-way ticket to California, where he knew some friends. Within a week, he had gotten a job as a waiter and an apartment of his own. Slowly he strung together credits, determined to speed past his former life: Acting class. An agent. Auditions. Callbacks. The regular actor's carousel, which he made to sound simultaneously wearying and glamorous. Almost right from the start there'd been close calls. Roles he narrowly missed out on, and which, instead of being regarded as setbacks, encouraged him even more. Hell, if he'd been this close, who's to say that the next time out wouldn't go his way . . . And what did you know? The jobs started coming in. Had I seen him in his television appearances? He rattled off a bunch of names that were insignificant to me. Oh, that was all right. How about the movies? He mentioned two in which he'd recently appeared. Again I shook my head. He looked at me with censure, as if I was determined to be unpleasant. I apologized once more. But there was no dampening his mood. He seemed genuinely glad to see me, and for a while I felt bad about not feeling happier for him. And then suddenly I realized that of course he'd be glad to see me. For him I was a godsend, somebody from the old days against whom he could measure the progress of his life, left behind and to be treated like a charity case.

Jokey got up. He told me he had to get going. Voice lessons. Somehow, more than anything else he'd revealed all afternoon, I found this the most depressing, although I couldn't say why. I thanked him for his treat, and he smiled once more, saying how lovely it was to have bumped into me. And if this was any indication of his abilities as an actor, I could tell he was going to go far. We walked out into the streets, which were now much busier, schoolkids and workers having been freed to resume their lives. We parted at the corner of Broadway and Sixty-second, shaking hands.

By the time I got home, I had a headache which was making me see things twinned: first there was the object, and then surrounding it was a larger, vaporous version of itself that was like an aura or soul and which jiggled and danced with a psychotic intent of wanting to exhaust me, like a merciless child. The effort of suppressing the ill will I felt for Jokey was now making my jaws ache, and looking in the mirror, I discovered a mushroom zit on my left jaw, which made me wince when I put a dainty finger on it.

In the kitchen, the roach bait I had bought three weeks ago—its poison in the shape of a small bouillon cube sitting in the center of a hexagonal structure capped by a see-through plastic dome which allowed me to observe how much of it was being taken—remained untouched. The roaches were getting smarter, or maybe the lure was no longer any good. I threw them away, wincing when I remembered how much they cost. In my mind I saw that figure exchangeable for at least seven McDonald's hamburgers. I went to sleep thinking of my waste: useless poison in lieu of good, hearty food . . .

I luxuriated over the words, pored over every clue even if I knew I was only being bamboozled. I read a description of a character more than once to see if seeds were being planted for eventual guilt, but of course, each was supplied with more than his or her share of shadows, so that they all turned out to be on equal footing. And following the logic of these stories where virtue was a frequent cover for villainy, I also reread the sections pertaining to the blameless characters, imagining for each a scenario of being unmasked. The descriptions were colorful and contrasting, setting the characters off against one another so that the book was full of "types" who in real life would never deign to rub shoulders with one another.

The plot involved a group of people being invited to an island and then being systematically, literarily, killed off one by one . . .

Before I knew it, there were only twenty pages left. Somehow I didn't want the culprit to be revealed. I would have been just as satisfied if he or she had gone on killing and was never found out. In other words, if he or she had gotten away with it. It was this killer's side I was on, both of us arrayed against . . . well, the rest of the world. But I knew I was bound to be disappointed. So I put the book down.

There was a knock on my door. Standing there, looking elegant in a long black dress and wearing dangling gold earrings and carrying a rubber-tipped walking cane, was Preciosa, who purred out my name. I kissed her on the cheek and stood aside as she came in. Looking at her all dressed up made me nervous. Was it that kind of evening?

That's all right, she said. You're young. And you're a boy. Wear anything you like and you'll still be OK.

I excused myself to go put something on. When I came out, I could tell that even Preciosa was disappointed. I had on black slacks and a simple white long-sleeved shirt which, admittedly, made me look like a waiter. Is this OK? I asked. She smiled and lied.

Someone Preciosa knew had given her tickets to Lincoln Center. I had often daydreamed about the things that went on inside, though I had never had a chance to find out. In these daydreams, expert performances transpired in front of a handsome and worldly audience which included me, and our appreciative applause was like the tinkling of many small bells.

The lights were on, casting a golden glow on the premises. The fountain had been drained, revealing several coins, mostly pennies, stuck at the bottom. The sculpture in the middle, a rising abstract slab representing I didn't know what, had a green waterline a foot from its base.

As we drew nearer, the joyful sound of women's high heels grew louder. But as soon as we entered, they disappeared, being absorbed into the plush red carpeting that extended in every direction to become pedaling sounds like a convention of organ players warming up.

We let the crowd lead us along. This way, we found the box office where Preciosa waited in line for our tickets. The floors were bare once more, and again I heard the women's heels that suggested perpetual nighttime in the city. A picture came to me from a movie I'd seen once: a scene of boys and men kept awake, disturbed and exhilarated, by those very same sounds outside their windows.

Tickets in hand, Preciosa took me into the auditorium. There were chandeliers hanging above our heads which looked like giant petrified spiders. But nobody seemed to notice anything, and so I followed their leads. We were directed to our seats by a young girl, and then again, barely a few steps later, by an old woman with hair that must've been a wig—she insisted on telling us where to go, but neither Preciosa nor I said anything. There were no curtains obscuring the stage and we saw what appeared to be a desert vista, barren and dusty. We got to our seats without having to step past anybody.

The curtain was held for ten extra minutes, as if waiting for some mysterious late person to arrive but everyone who had come to see the play was already in their seats, and what's more, were beginning to make their impatience heard, and so finally—defeatedly almost—the lights went down. I held my breath. I did it automatically. I wanted to be bowled over. I wanted to forget my name, or that my life had come to nothing. The lights came up onstage and actors, who had entered during the darkness, were revealed. They were supposed to be a mother and son, reunited after some time, but whose enmity still showed. The lines were bitter, and sculpted in a way that called attention to the fact that they were sculpted. The audience around us giggled in spots, but the prevailing mood was one of respectful contemplation. And anticipation of heavier things to come. Somehow, though this was contrary to what they wanted and demanded from life, they gave the feeling that unless unpleasant things occurred—that is to say, unless the decibel level was raised—the evening would be a failure.

It didn't take long for the audience's wish to be granted. The actors continued their brittle dialogue, but the volume was certainly louder than before. I could almost see the exclamation points come out of the actors' mouths and hit the audience, whose shoulders lurched back gratefully from the impact. *desperation → new identity (savoy) (parties)*

And then the scene shifted—the desert vista turning into a modern apartment fitted with clean-lined furniture that seemed designed to be looked at more than used: the smooth changeover making the audience coo with pleasure—and still the language kept circling around uselessly—cooked up to showcase the author's having rehearsed lines in front of a mirror in anticipation of applause. They

in party

surfaces more important than value

Concept of "fungshuey"

nothing is what it seems

Shakespeare "All the world's a stage"

spoke with pat summations accompanied by aggrieved expressions
on their faces like lawyers, to the great delight of the audience, for
whom such things referred back to their punitive years of schooling
when they first learned to differentiate between art and dreck: Art is
the thing that is graceless and obvious, but always "serious." The
chandeliers above our heads seemed no longer like spiders but like
skeletal fingers threatening to press down on my skull.

Finally intermission came and I followed Preciosa outside, where
she smoked a clove cigarette, looking chic. Other theatergoers formed
discussion groups around us. Their faces were so happy it made me
feel estranged from all humanity.

You holding up? Preciosa asked in between puffs of her cigarette.

I smiled wanly.

Preciosa took my arm. We walked away from the crowd, whose
buzz had gotten louder. We stopped near the fountain, at a planter
filled with new blooms that had tiny, wispy petals. Preciosa leaned
against it. If you want, she said, we could just keep going. We don't
have to stay. There's a choice, you know. You don't have to be unhappy.

Why? I asked. Aren't you having a good time?

It's theater, you know, she replied, and I took that to mean that
she felt the same way as I did.

But still I shook my head no.

We both looked back at the glass facade of the theater lit from inside. It was so beautiful, like the simple things in a picture book,
but for me a crack had revealed itself: Inside, torpid things happened. But maybe I had had unfair expectations all along. Maybe it
was built to show just the things we were watching tonight. Next to
it was the library where I got Preciosa's movies. It looked dark and
beckoning.

I looked at the crowd, at isolated persons who were beautiful and
cherished the burnishing glow of the floodlights trained on the
premises. They were attired in what looked like expensive things,
and were continually smoothing out these things in rituals of fetishism that baffled me. Were these the people Shem had referred
to in his diatribe, and did they come to places like Lincoln Center
in a collective will to celebrate their separateness, requiring brittle

things overlaid with the patina of art to match the rest of the upholstery in their lives? Suddenly, the evening began to clarify, and
equipped with the words to match my inchoate resentment, I began
to feel better.

Where was Shem? When would he call? Would he ever call?

I caught the eye of a middle-aged woman, who smiled at me politely and looked away to resume a conversation she was having with
a male companion. It made me feel better but also made me feel like
a fraud. Some of the people were herding back into the theater. I
looked at Preciosa and made my decision: I didn't want to be unhappy. I remembered Jokey, who had certainly done something
about his dissatisfaction.

Preciosa and I began walking to the subway. My steps were light
from tonight's discovery: I could just walk away. It seemed an important first. The night had grown chillier, but it was still lovely,
and the city was like a poster everywhere you turned.

The ride back on the subway was unexpectedly pleasant. I guess
we'd gotten the jump on the rest of the theatergoers . . .

Lying in bed, I found myself fingering open the program for
tonight's play. Some revelation triggered by our turning our backs
on what everyone else was celebrating seemed about to come to me.
Flipping past pages of advertisements, I stumbled upon two pages
toward the very back that were filled with pictures illustrating various highlights in the theater's history. One picture in particular
caught my eye. Below it, a caption that read: *Primitives*, by Max
Brill Carlton/1987–88 season. In the middle of this publicity still
stood two white missionaries. The man cradled a wooden crucifix
against his large belly; the woman clasped between both hands a
thick black book that I took to be a Bible. They were flanked by a
chorus line of dark-skinned men and women wearing only loin-
cloths and with nothing on their feet. The two men at both ends
were carrying spears, like sentries. All the women had long necklaces of multicolored beads that were looped around their necks over
and over. Among these women, standing third from right, was—
Preciosa! Her exposed breasts were droopy and small, like unripe
fruit. In the photograph, her head was no bigger than a comma, yet
there was something queenlike about her stare, and that made her

stand out, contradicting where she was placed in the photogra ph. I could tell just from the picture what the play was like, and understood Preciosa's sullen, from-a-distance look, the look of someone who realizes too late the farce they've agreed to be part of. My mind kept asking: Why didn't she tell me? And then: Why would she? I looked at the picture over and over.

Was it her first role, and if it was, did it become a sort of launching pad into other, perhaps better roles? Why had she stopped acting? Maybe instead of being the first, it was the last role she took, the humiliation of having been assigned a naked character—and the humiliation of accepting—the final discouragement. A title occurred to me, fit to emboss on a paperback cover: *The Mystery of Preciosa X*. When I saw her again tomorrow, how could I broach the subject? And would she be forthcoming, or, as usual, committed to a tantalizing, flirtatious silence?

Perhaps the person who'd given us tickets for tonight was a former colleague, an actor perhaps, or maybe the director, or even the playwright.

The next morning, before I could find out the answers to my questions, I discovered that Preciosa had been taken by ambulance to the Bronx. How had I managed to sleep through that? This neighbor—a woman who lived alone with several cats and whom I had seen once or twice before in the stairwell but had never spoken to—said that Preciosa's hips had finally given out on her. She told me the name of the hospital. And then told me how to get there by subway. She revealed that she'd lived next to Preciosa for close to fifteen years but had rarely taken the time to discover how she was, and Preciosa's accident had put things in perspective. She asked me to relay news after my visit.

That same afternoon, coming back from the hospital, I bumped into Shem C.

8

At first I stopped in my tracks. And then the motion of the crowd pushed me along, and I found that I was trailing him. When he stopped to look into the window of a store, I stopped too, doing the same thing with whatever window was beside me. At one point, I found myself staring into some restaurant, directly at a couple who were eating. They stopped what they were doing and glared back. I pretended to be tying my shoes. When I looked back up, Shem had disappeared. My heart was pounding. At the first corner, I turned my head in one direction and then another. Not a sign of him. I decided to turn back. Perhaps he'd seen me and ducked into one of the stores on the block. I went into the first, which sold shoes, and there were only a handful of customers, none of them Shem. Next, I stood outside an optometrist's. Again, no Shem. On my third try . . .

I had a sensation of walking into the pages of the books I loved. A woman came up and asked if I wanted a table. I told her that I was with somebody, my head acknowledging where Shem was. I heard what I thought was a conversation he was having with himself. But as I came nearer, I realized that there was another person at the table. A little girl with big blue eyes. I caught her saying, Don't cry, Daddy. And as soon as I heard what the girl said, I noticed that Shem's shoulders were indeed shaking. I knew I only had a few seconds before the girl would look up and, looking up, would call Shem's attention to me. I turned around. The woman who had approached me when I came in gave a curious look, and I told her that I'd been mistaken after all. How would I proceed? What would a detective do? I noticed the counter. Facing it was a mirrored shelf in which Shem and his daughter could be seen. I told the woman I'd have something at the counter. She smiled, handing me a menu. I fingered the money I had in my pocket. Five dollars and change. That would buy me soup and coffee. You know what you want? asked a burly waiter with a grease-streaked apron on. On his face he wore an expression of thick noninvolvement. I gave him my order.

In the mirror, I could see Shem and Shem's daughter, who was exactly as he'd described her: a head of bright blond curls topped her wide-awake face, and her mouth, always moving, was like the scan line on a seismograph. Shem, I noticed, had an eloquent back. Looking at it I could guess what he was saying to Beulah. The kid kept nodding. She was spooning some mushy pink dessert from a tall glass into her mouth, miraculously keeping both the table and her dress tidy. She had large hands, which were constantly in motion. With them she drew pictures in the air while she answered her father's questions. I could see Shem's hands caressing the tablecloth where only a moment ago, before she'd embarked on a tale, those hands had lain. And when they landed, father and daughter joined fingers once more. Shem was wearing a wedding ring. Was he hoping to be taken back into the family?

Now Beulah was gesturing with both hands placed wide apart. Shem was mirroring her.

Now Shem was turning his hands into claws, changing the word "big" into "scary." For a moment, I had a flash that he was telling her a story about his transformation.

My soup arrived, and I made a few obligatory gestures of testing. When I looked back up, a black woman wearing jeans and a zipped-up hooded windbreaker was at their table. Shem made a halfhearted gesture of looking at his watch, while the woman proceeded to wrap Beulah in a tiny gold jacket whose edges shook with fringe. Once more Shem's face turned the way I remembered it, like a punch restrained, and his eyes had that faraway, almost hopeful gaze, as if he were thinking of some date in the future when his enemies would kneel before him, turning *them* into the supplicants. Give Daddy one last kiss, said Shem to Beulah. He knelt down to receive her kiss. And then stood up, taking Beulah's other hand, to walk them to the door.

We'd better go alone, sir, said the black woman. Beulah looked up from one adult to another.

He watched them go, the kid immediately forgetting her father. And then he walked toward me. I opened my mouth, but Shem was so hypnotized by his own rage that he didn't hear. I quickly put down some money, and walked out after him. The hostess, looking at me following Shem, registered a look of understanding on her pixieish face.

He walked down Broadway. At Eighty-ninth, he crossed the street and entered a stationery store. When he came out, a thin packet stuck under one arm, I continued following.

On Eighty-sixth and West End he entered a building with an entrance fitted with dark green tarp above gold-colored poles. A uniformed doorman greeted him. Was this his new address? It was certainly an improvement over the New Yorker.

I stood across the street, trying to think. But then Shem came out, making my decision for me. He looked exactly as he had when he entered, except now he had a thicker packet stuck under his arm. He made his way to the corner of Eighty-second, turned, and then began to take Broadway downtown.

He didn't once allow himself to be distracted. Who was he meeting? Perhaps somebody to carry out his plans, my replacement. How many people had he confided in besides me? I would ask Barney if Shem had been talent-scouting at the Savoy any other night.

At Fifty-seventh and Eighth, Shem braved a red light and dashed onto the path of several oncoming cars, leaving me stranded.

When the lights going the other direction turned yellow, I re-

peated Shem's daredevil act, in the process receiving what I thought
of as the congratulatory belches of a few horns. There he was. My
God, what a godsend to have for my virgin assignment tailing this
Shem with his beaconlike backside. Two blocks turned into one and
a half, and in just a few seconds, I made up the difference of another
block, and again we were back to our original distance of being separated by about four or five pedestrians.

Suddenly, there was a bright-looking boy who came out of
nowhere and almost hit me in the face, and when I stopped to avoid
an accident, so did he. He had the kind of face which I'd always
wanted for myself, but which, despite my best efforts, had always
eluded me. His was an awake face, a purposeful one. And seeing
him, hate effortlessly surged inside me. For a few seconds, we stood
there on the sidewalk just staring at each other. And then reality did
its firecracker pop and I realized that that was no bright-looking boy
at all. It was me! I had caught my own reflection in a giant mirror.
How come I was awake? Was this a sign of the new life?

We were crossing at Forty-second, heading east along the strip
once studded with all those colorful porn shops. Behind one gated
and padlocked front, I could just barely make out haphazard con-
struction going on. To put up what? Outside a newly restored theater, tourists lined up to catch a "family" extravaganza at which the
papers had thrown adjectives splashed across bright plastic boards
tacked above the theater's doorways, words rendered so bold they
added to the neon surplus of Times Square. *Magnificent! Exhilarat-
ing! Once-in-a-lifetime! Stunning! Amazing! Unbelievable! Confound-
ing!*

I didn't need the exhilaration of whatever went on beyond those
doors because suddenly there was Shem with his up-and-down, purposeful gait providing in the flesh the very things I sought for in my
paperbacks and in the *New York Post*: a little shadow; a string of
question marks; the thrill of a real person's life lived in real time—
each footstep and each decision, having occurred only this instant
and not a moment before, possessing a newborn significance that
would take a while to settle into a legible pattern.

We had made up the distance of three blocks before it occurred
to me where Shem was headed. He was going to my place! Talk

about duh! *I* was the one he was going to meet. By now it had become shockingly clear. The door to my building, beneath the two eyes of Peep Corner, now turned into a gaping mouth: the Oh! of delayed recognition. How did he know where I lived? A picture began to form following that first encounter at the Savoy: afterward I had staggered home beneath woozy streetlamps that looked like things submerged underwater, and he had, taking advantage of my pinprick consciousness, trailed me, the same way I was trailing him now. Well, well. Cat and mouse, announced my brain, recalling a favorite phrase from my paperbacks. What was he going to do? He stopped right outside my building. He pushed the front door open. He went in. I crossed the street to observe at a safe distance. I could see him consulting the mailboxes. He would see . . . what? My last name was the only thing on my mailbox. Had he discovered what that was too? How? Nobody at the Savoy knew. I could see him pressing the button for an apartment. Even if he'd guessed correctly, I would not be there. He kept on pressing. He paused to consult the dead eye of the surveillance camera. Might as well be scratching his head to complete the picture. He acted as if certain that I would be home. What would he do next? He turned around and seemed to be taking me in, standing right across the street. But I decided it was only my imagination. But just to be sure, I found the cover of a phone, behind which I had a partial view of the doorway.

Suddenly I saw Shem leaving, the packet no longer under his arm. I rushed across the street. Shem never once turned around. As I made my way in, I saw the envelope on the floor, leaning against the wall. It had on it my name written in thick red marker and then underlined. I picked it up. Weighed it in my hand. I tore open the top and out slid two magazines. One was something called Condé Nast *House & Garden*, and the other something called *Metropolitan Home*. There were yellow Post-it stickers earmarking pages for my attention. These sections turned out to be a suite of photographs plus short articles on the same person's luxurious digs on the Upper West Side in Manhattan: Suzy Yamada, a Japanese-Canadian transplant who had made her fortune by trading with Japan. Just what exactly she traded I couldn't by quick skimming find out. There were pictures of her in both articles. A handsome, elegant woman in her early to mid-forties with a pink-cheeked face and a prominent forehead made even more prominent by her tendency to scrape her long hair back into a tight ponytail. Beside her in both pictures was a beautiful young man identified as her son, Kendo. In one picture, he wasn't so beautiful but instead looked rather perturbed, his lips a quivering line that suggested disapproval or uncertainty. But in the other, oh brother, I said. My eyes popped out in disgust and jealousy. Here was a matinee idol. With liquid eyes and thick brows and a nice long nose hooking just slightly to the left, rescuing his face from a perfection that would've been no different from blandness. And underneath everything were bones that looked custom-designed. And I thought: The whole world is looking for someone to fall in love with.

There was no note anywhere for me.

I looked at the beautiful Kendo once more and then hurried out the door. Shem was long gone. I shook my head and went back in.

On the stairs, just as I was pulling my keys out, something else plopped out of the envelope. A pocket-sized pamphlet with two words in white on a black cover: *Feng Shui*. What was that? Was that like jai alai? A subtitle declared: *The mystical Chinese art and science of harmonizing with the environment*. OK, I thought, waiting for a laugh track to play above my head. At the back of the front cover, I discovered a message from Shem. Read everything, he scrawled in pencil, and we'll talk in two days. At the Savoy. Same time. What time was that? Oh right: midnight. The wedge mark between today and tomorrow, the old self that was dying a death by drink so that the new self could be slapped awake into existence.

Two flights before mine, on Preciosa's floor, I heard a door opening. The woman who lived with her cats peeked out, and when she saw me, she came out, gathering the uncinched folds of her terrycloth robe around her. How is— How is— It took her a while to be able to pronounce the name.

I told her everything, standing there in the corridor. At one point she invited me in, but I declined, saying that I was expecting an important phone call. Her face registered a look of disappointment, and seeing this, I reconsidered my decision for just a moment, knowing that I had penance and volunteer work to catch up on.

At the hospital, Preciosa had looked waylaid, diminished. It was the same look of people conditioned by having to wait in line, slouching in the corridors of anonymous-making institutions before passing through door after door to get endless forms stamped. She was in a room she shared with three other people, each one more miserable-looking than the last, racked with mysterious ailments which I was assured were not contagious, but which nevertheless warranted the protection of thick vinyl curtains between the beds. The whitewashed stucco walls radiated with the exhaustion of witness, reminding us that we were no more special than the countless other cases of death and numbness it had been forced to contain over the years. In the two hours I spent visiting, not a single nurse made an appearance to check on anyone. I was the only one there, sitting at the foot of Preciosa's bed and keeping up a continuous, largely one-sided stream of idle chatter. At one point I told Preciosa what I had discovered the previous night, about her being an actress. She looked at me stone-faced, as if daring me to go on. Cowardly, I dropped the subject.

I told the neighbor none of this, and instead used generic descriptions to paint a scene: Preciosa was "well." "Rested." The pain was "under control." The nurses had been "helpful." They were waiting on X rays to see whether an operation was necessary. That would take another day, at the very least. But she was "well."

The neighbor looked so grateful—having projected herself so thoroughly into Preciosa's condition, being the same age—and I understood immediately why I had told the story the way I did, and realized that, after all, I had done my penance, my volunteer work for the day.

9

The magazines seemed to have been published just to bring the capital O of disbelief to my lips, and then keep it there. In *House & Garden*, there was a page devoted to pillows and what were called "throws." There was a picture of all these items piled atop one another. A cashmere "throw"—which, as far as I understood, was like a blanket, except instead of people, it was meant to cover a piece of furniture, adding some color, or immediately changing the texture or the "look" or "feel" of a room: these were two words which I gathered were interchangeable and were peppered throughout the pages of the magazine—was listed at a retail price of nine hundred dollars. Imagine my mouth. Nine hundred dollars for a blanket. The word "cashmere," I gathered, was supposed to balance the weight of the nine hundred dollars. I had to turn back to the cover to see if I had missed the words "a parody" anywhere, but there was nothing. What was Condé Nast? Was that like Feng Shui? What a name. If I were Agatha Christie and wanted a character with the dubious air of fake aristocracy, I might come up with that name. A Hungarian count, say, with a blackmailable past. That would make for a nice mystery right there. But murder victim or perpetrator? I couldn't decide. Perhaps a victim after all, his corpse discovered underneath a blood-soaked cashmere throw that retailed for nine hundred dollars, in which case the detective—who would be myself—would be hard put to decide which was the more urgent crime: corpse or cost?

There was another page filled with things that were made of leather: shoehorns, place mats, ottomans, lampshades, picture frames. The prices . . . But then I could go on and on.

I turned to the sections that Shem wanted me to study.

In both, the pictures showcased the same spacious, light-filled apartment from various imaginative angles. In the words of Condé Nast *House & Garden*: "What was once a cramped duplex has been transformed by Suzy Yamada and the architectural firm of Stowan & McKettrick into an expansive habitat that resembles, in feel, a SoHo loft." The floor was dark cherry wood and it glowed. Inside a fireplace stood three glass vases filled with tall flowers of orange and red like sparks of flame. For a coffee table, there was a large sheet of glass which sat atop four low metal wheels. There was a bank of windows in the living room which let in enviable sunlight and looked out across the street above the roof of some red-bricked building that a caption identified as the Museum of Natural History. There were pictures of bedrooms. Suzy Yamada's, yellow and red. Her son Kendo's, a neutral white. Two others for the use of guests. There was the kitchen, with a lot of shiny metal surfaces. And three bathrooms, each with its own distinct "look": one to make you think you were in Rome; one that linked up with the kitchen, having the same shiny metallic "look" that put me in mind of a morgue; and another that resembled a ship's cabin. And finally, adjoining Suzy Yamada's bedroom, a beautiful terrace that was like a private box looking out onto the drama of the city, filled with pots overgrown with tall grass and various flowering bulbs, and to sit in, artfully rusted wrought-iron chairs.

I was intrigued by the recurrence of the same sentence in both articles: *I need better Feng Shui.*

Suzy Yamada talked about moving furniture. She talked about

the placement of mirrors. She talked about the relationship between the doorway and the foot of the stairs which led to the second floor, where the bedrooms—and thus "our souls in repose"—were. She talked of being disappointed by one Feng Shui consultant and being on the lookout for another . . .

This brought me to the pamphlet, and as much as my instincts were to parodize—as I was beginning to understand that Feng Shui somehow meant the rearrangement of furniture to attract luck and "good spirits" into the house, the same way that a throw could automatically change the "look" or the "feel" of a place—I forced myself into the material, and as soon as I did, I was caught up once more in the engine rhythm of my hunger for learning. Within an hour, I'd finished all fifty-five pages, complete with illustrations. My roughshod definition of Feng Shui remained unchanged.

My only question at the end of my reading was: Who was Suzy Yamada? And what kind of scenario did Shem have in store for her, involving me?

I looked back at the statement she had made about wanting better Feng Shui. Certainly, the apartment, arranged and photographed to great effect, bore no clues. I looked at the photographs of her, beside her son. The only clue was in the one picture: Kendo with something like discontent on his lips. Was that what she wanted remedied through this thing that to my mind was no better than the pagan superstitions of my Filipino grandmother, hemmed in inside her house for most of her life because of the paucity of days deemed opportune by her fortune-teller? A woman unwilling to leave her crumbling Tondo residence, much less the country, and who had to be eventually left behind by her family heading for America. Could there have been more than superstition—perhaps, after all, a premonitory wisdom—in her decision not to set foot in this country?

I returned to the pamphlet.

"Very popular" and "trendy" were words that kept recurring in its pages, and behind those words, I got the feeling that somebody was winking their eyes and licking their lips.

* 10 *

The skeletons at the Savoy were applauding. A young white guy with an unshaven face and a small potbelly was being cradled, motherlike, in the arms of a pretty black drag queen. The song was something by Patsy Cline. Barney saw me and nodded, and for him it was as close as he would ever get to normal human interaction. I sat at the bar and ordered a beer.

No tequila? Barney asked, surprised.

I resisted the urge to tell him that I'd had my quota of water for the day.

I nursed my drink in silence. The clock with the tinfoil rays said that it was midnight. Any minute now . . .

There was Shem, looking directly at the bar and seeing me. His impassive face was like a senator's or a preacher's, with important information that he didn't want to surrender so quickly.

We shook hands. He ordered a beer, which Barney brought pronto. Did you read the material? he asked. What do you think? he asked.

I had a feeling that I was not expected to think but instead to make myself blank and pliant, ready to translate whatever information I received into action.

His plan was very simple. He needed me to pretend to be an expert on, what else, Feng Shui. That way, he could take me into a series of homes owned by those people who formed the circle he so detested.

In these people's self-projections, they appeared as colorful characters given distinct outlines by private areas of expertise—admen, screenwriters, Wall Streeters, realtors, magazine editors—but really they were nothing more than blind lemmings with the instinct to follow. And what they all seemed so eager to get behind was this new trend.

They fancied themselves to have artistic sensibilities and/or sympathies—who talked about "inspiration" and "the muse" as things more concrete and vivid than anything from their hidden pasts— and therefore had a natural predisposition to believe in the unseen. And if this unseen was given the weighty cultural imprimatur of two thousand years of Chinese civilization—well, that was as good as gold!

It was a group that knew how to perpetuate itself. What was that bit of Catholic prayer? World without end? For them, it was the very same thing.

More new people kept finding themselves suddenly prosperous and, desiring the inoculation that prosperity can buy, would get referrals from members of the established circle for brand names—interior designers; books to catch up on whose titles could then be conspicuously dropped at parties; restaurants in which to be seen; charities to support—and in this way, would build up the same glass bubble by which a group begins to recognize and protect itself . . . Marianna, Bill Hood, his own disgusting father, the people who stood in for the entire circle who not only laughed at him but, what's worse, had by this time forgotten all about him.

The way he talked reminded me of Preciosa and myself discussing Divina Valencia as she swam to and fro inside her goldfish bowl: everything seen from a giant's distant, haughty perspective.

As he talked, his hands moved the same way that his daughter's did, first going from a position of holding an invisible football, and then dropping it and lengthening the distance between his hands, and then keeping his hands in the same position but adding a single, subtle touch: turning the ends of his fingers crooked, into claws: from "big" to "scary": this time he really was talking about himself.

What exactly would *I* do?

Study the book he gave me, by which he meant the pamphlet. And study some more. Check out titles from the library—there was an ever-growing list on the subject. Learn the terminologies, get comfortable with those foreign, shaken-out-of-a-bag syllables because I would be counted upon, when declaiming and performing in these people's houses, to have a flair that was the decisive complement of authority. Once more, I ran my Agatha Christie vocabulary list through my head: obfuscate, obstinate, obstreperous, ostentatious, oracular. The last word, in particular, began to ring bells.

And he needed me to know exactly what principles to follow, how to rearrange the furniture and suggest color schemes and locate props that would assist these people in their quest for buffers against the harsh world of New York: *peace*, *harmony*, *prosperity* settling over their frantic modern lives: words to which the Chinese, by virtue of age and an evanescent sense of spiritual superiority, have become attached as experts and expediters . . . Except . . . He paused tantalizingly . . . Except he needed me to do just one thing wrong. Do one thing that was the exact contradiction of what those manuals said to do. For a banker, for example, he needed me to do the one thing that would ensure that his money schemes would be met with failure. He needed me to familiarize myself with that one thing, and then carry it out, like planting a secret, ticking time bomb.

But, I asked Shem, wouldn't that be contingent on the veracity of this Feng Shui thing? What if it wasn't true at all?

If it's not true, we'll still have scammed them. And it'll still be like a big fuck-you in the middle of where they live. Like a rape, he said. Like sneaking into their homes and doing ugly, hateful things to the things they love. And what's worse, all with their cooperation. And if this Feng Shui is true, so much the better. Suffering and pestilence. I've got the best of both worlds.

And my second question was: Why me?

He looked at me, as if the answer couldn't have been more obvious. I need an Oriental, he said, because this thing, this Feng Shui, is the province of an Oriental. And I've looked. I've looked and haven't found anyone who can go as low as you've gone. You've gone low, you can go low again. He made this sound like a compliment. You and me, he said. You and me are the right team. With your face and my plans . . .

And I sat there, mentally going back years to when I knew this guy, Sam M, a confidence trickster. He conducted his various scams on the streets, in pool halls, bus depots, airports, at the racetrack, anyplace where the flurry of crowds ruled and which helped give his face an erased-over aspect. He put on a show and hustled. And oh boy, what a show that was, aided by his aging priest's look, which, when you encountered it, made you blindly drop all your defenses, and then he'd cinch his hold over you by lubricating Ripley's Believe It or Not hard-luck stories with expertly squeezed tears. But it was strictly small-scale, one sucker at a time, and only for whatever pocket money they happened to have at the moment. A mom-and-pop operation. Had he graduated by now?

What Shem was proposing was bigger. Could we pull it off? The books I loved, after all, depended on apprehension and punishment as part of their ritual satisfaction.

When I came to, Shem was looking at his shot glass as if trying to divine something from the oily smudges of his own fingerprints. There was a mirror behind the bar, a yellow thing with my face on it. Looking at it made me afraid. Oriental, said the invisible caption beneath my face. This caption was crowding out another, which said: Saint. My heart was beating fast. And I realized I was feeling the kind of big fear I'd vowed I would be smart enough never to open the door to next time around. But here I was nevertheless, poised . . . Oh, wait a minute. There was another question I wanted to ask Shem: Who's Suzy Yamada? But when I turned to him, there was only an empty shot glass and neatly arranged bills on top of it. The indentation on his barstool was slowly filling up again. The vivid red doorway bore no trace. And when Barney collected the bills, he found a piece of paper. I think this is for you, he said, handing it to me. On it was a phone number.

11

I went to the library, this time to check out two books on Shem's subject. That was how I thought of it. Belonging to Shem. Apart from myself. Something I could borrow, put on, and then return when everything was said and done. But then again, the same thing could be said of almost everything I encountered: Sometimes an object may possess a force field which repelled me, but more often I was the owner of this shield, and I made sure to put the proper distance between myself and my surroundings. But whether it was to protect me from them, or them from whatever contamination I believed myself to have, I'd long since forgotten.

I took the books to Central Park. Another beautiful day with the sun unfettered by clouds. Green trees everywhere held up a light blue sky. I took off the jacket I'd put on earlier and walked to a bench, one end of which was held down by an old man wearing plaid golf pants and eating what looked like a peanut butter sandwich. On top of his balding head he wore a golf cap, turned at a crisp angle. He moved his body away from me, protective of his own eating. I could see him peeling off the edges of the bread, and after he'd amassed eight of these pieces he took them up one by one and threw them on the ground, making small brown sparrows appear with a sudden whoosh. They dismantled the pieces with great industry, needing three or four tries to break off a piece they could then swallow. The old man stood up, dusting crumbs from his pants, and walked peacefully away. He showcased a backside creased in the shape of the bench's wooden slats.

I could hear, but not see, children playing somewhere. Even at this distance, their shrill cries were enough to send the birds scurrying in fear. And then Third World nannies came into view, pushing their towheaded wards in strollers upholstered in flowery fabrics, fabrics that echoed the surrounding scenery. Suddenly, among the towheaded wards reared the smiling, cackling presence of Beulah, her nanny behind her. They were stopped so that the nanny could converse with colleagues. Among these were a couple of Filipinas, who didn't see me.

Beulah was looking at me with what seemed to be a look of recognition, but that couldn't be. For the first time I realized how closely she resembled her father. It was unnerving, like Shem looking right at me, keeping an eye to make sure I fulfilled my part.

Being here, cut off from any city feeling, and just like a tourist, filled with a gauzy impression of having left my real life far behind, sitting here, witnessing spring and the resurgence of green and more lulling green, reminding me of my newfound appreciation for nature, and therefore my age, my having slowed down, which seemed a preview of more to come, though my new job would seem to refute it, idling here, I could hardly summon the energy to visualize the group for whom I would be performing this Chinese magic, but reversed. Who would believe, sheltered here by cottony trees and entertained by the hypnotic, squeaky metronome of birds, that these fanged, long-fingernailed people could be in the same world as me, that I could even reach them? The twin towers of a West Side building peeked shyly in the far distance above trees, but they looked about as fake as a billboard.

But wasn't Beulah here? The youngest citizen of that fabled group, infecting the tranquillity. I looked at her closely and realized that her resemblance to Shem lay in her startling aliveness—a look of pleasure on her miniature face, not in appreciation of the blessings in her young life, but in anticipation of more, much more to come. Underlined by a strong, inherited sense of deserving. I understood why the nanny looked so exhausted. She was the guardian of the future, and in this case, there was nothing mysterious about the future, it would be a furthering of the past and of the present, the same power, same money, same straight, unperturbed line through the American landscape, recalling another Catholic phrase: Now as it shall be forever. Amen.

I cracked open the first of the library books. The first lines my eyes lit on said: "The term Feng Shui literally translates as 'wind water.' These are two elements thought to be essential to the life of any living thing, and are equivalent to what the Chinese call 'chi'— 'energies' or 'currents'—through which Feng Shui operates."

New York, though it was hard to believe from the evidence in front of me, was a desert, and in it, the people yearned for wind and water. In this simplification lay Shem's genius.

I closed the book. Shut my eyes. Wind water, I said to myself. And then aloud. Wind. Water. Feng. No, Fung. Shwee. Fung Shwee. Which was what?

I opened my eyes and I was no longer in the park. I was inside the pages of Shem's magazines, walking around in the spacious rooms, pretending to see something I couldn't. I said, trying out the words on my lips: It's an ancient Chinese philosophy, known in the West as "geomancy." Was that right?

I verified the information. I was exactly right. Geomancy. A perfect Agatha Christie word—a training that Shem, in deeming me the man for the job, could not have known about. To an imaginary dupe, money jammed tight into his pockets but which could be made to fall out by the polish of my performance, I continued: It's something we Chinese—that's right, good, you're Chinese now—it's something we Chinese have grown up with but which only now seems to be making itself known in the West. It's nothing more than a combination of common sense and intuition. We Chinese believe that the way your house is arranged is instrumental in determining and forecasting your fortunes, financial and otherwise.

refer to pg. 40; unused furniture to look @ = rich?

I walked home repeating the words over and over: Fung Shwee. Hello, I imagined myself saying, not proffering my hand because I was now Chinese, Old Worldish and distant. I am Mr. Fungshwee.

Hello I've come to do your Fungshwee.

You ordered Fungshwee? Extra topping with that?

I tried squinting my eyes but found myself unable to see.

On the streets I must've appeared insane, but I didn't care. I practiced first one walk, mincing like a geisha, and deciding it wouldn't do, tried long strides accompanied by a showy swinging of both arms, like a pasha, but that was too much. And then I decided on a walk that was my normal—that was to say, pitched exactly between geisha and pasha, signifying nothing.

These people want wind and water, I said to myself, continuing into the night and hoping, by infecting my dreams with that image, to seal my new identity: in one hand I would be holding a watering can, in the other a swiveling fan. Water their couches, watch them sprout money. Blow air through their bedrooms so that dust, long-settled and unhealthy, could be cleared out the window. Hey, I thought: just like what I do for Preciosa. But better paid. In league with the sellers of nine-hundred-dollar throws. A thrower. Or rather, they would be the throwers—of money—and I, the catcher.

But still, there was a frightened part of me that wouldn't believe. Could Shem be wrong after all? What if I couldn't pull it off?

12

H ere was the next step: Oldero Barbershop. The sign was fired by bright noonday sunshine. Through the doors I passed, following Shem, and it was like gaining access to a sepia-tinted world in the middle of modern New York. Old men wearing the slightly transparent starched shirts of another way of life looked at us. The crisp straw hats on their heads all swiveled simultaneously.

Shem took the initiative and smiled. Greeted with a silence which he confidently took for friendliness, he began his inquiries, addressing them all together because he wasn't sure which was the "boss." He slowed down his English and pointed at me. Finally he finished and one of the men got up from his seat and indicated for me to sit there. He did this without speaking, without answering Shem. This gave him the air of a master. And it gave me a clue as to how I myself would behave later, in front of an audience. The other men went back to the magazines and racing forms they'd been consulting before our entrance. We were the only outsiders in the shop, and in the space of the few minutes that we'd been here, the sun had slanted further downward and, shooting through the dusty windows, was casting backward letters on various surfaces, including the legs of my pants. Shem gave the man instructions, using the words "handsome" and "conservative." The barber took in his words in silence. Consulting my reflection in the mirror, he frowned. Apparently he had his work cut out for him: He seemed to be thinking: How can I fashion from the junk of this unruly boy's face and hair a result that would come close to being described as "handsome" or "conservative"?

Whether he had any idea of how to bring this about I didn't know. Nonetheless, he began. Pushing my head down, and turning the chair at various angles to suit his needs, he took swatches of my hair between fingers and began cutting. I could feel the deliberate snipping of scissors against the nape of my neck, like being seduced by mischievous fingers.

To our right, the men were engrossed in their reading materials still, their jaunty hats protruding like emanations of their elegant heads.

And then, everything was done. The barber announced this with a small tap on my shoulders, clearing away fallen hair. I could hear Shem standing up and approaching us. We were a trio in the mirror, which was now flooded with blinding light, as if for a curtain call. The two of them were looking, but with my head bowed, I had yet to acknowledge the finished product.

I could feel the hush of anticipation coming off the barber's colleagues like vapors of heat. Five hats sat tensely in a row, waiting for a signal from me before allowing themselves to be bowled over.

What did I think? asked Shem. Up until then, I'd been too nervous to look at myself. But now, the barber had two fingers placed at the nape of my neck and was using them to guide my head ever so gently upward until finally—my eyes locked into their mirror twins. My head was not my head at all! What do you think? Shem asked again. Nice, I replied, which admittedly was a telegram version of the actual thought running through my head. Which was this: The whole world is looking for someone to fall in love with. I remembered Jokey, on his way to being a matinee idol. I remembered

Kendo, the beautiful Kendo, making his debut in the pages of *House & Garden* and *Metropolitan Home*. And then I thought, acknowledging my transformed, beautiful head, and letting the nagging voice of self-commentary recede for once into the background: If the whole world is looking for someone to fall in love with, why couldn't it just as well be you?

13

I brought with me a surplus of confidence. It transformed the waiter's outfit I had on, making its humbleness seem like a choice.

Shem was leading me into the lobby, its red-hued marble newly waxed, forcing us to walk with mincing steps. He was playing the role of the great familiar, shaking hands with the black doorman, who acted as if the event was a privilege. As the elevator doors slid shut, the doorman announced ceremonially, because this was part of his job: Fourth floor. Which was where we found ourselves in no time.

The door to the apartment was open, and standing in front of it was the poet we'd come to see, Lindsay S. He smiled on seeing Shem, as if amused that Shem was still alive, and what's more "Looking good, my friend." The two of them shook hands.

And this must be . . . , he said, turning to me.

Shem introduced me: William Chao.

It was the name he'd decided on. He didn't consult me. He knew

I would accept. He'd greased my palm with five hundred dollars. Another of his various signs of good faith. Five hundred dollars with which, on his advice, I opened a savings account, using my real name: Paulinha, William Narciso: a name whose very ornateness was nothing more than a decoy. This is what I want to say: I have long been singed by my experiences, turned—for lack of a better word— "modern," acidic; every attitude you thought of as urban and mundane I owned; but these people—the first of whom was Shem, and now this Lindsay S, who, admittedly, looked like a sweetheart, a lamb—were more than happy to preserve me in the brine of ancient stereotype: a soul directly linked to the ancestral past, shot through with the very thing which the white man had given up in exchange for technological advancement—spiritual enlightenment—and the lack of which now made him inferior, in need of guidance . . . I felt trapped. All right, if that's what you want, that's what I will become. I will turn myself into something I am not. I will be your Condé Nast for you . . . The night before, lying in bed, my future had seemed boundless, stretching before me like an eternity. Mainly I saw myself surrounded by waist-high piles of money. Whichever way I moved, I made a sound. It was the kind of protection I didn't know I had been looking for until I found it. Or, at least, was this close to finding it. The words Condé Nast had appeared, taking hold of my thoughts. Black type on white paper. Stared at long enough, the first word began to molt: Condé breathed, expanding: Condé . . . scend.

I bowed my head at this poet whose poems I had never heard of, much less read, and he did the same, and then he took my hands in his. Lindsay, he said, introducing himself. I smiled. Pleasure being mine and all that.

How are you? he asked. Though a white American, he had a foreign accent that I couldn't place. A twinge of—South American, could it be?

Come in come in, he told us, ushering us into a long narrow hallway fitted with hat- and coatracks and with a mahogany sideboard pushed against one wall. On top of the sideboard stood a jumble: vases of dried flowers and crystal dishes of many colors which were filled with loose change, keys, matchbooks, and candy. I had nothing to surrender and waited as Lindsay hung up Shem's oversized blue blazer. He motioned for us to walk ahead of him, down a path that led to an open doorway, behind which rosy light beckoned.

Through the doorway. My heart beating fast. My newly cut hair brushing against the top. When had I gotten so tall? Eyes wide open, surveying everything: an avocado green couch facing two armchairs, also avocado-colored, all upholstered in what looked to be velvet; multicolored pillows bouncing on top of these; a fireplace with an iron sculpture of logs aflame; various precious-looking knickknacks—a pair of dull silver candlesticks with dragons going up their sides; three ivory brooches with the yellowish color of age—a pair of dragons, and a phoenix with an elaborately carved tail; a miniature jade sculpture of cherry blossom (?) trees encased in a glass box; and various postcard-sized reproductions of Chinese Cultural Revolution propaganda posters framed in handsome dark wood—on a marble mantelpiece; heavy wine-colored velvet drapes drawn over two windows; four floor-to-ceiling bookcases—two on each side of the fireplace—painted white: every single shelf jammed with the spines of new-looking hardcovers. Cursory glance at the titles. Some in French, some in Spanish, some in Italian. Among the English: Victor Hugo, Thomas Hardy, Mary Barton, Anthony Trollope. Names I didn't recognize but recognized, in that way that dead people of a certain repute had: washing over daily life in snatches of overheard murmurs, or momentarily stopping the eye in curious bits from newspapers and magazines. Who was this man, this poet? And how could he afford this beautiful place on the Upper East Side? Shem told me very little, perhaps not wanting me to be intimidated before anything had even begun. Beyond the room was a doorway which promised more space, more luxury.

All the time he'd been talking to Shem, the two of them catching up, he'd been staring unabashedly at me. I stood myself by the fireplace, my back to the artfully darkened and cracked mirror above the mantelpiece. Across on the other side of the room, was a small desk meant for letter writing, and a chair. Lindsay and Shem had both turned to look as if I had become part of the apartment, another object put out on display. I didn't say anything. And tried to make my covetous sweep of the contents seem like a professional duty. What would I say? Shem and Lindsay both waited. I looked at Lindsay.

Drinks, he said cheerfully, as if having inferred that from my look. What would you like?

Scotch, said Shem.

None for me, I said.

Are you sure? No water? Juice?

Oh. Water. Water would be good.

Sparkling?

Tap, I said. A beat later, I realized this made me seem cheap, ordinary, two things I was not supposed to be. But Lindsay didn't seem to notice. He said, I have Evian.

That's fine too, I said, trying to cover my embarrassment.

All right. Evian and scotch. He turned to Shem: Straight up or on the rocks?

On the rocks, replied Shem.

Lindsay disappeared. In his absence, Shem and I didn't say anything. He smiled at me, that was all.

When Lindsay came back, he found Shem seated on the couch and me exactly where I had been. I had time to look at the titles while he was gone. I couldn't find a single Agatha Christie. But then, I remembered, he was a poet. And besides, the library seemed like a museum built to advertise someone's erudition, with no time for casual reading, no time for fun. And to showcase wealth, to judge by the books' handsome spines, their rococo gold letterings sunk deep into the luxurious leather.

He brought me water and ice in a glass that felt like a dead weight in my hands. There was a single small diamond etched inside the rim, and as I lifted the glass to take a sip, it caught the light and sparkled. Immediately the water I drank gained in taste and value. I sipped. I said, You have a beautiful place. Just that. Beautiful. Noncommittal. Something he'd have heard a million times before. But it seemed to have woken him up.

Oh, he said. Let me show you the other rooms.

Beyond the living room was the dining room, a mini-chandelier hanging from the low ceiling. And I realized, the man had had the apartment built to suit his shortness, with everything lower and closer to the ground, like a Japanese residence. I hadn't grown taller after all.

Beyond the dining room was a hallway that had two small doors on each side and which ended in an open doorway, its black square appearing to be without depth. Lindsay opened the doors at our sides. Each was a guest bedroom, outfitted with every luxury; each with windows opening onto views of green now made black by lamplight. He closed those doors and led us to the dark square.

He turned on a light: It was a small alcove which had to its right a wrought-iron spiral staircase. We followed Lindsay's ascending figure. Another full floor was revealed when he turned on dim, rosy overhead lights. More bookcases flanked a huge center window that looked out onto empty Park Avenue. Textbooks this time, a profusion of bright colors, which made me think momentarily that they were bought solely for purposes of decoration. A whole shelf, however, was streaked by the same black: multiple copies of the only book Lindsay S had ever published, a suite of poems entitled *Despair*. Yeah right, I thought, looking at all his possessions. Lindsay presented me with a copy, bowing. I bowed back. I had a premonition that this would be a frequent m.o. from now on, and my neck ached in advance.

There was a large bathroom with artfully uneven slate tiles of contrasting shades of gray and green, and a Jacuzzi and shower stall standing at opposite ends.

And then Lindsay's bedroom. Eyes giving a quick survey: Ah-hah! Something to declare. I looked at Lindsay. And smiled. I could disavow everything. I still had time. That was what I was thinking, confronted by his short figure swathed in cotton. Why do things to this guy on whom a child could draw bunny ears and not be said to be caricaturing but instead completing? He was responsible for nothing. He was like what I was to him: a symbol, a cardboard cutout.

And then I jumped in with both feet, and said: The mirror facing your bed should not be there. Because when the soul wakes up at night to move about in your dreams, and it sees its own reflection, it might scare itself to death.

Though I wasn't facing him, I could sense Shem stifling a smile.

Lindsay obediently took the mirror down from the wall, revealing what it was put up to cover: some stain that looked like the print of a bird's feet. He paused to consider this, putting a hand below his chin. His fingers made a bristling sound as he moved them back and forth in contemplation. And then he lit on a solution, saying cheerily: I just bought a new painting that could go very well there.

The second thing: The view outside his window was marred by a telephone pole.

Hmm, said Lindsay, awaiting an explanation.

The Chinese, I said, believe in secret arrows which drain away and threaten life. They call this malignant force *sha*. Telephone poles outside a window create this unfortunate phenomenon. I knew that I sounded like a textbook, but how else could I have phrased everything and still sounded the part?

Yes, Lindsay said, nodding.

Meanwhile, Shem had sat himself on the bed without asking. He looked at me eagerly to see how everything would unfold.

You could, I told Lindsay, counter this by placing a tank of goldfish directly across from where the poles are. This would absorb the *sha*.

Lindsay frowned. He explained that he traveled too often to be able to maintain an aquarium. I told him then a plant would do, something green and with a red bow tied around its base, or better yet, planted in a pot painted gold.

He paused to consider the aesthetic effect this would have, and then said yes, he would do as I said.

I gave his bedroom one last glance and then nodded my final approval.

Lindsay saved the best for last. He opened the door and turned on the lights like a master of ceremonies, with a little flourish that ought to have been followed by gasps, but unfortunately we didn't oblige. Not that we didn't feel like it. I'm sure Shem had the same reaction. Or perhaps he'd seen it all before and was merely curious about what effect it would have on me. It was all I could do to keep my mouth from hanging open. The man had it bad. His huge crush on Asian culture was much bigger than Shem had led me to believe.

Special pin lights in the ceiling isolated three beautiful Chinese scrolls hanging on the wall directly facing us: A pavilion scene with two maidens attending a musician, the folds of their sleeves rendered in simple strokes that miraculously conveyed their billowing textures; a wineshop scene of traveling scholars pausing for a rest and drink; a painting of blue-green mountains festooned with trees that looked like tiny, arthritic hands and the tops of which jutted against inky, low-hanging clouds. All this had to be explained to me, of course. Ostensibly, he was speaking for Shem's benefit, because, since I was an Oriental, of what use was all this instruction to me? Lindsay's voice turned deeper with authority. His eyes were— Dancing, that was the most accurate description. His own private museum. Built with love, I was sure. But with my own blithe disregard for the very things that he was venerating, things forming a sort of past for myself and which I therefore did everything to get behind me, his love could have no value but as comedy.

Sitting on shoulder-high pedestals and kept under glass I observed various teapots and teacups, Japanese swords, calligraphic ink sets, plates with blue flowers and swimming carp painted on. Lindsay with one gesture of flourish after another.

And then best of all, as he turned on another of his innumerable switches: Ensconced behind glass, hundreds of Buddhas of dazzling variety—made of gold, silver, copper, porcelain, jade, different kinds of wood, even plastic; pendant- and TV-sized, and everything in between; some were toys, some jewels, and others ancient temple relics (this last one Shem would later reveal as having been bought on the black market): They were all sitting inertly on library shelves made out of some dark wood, filling up an entire wall. Their eyes stared straight ahead of them, confronting eternity, an eternity which we were now blocking. Some were smiling at this view of the three of us, perhaps being in on the joke. But mostly they had a straight line for a mouth and eyes that were the stock illustration of wisdom: a refusal to be amused. This bank of serious, faintly disapproving faces, with their collective air of sitting in judgment, was powerless to warn Lindsay, who acted not so much as a believer but as a parent, a collector, an owner, with powers far above those possessed by—and accruing from—the very things he owned. Turned novelty, these statues had lost their native force. I had a sudden flash of myself as a revenger, sent by the fat, contented icons before us to show Lindsay their true powers.

Having completed the tour, Lindsay was now silent, awaiting comment. I knew exactly what to say. Marvelous, I told him. You have done my culture proud. My instincts told me to put my arms around him, and I did, welcoming him to a club that he had already long ago been a member of, without any help from me. Again I bowed. My eyes confronted the patent-leather shoes I had on. Two days ago these shoes had sat inside a box in a Florsheim's. Today they were taking me through the paces of this museum tour. In Lindsay's brain, it was he who was giving the tour. But Shem and I knew better: The clearest layout of things was the one in our heads.

Was it going to be this easy?

Scuffle of shoes on wood floor. Polished, clinking. A sound I will forever associate with being in the presence of money. Retracing our steps. I gave everything another once-over, as if trying to look out for things to be fixed. Lindsay followed my eyes with nervousness, which, when he noticed me noticing, he tucked beneath a look of quick, contemptuous challenge: if friends and family had only the best things to say about his connoisseur's arrangements, would I daringly, insubordinately break rank? I decided to keep quiet. Perhaps the man didn't want Feng Shui so much as applause.

On a side table by an armchair next to the paperbacks was a picture frame. I took it up and looked, turned even bolder by Shem's seeming ease in my performance. For stretches I noticed that he went without paying attention to us. He looked either out the windows or at the floor. What could he be thinking? Perhaps he'd become bored by the smoothness of everything.

I heard Lindsay's voice intrude on my thoughts. That's me, he said. It took me a beat to realize that he was referring to the picture in my hand. In it, a young boy dressed in a stiff white shirt and matching white knee-length shorts looked uncomfortably at the camera, squinting his eyes at some unseen glare. The costume looked like a uniform of some kind. I asked Lindsay.

Catholic school, he replied. My heart skipped a beat. I wanted to ask further, comparing notes from my own boyhood spent in Manila's Catholic schools. But that was not my history now. And so

I smiled instead, making some comment about how adorable he looked. Without prompting, he revealed that he was no longer Catholic. Lapsed, he said of himself, laughing a laugh that sounded self-congratulatory. He added, It happens to the best of us. No hint of regret or apology in his voice. He only made it sound like he was talking about yesterday's fashion discarded on the closet floor. Once more I had to stifle the urge to relate my own parallel story, one of disillusionment and turncoatism. In light of what I thought of as Catholicism's betrayal, every move I made thereafter, every sin committed, seemed to be to taunt the watchful eyes of ever-present saints behind my shoulders, saints who were first stand-ins for my parents, and then—when the years of no contact caused even my parents to fade into washed-out carbons—saints who became only themselves, but even more so: malignant things that trailed me with taunting whispers whispered into my ears in my very own voice, convincing me, despite the advances I had made through petty crime, that I was still at heart a Catholic, and therefore worthless, perpetually worthless.

Here we were now, sitting once again in Lindsay's living room with the fireplace and the bookcases. In front of us, on a table, was tea. Lindsay put a cup to his mouth. He wanted me to tell him about my childhood in Hong Kong.

I had a peripatetic life, I told him. This was a word taken directly from Shem, the writer: Peripatetic. Meaning to and fro, suitcase-based, a wanderer. Thus instructed, I told Lindsay, the poet, and he nodded with appreciation at the introduction of this fine word to match the fine things in his room, another collectible.

My grandfather was a merchant whose ventures were never successful. Frustrated, he consulted a Feng Shui man in Kowloon who turned out to be the miracle cure he was looking for. And soon my grandfather was applying the principles of Feng Shui to everything in his life: down to the most propitious dates for the birth of his children, forcing early delivery or delaying painful ones if necessary. My father's life, in turn, was guided almost entirely by Feng Shui. Which school to go to, what degrees to take, what business proposals to entertain or reject. Feng Shui, I told Lindsay, is really nothing more than the merging of intuition with common sense. My father, as a result of Feng Shui, emerged with a wonderful education, a thriving business in textiles, a wife whose personality suited his, and three children who were sure to carry on the family traditions. A more perfect definition of felicity you couldn't find.

Another of Shem's words: felicity. Like a musical notation.

How interesting, Lindsay said. You must have had a strict life then. Maybe, despite our cultural differences, our childhoods were very similar after all.

How so? asked Shem, the Jew.

Well, my childhood, you know, the childhood of most of my Catholic friends—and factor in the fact that this was a childhood in the South, the serious South—our childhoods, looking back on them now from my grown-up perspective, were so hemmed in. Don't do this, don't do that. I mean, the Ten Commandments. Plus a hundred smaller Orders. And going to Catholic school, my God! The uniform. Which—he turned to me as he said this—you saw in that picture upstairs. I keep that picture as a reminder to myself of everything that I've risen above, not as a cherished memento. That picture drives me even to this day. I mean my poems. People ask me what my sources are. They look at my house, and they ask how can you possibly write a book called *Despair*, and I tell them that I went to Catholic school, and of course, if you're a Catholic of any stripe, lapsed or not, you'd understand immediately.

I looked at Lindsay with encouragement.

He continued: Catholic school, don't get me started. We didn't realize it then, of course, but now! I mean, all those stories of saints and what do they have in common? These people earn their Catholic stripes through the most incredibly masochistic rituals of suffering. That's how Catholicism tells you to become a legitimate Catholic: suffering. Jee-sus! What a fucked-up indoctrination. The people who survive do so through a kind of great, gigantic will. Or through sheer blind luck. He laughed.

Which one are you? asked Shem.

Which do you think? Lindsay retorted, his laughter exploding even more. The first of course. I sure didn't inherit my money from my family.

How did you inherit your money? Shem asked, with the air of someone who already knew the answer.

I meh-reed it! Lindsay replied.

Shem turned to me and even when he continued speaking to Lindsay, he didn't turn away, eager to gauge my reaction. He said, Tell William how your wife died.

A skiing accident, Lindsay replied without skipping a beat. A sour note was struck again, but both men were careful to keep the tones of their voices level, as if simply asking for the sugar to be passed.

Mysterious circumstances, Shem said to me.

For the first time, I had a personal glimpse into what Shem had only claimed in his stories: His great disdain for the things that came with ease. Like this project. Everything was going along so well, and now he needed the challenge of looming failure to keep him interested.

Yes, Lindsay said. My wife was said to have died in mysterious circumstances. But I was not responsible for her death in any way. Those, by the way—he spoke this directly to Shem—were the words of the court.

I felt it was up to me to catch the ball. Death, I said, often comes for reasons we cannot gauge until after a long time. Perhaps a lifetime.

Oh, retorted Shem, the reasons are clear enough. How many millions did you say you inherited? he asked Lindsay.

Come on, Shem, Lindsay replied. Mr. Chao doesn't need to be witness to all this.

William, please, I said.

William, conceded Lindsay, with an almost imperceptible bow. This, he explained to me, is our way of catching up. It's mostly harmless.

Little bites

Is it? asked Shem, like a dog refusing to let go of a pant leg.

I interrupted once more. You were telling us about your Catholic childhood, I said to Lindsay.

Hemmed in, echoed Shem, nodding.

Being a Jew, you'd understand, said Lindsay.

Understand what?

Hemmed in, Lindsay replied. More tea?

I shook my head no. And as for Shem, Lindsay didn't even acknowledge him. Lindsay merely poured himself a cup, sipped, and then waited with an expectant air of receiving a grenade through the air. But Shem kept quiet. I could sense a truce forming.

And so could Lindsay. Taking advantage of momentary quiet, he said, But my point was never to talk about myself and my boring history of Catholicism and whatnot—which all my friends have heard a billion times anyway. You were saying, Mr. Chao—

William, I corrected him again.

I'm sorry, William. Old habits die hard. It's just. You're a master. And you know—I hate to invoke my Catholic school training once more but— Well, one of the good things I've retained from that training is calling people by the proper appellation. But yes, William. See? He smiled. I can do it after all. One more thing I've outgrown. Thanks to you.

I smiled sweetly.

Please, William, he encouraged. You were telling us about your family.

I thought he'd finished, said Shem.

I didn't bother to turn my head, adopting Lindsay's tactic.

And your parents, Lindsay asked, are they still alive?

 shem's bitterness

No. I'm afraid they've both passed away.

I'm so sorry.

Well, said Shem with a shrug, that's what parents do.

Lindsay laughed indulgently. Shem tells me you were educated in the States.

The Feng Shui man advised my parents to send me abroad to study.

Which explains why he doesn't speak the least bit of Chinese, said Shem.

You don't? Lindsay inquired.

It's tragic I know, I agreed, nodding. My parents thought it a great tragedy. But ultimately, it was something they were willing to sacrifice in exchange for my life.

Your life? he echoed dramatically.

A fortune-teller, I said, lowering my voice to an expert hush, prophesied that I would not live long if I remained in Hong Kong. That I would die in not very natural circumstances. My father, it turns out, had made enemies in the competitive textile industry. So many jealous people without the right Feng Shui to replicate his business success and who therefore had to resort to other means. And so when my father heard those words, he knew that they must be true. The Feng Shui man, of course, didn't go so far as to echo the fortune-teller, saying that my life was in jeopardy. But he did confirm that training abroad would do me a world of good. Be the first in my family to widen his horizons, and who knows, might even someday take the family business to the next level of global expansion.

But surely you could have received a Chinese education even abroad?

I paused. Inhaled for effect. Even Shem was mesmerized. Then I replied: The fortune-teller told my father that in the likely event his enemies sent scouts to track me down in this country, who I needed to become was someone who would not be found in the places that someone like me, someone like a member of our family, would be. Because of that there could be no Chinese education for me. I had to become this new person so totally that the footprints would be completely wiped out. Even my name, I said, Chao: even that is a false name. Inwardly, I smiled, savoring the truth of the statement.

But, I went on, I've been adopting it for a lifetime and have come to think of it now as truly mine. And it has saved me.

And I added: And thanks to the Feng Shui man, all threats against my father, though not entirely dissipating, have remained only threats, without materializing. Still, for my safety, I'm obliged to live in secret.

The touch about the name was completely unrehearsed, and Shem had to pull in his breath while I had been narrating. Now he looked at me with the unspoken but implied apology of one expert being reminded that another was in the room.

How dramatic, intoned Lindsay, who was putting on such faggy airs that I was beginning to form a picture.

And yourself, I asked, do you have any children?

Shem was trying hard to restrain himself from commenting.

Unfortunately no, Lindsay replied. But such is life.

I'm sure, said Shem, that with all your millions you wouldn't have trouble finding another wife to give you kids.

I don't want another wife, Lindsay said resolutely.

Everyone in the room could sense that the evening had come to a stop. It was only left for us to tie up the threads.

Lindsay took the initiative. He asked Shem, trying hard to tread lightly, as if embarrassed to have to bring this up, though God knows what else I would be doing there—he asked: So when can William come back and do a full consultation with me?

I replied for Shem: Anytime that's convenient for you.

Lindsay's face tilted with surprise at such an easy answer. He asked, How about next week?

I gave him a card Shem had had printed. On it was the name William Chao and below it my home phone number. Call me, I said.

Yes of course, he replied. He stared at the card as if something profound would reveal itself. Finally, he looked up. Coughed. Then said, again afraid of looking at me, Ahh . . . about the . . . the payment?

Please, I said, getting up. I should leave you two to discuss this. And without waiting for their replies, I left and stood in the vestibule with Shem's blue blazer hanging forlornly on the coatrack.

A few minutes later, after a bare minimum of dialogue, there was Shem smiling his wolf's smile. He had one hand cradled behind Lindsay's elbow, the two of them back as best friends.

Lindsay stopped at a distance of about a foot from me. With him, you got the feeling that everything was measured according to a series of arcane formulas and recipes that, put together, created a kind of ceremony by which his life was lived. In other words, when he stopped a foot from me, he intended to stop exactly a foot from me; this distance for him spelled a form of consideration for the Old World in which I stood, behind some invisible painted line on the floor that he wouldn't dare traverse. (There was a reason, after all, that Shem had chosen him for our first mark: inclined to think of me as the living embodiment of a part of the world he had been honoring for nearly a lifetime, he would have nothing but acceptance in his heart.)

The foot distance between us made the next transaction a bit funny, considering that his hands, like the rest of him, were rather short. He revealed a red envelope—the kind the Chinese use for gifts of money—and stretched it in my direction. Here you are, he said.

Something had to give, because I couldn't reach the envelope, though you could see by my face how hard I was trying. The idea that this was perhaps a joke flashed for a brief instant through my mind. And then Lindsay, taking a few cool steps forward and breaking through the perfect crystal of his planned decorum, and with a completely derisive look as if to say that despite my expertise his was still the upper hand doling out the benediction of money, put the envelope within reach, and I grabbed it.

We all smiled.

Shem moved over to where I was.

Lindsay asked, as he saw us to the door, Do you know the work of Yasu-jeer-o Oh-zoo?

Who? I asked.

Yasujiro Ozu, echoed Shem. The Japanese director?

The greatest, replied Lindsay. The most sublime of all movie-makers.

No, I had to admit. I stole a nervous glance at Shem: Was this part of what I had to master as an Oriental as well? It occurred to me that I just might have revealed a chink in an otherwise smooth performance. But Shem's face, with its easy smile, betrayed nothing.

Well, you're in luck, Lindsay said to me. The Walter Reade Theater at Lincoln Center has a two-week-long retrospective. You should go.

Oh yes, Shem said, looking at me. You must. The Chinese and the Japanese are great complementary cultures, he declared, like an irritating docent, but I could see the comment had its intended effect: Lindsay smiled his biggest smile of the evening, and asked, So you think so too? I couldn't be more in agreement. The two greatest cultures in the world. Bar none.

The way Lindsay's face looked as the elevator doors closed I had a feeling that I had just narrowly escaped being pinned to the wall as a trophy.

Shem caught my look of relief and let me have it. Put your goddamn face back on. You don't have time to celebrate. You have a new client tomorrow.

I couldn't believe it. So soon?

You better get used to it. Why do you think I chose this jackass for our first anyway?

Why?

Cause I knew he'd be as good as a town crier. He's probably on the phone to some other fool raving all about you as we speak. Saying which, Shem breathed a weary sigh, as if as soon as the elevator doors opened there would be the line of fools he so confidently believed existed, right there, ready to wash over me with their deafening requests and drown us.

PART 2

* * *

14

There were so many sick people here tonight. And they were all given a momentary outline by lights in the ceiling, illustrating some unknown lesson, before being returned once more to the ashen crowd.

A noisy group, buzzing away, and as they buzzed, they were busy examining each other's clothes and jewelry and new tans and fixed-up lips or eyes or noses with the squinched-together expressions of old women inspecting price tags.

Everyone seemed to be connected to me. In my mind they were all gathered in a circle, reaching out an arm toward my rotating body in the center, and it was my job to touch them—a hollow gesture to me but to which they brought all the transporting belief of children as to a fairy tale.

I heard so many words of calm that belied the sick and tortured natures of their speakers. These words were like the sound of insect wings flapping very close to my ears, and gave me a sensation of swimming in a gentle tide, a feeling of being buffeted and laundered, pushed around and molded into a shape by some unknown force to which I had to surrender if I wanted to be changed. And I did. I wanted to be changed just like these people wanted to be changed. I wanted to put on a new shirt and discard the old, sweat-soaked one I had.

I was standing in the vast living room beside some kind of shoulder-height totem carved out of dark wood. Was it African? It looked African, with lips that protruded like a movie star's and eyes that were big and hooded as if in warning. Yes, I was sure it was African. I was beginning to become more knowledgeable about the things I'd begun by regarding with the same laughter as children's at a Sunday matinee.

In the distance I could see a glass door open, and beyond it, more people were gathered on the red-tiled veranda, under skies that shared in the refracted glow of a thousand jiggling lightbulbs strung around four bamboo poles planted at each corner.

Most of the women wore sleeveless shirts and slightly above-the-knee skirts, or slip dresses with barely-there straps, made of light materials like cotton and linen, that upon contact with the breeze were revealed to be things made explicitly for seduction. The clinking of ice in glasses and the scootch-slide of footwear on the wood floors made everything seem inconsequential. There was a heightened feeling that we were truly alive only for this length of time, bracketed by the hours of the party as printed on the invitation cards mailed three weeks ago: 9 p.m. and 3 a.m. And whatever else had happened to us or would happen to us—all these things seemed very far away.

And then among all the sick people there was Shem, who wasn't sick at all. He circulated freely, a gold-colored drink sweating in his hand. I didn't always know where he was in the apartment—which was palatial, and which I realized neither Condé Nast nor *Metropolitan Home* did any justice to—but every once in a while, like a dot pulsating on a tracking screen, there would be Shem's shirt, a shimmering, billowing thing that was neither purple nor gray but instead combined the worst qualities of both, making him stand out like a signal flare even among a field of Mardi Gras tones. He would hold forth for minutes at a time, surrounded by people riveted by his speech, and then he would move on, begin another conversation with a whole new group who would just naturally cluster around his standing figure or he would interject something into a conversation already started, adding expert comments that were either serious or flippant depending on his reading of the crowd. He freshly insinuated himself into a corner by the kitchen doors where a bunch of teeny women were gathered. At the sight of him their eyes lit up. What could he possibly be talking to them about? Certainly not Do you suck cock? Riveted, they were riveted. Look at those hands, flying as he narrated. Those skeletal and wide-spaced fingers that always led people to ask whether he played the piano. He touched them on the shoulders, the elbows, why was he expending such energy on these women? Knowing him, it could only be disdain. Maybe I would be ushered to them later on, introduced by the name of my new religion: Master Chao. Oh, they would think, he's too young to be a master. And this disparity, this chasm between my age and my publicized skills, drawing disbelief at first, would very soon develop a skin of truth around it, as if these listeners were sick and tired of listening to the credible and wanted to cast their lot with the fantastic instead, hoping to be rewarded with whatever the fantastic rewarded its believers.

Riveted listeners, nodding along with his musical speech. As I suppose I had been. Not that I no longer was. Shem still exerted his beautiful control. Intelligence did indeed shine forth in the eyes, and Shem's eyes were— They blazed. Behind them were the fires of a plan in motion. He was back in a circle of people that he saw as tormentors. They had opened their arms once more, courtesy of me.

So many of these people I had helped. They each took me into their homes and revealed the thing that they would never dare speak of in public, the thing that was their big shame, for which their reputations were no more than paperback covers—about to be blown open. They had sons and daughters who were drug addicts. Spouses with drinking problems. They were the children of country bumpkin parents they were embarrassed to present to city friends. They had ailing health for which they held themselves responsible—unwholesome inclinations finally metastasizing into little balls that were blocking their windpipes and arteries and intestines.

Shem pointed out a common denominator in their homes: stacks of glossy magazines underneath coffee tables or beside beds or piled high at the foot of bookshelves. Shem said: They read these things, gulp them down, and cannot avoid seeing themselves as falling far short of their magazine counterparts. They do not have—and will never have—enough possessions, and the ones that they have will never be as shiny, or quiet, always requiring upkeep. And as for their careers—the magazines are always raising the imaginary ceiling of accomplishment. Picture it this way, said Shem: These people on treadmills with speeds which can only go in one direction: plus. Never enough. They covet, said Shem. As I once did.

He had typed up a fake article about me, giving it to me to read. I was impressed. From it I could gather something of the talent he claimed to possess. Its tone was one of casual validation, as if I had been interviewed on a Sunday afternoon, with my feet up on a table, interviewer and subject merely passing the time companionably. It tossed made-up facts carelessly, putting in quotes that sought to establish me as everything I wasn't: offhand, serene, gifted. The picture that emerged of this person, this Master Chao, seemed entirely accidental. You read, not aware that points were being made, or themes being engaged, and in the end you had this sudden sensation of a whole world assembled, a clarity that emerged from sentences that had the look and feel of rubble. This m.o. described Shem's style perfectly: under the radar.

He then had the article designed and then printed up—complete with a photograph—in a copy shop. The entire thing cost him less than five dollars. The article was attributed to a made-up "lifestyle" magazine from Europe. He xeroxed a hundred copies of the article and this was the way I was legitimized, my existence verified, poked into, but only superficially, to give a little "flavor," a little human face to a trend that was on the upswing and didn't seem likely to die for at least the next five years, which, in magazine time, was an eternity. Feng Shui Master Chats with Us, said the subhead beneath the main title, which said: Go East! And there I was, in the lower right-hand corner, above a caption that read: Young Master Chao. I looked like I was smiling, though I wasn't smiling at all. This fact alone made me look more Chinese, more mysterious, gifted with powers that the magazine article didn't even have to elaborate on.

For the photograph, he'd taken me to a furniture emporium in Brooklyn. We'd found an empty showroom for couches and Shem had simply sat me down and started snapping away. This one serious, this one casual, here I'm even smiling, this one looking to my left, then to my right, at some mysterious source of light outside the frame that was nothing more than a dinky floor lamp with a broken glass shade.

In the photograph he eventually used, the plush red velvet of a sofa behind me was cropped in such a way as to suggest that it was so much more: a painting, a flag, the red of a column in a Chinese pavilion. Red for luck, a Chinese preoccupation. And besides, Shem said, it was the one picture where I looked handsomest, the most serious, without any hint of mischief, or of betraying our true purpose—which, in me, came out as a clear shine in the eyes, complemented by a slight arching of my left eyebrow—and this look seemed to come out in picture after worrisome picture that Shem took. I was familiar with that look. I had seen it in many photographs taken of me before and had always thought it made me look more handsome, which was why I continued doing it. But now I realized it was only that I confused handsomeness with inane mimicry of pop star poses in magazines, poses calculated to establish a pop star's integrity by aligning him with black traits: surliness, indifference, mischief. Well, Shem and I didn't want any of that. What we wanted was a look that was the opposite of a pop star, or rather a pop star whose aura was white rather than black, sexless and filled with wisdom.

In the picture, my hair was greased with newfangled pomade that was supposed to coat the hair with protective proteins. The amount of money it cost, though it made me wince—forty-two dollars for a six-ounce container—was like a down payment for a future of returns, a thousandfold.

Every picture tells a lie, Devo the stylist for photo shoots, the concealer, the fixer, the rearranger, quipped to me once.

Well, this picture Shem took was the image these people were projecting back onto the blank screen of my face tonight. It was that man these people had shaken hands with, behind whom doors had closed with little ceremonies of embarrassment and supplication. Please come into my humble home, more than a few of them had said, stepping aside for this man. And the truth was, not one of those homes could even be remotely described as humble. Ugly, yes. Intimidating, of course. Palatial, some. Even the ones that adhered strictly to the modish principles of minimalism, given the buffed sensuality of a Japanese or even a Shaker environment—even those homes could not be described as humble: There might only have been one table and one chair in a vast room that could easily house a family of five, but that table was made entirely of marble and the chair, of hand-sewn double-stitched leather. See? My eyes were beginning to wrap around confronted objects better. With the first big money I got—five thousand dollars from Lindsay S, minus Shem's cut—along with a second savings account that I opened in another bank, I bought subscriptions to three magazines: *Metropolitan Home*, Condé Nast *House & Garden*, and newly, *Elle Décor*. This was my little joke to myself. Even my own slummy apartment was beginning to show the influences of this reading: like a rusted tin can repainted and then pierced with holes and then, with a lighted votive placed inside, made to shine.

Some of my clients and their homes I first encountered in the pages of these magazines. I enlarged on the revelations in the various articles or read between the lines, deciding on likely troubles for the subjects—taken for diagnostic clairvoyance and greeted with breathy But-how-do-you-know's—before offering my occult solutions.

For example, there was a woman whose child's spine had been permanently crushed in a car accident and who stuffed every single seat in her home with thick pillows, referring to them as "posts of much-needed comfort": I told her to get rid of those pillows. I said that I "sensed" a tragedy that had occurred in the past hanging in the air and for which the pillows had been trotted out as "palliatives."

You feel guilt about this accident, and the guilt has been building and concentrating on your back (giving her back pain; hence the pillows), but as soon as you get rid of the pillows, your back will have to learn to straighten instead of curve and, straightening, will have to release the guilt locked inside for a long time.

This woman, hearing me speak, opened her mouth but could say nothing.

The music that had been permeating the thin air at the party—dominated by a drum-kit machine that sounded like what would happen if I asked you to run at a furious pace and then plugged speaker wires into your heart—suddenly stopped. In the abrupt and disconcerting silence that followed there could be heard exaggerated groans of protest, mostly from the younger crowd. Heads turned. Mom! I heard a male voice say. Conversations started up to cover the embarrassing void, and very quickly everything seemed to have been forgotten.

Suddenly, music came on which sounded like water being struck inside several bottles and which took me a while to realize was actually coming from a guitar. And then there was the young man I presumed had spoken earlier: He lumbered into view, with a face trying to rebel against its own handsomeness, like someone had slashed X marks over his clear eyes, and turned his hair into a series of scribbled-together circles, and when our eyes traveled past the glue trap of that beautiful head, down to his shirt, there was a final, decisive claim on our attention: In big red letters on his chest were the words Fuck Life. Kendo made eye contact with no one but it was clear that he relished being looked at. Hi, Kendo, how are you? asked a few people who, as he began to move awkwardly forward, he made a point of bumping into, in the process upsetting more than a few drinks. A trail of Oh's like popcorn popping followed him all the way to the veranda, where he sat himself at the farthest edge away from everyone. He didn't see me.

It was my first confrontation with celebrity—the beautiful Kendo of *House & Garden* in the flesh!—and for a moment, the easy smile that had been pasted on my face since crossing the threshold was replaced by the open-mouthed awe of Paulinha, the man from the Philippines.

When I looked back at the room, my peripheral vision snagging on a bright, pearly streamer quickly fading from view, I realized I was staring at the quickly exiting backside of tonight's hostess. Even more than Shem, this woman was a runny, liquid presence, always seen in profile, or with her back turned. If pressed, I doubt any of us could have proven that she was really there, though a picture formed from details whose accuracy was rendered moot by constantly whirling motion: hair pulled tight and secured in a bun at the back of her head, with two (jade?) chopsticks stuck through and some jangly gold stuff dangling from the end of one of the chopsticks; red low-heeled pumps (with gold buckles?); pleated silk skirt matched with a short-sleeved shirt with a Peter Pan collar; for earrings, two black buttons surrounded by rings of gold, like miniature plates; hands turned festive by too much jewelry: various-sized and -colored bracelets and rings and a watch; and always she left behind a lingering trace of too strong—though not unpleasant—perfume.

Beside one door I spotted Brian Q, jutting his chest out in a formfitting suit of iridescent gray.

He was a banker. All of thirty-three, and already with two homes, one on each coast. Not to mention a share in a converted farmhouse in the "Hamptons," a brand name frequently mouthed in the houses I visited. Hamptons? someone would ask of another, and in the replies that followed—both parties toting up competing addresses, itineraries, invitations—would be coded a laser-clear index of how useful you were . . .

Tonight's party had, in fact, been scheduled in deference to that word. A Thursday evening, the last night of the week in the city for most of these people before they flitted off to "shares" or properties in the Hamptons. There, they could slough off dead, dulled skins brought on by a daily grind that was the price paid for things like a share in the Hamptons.

Brian Q had parted his hair near the crown for me when I'd gone to visit him in his duplex apartment on the Upper East Side. It was bald in the center, and to conceal this he'd combed over surrounding hair, making sure it stayed in place with industrial-strength hair gel. But for me, sexless, wisdom-filled me, he'd been willing to reveal his humiliation. I'm only thirty-three, he'd said, in a tone of scientific bewilderment. Accidentally, he'd tossed his hands in the direction of a photograph that had lain on a low table by the windows. And this photograph had elaborated his complaint for him perfectly.

You could tell this was a prized photo by the frame: the bone of some animal had been smoothed and buffed to a shine and it had edged the picture and seemed to give it its own light. In the picture, chubby Brian Q had been surrounded on one side by an Asian pal and on the other by two white ones. They had arms slung over each other's shoulders, and squeezed tight to emphasize their friendship and also to fit better into the frame. They all had healthy, bouncing helmets of black hair, and standing out there in the sun, given animating ridges of light and shadow, all that hair had suggested an animal, a dog say, each face and body beneath it a knobby leg.

He'd filled me in. Each smiling face had acquired a name, an accompanying history whose center was himself. I'd gotten a better idea: These four friends lined up for a photograph had become four competitors straddling a starting line, waiting for the gun's crack. Now, years later, they were in mid-race. Who was in front? My guess had been Brian Q by several strides . . . And yet. The other three still had their bouncy helmets to boast of. That had also been a guess. But one Brian Q's distressed face had come close to verifying.

Baldness did not run in his family. The men took thick, arrogant crowns of hair with them to old age. Surely, this was a psychic disturbance. He'd visited doctors, who'd as much as told him so. They'd frowned over what could be the cause, and having written prescriptions, had still been frowning about the apparent failures of these medications, medications which, in every other healthy human male, had justified marketplace claims. You, he'd told me, unable to look me in the eye, are my last chance. But not a drastic one, I'd noted to myself. In his refusal to part with glasses he wore for good luck had been a clue: a long-standing belief in the irrational.

I'd wished him no harm, this fat, slobby kid with the common dream of wanting to be more dangerous than he actually was. On his left chest had been a small serpent tattoo, hidden daily by his beautiful shirts and suits. It had helped, along with a goatee he wore which looked glued on, to corroborate his true rebel's identity. He'd only wanted the "look," the "feel" that went with his success. This had been true of a lot of the people I'd visited. I felt just like a gardener, a barber, somebody who kept things clean, pushed bothersome nature back, and restored a hermetic, an amniotic order. Every week, to maintain my handsomeness, I went to visit the old Cuban men of the Oldero Barbershop, and from its doors I would emerge, ready to continue the work I myself was a beneficiary of. Everything in my life extended forward and backward like a long, smooth line now. This was another first. Before, my existence could accurately be summed up by the Morse code, full of short dashes and then full-stop dots, lurching and lurching.

What had I done for Brian Q? I'd looked at his beautifully furnished apartment. I'd gone from room to room, listening to the back story he'd given to each piece of furniture. Then, in his reading room, I'd told him to move two bookcases and a worktable so that they wouldn't be next to the windows, casting darkening shadows.

I'd explained: Your worktable shouldn't be made so vulnerable as to be directly exposed to an opening where precious *chi*—energy or life force—could be drained away and malignant force—known as *sha*—could come in. *Chi! sha! chi! sha!* my brain had sung, in the rah-rah tones of a bubbly cheerleader.

I'd told Brian Q in a triumphant voice, praising my new arrangement: Now energy can flow fully in this room. As opposed to before, where pools of it simply collected to stagnate. Also fear. I sensed very strongly when I first walked into this room . . . Is this the room where you do your work? He'd nodded. I sensed that sitting here, stagnating, was a great pool of fear. A fear of . . . Punishment. But now that I've cleared a path for it to flow out of the room and out the house, now will begin your new, peaceful life.

He'd lowered his head, knowing how right I'd been.

I had had Shem dig up some dirt on this man. Through an acquaintance who was a "professional source," Shem had come back with a story about how Brian Q had once been accused of mismanaging a client's funds and been put in jail. Though eventually exonerated, he had had the fear of God put permanently into him, always turning his head to see who was behind him, tearing his hair out to reassure the clients who'd stuck with him that he was as morally upright as any banker could be.

In the bedroom, having already learned the lesson of *chi* and *sha* in his workroom, he'd offered to move his bed, which had been by a window. And of course, he was right. Why shouldn't he be? He'd rubbed his scalp, a habit. I'd told him to stop doing that. He'd reacted with the dejected look of a schoolboy found out. I'd told him that his bed was in a bad position. I'd pushed my head out the window, hoping to get some flash of inspiration. And there on the spacious ledge, I'd found it: pigeon droppings, some new and dewy with the morning coolness, but most hardened into white and yellow speckles, making a kind of stucco against the gray concrete.

No no no, Brian Q, I'd tsk-tsked to myself in the voice of a fussy housekeeper. For the rest of the visit, as I'd inspected the arrangement of the other rooms, in my mind I'd been dressed in the uniform of this fussy housekeeper: an outfit of pink and black held together by a final touch of a ruffled silk apron, the swoosh of which had been so clear in my ears. Days later, I realized this had given to my tour of inspection a blitheness that had been responsible for the impressed look on Brian Q's face. From then on, for each house I visited, I had called up this housekeeper to help in my performance.

I'd looked around the perfect white square, then had decided that the best spot for the bed would be right by the door. This would get it away from those damn pigeons, and free up needed space. But this meant that something had to intercede between the door and the bed, because "you don't want the bed immediately visible when you enter, and besides energy from the outside would immediately clutter up what should be an area of rest." Rest and peace had been his key words. I'd suggested the most obvious thing: a screen. Brian Q had perked up at the idea of buying something, anything.

Before I left, I'd stood at the front entrance. What? Brian Q had asked me. He had a whole library of books written by obscure dead people, mostly Germans, Austrians, Swedes, books full of brooding, nihilistic views punched up in tight, fortune cookie sentences: Life is a goal none of us truly attain; Death is a reward very few actually deserve; Hindsight is wisdom turned accusatory, useless; etc.

He hadn't been able to take my silence any longer. What? he'd asked again, cued by his extensive reading to expect the discovery of a cyst, of several, in his life, and for each of them—accompanied by a gavel banging away—to be diagnosed as just. What a burden it was to be both liberal and wealthy!

Brian Q's front door had been right where the elevator doors opened, just like Lindsay S's. This had been perfect, a problem directly from the books. For Lindsay S, I had suggested putting up a totem, a "guard" that would scare off evil spirits which could so easily ride up that elevator and straight into his home as if having received an invitation. For Brian Q, I'd given the exact same prescription.

Conveniently, I had had the name of a shop in SoHo which sold beautiful, decorative "guards" such as winged frogs, winged pigs, bats in flight, or sentry lions, all carved out of Indonesian teak and painted bright, cheery colors. The name of the proprietor was Pratung Song. A man in his late thirties, originally from Jakarta.

What a beautiful name, I'd said in greeting when I'd first entered the shop, but he'd only rolled his eyes. I'd realized I was doing to him the exact same thing I'd been complaining was being foisted on me. Beautiful as indeed everything from his past had been—though all I had been able to imagine was a monotonous expanse of verdant countryside, a perfect diorama constructed as much from my ignorance as from hopefulness—he hadn't wanted it highlighted at the expense of his present. Why else come to this country unless you specifically wanted the past displaced, turned inconsequential? The only thing he was interested in, he'd repeated in an exaggeratedly coarse voice, was money. The beauty of his name and all the rest of that had only been the beauty of childhood, which, having left Jakarta, he'd also left behind, without regret. Now it was time to grow up.

This had been what I'd proposed to him: I'd said, I'll send you clients. A lot of clients. Ten. Twenty. Even more. And they'll come to your shop to purchase items. For that, I want a cut. It doesn't matter how you pay me that cut. You can mark up the original prices by exactly the figure you want to cut me. You decide what that should be. It doesn't matter.

He'd mulled it over, looking at me the entire time. I'd instinc-

tively known that I had to hold his gaze. That had been his
And I had. I'd looked at him the whole time I'd talked. It'd
easy. My plans had no shadows. I'd known I was offering him a
great deal. I'd also given him Shem's article. He'd looked at my picture, glanced at a few sentences here and there. I hadn't even been
sure whether he'd grasped any of their claims. But in the end, he'd
looked up, only to find me still looking at him. And he'd said yes.

I'd brought him a dozen clients since. All these clients had
needed screens to hide furniture from doorways; curtains; totems;
good-luck charms; bamboo mats; light sconces crafted from exotic
materials like capiz shells; incense; polished stones intended for
meditation; little medallions to wear around the neck to protect from
vampiric forces—items that, lo and behold, had been found in one
easy stop: Pratung Song's shop in SoHo called the Very Far East
Trading Company. A dozen clients, spending upward of two thousand each. Brian Q had been lucky thirteen . . .

. . . I could see Pratung Song, smiling as we entered. The bells
tied with red cord at the top of the doors tinkling. Him seated behind his small bamboo desk at the far end of the shop, directly facing the glass entrance—bad Feng Shui because there was a direct
line of exit from the *chi*-concentrated desk to the door every time a
customer entered, but who'd be willing to believe any of that with
his newfound prosperity? He'd been smiling, bowing his obsequious
bow. A short man, made for just that gesture. Wearing a nice white
linen shirt with his cuffs folded up to his elbows, exposing tan arms
with a few chalky patches. The introduction: This is Brian Q. Another bow. And then the tour of the shop, each item stopped at, admired. What are the gentlemen looking for? Pratung Song had asked
with a beautiful, lilting accent. Well, I'd said. And then Brian Q had
taken over, enumerating: Curtains? A screen? Two? He'd looked over
to me and I'd nodded in approval. We need, Brian Q had continued,
a guard? I'd explained to Pratung Song and he'd said, Ah, yes, and
had directed our attention to one corner of the ceiling, hung with
innumerable animals given wings by the fancy of Indonesian superstition: pigs, frogs, cats, dogs, fat infants turned seraphs, mermaids.
It had been like being in a crib and looking up to a giant mobile of
fairy-tale animals. Not Brian Q's style, perhaps, but what had he to

lose? Well, a lot, actually. So Brian Q had feared. And so had a lot of the people I'd encountered. Shem was right. Fear of even the slightest decrease in the prosperity that they'd become so used to (that was, of course, if the world was still turning) had paved the way for our entrance onto the scene. For Brian Q the list was long: Two homes. The Hamptons. A great business. And with it, an assured social standing and the ability to purchase the latest, hippest suits to aid in seducing the ladies. And there had been his hair. But with me, he would lose none of it . . . At the end of the viewing had come the best part: the tallying of prices with an old cash register, making a tin can sound with each purchase, and, to announce the grand total, a ring like a windup toy being goosed to start . . . The grand total, ten percent of which was mine! . . .

. . . Brian Q had followed my instructions. The amount of money he'd spent had been like the forty dollars I'd laid down for a container of hair grease: a down payment for a chance at greater rewards.

At Suzy's party, Brian Q had a short, unattractive girl with a too long nose cornered. He was talking about something that took all her energy to feign interest in. Her jaw was set determinedly, as if gripped around some hard shell she was trying to crack open. And when she opened her mouth, to smile, or to interject with some little pearl, her jaw still didn't relax. Face-lift? My reading of the scene came quick and immediate, like it had been coming for the last few months, senses pricked: She was more interested in the suit than in the body inside it. She had both eyebrows pushed to the uppermost limits of her skull, her open, silent lips implying a wow about to be surrendered—just what a guy wants: a girl to make him feel like a pro. Her eyes scanned his figure up and down several times during the conversation, and in the very center of them—if Brian Q only had better glasses—could be seen the dollar figures of a cash register ringing sales.

Brian Q saw me and waved. How are you? he mouthed, smiling.

We were far across the room from one another, and he seemed to be beaming. Surely, it couldn't be because he was glad to see me. It took me a minute to realize that he wanted to show off his position.

He made a perfect diagonal crease in his suit which ran from his right armpit down to his navel. The exposed, jeweled buckle of his belt sent out several gold asterisks. This was new. A signal of recent weight loss? I couldn't tell.

I waved back, thrilled to have become the familiar of this young man on the rise.

He continued to move his hands, making a gesture like hailing a cab, and I realized that he wanted me to come over. I ambled over, sliding my stupid kung fu shoes on the beautiful floor. They were part of the "look," though they made me "feel" stupid, and what's worse, naked, vulnerable, as if about to be stepped on at any moment. But two things were in my favor: first, they fit the beautiful summer weather; and second, their humbleness was like an endorsement of my unearthliness, a monklike creature with no concern for his material well-being. Still, sliding across the beautiful floors, they made a ridiculous sound, and in that sound—had there been anybody paying attention—were all the personas my act was meant to push down: a janitor, a scraper, a beggar, a lowly thing these people would never deign to acknowledge on the streets, much less spit on. But they were deigning to do more than spit. They nodded their heads and opened mouths studded with bits of cracked glass, and by the way they touched me—with a kind of sheepish reverence— you could tell that they believed something would rub off of what I was wearing and onto them. All these small tributes I received from the people who blocked my path to Brian Q.

How are you? I asked Brian Q when I finally reached him.

Fine, Master Chao, he replied. This, he said, indicating the girl, is Norma.

Hi, how are you, said Norma. She had the metallic voice of a spoiled teenager and the quick delivery of a thirties movie heroine, though her worn horse face put her in another category altogether.

I shook this girl's hand, despising her for homing in on Brian Q, who stood there with moony eyes. Despising her, in other words, for being like myself, the contempt of one professional for another.

I've heard about you, she said to me.

I merely smiled, saying nothing.

Thank you so much, Master, Brian Q said to me. And then he winked.

What did that mean? Did it mean that his hair was growing back? As I walked away, I tried to get a vantage point, but he was taller than I was, and there was no way for me to see the top of his head. Behind me, I heard him laugh, and that would have to answer my question for now.

Suddenly, I found myself confronting the open door of the kitchen, and beyond it, sitting in a perfect angle like everything else in this immaculate apartment, was a glass pitcher filled with margarita. Its curved, sparkling surface was sweating, and seeing it, I began to sweat too. I'd been stuck with iced tea, and caterers, told to give me special care, kept coming over to refill my glass. The effort required to put up a show of enjoyment was demoralizing.

There was no one in the kitchen. I did a spy move of slowly turning my head one way and then the other. Everyone seemed completely absorbed in their own atmospheres. I slid into the kitchen and with an imperceptible move nudged the door closed. The pitcher sat solitary on the tile counter. I moved to a batch of cabinets above the sink and opened and closed them in a flash. They held only shiny plates with overembellished rims, so precious that they looked unusable, like expensive toys. Cabinets below the sink revealed no glasses either. In the sink, however, stood a few used ones. I took the first one I could get my hands on and quickly rinsed it. In one fast movement, I took up the pitcher and poured a drink for myself. Then I set the pitcher down, picked up the glass, and put it to my mouth. But I didn't have time to swallow, because in walked a young girl to surprise me. Sir, the girl—who I could see was wearing the black-and-white uniform of a caterer (a button was missing just above where the shirt disappeared into her waistband and there was an unfortunate spot the color of soy sauce hovering near the right cuff; my eyes went instinctively to the things in need of correction)—called out to me, approaching hesitantly. That's alcohol, sir.

Oh, I said. I was glad that she hadn't used the word Master to address me. Alcohol? I repeated.

I'm afraid so, sir.

I thought it was, ah, lime juice, you know, I said as she took the pitcher, smiling, and left. I hoped my face hadn't turned red to betray me.

As soon as the door swung shut, I gulped the whole glass down. It sent an electric kick from the base of my stomach to my guts and from there to the rest of my body. I momentarily felt my skin pop out of bounds, and then return.

When I went back to join the party, I no longer heard the limp slapping of my kung fu shoes, and the world seemed even more beautiful, lastingly so. A couple close by were kissing.

A stray piece of paper on the floor crawled toward a pair of low white heels. My eyes followed those heels up, until they stopped at the yammering mouth of Cardie Kerchpoff.

Her father was a cardiologist, hence Cardie. Kerchpoff: Jews from Russia. She let you know as soon as you met her. As if this was the most important fact about her life. The thing that marked her as original. As if she were the only Jew with a lineage traceable to Russia in the entire history of the world.

A short woman, with a natural frizzy pompadour, cut short on both sides and sticking straight up in the middle, so that the impression she gave was of the Bride of Frankenstein, but with red hair. Bulging eyes, and thin, cracked lips the color of her skin: pale and sickly like dried bone. But unhealthy-looking as those lips were, it wasn't their appearance that made you cringe but rather the things that came out of them.

Lindsay S had brought us together over a dinner party.

Some woman at the table had begun by announcing that she'd turned vegetarian.

You have? everyone had asked, surprised at this woman's willpower, which her history of various addictions could not have led anyone to expect.

The conversation had then turned to other "healing" and "cleansing" rituals the other guests had taken up, trying to reverse the damages of a lifetime of bad habits. In this vein, Lindsay S had turned to me and, beaming, told everyone that I had done him a world of good.

How? various people had buzzed. What did you do?

Feng Shui, Lindsay S had declared, and then he'd turned the spotlight over to me.

I had given them a short speech, making sure to mark myself down.

Oh yes yes, someone had said. I've read about it.

And so had more than a few people, and in this way the die had been cast, my number passed out, with promises having been echoed by a lot of voices to set up consultations in the following weeks.

You must, you simply must, Lindsay S had said.

Someone had mentioned that, come to think of it, Lindsay S's place had indeed looked more "harmonious." And hearing this, Lindsay S had again looked at me, with a lengthy wordless compliment.

Cardie Kerchpoff hadn't been able to stand it, her knuckles whitening from the way she'd been gripping the edge of the glass dining table. So she'd done a maneuver in which she had set up her subsequent monologue, circling back to the subject of vegetarianism introduced earlier.

Oh, blah blah blah . . . my children's nanny's a vegetarian, she had begun.

People had turned to look at her: Step one accomplished.

Yes, she'd continued. She's Indian. This fifty-year-old Indian woman.

Oh really? Lindsay S had asked, giving Cardie Kerchpoff just that tiny bit of encouragement, and having received it, she'd taken it and run, never once letting up. The subsequent monologue remained the low point of my recent life. This had been another sign that the plan proposed by Shem—which I had agreed to in the spirit of a dare, without thinking through its potential repercussions—had turned serious: I had entered this world of privilege where the people had taken me in as one of their own, and had been entirely comfortable divesting themselves of ugly things in my presence. These people, in my imagination, lived in a glass bubble filled with money, aerated and sent flying in all directions. They flew up to catch as much as they could, swatting away everything in their way.

The Indian nanny monologue, delivered in a fitful whine like singing an aria while being tickled: *This woman*, Cardie Kerchpoff has begun, *every little bit of bother that comes up in the house, she feels she has to call me. Like I don't have a job of my own to take care of? Why can't she call John?* (Cardie's husband.) *Because John's a man. And she feels—I mean I've never been to the Third World, but let's face it, they raise their women to believe that the home is still exclusively the province of the woman. So this woman calls me up. In the middle of my meeting with Bill. Bill fucking Hood! Only one of the two or three greatest contemporary novelists this country has ever produced, excuse me very much. I'm trying my best to convince Bill to let go of a passage in his new novel that's absolutely, totally unnecessary but which he's very fond of and won't part with—I mean, pulling teeth, right? And I'm using all of my—well, even if I do say so myself—considerable intellectual resources to convince him to let go of this, this passage that's totally unworthy of him and who should call, who should not only call but convince my secretary—who I had told not to disturb me—to buzz her through? And what do I get when I pick up the phone? An earful about how my daughter's chew toys that she plays with in her crib need to be sterilized every so often and that I should always be on the lookout for bacteria because— If she feels—I mean, if she absolutely feels the need to sermonize anyone on the topic of child rearing, which I can understand because anybody cooped up in a goddamn enclosed space for hours on end is bound to go crazy with lack of conversation—don't I empathize!—but if she* must, *if she absolutely* must *talk to somebody, can't she call up John every once in a while?!* (A loving, teasing look at her husband.) *I mean, come on, so he's a big-shot lawyer, so what?! I'm a big-shot editor! People's livelihoods depend on me! Why can't she understand that? Well, what she can't understand is the concept that women—well, I don't know what the fuck she* can *get through that thick aged skull! She feels—at home, OK?, when I'm sitting there with my feet up just trying to unwind after a long day—she feels the need to instruct me on how to clean house, what to do for fire safety, oh my God the list goes on and on, what could Cardie the more than very successful editor but inadequate* woman—*that's what she's thinking, I know it! and granted she might have a little bit of allowance for women who work, but only in very specific professions that seem an extension of being a mother, like nurse, like I don't know what, teacher!, you know, motherly types, but an editor? making decisions with words which convey truth and are then printed up and bound for people to read which could possibly affect their way of thinking? forget it! that's a man's job!—what could Cardie the fake male, the wannabe male editor—she probably doesn't even know what an editor does!— what could Mrs. Cardie—actually that's what she calls me: Mrs., which she emphasizes like what? like she's reminding me of my proper place?—so what could Mrs. Cardie possibly be remiss on, let's make a list and then call her up in the middle of her very busy workday and disturb her about them! Or let's wait for her to come home and just as she's relaxing ambush her! Oh Jesus Christ! I've tried.* (John had nodded to verify.) *I've tried to tell her that she should only call me if something important comes up, an emergency, something like that. But of course, she always comes back with her famous rejoinder, But this is important! Cleanliness is important! Child safety is important! Of course, I agree. And this is where things get dicey. Because you have to differentiate between two different kinds of important and believe me, if you've never talked to someone not from this country about things like that, things which we're already acculturated to, little you know, what's that word, nuances!, little nuances, my God, if you've never tried to explain American nuances or Western nuances to a Third Worlder, are you in for a marathon! And you know what? Ultimately, I don't even have to explain to her the difference between important lowercase and important capital letters, because it's my goddamn house and I have sovereign rights, excuse me very much. So she should just take what I say as divine truth. And shut up. And put up. My God why do I allow myself to be tyrannized by this short woman—I mean, it's ridiculous, she barely comes up to my armpits!* (Laughter.)

John, an English lawyer with skin the color and appearance of uncooked dough, and with a character to match, always at the side of his talkative wife looking abashed, as if about to apologize for her, but always remaining silent, complicit, a complicity which in all respects had grown into a kind of encouragement, even pride; John, without the power to contradict, henpecked, hard to imagine him being a lawyer; John, at this point, had surprisingly interjected: Well, he'd said to Cardie, you get what you pay for.

What's that supposed to mean? Cardie'd asked.

Well, John had said, introducing a welcome note of dissent: Nannies, they're either too careful or not careful enough. You pay top dollar to ensure that you're getting a top-drawer nanny, don't be surprised if that's what you get.

You're only saying that because it's not you she calls!

Laughter. Which, of course, had encouraged Cardie. From the nanny, she'd begun to enlarge on some other microscopic topic, but not before her run had been momentarily stopped by someone proffering advice: A well-to-do Asian man wearing the same waiter's outfit I had on that evening and which had turned him cold against me, though his outfit had probably outcost mine by hundreds, if not a few thousand, had looked at Cardie and said, Well you should dump that nanny. She sounds like she's more trouble than she's worth. What you should get, he'd leaned in and, without any trace of irony, had said, what you should get yourself is a Filipino. They make the best servants. This remark hadn't been helped by the immediate entrance of Lindsay S's Filipina maid, a fortyish woman who'd been bearing another dish, as well as a look of permanent apology on her face. And Lindsay, seeing her, had smilingly echoed Mr. Asian Man's statement. The maid had retreated into the kitchen, afraid of bearing witness.

Cardie'd seemed to be taking note of all this, though I could tell that she had merely been catching her breath. And when she'd opened her mouth to continue, it had been with depressingly renewed vigor.

By the end, even after she—made thirsty by all that talking— had retired into silence, I had still been able to hear that voice echoing inside my ears. So when she'd grabbed my elbow at the end of the party, and had started talking softly into my right ear, about how she would love for me to come to her New York apartment and help guarantee that its arrangement was proper, it had taken a great deal of effort not to scream. And for the first time since adopting that name, I'd felt that I had truly—with the superhuman skill required not to betray my murderous feelings—earned it: Master indeed.

So I'd gone to her apartment the next day. She had been leaving for San Francisco and so the consultation had had to be expedited. I had looked carefully, knowing exactly what I'd wanted: This was a woman whom I meant to harm, so I would do everything wrong.

I'd encouraged her to move a vanity right in front of the bed, so that waking up, the first thing she saw would be her own ugly reflection, a slap and a curse to begin her day. I'd advised her to keep her front door free and open, getting rid of two potted plants that had stood like a protective hedge. Her front door had opened out onto the top of the stairs, which, per my Feng Shui textbook, was a no-no, for the same reason that a front door facing an elevator was a no-no. The malignant spirits, having to climb stairs instead of simply pushing an elevator button, might be winded by the time they got to her doorstep, but still, without anything to conceal the entryway—such as the protective hedge Cardie Kerchpoff originally had—or to scare them away, they would merely take a moment to collect themselves before entering, making themselves right at home as if having been invited to stay—sitting on her bed, eating off her dining-room table, which had faced an unprotected window, a window that had perfectly framed television cable lines dropping from an apartment several floors above and which had emanated poison arrows of *sha*.

Never had I needed for anything to work more than then.

There had been a small, cramped space with a long, narrow window which had looked down onto garbage cans. This room had been outfitted with two naked mattresses on spring platforms and above these simple beds had been squares of color lighter than the rest of the wall where pictures had been removed—this she'd introduced as the servant's quarters, and this had been the only room I'd been careful not to touch, having seen in one bed Preciosa and in the other myself: Filipinos make the best servants. I hadn't been able to help it. It was a catchy line, and it had echoed effortlessly in my head like a pop refrain past any powers of contradiction I might have had. Filipinos make the best servants Filipinos make the best servants! Why? Asked not in opposition, but to ease the joke to its punch line: Because they kneel by instinct and bend over like clockwork . . .

I had made sure important details in all the other rooms had been off by just a few crucial degrees. Individually, they hadn't seemed all that malignant, but the way I'd seen it was this: it would be like chipping into a bank account bit by bit, day by day: the sum total would still eventually turn out to be one big minus sign.

Now at Suzy's party, I looked for signs that my plan had worked. But I couldn't find any. I felt myself too close to her, looking nakedly. She was standing next to Japanese lantern light sconces casting a pearly glow which made her seem softer, hard edges blurred. A group of people were clustered around her, but I could tell that they were struggling to get away, all of them caught up in the torture of being too polite to say anything.

A last grasp: Were those red rings around her eyes? I wasn't sure, but I didn't want to look too hard lest they disappear.

Suddenly, between me and the scene reared a white thing that disappeared as quickly as it came into view, as if borne on wheels. I followed it.

It had turned a corner which dead-ended at the bottom of a smooth wood staircase. I followed the staircase up to the second floor, which was off-limits for tonight's party—though nothing had been said. Recalling the spread in *Metropolitan Home*, I knew that I was walking to where the bedrooms were. Was that white apparition none other than Suzy Yamada, and what would I be catching her in the middle of doing once I opened any one of the three doors that I was now facing, as if having come to a crucial spot in a maze? All night long I'd been waiting to get her alone, and I was strangely unafraid.

I opened the door nearest me with a preemptive gesture of challenge. But there was nothing dramatic to greet me. Only darkness. At first. Then the Christmas lights of Manhattan outside the window focused. For the longest time they were the only things I could make out. But slowly their glow extended to the rest of the room. And with their help I could make out bookshelves. I could make out a bed, and then on it, the white figure, lying there, its body curved into a tight little letter C. The white of this figure turned out to be none other than the Fuck Life ad Kendo had been displaying at the party. He was quiet, and so was I. Standing there, I felt like a ghost, unseen. The entire scene had a quality of being composed just for me, an occasion of privilege. My heart was beating fast. I could make out the sheen of Kendo's longish hair, loosed and falling over his eyes. Was he looking at me? His lips were open, puckered and twitching in a kind of dream speech. He had the perfect skin of certain young men before they are loosed from the pampering world of adolescence into the workday realities of common life. His sneakers were still on him, oversized basketball shoes that looked like they never got much use. Handsome as I had become, there was still a great gulf between my face and Kendo's. And though this was another fact that I could marshal as evidence to support Shem's campaign—to think of these people not as human beings like myself but rather as physical obstacles to the material benefits long due me—I found myself instead as if at school and accepting everything on the blackboard as essential, as insurmountable because they'd been set down before I walked in. Close the door, he suddenly said aloud, and it took me a moment to realize that this was not part of my imagination. It was Kendo. He'd registered my presence. I was too shocked to reply, and merely closed the door without uttering the apology I meant to give. Did he know who I was? I was certain that all he could make out was my silhouette, backlit as I was by the ceiling bulb in the hallway. And what if he knew who I was? All that would have registered with him was the fact that I was from the same detested circle as his mother, sharing the same laughable concern for surfaces that put me across a definite divide from his own concerns, whatever they might be.

I walked away from the closed door.

There was another—Suzy's? I opened it, knowing what I had to do. But there was no garbage can beside the bed. And none underneath the vanity with its containers of makeup concealed inside clean dark shelves. A small door led to a bathroom. By the toilet was a plastic trash pail, newly cleaned out. There was nothing to be gone through to provide a single clue. And then I saw the medicine cabinet—of course! Inside, I found my potential weapons and smiled: a row of prescription bottles, each one a legible caption underneath a picture of the "disturbed" Ms. Yamada. I memorized the names: Seconal (she had trouble sleeping); Estrogen (just like Preciosa, for whom I bought the same prescription: menopausal: which meant

that Suzy was older than her advertised forty-four: vanity, vanity!);
Dexatrim (oh puh-leeze!); Claritin (allergic to what?); and something
called Guanfacine (have to ask Shem). No condoms, no spermicides,
no diaphragms: the woman wasn't having sex. But then she wouldn't
need any of those, being menopausal. Or if, to judge by the Dexatrim, she thought herself inadequate.

I gave the room one last survey. What did I miss? Sheets were
smoothed over the bed, the pillows fluffed, the curtains drawn over
the windows, the carpet newly vacuumed. Next door, Kendo remained quiet.

I closed the door behind me and quietly backtracked my way to
the din.

I didn't even have time to catch my breath because the first thing
I saw was another scene.

There by the empty fireplace were Shem and Paul Chan Chuang
Toledo Lin, a novelist, the celebrated author of *Peking Man?Woman*?

Lin's pudgy face, as he spoke, gave the appearance of tasting
something he found unbearably delicious. He had an embarrassed
chin, and a nose that looked as if it was being squashed against an
invisible windowpane. All of this was topped by a delirious and
stiff—and thinning—pompadour, gelled to within an inch of its life
and then furiously blow-dried to create a look that was nothing if
not a hilarious tribute to the continuing primacy of the seventies. He
was always seen wearing slouchy suits that emphasized his sorry
physique—more stomach than shoulder—suits whose expensive
names he always casually let drop in conversation, or in interviews
in newspapers, because he knew he was inadequate and needed the
backing of brand names, but on him they always looked thrift-store,
secondhand, as if passed down from sad, spendthrift immigrant parents—and not even altered to fit! Tonight his sack outfit was a thin,
pin-striped gray, matched by suede Hush Puppies the color of red
bean ice cream, and when he lifted his foot every once in a while in
an inexplicable flamingo gesture, as if to test an injured knee, I
could see that he wore no socks.

I circled the periphery, turning my back on them, and heard the funny-sounding words hegemony, proletariat, diaspora, dichotomy, hagiography, calligraphy. They were all coming from Lin, who was using them to make political points that were, however, undone by that voice of his which belonged to a glee club member soliciting for a candy drive.

Finishing, he moved on. I watched Lin sashaying from room to room and air-kissing familiars, moving with the ease of the wealthy—he had a millionaire industrialist for a grandfather. He and Lindsay S found each other and promptly gave one another embraces like a secret handshake of a private club.

Around Lin had swirled long-standing rumors of gayness. Which he thought he had finally and decisively put a stop to by two strategic maneuvers: first, a new wife, and with that, a new baby; and second, his hocus opus, *Peking Man?Woman?*

In this work, he had divided the world he knew into two: the East and the West. And since this was the same scam we were pulling, I had grabbed at the chance to read the book. What was I looking for? Some intelligent-sounding theology to help back up what I was doing—the East and the West, like salt to rub into a wound. I was looking, not realizing that I already had a theology to back me up, and the strongest: money.

It turned out Lin had other interests to pursue. He argued that the West saw the East—particularly its men—as essentially feminine. This I had no problem with. As Shem had said: It's all in the handling. And as it turned out, Lin's handling was, well, stupid. He had his characters mouth off in thesis statements like— Well, one character who was his stand-in, that is to say he was clearly gay, was thought by the public to be gay, but in the book he was given one triumphant moment when he scolded a misinformed gathering— Lin had this character mouth off the following lines seemingly plucked from an essay: *You've wronged me! You thought I was like all things Oriental, soft and mysterious and effeminate! The West and the East, yes, the feminine East, of which you thought I was a charter member! It's a thinking typical of your race, a constant subjugation of other races you have had a history of conquering or yoking! You treated me like the porcelain doll that you thought I was, fearing that I would break, but I was steel, only you, with your foreshortened historical sight and your lazy conqueror's worldview, didn't know! . . .*

I'd thought to myself, bored beyond belief: This guy has a big fucking chip on his shoulder. (And meeting him, of course, I'd understood.)

And though there was a seed inside his book that pertained to my situation—which was that sometimes a face other than your own could be grafted on top by the outside world—I thought that there was a world of difference between what he chose to do with that knowledge and what I was choosing to do. In essence, it was the gulf that separated a screed from a plan. Paul Chan Chuang Toledo Lin was the author of a screed, a rant, a complaint, huffing and puffing. Versus? My plan, a definite course of action: revenge. (Well, to be honest, it was only in the middle of things that I had given a name to this plan: suddenly I looked around and the word suggested itself.)

Peking Man? Woman? was a definite screed which, though bitter, was written from hope. A hope that people's minds could be influenced, made to see the error of their ways and then corrected, and therefore linked with the idea of progress, moving forward. In his own way, then, Toledo Lin possessed a kind of grace, believing that human beings could be made better, shamed into improvement. While as for myself, I started from the belief that human beings, having begun low, only degenerated further, and that the only correction possible came from a kind of violence, a kind of wresting away of privileges which were undeserved, things granted which it was time to repossess, to reveal the naked, fatty, vulnerable thing underneath; a feeling closer to death than to life.

Shem had consoled me and had laughed heartily at this state of affairs. He'd said about Lin, in a tone used for an aside: *If truth be told, this East West man woman thing is really Lin's way of trying to rationalize and shrug off rumors of his own faggotiness.*

I really should have been sorry for him. Why was I so repelled? Maybe because he'd seemed like he was moving inside a protective bubble of money and privilege, arrogantly unfettered. But the same thing could be said of everyone here. So why did I seem to single him out? He'd been nice to me. He'd smiled when Shem had introduced us, and had given me the requisite five minutes of conversation, clocking in time for politeness.

But in those five minutes I had an inkling that he had spotted me for a fake, but hadn't said anything because, not having been born in Asia, he could not be sure that my "fakeness" was not just some small whiff, some nuance of foreignness he was sorrily un-privy to.

That was another thing about him: he carped about being born in America, in the process having lost an important connection to the "motherland." Always moaning about the "motherland," fearing lack of authenticity. Even that ridiculously long name was like a lo-comotive assembled to chug backward toward some kind of fake his-tory of purity. When I'd asked Shem about this, he'd said, Why live in America and then bemoan your inevitable Americanness?

All I knew of his work was *Peking Man?Woman?* Afterward, I hadn't wanted to crack open another book. In Feng Shui terms: The writing was nothing more than a thicket of expensive words form-ing a wall, not a window. Even Agatha Christie, with all her red her-rings, was more illuminating.

Shem, recovering from his shocked encounter with Lin, caught me regarding him. We nodded politely at one another.

There was Brian Q, introducing his conquest to tonight's hostess, and then catching me looking, he included me in his happy ac-knowledgments. Paul Chan Chuang Toledo Lin was talking to some white guy handing out blue flyers. And Lindsay S—it was his turn to charm the teeny women who'd been enthralled earlier by Shem. Somebody was asking Suzy about Kendo and she was shaking her head in cheerful ignorance.

Then I felt a tug at my knees.

Rowley P, looking up from his wheelchair. A seventy-six-year-old man whom I had paid a visit to a couple of weeks ago at his palatial apartment on Central Park West, in a sparkling building given the fitting name of El Dorado. Since then, I had seen him four times more. Mostly I'd gone to listen to him talk about his life. We would sit in his living room, which was the size of a city block, and he would pour me cup after endless cup of tea, while outside the sun, slowly setting, would be turning the big rectangle of Central Park into marmalade toast. It was a king's promontory, and looking out

across everything from where we sat, I had once again been reminded of the newness of my situation, making my skin tingle
and my head tip to one side from the weight of having been let in
the door. Rowley's words, like balls lobbed into the air, each important point underlined with a thwack, had invariably brought me
back to the world of the living. They, who were all miserable with
stories . . .

I'd known that in assuming my new identity I would have to affect many traits, talents, and tastes that were not mine, and I had
been prepared to make every effort to take them all on, some of
which—like the fucking kung fu shoes, or the occasionally cryptic
speech which had felt like a deforming lock on my lips—had been
clear sacrifices, but never had I imagined that among the hardships I
would have to endure would be having to drink cup after fucking
cup of *tea*! In real life, I never went near that shit. As far as I was
concerned, it tasted like pee warmed over. So imagine my forced
smile, my constantly having to remove myself from what the old
man had been saying with every bitter drop swallowed. Imagine the
scream suppressed as he'd poised the spout of the teapot over my
empty, rattling cup.

He was a man convinced of his imminent death, and had wanted
somebody to listen to his history before it all fizzled out.

He was a half-black, half-white man who had made his fortune in
the early fifties building a ball-bearing business in Pittsburgh.

Like him, his first wife was mulatto, with the lack of clear bound-
aries that that word implied: shuttling back and forth between two
worlds, neither of which had been prepared to welcome them because each had seen the opposite world inside them as a taintedness
and as a betrayal. So it had been a comfort at the start to have found
someone for whom hurt and ostracization were commonplaces, to
have thought of themselves as being two lovers united to form a
solid wall. But, of course, he hadn't counted on the fact that if they
were to draw their strength and solidarity from prejudice, this
would require the world to keep up a steady supply—and what if
the world had suddenly decided to stop fulfilling its part? His success in business had slowly freed him from his original way of thinking, allowed him to let go, and anything he couldn't overcome he'd

steadily learned to live with: after all, what was the point of material improvement if you yourself couldn't improve right along with it? But not so his wife, whose idea of her own self had still come from storing away and reliving particular hurts, as if her identity and her politics, having been galvanized by those crucial heartbreaks, would all be lost if she ever allowed their opposite—calm—into the equation.

Rowley P had said, At some point, I decided to become the sum total of all the good things that have ever happened to me, while she decided to become the sum total of all the negative ones.

As for the children, his wife had succeeded in alienating him from their affections.

To this day, Pittsburgh was where his family, with their—thanks to him—easy aristocracy and their limited ambition, lived.

He'd come to New York in the early seventies on a honeymoon for his second marriage, and it was then—with his new wife Adela's encouragement—that he'd fallen in love with the city.

Even after Adela had passed away a few years later, he'd decided to stay on in New York because, well, the break had already been made and there had been no going back to Pittsburgh. Besides, if this had been the place where his heart had been broken (poor Adela!), he'd owed it to himself to make this the place where his heart would heal. And it had. Eventually. What with the many activities he had soon found himself in the middle of.

Before, his world had revolved entirely around Adela, his view shuttered by total devotion. And now with her gone, just when he'd expected to find himself stranded in a city that had no use for the likes of him—the exact opposite had happened! Life had incredibly opened up to reveal springtime facets. He'd started golfing, had taken dancing lessons, played bridge—knowing that Adela would've wanted him to. And all the time surrounded by people who, like him, had come from varied and mixed backgrounds which they'd treated in a matter-of-fact, almost blithe way that had liberated him. By this time, he was in his fifties, and his life had seemed to turn a corner. He'd started philanthropic work, donating to various hospitals in the city, particularly those in depressed areas like Harlem, the Bronx, certain sections of Queens that were beginning to be associated with the new black immigrants, like the Jamaicans and the Haitians. (Several plaques in several wards bore Adela's name.) He'd sat on a public school advisory panel for the mayor several mayors back. His opinion as a businessman, a *successful* businessman, one able to translate progressive ideas into practicable plans, had been highly valued. Although, he'd confessed to me, he hadn't been sure how they had thought of him as progressive. Perhaps, since he was racially mixed, they'd inferred that he couldn't have been any other way. Also, around this time, he'd become a grandfather, and for a while that had brought him back into the orbit of the family, but only at a remove, as the provider of gifts and of money. His family still had not been able to understand how he could be so happy without them, and ultimately they hadn't been able to forgive. But how could he explain everything to them without further alienating them? They were so much like their mother—committed to inherited histories of racial hurt for which they'd sought to find present-day equivalents, checking grievances off a list that—had they only opened their eyes— they'd have recognized as ludicrous, considering how their wealthy upbringing had safely cocooned them from very real and poisonous prejudice . . .

Rowley took me by the arm and with a casual flicking of his hand dismissed the nervous-looking nurse hovering three steps behind him. This woman Rowley had tagged a bothersome Swiss, with that nationality's characteristic fastidiousness, which he'd described as having been "custom-bred to protect, serve, and irritate." She remained standing there, looking on disapprovingly, while I had taken up her position behind the wheelchair. We passed Shem, who smiled as if to detain us for a chat, but Rowley only had eyes to scout for that elusive place where we could be alone. A few other guests greeted him but again he took no notice. Having been singled out by Rowley, I was regarded with thrilling jealousy by several pairs of eyes. Here, he said, and we entered a small room filled with books. Close the door. I obeyed him.

How are you? I asked.

It took him forever to answer, as if the energy required to smile was all that he could afford.

Fine, fine, he finally replied, breathless. I waited for him to say more, but that was all he would give up for now.

An eternity went by, but I was prepared to wait. Filled with books, the room gave off a hearthlike feel. Along one wall were shelves stocked with well-thumbed paperbacks. Was that an Agatha Christie I saw among them? If it was, that certainly spoke well for Suzy Yamada.

Rowley's voice came back to him lighter, as if he'd just sucked from a pipe of helium. I wanted to ask you, William, he said, and then stopped to take another pause.

This second silence allowed me to assess his face more closely than I'd ever done before. Well, to be honest, there was nothing else to assess. His body, shriveled, lay inside its casing of custom-made clothes like a wisp of smoke held inside a plastic bag. Five years ago he had fallen down a flight of stairs and ever since then had needed a wheelchair to move around in. His face, on the other hand, retained its vitality. His skin, though lined with fine creases here and there, was remarkably clear, without the fish spots that were a commonplace among the complexions of his contemporaries. As for its color—I'd heard the expression "coffee-colored" before, but meeting Rowley was the first time I'd seen this phrase given life. His eyes were shiny and unclouded, proving the soundness of his life's philosophies.

Could you please open the window for me? he asked.

I hadn't spotted a window in the room. The single lamp I'd turned on was more for mood than illumination. But of course, Rowley was right. There was a window behind silk purple curtains. I opened it. Rowley took a deep breath and then smiled. Damn smoke, he said. Couldn't breathe out there.

I didn't know you were part of this world, William, he said.

I've helped a lot of these people, that's all.

The same way you've helped me.

That's what you wanted to talk to me about? I asked, surprised.

And you're paid well? he continued. To help these people?

They pay what they can and what they think I should get. As a sign of gratitude.

The same way I do.

Yes.

Which can mean a lot.

Or a little, I offered.

Come on, William, Rowley said, smiling. Look at these people. Even a little for them must be a lot.

It's a skill, I reasoned. What are you surprised about?

That you're part of this world.

I told you. I'm not.

Just a guest, he echoed, with a faint trace of mockery.

Just visiting your world, Rowley.

Hah, he laughed. It's not my world. I've been very lucky but it has never been and will never be my world. He paused. What is it you see yourself accomplishing in life, William?

What? I asked, surprised.

He'd never appeared interested in me or my life before, and I thought my role with him had been marked out very clearly from the start: someone who, besides being engaged to help rearrange his house, listened to his stories, made him feel important that way.

What is it you want from life? he repeated impatiently.

I wanted to say, in character: To help others. But I held my tongue and a better answer suggested itself: I don't know, I told Rowley.

You don't know?

I'm not sure.

But you have an idea.

I began rubbing my elbows with my palm, an act of nervousness Rowley misinterpreted. Are you cold? he asked. Maybe you should shut the window.

I moved to the window to close it, turning my back on Rowley. I was careful not to let my face lose its composure lest my reflection in the window tip him off. Why was he asking these questions? Maybe I'd been found out. But how? Surely I must have known the day would come—Shem had severely underestimated the group. When I turned to face Rowley, I volunteered an icy smile which was meant to warn him from going any further with his questions, but which he again misinterpreted.

You remind me of Adela when you smile, he said. Are you sure you don't have any Portuguese blood in you?

I steeled myself. Portuguese, Filipino. I thought: He's found out and he's just prolonging the moment before his announcement. No, not that I'm aware of, I replied calmly.

You're turning red, William, he said.

Why do you want to know, Rowley? What does it matter what I want to do with my life?

Because I've been thinking about things. My life. And you. Since you're part of it. You're so red, he repeated.

Must be the smoke, I lied.

Well, make up your mind. Either open the damn window or keep it closed.

I moved to open the window again, just to give myself something to do. Behind me, I could hear Rowley's wheels rubbing gently on the floor. When I was done, I returned to my seat, crossing one leg over the other.

I thought about Rowley P and his wheelchair, and I thought about the window—which I now realized had been opened for a reason. The plunge was seven stories high. And yes, I could do it. And cover up afterward. "You have a smile like Adela." Didn't he say that? He did, he most certainly did. I could say he came forward, like he did during my past visits, with sexual advances, and that this time I'd had enough. I could say everything happened so fast, clearly I had no idea of my own strength, it was only that I wanted him as far away from me as possible. Self-preservation. Defense. Yes. These words were there in the air waiting to be plucked.

Suddenly, to make matters more interesting, Suzy Yamada came in, making me hold my breath. But when she saw Rowley P, she seemed to grow cowed and so merely backtracked, apologizing. The party sounded to be in full swing, the words coming across, as the hours and drinks piled up on top of one another, more slurred, with warm undercurrents of mutual congratulations buoying up the buzz.

Rowley curved his brows. He asked, Has Suzy asked you to consult on her place?

No, I replied.

She's a finicky girl.

Is she?

You don't know her? he asked me, surprised.

I've never met her till tonight, I confessed. Mutual friends asked me to come.

Ahhh, Rowley said knowingly.

How do you know her? I asked.

Mutual friends, he replied.

What mutual friends?

I could ask you the same question.

I had a feeling of being drafted into a chess game I was unwilling to play. Shem, I replied. The writer.

Rowley shook his head to indicate he didn't know who I was talking about.

And you? I asked him.

He replied, Adela owned the trading company Suzy now has. It was started by her family in Portugal.

She bought it from Adela? I inquired.

Suzy used to work under Adela, began Rowley, scratching his nose. He looked away from me, as if distracted by something that only he could see. After an interval, he continued, And then she rose in the company. And then she rose a little bit more. And then she convinced the stockholders that Adela was getting on—which she was—and that they should let Adela go and put her in charge instead.

Shouldn't that make her an enemy? I asked.

It was underhanded, but it would've happened in a few years anyway. Besides, Suzy has her ways of getting back into your good graces. She was very kind to Adela when Adela . . . just before Adela died. They reconciled.

Was there something more to all this? I didn't have a chance to find out because again we were interrupted. The perturbed, scowling face of the Swiss nurse flashed through a section of the open door.

Rowley looked at me to explain: Bedtime. Then he told the nurse, Five more minutes.

She stood her ground at first, but eventually ceded the room back to us.

Where was I? he turned to ask me. And then he remembered—

what did I want to do with my life?—but a look came over his eyes, as if he wanted to spare me, and instead he said, cheerily, I have you to thank for a lot of good things that have been happening to me recently. He slapped his hands on his knees.

Like what? I asked, raising my eyebrows, as if irritated to be reminded of having done a good deed.

He began rattling off a list: how he slept more soundly now (a jumbo flying pig hanging from the ceiling like a mobile and muslin curtains to section the bed off from the rest of the room, effectively turning that area into a giant crib, in turn giving him a baby's sleep); how he was eating better (a small table was installed right inside the kitchen so that he could eat his food while it was still hot, and so that he could be gotten away from the long dining-room table, which was clearly meant for dinner parties and which, when used day to day, would only emphasize his widowerhood); how he was beginning to read more (using five new bookcases in place of a screen to section off his living room from the front hallway—a spot previously taken up by antique cabinets he had had auctioned off for money for his philanthropy—new bookcases whose empty shelves inspired a bout of book shopping and, consequently, book reading); how he was even entertaining more, seeing friends from his past with whom he'd lost contact or inviting newer acquaintances over for chats over cups of tea (Adela's beloved overstuffed furniture—pieces that he was famously too fussy over—were removed and put into an unused guest bedroom; and then the empty living room was filled with contemporary furniture that could be used without fear of sacrilege); and lastly, how the Swiss was giving him more room to breathe (making access to the rest of the apartment from the nurse's bedroom harder by constructing a wall using screens, on which Rowley could hang pictures of his beloved Adela; in effect using Adela as a ghost to haunt the premises and as a subtle warning to the nurse about who was still in charge) . . .

I have to go, William, he said, sounding vaguely sorrowful. But I want you to think about what I asked you. And maybe we can talk in a few days. Why don't you come over on Thursday. Can you?

What does it matter what I want to do with my life?

Of course it matters.

To you? I asked.

My life is almost over, and yours— You're right in the middle of it. Things can still happen for you.

I, I . . . I stammered, then blurted out before I had an idea of what I was saying: I want to be good.

This shocked Rowley. I could tell from the way his lips hung open. It shocked me too.

What did I say? I asked, as much to myself as to anyone else.

Aren't you good? he asked.

No, I confessed. Now I wasn't sure who the enemy was: Rowley or myself.

You're not good, he said, trying it out on his lips. And then I could see his shock slowly give way to something else. His eyes had a glint in them. It seemed he was considering the thrilling possibilities of my not being good.

I repeated myself cautiously: No.

But you've done good things, he declared.

When?

For me, you've done good things for me, he said emphatically, all of a sudden needing to be convinced himself.

I guess, yes, I conceded, but I remained unconvinced.

You mustn't undervalue your gift, he lectured.

This made me want to laugh. No, I mustn't, I replied, like catechism, a blind echoing.

You mustn't consider what you do not good simply because it's second nature and comes without effort. Sometimes goodness doesn't require a great effort. You can sometimes just *be* good. Or do the things you do naturally and out of that comes goodness.

Rowley . . . I ventured.

You can wheel me back to that damn woman, he ordered.

Rowley, you don't mean me any harm, do you?

What?

You don't mean me any harm, right?

What harm could I do you?

You didn't answer my question.

William, a stupid question does not deserve an answer.

Is that a no? I felt both hands tighten at my sides.

What harm could I do you? he repeated. Even if I wanted to, what could I do? Don't be silly. Now wheel me back.

I did so, and when I transferred him to the Swiss, I uttered something glib: I said to her, He's all yours now.

You take care, barked Rowley, who suddenly turned back. You can make it Thursday, can't you? he asked.

I'll find out and give you a call.

Get some sleep, he said. You probably have too much alcohol in your head. He said this within hearing distance of a few people, but nobody seemed to notice. But just as I thought the coast was clear, there was Paul Chan Chuang Toledo Lin, giving me a look to let me know that he'd heard. Smirking, he rounded a corner and disappeared, his ruddering hips a final insult.

I watched as Rowley and the nurse bid goodbye to Suzy Yamada. Suzy bent down to kiss Rowley on the forehead. He took both of her hands in his and squeezed warmly, with a meaning I couldn't guess.

I returned to the room where I had spoken to Rowley. I opened the door, and then turned on the lamp. A breeze tickled my fingers as I passed them through the spines of the shelved books. I didn't have to peruse the titles long before I found what I was looking for: there, just slightly above eye level, was, indeed, an Agatha Christie: *The Mystery of the Seven Dials*. I took it down immediately and put it in my pocket, which I gratefully discovered was so large it swallowed the book whole. As I turned toward the door, I saw a figure about to appear, which gave me a start. Seconds later, Kendo and I were staring right at each other. I wondered if he could've seen me take the book, but I'd seen him first and had had time to right myself. Still, what was he staring at? Did he remember me looking at him in the dark upstairs? What would he say? I didn't wait to find out. I spoke first. I heard a noise, I told him, and then pointed to the open window, revealed by the upturned curtains. He merely scowled, but didn't move. I turned off the lights and then stepped outside, closing the door behind me. Suddenly, Kendo moved forward and gave me a tight embrace that I swore was meant to injure me. You're OK, man, he said, refusing to let go.

Thank you thanks, I rasped out, breathless.

You're really OK after all, he said.

He was squeezing so tightly that I could feel the pocket book caught between both our legs, its covers giving a scratchy sound that made my heart skip a few beats. Finally, when he let go, I could see the book's imprint on his pant leg, but he didn't bother to look down there. He had his eyes pinned mischievously on me. I couldn't recover quickly enough to turn the stupefied look on my face into anything else. Oh for fuck's sake, what the hell did this kid know that made him smile that smile of owning the upper hand? That made two times tonight that I felt myself to be at the mercy of an unmasker. What could I do to him, this imbalanced fuck? That was it: imbalanced! He'd acted out just that role in front of so many witnesses. What would I say, after they discovered his dead body on the ground floor, that body that eyewitnesses below saw flinging itself over the window and were powerless to stop from smashing right past the flimsy tarp of the building's entrance and onto the concrete walkway? He jumped, I would testify to a sobbing Suzy Yamada. He just jumped. That was what imbalanced kids did. They lost their footing while preening from the ledge, making a show of their juvenile desperation, hoping for some needed attention.

But, perhaps sensing my intent, Kendo started to move away, and very soon was gone.

I smoothed my pants, made sure the outline of the book was subsumed into nothingness.

There was a clock on the mantelpiece above the empty fireplace, but its hands were too fine. I ventured nearer. It said one o'clock. I turned to see Shem coming toward me.

How are you, Master? Shem asked me. Having seen my tired look, he hissed under his breath, Snap out of it!

What's Guanfacine?

That a joke?

It's medication. What's it for?

Beats me. Why?

Suzy takes it.

You talked to her? he asked.

She's always somewhere else.

Well, I don't think she's gonna give another party anytime soon, he warned.

I'm waiting for an intro, I told him.

But she knows who you are.

Not according to the way she's acting.

All right. You still holding up?

Not for very long.

There by the glass doors to the veranda was a stack of blue sheets on top of a tall display table, empty of its vase. People leaving the veranda were encouraged to take a sheet. The man doing this wore a yellow shirt with a crocodile stitched on a breast pocket. Like Chan Chuang Toledo Lin, he wore no socks. On his feet were worn-out loafers that were beginning to warp upward in the toes. I asked Shem who this man was whom I'd caught conversing earlier with Lin.

He's a writer, said Shem. The last word was tinged with disgust.

What's his name?

Max Carlton.

Why does the name ring a bell? I asked aloud.

He's looking at you, announced Shem.

I walked over to the man. Viewed him caught in the crosshairs of my campaign: What angle did he have that could be exploited by Chao?

Here, he said, pushing a flyer into my hands.

On the sheet was an announcement for a reading of a new novel by the playwright Max Brill Carlton. It would take place at Columbia University a week from tonight. There was a picture of the author that I was now assessing against the man who'd given it to me.

Please come, he said to a pretty, wafer-thin model type, who was on her way to the front door.

Looking at her, I recognized an easy mark slipping away: I would glance at her apartment and speak of "the deprivation and starving of your soul," not once mentioning food, and she would confess.

Max Brill Carlton. The name meant something to me, though I couldn't figure out why.

So I read on: "*Set among several blocks in the West Eighties, near Riverside Park*, Blind Souls *tells the interconnecting story of a group of Manhattanites each engrossed in their quest for a piece of the "American pie." Filled with vivid details of such perennial New York subjects as uptown versus downtown, the personals, the hottest nightclubs and the oldest wealth—and how to get into both—and finally, the high cost of trying to stay sane, it is also ultimately about the state of our nation's soul, circa the late 1980s. It is about the haves and the have-nots, the well-healed and the down on their luck, all scrambling to turn a piece of this city into their own heaven on earth . . ."* I noticed the misspelling. Well-healed? Or was it intentional? I continued reading: *". . . This sensational debut by the playwright who brought us the acclaimed play* Primitives *(1988 Tony Award for Best Play) has been excerpted in* The New Yorker, *and will surely be among the most talked-about books of the year!"*

Primitives. That was the play Preciosa had starred in! And this man who was now smiling gaily at me as if expecting everything to have clicked, but click in a way that meant, number one, that I'd seen his play, and, number two, that I'd liked it, was that same Max Brill Carlton whose name was in the Lincoln Center program!

His voice cut into my thoughts. What's your name? he asked. After I introduced myself, he said, Oh, you're the Chinese voodoo doctor.

This took me aback, though it probably wasn't so far from how I would phrase things myself. I beamed him a tolerant, indulgent smile, stretching my lips wide without revealing any teeth.

I'm sorry, he said. Did I offend you?

Oh no, I replied. I went on automatic pilot: Faith is a funny thing. When you're inside it, it never even occurs to you that other people might find your beliefs funny or misshapen. All the while, I thought: This man is not a customer.

I'm sorry, he repeated. He sounded sincerely contrite. He said, I hope you'll come and make the acquaintance of my work. So that you can see for yourself that I'm not usually this— Well, this moronic. He grinned.

I grinned back.

He was a white man in his mid- to late forties, with a rosy-cheeked face and a long cascading top of chestnut hair, wearing clothes that bespoke an ease in—and a basic indifference toward—the kind of event tonight represented. And I was . . . well, me. We had nothing in common. And I was sure that nothing would induce me to show up at his reading. I'll *try* to make it, I told him.

Owww! he said, pantomiming being hurt by an arrow stuck in

his chest, right where the crocodile sat, grinning its Master Chao grin.

Again, I grinned right back.

There was no one else around to hand flyers to.

It says here that you wrote a play called *Primitives*, I remarked.

Yes, he replied, smiling.

Shem was watching us from his perch on a love seat. Kendo, making a sudden appearance, flopped himself onto the cool tiles by the fireplace. Is it over? he asked the ceiling. Is it over? he repeated. Cued by this, four people began to gather their things. Suzy magically reappeared, seeing them to the door and thrusting bottles of wine into their hands, which they made a show of refusing.

There was Brian Q, escorting the horse girl to the door. He had an arm underneath her elbow, and was continuing to beam. Had he ever stopped beaming during the whole evening? He spoke to Suzy, who was clearly keeping her distance from the girl. Like me, she'd smelled something untoward about that horse face, that gunfire delivery.

How much they both enjoyed the evening, said Brian Q, speaking for the horse girl.

Next in line was a chic blond duo with matching haircuts. Ice would not have melted in their mouths. The woman was absentmindedly pulling at a strand of pink pearls around her taut neck. The apartment was looking swell, better than it'd ever looked before. Replying, Suzy hinted at future improvements. Would they be seeing each other out at the Hamptons? asked the couple. Would Suzy be visiting them at their home on Gin Lane?

A few hours before, I'd felt myself to be the unofficial center of the party, even though there were so many faces that were new to me. But these faces, judging from the whispers I caused whenever I walked by, wouldn't be new for long: I had made good on the promise of tonight.

I had these people's numbers. I knew exactly who they were. The Catholics among them had been taught—as I had been—that all those who were not Catholic would be sent to hell on the Judgment Day to become kindling for the devil's fireplace. The Jews among them were taught—so Shem confirmed—that it would be the non-Jews who would burn. They would be made to cross a chasm of fire on a bridge unfortified by the strength of the Jewish faith, and would consequently fall to their horrible deaths. And from that, it would be safe to extrapolate the same story for other religions: Join us or risk hell, would be the wording on each recruitment poster. And the nagging awareness that the year 2000 was around the corner had as good as driven these people back to the time-consuming faiths of their parents and their grandparents. Their return was like an insurance policy for the next life. And as for this one— If you stubbed your toe, went the logic, it was only because something in you pulled you to that spot where your toe would be stubbed. Something dark, twisted by the imbalance in the environment. To redress this, people were being encouraged to go further inward, where true peace could be located. *Stability. Family values. The good old days. A return to tradition.* You even heard that phrase in the magazines I perused—"Tradition makes a comeback!": People were again living in environments that reminded them of the way their parents' lives were, when things were "simpler," and the homes cocoonlike. They were forgoing the chicness of steel and leather in their interior decorations, for instance, and going instead with materials that suggested "the human touch," "warmth," as if in anticipation of a long, cold winter: wood, wool, cotton, unpolished stone; or they might use leather and steel, but it was leather and steel treated in such a way as to diminish their essential frigidity.

It was only because I was the blithe housekeeper, with a complete disregard for these people's beliefs, standing outside their lives and passing comment on every single thing as I dusted them clean, that I was able to see so clearly. It was the total and unforgiving sobriety of a man who owned nothing, to whom nothing belonged . . . And now they were all deserting me.

Max Carlton had been speaking. I'm sorry? I asked him.

He repeated, I said have you seen the play? He was referring to *Primitives.*

No, I'm afraid not. But the title is so . . . intriguing. What was it about?

He looked crestfallen that I hadn't seen his play, but plowed on: It's about a group of missionaries who go to some country in Central America and try to set up its first Christian village.

Finally, I took a deep breath, and heard the words that I really wanted to ask (unlocking *The Mystery of Preciosa X*) come: Did your characters who were the natives, did they, uhhh . . . they spoke?

I wanted to learn if Preciosa had been a star before her career had ended abruptly. And to have been a star, at least in the theater, she had to have access to lines that made an impression, persuading the audience to come over to her side, despite the distancing effect of that photographed noncostume.

How'd you know I had characters who were natives? asked Max Brill Carlton.

I . . . Well, it just seemed likely, the title and all, I blubbered. Why? Didn't you?

Yes, he said, I had. And yes, they spoke.

Oh. What did they speak?

You mean what language?

Yes.

English. You have to cheat, you know. The object, after all, is communicating to the audience.

Did they speak good . . . I mean what kind of English?

What do you mean? he asked, sensing a trap. Perhaps he'd been accosted by activists during the run of the play and was understandably nervous. But if he only knew my reasons, he would've . . . well, would he have laughed, or been made more shamed?

What kind of English did they speak?

Well, first off, he started cautiously, only the chief and his translator spoke.

Oh, I said, making a little hole of my lips which stayed put as he continued to speak. I took his revelation in: Preciosa had had no lines. Not even Ooga Booga bullshit lines—*no* lines, zero! Only unripe tits and a passive, out-of-it stare, like being on dope. She was not, and had never been, a star. The rest of what followed became a blur. And when he was done, I was more than glad to let him go.

Shem came up and guided me to where Suzy Yamada was. I was still dazed.

He presented me to the hostess. Finally. She had let her hair down, with the effect that her face was now more rounded, with chipmunk cheeks suddenly visible. They were fever-rosy from drink or exhaustion or a combination of both. Somehow, she looked more approachable, though of course I immediately realized how deceptive this was. If anything, invisible straps seemed more than ever to be securing her arms and legs in place, governing the limited arcs they traveled as she extended her hand for me, pretending to move a few steps closer, and then immediately retreating. This was certainly not the way she had behaved toward the departing guests. Why did she turn cold with me? Or was I simply imagining things?

Hi, she said. Nice to meet you.

You have a lovely home, I told her. It was the same way I'd begun with Lindsay S. Would it produce the same results?

Thank you, she said, refusing to take off her poker face. *Nope.*

I'll leave you two alone, Shem said.

No, stay, Suzy told him.

Shem and I exchanged noncommittal looks. Please, Suzy said to me, have a seat. After we were all seated, she turned to me and seemed about to speak. But she said nothing.

Wonderful party, huh? asked Shem, who was the first to capitulate to the uncomfortable silence. I gave the appearance of not noticing this silence, which in my mind was engineered by Suzy Yamada as a test, and so the way I saw it, I'd scored a point. I could've relaxed and echoed Shem's sentiment about the party, but I merely smiled. I had a sudden insight: Maybe this was why I had turned handsomer, being forced to smile so much.

Suzy Yamada said to Shem, Thank you.

I still didn't speak.

Lin came to pay his respects. Good night, Suzy, he slurred. Are you going to get home OK? Suzy asked. Lin's trademark pompadour looked like some exhausted fowl.

Suzy excused herself to walk the writer to the door. Suddenly, to my eyes, he appeared like a lost man. It was as if I could see right into his future: he would be forever alien to happiness. Without knowing it, I was up and moving to where he and Suzy stood. I caught them just as she was helping him into a jacket. The door was open, the hall behind it empty.

Is there anything I could do to help you? I asked Lin. Everything seemed outside my powers of censorship.

What do you mean? he said. He could barely get the words out of his mouth he was so drunk.

Here, said Suzy, fitting the final arm in. And then she left us alone.

Do you need any help? Help that I could provide? I asked, looking at his hairline, where sweat was beginning to accumulate and then drop.

He furrowed his brows, as if considering the opportunity I was providing him. And then before I could prepare myself, he was cawing, a loud, vulgar laugh like a slap across my cheeks. Excuse me, he said. I'm going home.

I watched him go to the buttons, which he pressed again and again. He knew I was looking at him, and that was why he stood so stiffly, refusing to turn around. And for the first time, I realized: Lin knew that he was a sham, and only in moments like this, moments he himself engineered to be able to loosen the mask and catch his breath, did the evidence of his humanness, that is to say, his sadness, show through.

I closed the door on him.

A lot of people seemed to know you tonight, Master, Suzy said, when I returned. She was finally turning to me and throwing in her chips. But you could tell she found it distasteful to have to defer to someone so much younger than herself.

Please, I said. Call me William. I sat next to Shem, who put a question mark into his face—what had possessed me to accost Lin like that? I looked away.

William, Suzy said.

I nodded.

Yes, said Shem. William's been asked to consult quite a bit.

Shem showed me an article about you from a, from—

Shem graciously filled in the blank, giving the magazine's name.

Yes, said Suzy.

Oh that, I said, marking it down immediately.

I confess I haven't gotten around to reading it yet, she told the two of us.

I tried not to register the insult.

Still busy running around? asked Shem with his usual unflap-

pable good humor. God, Suzy, do you even know the meaning of relax?

Well, there's that one there, she said of Kendo, who was visible
from where we were. He was still lying by the fireplace, catatoni-
cally bored. He's a handful.

Lights were slowly being turned down by a maid. She was a Filipina. I could tell right off. Could the reverse also be true? Could
she, looking at me, see right through my claim? I was careful not to
look in her direction. The other maid, a white girl of indeterminate
nationality, was busy lighting candles which she then placed all
over the apartment. Both women wore uniforms of nun's-black cotton underneath ruffled white aprons cinched at the waist. Thank
you, Teresa, Suzy Yamada said to one of the maids, I wasn't sure
which.

Someone's crying, declared Suzy.

Is it over, Doctor? asked Kendo, who wasn't the one crying. In
fact, hearing the cries, he reacted with a sharp and derisive laugh, as
if he'd predicted all along that the party was going to be a disaster
and that at this late hour he was being proven right.

The source of trouble came to us.

Angela, Suzy said, and brought the young woman to sit next to
her. Shem made room.

The guru's dead, Angela declared.

What?! asked Suzy.

Is it over? repeated Kendo.

The guru. He's dead.

Kendo repeated once more, Is it over? When will it be over?

This sent Suzy into a rage. She screamed, Kendo shut the fuck
up! Go away! All the while, she continued to stroke the sobbing
girl's hair.

Where?! Kendo piped back.

Away from here. This is serious.

You mean away like outside?

I don't care! she screamed. You and your sarcasm are not wanted
here!

Sor-reee! performed Kendo as he got up. His eyes made sure to
pin curses on the open billboards of each of the others' foreheads

before he left. For me, however, he gave a strange wink—or was I imagining things?

What followed between the two women was a hurried exchange of arcane details about "the guru," who had died just hours before, under "mysterious circumstances," in New Jersey. Piece by piece, they walled themselves off from the men: An unknown woman had been found with this guru, the sole witness. Had he been assassinated? Or did he kill himself? If he'd been assassinated, who'd done it? If suicide, how? And more distressingly, why? It became increasingly obvious to the women that they ought to keep up the breathless pace of their inquiries lest the unsavory answers these questions deserved, encouraged by any kind of pause or silence, might develop. It was like trying to outrun consciousness.

Was Suzy a follower of this guy? And what was he a guru of? And was that why I was no longer needed—because she'd found another means of righting the wrongs in her life, her home?

Max Brill Carlton, who I thought had already left, suddenly appeared, putting a thin windbreaker on. Apparently, he didn't know what was going on between the women, because he looked at me and said cheerily, See you at the reading. And oh by the way, great shoes!

On the streets, my eyes were stopped by a jillion copies of the early morning edition of the *New York Post* strung on a line outside a newsstand like so much Christmas decoration. I gave the newsstand guy fifty cents and took a copy from the top of a stack dumped on the ground. The headline read: Curtain for Kuerten.

The guru's name was Georg Kuerten. His body was discovered floating in the Hudson near his five-acre estate in Alpine, New Jersey. Police made the discovery when they were summoned by a distraught phone call coming from a young woman at around nine in the evening. They came to discover the body of the famous self-styled "Eastern philosophy" guru in the river, with a dog collar around his neck and a possible smell of alcohol on his breath. Police found the young woman who called similarly collared, and appearing to be strung out from drugs, which she told police she and

Kuerten had been binging on for days. When asked whether there were other people on the premises, she replied that it had been only Kuerten and herself for the last two weeks. Police found Kuerten's mansion "spectacularly trashed," with pizza cartons and empty tins of tuna and pork and beans littered everywhere, staining the carpet and the walls. As yet, no drug-related items had been discovered, though the search was far from over.

Kuerten was the founder of the "Eastern Spirits Awakening Movement"—a sort of greatest hits of Hinduism and Buddhism and New Ageism all mashed together—securing a name for himself by holding seminars in Los Angeles in the late eighties, and then soon after across the country. Seminars on how to help heal the "neglected Eastern child inside," arguing to his constituents that they each had access to a vast body of mystical "Eastern" knowledge which life in the Western world had slowly occluded, masked over, like "the exteriors of buildings defaced over time by smog and neglect." His purpose, he stated, was to help bring people's "inner wiseman" out. Kuerten, a Jew, was born in Austria in the early fifties, and came to the United States as a small boy. His parents, both physicists, settled in Berkeley, California, where they taught at the university. There, the young Kuerten—who was a college dropout—was exposed to the "libertarian and hippie" atmosphere of the seventies Bay Area, and thus was formed the foundation for his later "progressive and slightly far-fetched" religious philosophies. Kuerten first became interested in Hinduism in the early seventies, when, swept up in the fashion of the times, he'd made a trip to India and discovered "what the Beatles and all the other hip celebrities were talking about." Converted, he came back and became a practicing Hindu, effectively dropping out of productive society. Still, there was no indication of the later messianic role he would take on—after years of practice, he suddenly claimed to have been visited by visions in which he was told that he was the reincarnation of Vishnu, the second God of the Hindu trinity, also called "the Preserver." Vishnu had had several human incarnations throughout the ages, the most recent and well known of whom was Krishna. So, in other words, Kuerten had laid claim to inheriting the mantle of a religious superstar. His "business" did not prosper, however, until he expanded his narrow claim of expertise to include Buddhism, and aspects of what was only then being termed "New Age" religions. Soon he was preaching a pantheism that would be the key to embracing life in the world to come, arguing that all faiths at their root were good, and sought to better the human condition by encouraging the alleviation of suffering and the propagation of beauty. His assets were said to be in the vicinity of thirty-five million dollars. His estate in Alpine, New Jersey, was equipped with the latest hi-tech surveillance and security gadgets, owing in the last few years to an increasing number of death threats. Most of which came from friends and family members of Kuerten's disciples. These people claimed that Kuerten was nothing more than a shrewd manipulator and brainwasher, and had persuaded his disciples to contribute heftily to his own private wealth. A sidebar made up of three very short columns on the lower right-hand corner entitled Fact or Quack? elaborated on these people's complaints, citing several cases brought to court but which were thrown out for "lack of hard, conclusive evidence," or which were shrewdly thrown by Kuerten's lawyers under the protective umbrella of the separation of church from state (?). Investigation was ongoing, continued the main article, and the statement of the cause of death would follow the coroner's examination. No funeral arrangements had as yet been made . . .

There was no mention in the article of Suzy Yamada or of the crying girl, Angela, two people to whom, by association, things *happened*, regardless of how malign those things were. This was what the new group I had been swept up by settled for eventually: lacking either the talent or the hubris to be able to pull off any kind of accomplishment, they were content to settle for connection, to be near the people who came back from the world with achievements that could then be suitably flattened for interesting dinner conversation, achievers who were more than willing to lend the distinction of their company in exchange for a taste of the generosity of the wealthy. Even the achievers with money of their own realized that theirs was nothing in the face of the money of the truly wealthy, which was sanctified by age and had a smell all its own.

The published photograph of the deceased was taken three

years ago. It was a publicity still issued by the Institute for the Advancement of Eastern Wisdom, an organization Kuerten founded and which had its national headquarters in Laguna Beach, California. In the picture, Kuerten had the clueless expression of a school-boy, as if he didn't know what the picture was being taken for. Behind that blank look, however, could be spotted a tiny, mysteri-ous apprehensiveness. Was it the fear that he would one day be found out?

Published in conjunction with his death, the picture seemed to take on a clairvoyant quality.

Wow, people get themselves into complicated, manufactured lives they end up having to put out so much effort just to keep up with, I thought, with the amazement of a momentary amnesiac. Well, duh!—the recognition dawned three beats too late, and by the time it did, realizing that the sentence I passed applied oh so neatly to my situation as well, it was too late, I was to be included among the group I'd condemned: complicated, manufactured, so much ef-fort . . . It was the worst kind of wisdom: to know and be trapped at the same time. And the weight it imparted was a million light-years from the spring in my choreographed steps when I first began . . . Walking into each of those people's homes, trying to contain my ela-tion at being put so close to wealth, with my hands clasped as if in prayer before me, not rigid but dropped naturally in front of my groin, as if I were taking a stroll through some museum where infor-mation was being relayed by a guide, information that I would not need to relay back to show that I had been listening, but simply in-formation that was just being offered to fill up space, to chat, just because I happened to be there, an audience, and these people needed me to complete the picture, that was why it was called a showplace, after all . . . Cut a scene this way: In between bouts of pretend-wisdom which he declaims with folksy gravity to the own-ers, have the young man, physically unrecognizable from his former life, have this new young man, in a voice-over, wonder which of the several items he sees in these various houses he could safely make away with to sell later on . . . And then crosscut the various homes which he's allowed into with the pawnshops in and around Times Square where he goes to to hock his goods, making sure the airiness and sunshine of the former form a machine-gun jolt contrast to the provisional, cramped, subterranean atmospheres of the latter. Cross-cut too the faces of the residents of each environment to see these two poles of New York made flesh: crosscut, for example, the pampered—if balding—head of Brian Q, with his gold-framed glasses, his easy smile, his cheeks constantly flushed as if having just ingested a hot meal, his unconvincing goatee like a miniature lawn sculpture tacked onto his chin and which did comic flip-kicks every time his mouth opened to talk—contrast that with the Arab man who sits behind a chest-to-ceiling panel of bulletproof glass, his brows constantly furrowed from having to regard people across the way who could potentially do him harm; his face a constellation of enlarged pores which, come summer and in the absence of an air conditioner, grow even larger; his mouth always pursed, shut tight, and then, when he opens his mouth to quote you a figure, marking your merchandise way down, you understand why: a man who owns teeth that even a horse would reject, ragged and pointy like stalactites, and colored yellow with skin-crawling lines of black in the spaces between each tooth; and on his chin a ragged mass of Brillo hair that was like the muscleman to Brian Q's ninety-pound-weakling growth . . . Also, have the young man speak the following voice-over to explicate the movie of his life: *In the beginning, when I didn't think too much, or hadn't yet allowed the fun word "revenge" to calcify into routine, when I was just going and grooving, coasting along on my hatred for God and my fellow man, in the beginning it was so much fun, and my life felt like it was about to start . . .*

All this time, I'd been standing on the street corner, the whole city sandblasted into oblivion by my concentration, and the night ending three feet from my skin—and so when I finally realized that there was a figure standing behind me and reading over my shoulder, I gave a jump. I was prepared for it to be Kendo, having trailed me from the apartment. I didn't know why I thought it would be him, but it was him that I saw in my mind. What the fuck? I opened my mouth to say, but the words, gratefully, didn't form. I found myself looking into the face of a black man who was grinning sheepishly. He got what he deserved, huh? he said to me in greeting. He was talking about Kuerten.

It took me a moment to recover, and then I said, blinking, You knew who he was?

Not till tonight, he replied.

Huh, I said, same as me.

I was as good as done with the paper, and so I offered it to him.

You sure? he asked.

Take it, I said.

He did, but he wanted to offer me my horoscope in parting. What sign are you? he asked.

That's OK, I said, making to leave.

No no, he told me, a death's a big thing, you know? When somebody big dies, you can tell that that's gonna be an important day for everyone, like you know, like all our lives, all our lives are gonna start to get better. No, I'm not kidding, dude, ain't no joke, trust me. Our lives are gonna get better cause someone big takes up all the good fortune that's raining down on the world, right? Sound about right? And when he dies, when that person dies, you know, it like frees up the good fortune for the rest of us, know what I'm saying? It's like, it's like some, like, a tall building, right? OK, a tall building, it blocks out the sun, right? And so when you knock it down whaddya got? You got more sun for everyone! OK. What's your sign?

His philosophy got a smile out of me. What do you do? I asked him.

He told me he was a janitor and was on his way to work cleaning office suites in midtown.

What sign are you? he asked again.

Capricorn, I replied.

He ran his fingers down the columns, and locating Capricorn, began to read aloud in a cracked, careful voice, putting a period at the end of every third word: Be wary of people who ask leading questions, especially if the direction you are being led in is one you would much rather avoid. It's unlikely they know enough to embarrass you, but you could easily say something that makes them want to dig deeper. Change the subject, if you can.

I just stared at him.

On the subway there were other livelihoods to consider. Long, narrow advertisements hung above the slouched-over figures of riders. One said: Everything breaks down. That was the lead-in, printed in

bold black. And then below it, the catch: Everyone is always looking for somebody to fix it. The list of potential fix-it roles filled a
thin column to the right, done in red letters: auto mechanic, TV and
VCR repairman, computer technician, watch and clock repairman.
The thickest letters were reserved for the name of the school that
put up the ad, someplace in Brooklyn, and next to it, a phone number. Call now, it said in parting. Next to it was an ad for the U.S.
Army: "Be all you can be" flanked a mean-looking man-boy with
camouflage grease marks slashing his impossibly even features. He
was staring right at the space above my head, with a hypnotist's
trick in his eyes. Next to him was an ad for volunteers for a medical
study, its exact nature unspecified. The people who were conducting
the study were looking for healthy males between the ages of eighteen and thirty-five. That's me, I thought. And for a brief moment,
because I had nothing better to do, and because it was in my history
to consider all sorts of ventures harmful but lucrative—in short,
ventures which poverty and indifference shape you to accept—I
thought about calling the printed number, which seemed like the
code for a safe.

I slid out the opening doors, eager to escape the other passengers,
and grateful not to be any of them.

On the streets, I stumbled upon a man in a doorway with both
hands busy. In one hand he was holding a crack pipe, which he delivered to his very chapped lips periodically, and blowing into it,
turned a very small flame on in the glass cylinder. And in the other,
he was scratching a lottery ticket with his thumbnail. He would
smoke, then scratch, smoke, then scratch another square of the
ticket, causing little bits of sparkly gray ink to flake off. He was
cackling, thrilled to have a chance in his hands. But in the end, he
threw the lottery ticket away. Still, he continued to cackle, because
in one hand, at least, he held a prize.

And when he puffed, making a ragged orange star fizz inside the
tube which he held to his lips like it was his own mother, he was
smoking in my mind for the both of us. Because I had, in a very different sort of way, a way that I hadn't been planning on, turned
"good."

Vishnu was dead, found floating in the Hudson. I could, continuing Shem's work of reclamation, take this man aside, clean him up, hook him to a new and sparkling history of repentance and salvation. He could claim to have seen the light, to have turned a corner and, in that turning, to have been granted a vision that he could pass on to the tired, hungry masses—for a fee, of course. He could be the perfect illustration for the abstract phrases "the next world," "the new life." Had Shem seen the same thing in me? Could he, looking at my end-of-the-race posture at the Savoy, have intuited a desire to play the lottery, to have that lazy, unfocused desire for improvement? And could he tell that I, once drafted, would—unlike the crack man who was now drifting off to sleep while standing straight up—stay on the path and not stray or slide?

Suddenly, as if occasioned by my thoughts, I found myself passing the dark open doorway of the Savoy. I heard tinny music coming from inside, as if from a child's transistor radio. But I could hear no voices raised in obnoxious challenge, no cackling, no slap of glasses on the heavy wood counter, no squishing of the cracked vinyl seats, no banging of the rest-room doors against the crumbling walls, no hands clapping, no steps piecing together a drunken dance routine—even though I was sure those things were going on as usual and it was just that I was now on the other side and couldn't hear.

The other side

15

William
starts
behaving
in E.S

The contrast between Suzy's loftlike apartment and my own little hovel made me awaken with disgust. I moved into the "living room" with its one window, outside of which I had secured leftover barbed wire taken from Brian Q (to drive away the pigeons), helping ease one blight, at least, but there was no sun to be had except for a kind of wispy film like thinned soup, and this, to me, perfectly exemplified my no-win situation. It wasn't that I faced an obliterating building that deprived me, but that somehow, by some magical means of arrangement that I could only describe as cosmic, almost no sun entered my apartment. It was mostly in instances like this that I believed in God—because, after all, there needed to exist a Punisher. Suzy's apartment, on the other hand, would probably be sunlit all day long. For a moment, I lost myself in a daydream of sleeping on her rich floors, lying on the stone tiles that marked the area around her fireplace, as Kendo had done, with all the windows, as well as the door to the veranda, open, to let the summer heat have its concourse through the place and be rendered impotent by the coolness of every surface. In this daydream, I was being fanned by sheer white curtains billowing inward, like the hems of the costumes of giant ghosts. A buzzer woke me.

I went to my intercom and, pressing a button, said, Yeah? It was Shem. I let him in.

When he came to my door, he had a package, which he handed over to me. He was smiling, and his smile cracked cruds of sleep from his eyes.

What's this? I asked.

Gifts for you.

Books? I asked, but he didn't have to reply, because I got the contents out in no time. They were three very slim volumes by a writer named Georges Simenon. An inside page stated that the books were translated from the French.

I knew you liked that kind of stuff, said Shem.

They're mysteries?

He nodded, moving me along to a wood bench pushed against one wall which served as my "sofa." With my new income, I had been able to purchase several cushions to make it comfortable. Shem, noticing the cushions, made a joke. Moving up in the world, he said.

Your butt noticed? I asked.

My butt appreciates.

I turned the books over to read the plot synopses, the blurbs from various periodicals attesting to the books' quality, and then I flipped back inside, catching a peculiar detail at the back of the title pages: the copyright dates were all in the 1950s.

These are old, I said.

Next to that Agatha Christie shit you read those are virtually contemporary.

The Mystery of the Seven Dials, I suddenly remembered, was still in my pants, which were hanging behind the bathroom door.

You've read them? I asked Shem, referring to the new books.

Years ago.

These are yours?

No. Mine I lost. They're on some shelves in the house that I'm no longer welcome in. Those I bought for you.

You didn't have to do that.

You just remember that.

They're French? I asked.

Belgian.

Huh?

Simenon's Belgian.

But he speaks French? I asked.

The Belgians speak French. You don't know this shit?

Self-conscious when it came to my ignorance, I shrugged it off.

What time did you get home? he asked.

I sat down on a chair close by. I got home as soon as I left the party. Why? Where else could I go?

The Savoy, he replied, like the most obvious of answers.

That's another life, I said.

So you mean to say it's behind you?

What if I get seen inside the Savoy?

By whom? he asked.

Clients.

Nobody we consult for goes to the Savoy, because if they did, number one, you'd have met them by now and the cat would be out of the bag and there'd be no need for us to go on, and number two, they'd be too afraid to touch any of the surfaces. Don't you get it? Nobody who wants Feng Shui can stand disorder, that's what they want Feng Shui for. And the Savoy, he said, is about nothing if not disorder. The Savoy is the antithesis of Feng Shui. Besides, those people have their own joints for picking others up, a higher grade of beef if you know what I mean.

You were there, I reminded him.

I'm not them, he snapped back.

You mean to say it's behind you? This time I was throwing the line at him.

Duh, he replied, and smiled in a childish way of pure satisfaction: This time it was he who was throwing the line at me.

So who's this guy? I asked him.

Kuerten? You read this morning's papers?

I nodded, replying, The guru. *Their* guru?

Ex.

What caused the split?

Maybe Suzy outgrew that stuff. Maybe it got her where she was and no further and she definitely wanted better.

You make her sound so easy.

With Suzy, Shem replied, things usually are very simple. She wants to move ahead. That's all there is to her. For us to give her the complex motivation that we think her success and demeanor deserve is definitely to confuse her for someone else.

If she dropped him just like that why would she still be crying? And by the way, how long ago did she drop him?

Three, four years? Maybe she had a change of heart and wanted to go back to him. Maybe she was just thinking about the money he owed her.

What money?

Oh, I'm sure she contributed heftily to his cause quote unquote.

A contribution's not a loan, I pointed out.

With Suzy everything's a loan. He tapped the side of his skull, saying, Remember: With Suzy everything's very simple. You know Japanese movies? he asked.

All I could think of was Ozu, whose film *Tokyo Story* I had caught at the Walter Reade, per Lindsay S's recommendation. It had been the slowest thing I'd ever seen. Nonetheless, I'd stayed, hoping for its uneventfulness to turn instructive. The main lesson it turned out to impart was the "secret smile" which, Mona Lisa–like, had settled on the faces of various characters at unexpected moments, giving them the appearance of keeping enlightenment to themselves. This I had copied for my consultations. Recalling the Ozu put an involuntary grimace on my face.

I'm not a big fan, I told Shem.

Even Akee-ra Kurow-sah-wah?

Who?

You gotta be kidding, he said. He made *Throne of Blood*. Ever hear of that?

Is that a mystery? I said this only half jokingly, but the look of consternation on Shem's face made it too hard to resist keeping on in this vein. Oh right, I said to Shem. *Throne of Blood*. That's the movie where the guy sits on the toilet and all he can do is scream because his hemorrhoids are killing him.

If I were you I wouldn't be so proud of my ignorance, he said sharply. *Throne of Blood*'s adapted from *Macbeth*. You know Shake-speare?

Duh.

Duh, he echoed. That's what they should put on your tombstone. William Chao: Duh.

That's not my name, I told him, shocked that he would forget.

You know *Macbeth*?

I know Shakespeare, I said, but not *Macbeth*.

What Shakespeare do you know?

To be or not to be.

What's that from?

Fuck you, I snapped. You ain't my professor.

You don't know what that's from, he said, laughing.

Hamlet, asshole. To be or not to fucking be. That is the question. And what's the answer? The answer is Just do it. You know Just do it? I asked.

Shem looked at me with an I'm-not-even-gonna-dignify-that expression.

Nike, I said.

Rent *Throne of Blood*.

Why should I?

The actress who plays Lady Macbeth is named Isuzu Yamada. Suzy is short for Isuzu. That's who she's named for. A rose by any other name . . . What's that from?

What?

A rose by any other name would smell just as sweet.

You ain't school, Shem, I told him. If you are, it's all extracurricular, know what I mean?

It's Shakespeare, he went on, heedless. Which one?

Shem, Shakespeare's like trigonometry, OK? Don't mean shit in the real world.

Unlike Agatha Christie, he said.

I know about as much as I need to.

You know, William, ignorance isn't always bliss.

Thank you, *Bartlett's Familiar Quotations*.

Rent *Throne of Blood*. Just watch that woman. That's all you need to know. Namesake for namesake. Call a dog Killer and don't be surprised if that's what you get.

So did she set up an appointment?

I'm not your agent, he reminded me.

What happens now?

You tell me, he said.

In the silence that followed, a question occurred to me. I put down the Georges Simenon books on a slightly wobbly side table by my chair, and then I put on an advance expression of apology for what I was going to ask Shem. Is she who you slept with?

He knew exactly whom I was referring to, but still he said, Who?

Suzy.

I slept with Suzy? He repeated my question but gave it an innocuous reading.

You told me you cheated on your wife—

I don't need you to remind me.

She's the one, isn't she?

What would she be doing inviting me to her party and acting so close if that was true?

But she didn't, I explained. She wasn't acting close. In fact, she was giving you the cold shoulder. Is that why she wants nothing to do with me?

That has nothing to do with me and everything to do with you.

I've done my groundwork, I told Shem, and she still won't budge.

So what's happened to Brian? Shem asked. He was smiling ear to ear like his dick was being stroked.

It was, I replied, remembering horse girl.

The plan was not for them to be smiling, isn't that what we agreed on?

What good would it do us for him to be crying? Where would that get us with Suzy? This is a small world. Word gets around. And we want that word to be good, don't we?

Of course he could see my point. Could see that there was no use clinging to the original plan. The clients would have to make do with the humiliation of being duped and fleeced.

Do you believe they *can* be harmed? I heard Shem ask.

By that thing? Do *you* believe?

The Chinese are no fools.

You sound just like Lindsay S, I said.

No, he retorted. Lindsay would've said, The Chinese are next to God. And that's not exactly what I said.

Better be safe than sorry, right? I asked lamely.

But what good is belief if you're not going to act on it? What's the good of owning a weapon unless you can take it out every once in a while and inflict some damage?

I told you why not.

But just one.

Suzy. She'll be our last and it'll be safe then.

Another one, he insisted.

And then I remembered: There'd been Cardie Kerchpoff. I'd acted on my hatred for her, hadn't I? But how could I tell Shem without acknowledging to him—and what's worse, admitting to myself— that I believed everything with the blind, heedless belief of a dumb-fuck conditioned by a lifetime of catechism, this time substituting the mumbo jumbo of ancient Chinese philosophy for the hoodoo voodoo of Christ's death on the cross? I had, in the end, despite all my protestations, a vast talent for faith, a great need for it, and as a hungry student trying to make up for the lack of formal education, I realized I had acquired in my later life a great desire to be overtaken by facts, by tenets, by rules, some order, some architecture to give meaning and purpose to my unraveling existence—which partly ex-plained Shem's importance in my life. He offered a *plan*.

Not all of them deserve it, I found myself arguing instead. I was thinking, of course, of Rowley P, perhaps Brian Q, and a few others. Paradoxically, those who *did* deserve it weren't hiring me—Paul Chan Chuang Toledo Lin, Max Brill Carlton: why did untalented people always have to have three or more names?

What did you say?

I said they don't all deserve it. Not all of them are bad.

Bad, he repeated, scoffing. What's the matter? They sat you down, showed you pictures, told you stories, poured out their hearts, little heartache here, a little there, got to you, made you have second thoughts, made you look away from all that money, huh, all that guilt?

Money equals guilt? I asked, though, of course, I'd come to the same conclusion.

These people wouldn't even look at you twice on the street.

Don't you think I know that?

So?

What? I asked Shem. So what? Aren't we— I mean aren't I still carrying out the plan? Aren't I still Chao-ing them? The sudden switch from we to I made me realize how alone I was, as if caught out by a spotlight on a deserted stage. Actually, if you want to know, I said, somebody's been harmed.

He looked at me. Harmed?

I did their fucking house all wrong.

Who?

Cardie Kerchpoff.

He didn't respond.

Why don't you check up on her? I asked. And when he continued to say nothing, I went on: Last night, I thought she was crying. But I couldn't be sure.

You fixed her?

Yes.

Why her and not anybody else?

My answer was very simple: Cause she pissed me off.

What could she have done to deserve that? asked Shem. This time it was he who was dancing backward.

She just pissed me off, I stated once more, not wanting to relive that particular evening with her.

What'd you do? he asked.

Everything. Damage to peace. To health. To the stability of her marriage. Her family. Listing everything, I couldn't help but giggle: It was so much fun being evil! All those books of my childhood giving to evil a cronelike face and a stooped, hunchbacked posture were wrong. At no point in my life had I ever been *this* handsome, *this* alive.

Well, I have something to tell you, Shem said, taking a breath. Her husband left her.

What?

He was having an affair.

What I saw was this: Cardie Kerchpoff burdened by her newly awakened face every morning, and underneath her skin a premonition of so much slipping away; what was this thing? If only she could put a name to it. That stricken face which was newly hers had turned up to look at her husband during dinner, and again across the bed at night. It had debuted in public while talking to their friends. And seeing it, he'd been given a push by a voice inside his head. Have an affair—if indeed he hadn't yet been having one. Or if he had—confess to her and end everything right now. Who could put up with a face like that for another day? Finally, she had an outside to match her disgusting inside!

And it had all begun because a mirror was pushed in front of Cardie Kerchpoff's bed. In it, every morning when she woke up, before defenses and excuses and reason could take their protective stance, shielding her, there would be her image: a small grain of discomfort buried beneath the skin, growing throughout the day, day after day. Without makeup, without the intervention of language, the professional pride that often provided a transforming lift, she felt herself no better than back at the starting gate, all her achievements as if erased overnight.

How long has the affair been going on? I asked.

Shem shrugged.

Who told you?

Suzy.

Cardie told Suzy?

Shem nodded. He said, And Suzy had to pry it out of her.

Well, I thought, that was a first: for Cardie to have to be forced to surrender information.

You fixed her? Shem asked again, before he would allow himself to feel what I myself was trying to hold back from feeling.

I did, I replied.

So what about Suzy? How are we going to get her to see you?

Something needs to happen to that bitch, I agreed, nodding. My tone was flat as a pancake.

16

The hair on his head was coarse and unruly like pubic hair. He was back in the Savoy! Well, come to think of it, so was I. Everyone who'd been there when I left was also there, as if frozen by time. Neil! I said, shouting. Hey, buddy!

He looked up and showed me a suspicious face with features pulled down by drink, like marbles rolling down a ramp. But this face soon warmed up and flashed me a smile.

I was overjoyed to see him, this guy who used to mop and change lightbulbs at Peep Corner, and it made me realize how few people I knew in the city. Could he be the man for the job, that man I had specifically come to the Savoy to contract, like Shem had come to contract me? What I was looking for was someone just like me, desperate and able.

He stood up from a banquette, gave me a hug. Please, he told me, it's Gurinder.

What happened to Neil?

Change of job, change of name, he said. Sit. We sat. Can I get you something to drink? he asked.

I'm not drinking, I told him.

You're not drinking?

Not anymore.

It looks like we've both changed, he said, with an undercurrent of disbelief, like remedial students finding themselves about to be handed diplomas.

Changed? Oh God, this made what I was planning to ask difficult, so I postponed everything.

Gurinder, huh? I asked, thinking it a strange match: Neil looked exactly like a Neil, with a long face and pointy nose and thin lips. What did a Gurinder look like?

Yeah, he replied. Suits my job better.

What kind of job are you in now?

I give tours for . . . He mentioned a name, which whipped its tail past me.

For what?

He took history students, he said, and tourists and UN workers and city lore buffs to various spots linked to the recent plots by a handful of Palestinians to terrorize New York—the World Trade Center bombing, which had been successful; and two or three others, including a subway bomb scare, which had been discovered and foiled in the nick of time. There were the crumbling apartments in Brooklyn and Queens where the terrorists hid out, devising their campaigns. There were the greasy spoons and bazaars hawking Palestinian goods that they frequented. There was the World Trade Center itself. And most fun of all, there were all the other places the terrorists had intended to destroy, names discovered on several lists the authorities found in the terrorists' apartments. Such as? He smiled at me, confessed that most of them were made up. But that it gave his audience pause for thought, which was what they were paying for. They wanted to be scared. Conspiracies all around. They wanted to find the devil, said Gurinder. What places? Well, he said, there's the New York Public Library on Fifth, Lincoln Center, the West Side Highway, the Brooklyn Bridge . . .

And as for his new name—well, it was just this side of mysterious and nefarious, and transformed his fictive reports into dispatches from the inside, which was also what they wanted.

The inside of what? I asked.

The inside of a cave, he said, laughing.

I told him how much I missed Peep Corner, though I had never once been inside. I told him about missing the smell of come, infringing on Preciosa's copyright.

Are you kidding? he replied. He told me how great a strain it had been to have to mop up the floors after each gentleman was through, in preparation for the next one, who would only muck up his work in a few minutes. And what a strain, he reminded me, all that Lysol had been on his nose. Fucked him up good. A whole world closed off. Looking down at his dinner plate to confront objects that sat there as if bricks. He grew thin, dropped ten, fifteen, twenty pounds—the numbers climbed steadily until there was no denying that something had to be done. So he left Peep Corner, even before the mayor had started his shutdown work. He was referred to a hospital where NYU trainees practiced on patients for next to nothing. His doctor was Indian, and though you'd think that that would have helped, the sonofabitch treated him with a caste disdain as if they hadn't bothered crossing oceans to find themselves at a new starting place. But never mind, the asshole did cure him. He'd recommended that Gurinder use some spray for three months. And his cousins Veejay and Sanjay—of course they didn't give a shit! It was the same old family order, their family looking down on his, his cousins, whom he called Vishnus 1 and 2 behind their back. Vishnu, I echoed, remembering Kuerten, about whom, after two subsequent lengthy pieces in the *Post*, nothing else came. Dropped cold. The death had been an unrewarding accident—nothing in it milkable.

Suddenly someone hit the jukebox. The air curled. It was a slow dance but nobody was dancing. The lyrics gave everyone an opportunity to reflect on their own misfortunes. It was Boyz II Men, four guys with honeyed voices who specialized in velvety pleading-for-pussy numbers hypocritically disguised as I'll-love-you-forever numbers which could be heard blaring from one end of the city to the other every summer as a mating call between young people.

Whose heads were bopping?

There was Barney, master of ceremonies, wiping glasses at the bar. Two black transvestites, not yet ten o'clock and already with the reptile glassiness of drink. They were the ones to whom the song meant the most. There was the guy with no name, whom nobody ever approached, and who always sat in the corner eyeing everyone like keeping score. No matter how much he drank he never got drunk. It was a great source of sadness to him. But he too was bopping his head. So was the guy with the Afro, whom everyone called Mr. Writer. He wrote Wild West books that nobody at the Savoy had read, and it was said that he'd once been quite handsome. There were the three Latina "sisters," each one more tired-looking than the next, and they were all entertaining men who were at the end of the road, who made the sisters' tiredness seem only preliminary sketches for what would eventually befall them. All six of them bopped their heads. It was like playtime at the Savoy. All of us not so far from childhood.

These people were not afraid of the end of the world, unlike my Feng Shui clientele, and needed no protection. Rather, they cherished its arrival. There was nothing in their lives they wanted saved. And as for the place's "arrangement"—everything was done to facilitate your journey to the bar, the seats encouraged slouching, and the red lights made everyone's ugliness seem just a bit more tolerable.

I etched into the song's sweetness before it walled me in . . . And if smoke could have risen from the words I spoke . . .

I said to Gurinder, Do you want to make some money?

He replied, How?

I prefaced everything in such a way that made Gurinder immediately know I was guilty. I said, Well, you don't have to really do anything, you just have to show up, and, and, threaten, but you don't have to do anything, just hold a knife— OK I know that sounds serious—but just *hold* it, nothing else, well, maybe say a few lines, you know, like I will fucking kill you, but you're not really going to kill them, just make them think that you are. Just a scare. I need somebody scared.

Who? he asked.

I told him about Suzy. I said I was in love with Kendo, which was a lie, considering it was Kendo's beauty I was in love with, something purely impersonal. And I said that Kendo was in love with me.

Only Suzy stood in the way, and so Gurinder could see that I needed to shake her confidence up a little bit. This way, I could come in and be the pillar of strength in the family, consoling Suzy, taking care of changing the locks and all that, and then ease myself into their good graces.

How much? Gurinder asked.

Five hundred? I replied, knowing that I should have started lower.

A thousand, he said.

Seven.

A thousand.

I can't afford more than eight. I love this boy but I'm not a rich man.

After you get in with the family, you will be, he said. A thousand.

I had no choice but to shake on it.

I knew that he'd roughed up more than a few guys at Peep Corner, matching belligerence for belligerence. Looking at his slender, reedy body, you wouldn't have guessed this. But Veejay and Sanjay did, casting him according to type—he was, after all, from the "dark" part of the family. I also knew that he had been an athlete back home, and coming here he had had to give all that up. It was a loss he tried not to think about. He wiggled his fingers nervously sometimes, as if to better handle a phantom ball. And when he walked back and forth inside his apartment, it was like a warm-up to a race that would never come. The entropy of a new life made Gurinder burst out in many surprising rebellions.

∗ 17 ∗

Brian Q sobbed and gulped in air on the other end of the line. Please come, he begged.

I came. He hugged me for dear life.

He whispered the word "herpes" to me. He had to repeat it several times for me to be able to understand what he was saying. The bitch he'd taken home from Suzy's party had given it to him. What should he do? he asked me.

Stupid man, I thought, shouldn't he be consulting a doctor?

Consult your doctor, I told him.

But can't you help me?

How? I asked. The deed, after all, had been done.

Yes, he was aware of that. But he wanted to make sure that misfortune of that kind, on that scale, would never happen again. He was lowered into a seat, almost begging. I had a perfect view of his scalp—miraculous hair sprouted to cover his bald spot.

Then, looking up, he said that I had fixed his place for him, he'd paid me a mint to ensure that such things wouldn't happen.

I looked him in the eye. I said to him, Your dick overrode everything. I said it just like that, breaking out of character.

He gulped. He had no rejoinder.

How stupid could this man be? Hadn't he been amply trained by those books of his? Shouldn't there have been in those millions of chic pages some character who was my counterpart, a big fraud? Resist me: the words scrolled across my brain as I beamed them to him telepathically.

I sat down beside him. I said to him, You have a responsibility.

He hated the word, visibly recoiling.

I continued, Yes, you do. You wanted your hair back, didn't you?

He didn't reply.

Didn't you? My voice was more forceful.

Yes, he mumbled.

And now you have it.

He brushed his hand through his scalp. Feeling his hair, he relaxed.

So now that you have it, I continued, you're going to be more attractive to women once more. Right?

He didn't want to have to say it himself.

Right? I repeated.

Yes, he capitulated, looking up at me to wait for the concluding moral.

So now, you have to be more patient. Don't just grab any girl you find. You'll have your pick. And be more vigilant. Use your smarts. Feng Shui can only go so far. Now go see your doctor.

Are you sure there's nothing wrong?

Please, Brian, I said.

Just take a look, he entreated. It wouldn't hurt, right?

Because he needed something to be found, I brought his attention to a missing egg on a side table in the living room, a jeweled egg I had stolen myself—and gotten a shockingly low fifty dollars for!

The bitch! said Brian Q, blaming herpes girl.

You have to have it replaced, I said. Harmony will once more come into your abode as soon as you do.

Thank you, Master Chao, he said.

Before I left, he tried to stuff some money into my hands, but I refused. No no, I said.

We had a comic tussle in the living room, which continued in the doorway, and then followed us out into the elevator. A neighbor saw us. We stopped for a minute, and then continued. I wasn't pretending. My fake contract with this man was over, I didn't want any more of his money. But he was so grateful, how could he let me go away empty-handed?

The thing about crime, I thought to myself as the elevator doors closed, the thing that nobody believes anymore in this day and age of smarts and cynicism and toughness, is how foolish the fools can still be. I refused to look back at Brian Q, who stood on the other side watching as the doors cut me off from him.

The doorman downstairs bowed and smiled at me.

18

I was sick and tired of the end of the world, miniature versions of which kept popping up in the residences I visited, so I decided to escape to the movies. But when I got to Times Square, I realized that escape would be impossible. I had a choice between four different destruction-of-the-earth pictures. Did I want to see the earth being pummeled by asteroids—two versions—or did I want to see it colonized by extraterrestrials, or did I want to see New York City terrorized by a mutant pigeon grown the size of the Empire State? Up at bat, and I heard myself saying in a resigned voice: One for *SuperPigeon*.

Ticket in hand, I opened the door, led into the theater by a group of Midwesterners who were smiling at everything, including me. I smiled back. The sound of traffic, suddenly and decisively, cut off. Waves of air conditioning made the hairs on my skin curl back. And then riding the air conditioning straight into my nostrils, the scent of popcorn, which stopped me in my tracks. It was a scent that immediately flattened everything around me, transforming the surroundings into a portable backdrop hauled intact, unmolested, from my childhood. My sinuses were tightening with each connection. The feel of much-trampled carpet underfoot, its fibers no longer springy like living things but staying pretty much in the shape of my feet. The bright curlicues of light fixtures on the wall, coloring posters encased under glass. It was like nighttime in the middle of the day. Walked right up to the ticket taker to hear his obligatory employee greeting. Hello sir welcome to Sony theaters enjoy the show. Except that this ticket taker was a teenager—a teenager from South America, it seemed—and was still too young to not put some effort, some human tone into his rote speech. I thanked him and walked in. A couple of teenage boys, who should've been in school, were just releasing the doors and so I moved up quickly and slipped in. Dim lightbulbs like holes punched into the ceiling and the walls. The theater nearly empty. The sound of plastic being attacked, munching, things hitting the uncarpeted floor beneath the seats. It was like entering the belly of some machine. There was a seat in the middle of the auditorium, near the aisle, which I took. Closed my eyes, forgetting my whole life, to better prepare for the life about to be shown me, blown up three stories high: it was why I loved going to Times Square—the screens were larger than in most parts of the city.

Lights went down. Everyone sitting up, like reacting to a teacher's entrance. Where were the Midwesterners? I couldn't see them anywhere. The previews came on, and I wished they would just go on forever—life reduced to a collection of high points. And at the end of each preview, just before the film's title was announced, when names like Mel Gibson and Jim Carrey scrolled across—in their place I imagined my very own. I tried various versions, unsure which would be the most convincing: My full name—William Narciso Paulinha? Or just William Paulinha? Or W. N. Paulinha. Or William Paul. Or William N. Paul. Or Bill N. Paul. Or just Bill Paul. Or William Chao. Then it occurred to me that there were a few Chinese movie stars, but as yet no Filipino ones, so William Chao might actually not be a bad idea . . .

Credits rolled, name after meaningless name of newcomers. Of course, we all knew who the star was. It was the pigeon, created with state-of-the-art technology. And the attraction was its death. That was what I was paying nine dollars for, to see my dreams realized: The pigeon must die! Or to some, a different dream: New York City must be destroyed!

Then it began. A great beginning, nighttime, when anything was possible. What would that first wrongdoing be that would set off a chain of events? A feeling like fingers stretching inside my throat. Up on the screen was a scientist's lab. Ominous shadows turning test tubes into a candelabra in a haunted house. A scientist, sitting in the darkness, is suddenly revealed by a flash of lightning. Close-up: he laughs, as if at a joke being told off-screen.

Next, it's daytime. He's feeding pigeons in the park, strangely proprietary, anxious that they should consume everything.

Then he's dead. Lying on his messy bed with eyes shooting straight up as if trying to read some inscription on the ceiling. A gun has fallen from his hand and lands with a precise thud onto the dull gray carpet. The police, when they are led to him by a neighbor reporting a foul smell, ignore the suicide note lying next to him. In the suicide note, he claims that he was a scientist in charge of the city's pigeon population control program, a man unfairly let go to accommodate the evil mayor's new fiscal budget. He says that the mayor will rue the day he made his heartless decision. He claims that New York City is on the brink of destruction. That the very thing that the city wants destroyed will destroy it. This neighbor who called the cops could've been ours, the woman with the cats, except that in the movie she had no cats and no shadow, with only enough attributes to secure laughs and dissipate the ghastliness of the setting. How slovenly she was, how could she have differentiated the foul smell in the apartment next door from her very own horrible scent, laughed the cops. They also laughed while they tossed the suicide note inside a Ziploc bag, to be filed under the deceased's "effects," thinking it would languish there for eternity, turning to mold. But they were wrong . . . It would soon be asked for by a colleague of the deceased, the film's hero. And when he reads it, everything will make sense to him . . . The attacks on children by unusually large pigeons, and then increasingly, fearlessly, on adults, the pigeons grown larger to match the size of their victims. Crazy

reports cropping up feverishly from one part of the city to another . . .
None of this was seen, only suggested. A flash of beak here, the flapping of wings there. Screams. Arms ineffectively held in front of
faces to ward off attacks. Spurts of blood. Everything wonderful
and satisfying . . . And then it was revealed that there were three giant pigeons, one roosting underneath the boardwalk in Coney Island, one in Central Park, frightening the horses drawing carriages,
and one in an abandoned subway tunnel, who was effectively taking
care of the city's rat population all by himself. The hero-scientist,
with the repentant mayor's support, and with the assistance of an intern whose job it was to provide anxious comic relief before being
disposed of later, sacrificed to one of the giant pigeons . . . And here
I was stopped, I couldn't keep from staring at the intern's face— It
was— It was Jokey! He hadn't been joking after all. There he was,
with his wooden, underwhelmed line readings which, given everyone else's conviction that they were in an opera, gave him a unique,
winning comic style. Wow, I kept thinking every time everyone
laughed along with one of his bull's-eye reactions or one of his
dumb lines, I know that guy. The sense of vicarious accomplishment
made me feel drunk. Again I was aware of a contest which I was losing, the gap widening further . . . When Jokey died, everyone was
sorry to see him go, and it further fueled their desire to see the pigeons destroyed . . . They fought, first two of them—the subway
one coaxed out by a giant stale bagel and the boardwalk one sprayed
with a vat of perfume and driven out into the open, where it was
then made to attack the first one over the bagel, revealed to be
spiked with poison. And then the surviving one, scratched and
weary, was in turn defeated by the third, in a spectacular fight
above the Empire State Building, while below Japanese tourists
clicked away.

The death of the last pigeon, achieved without effort, caught
everyone by surprise. Planning a sneak attack, the scientist-hero
and his team chanced upon its corpse, lying on the rooftop of an
abandoned building in Harlem, its feet up in the air. Dragging the
body to a hangar where an autopsy would be conducted . . . Thick
crowds congesting both sidewalks, as if convened for a parade,
watching the bloody beast leave behind a trail of foul-smelling in-

nard juice, which painted a ragged line on the streets. Noses held, mouths open in shock . . . And then at the hangar, the autopsy reveals a strange thing: teeth marks at the neck of the pigeon. Giant teeth marks. The other pigeon which had fought with this new dead one hadn't had teeth. So what was the deal? they asked each other, afraid to volunteer possibilities . . . The dark of a subway tunnel. A sibilant sound of air sucking in and out. Something breathing. The sound indicating—what was that? Hunger? And then in the blackness, two things glinting. Eyes. And with the shadows switching to a grayer, more legible shade, the eyes are revealed to belong to a giant rodent. From far off, the roar of an approaching subway car. The rat, SuperRat, hisses, senses pricked in anticipation of lunch . . . The End!

Going out, I once again encountered the Midwesterners. I asked them how they liked the movie. We loved it! the children, a boy and a girl, said in unison. I wished them a good stay in the city. It only occurred to me later that I was fulfilling a mayoral plan to help boost tourism by showing the kinder face of New York and I immediately regretted my actions.

The sun had slowly been pushed behind some clouds. The light, so unforgiving just a few hours ago, began to dim as if a layer of muslin was being lowered over the sky.

Uh-oh, I heard a voice say.

And then, in the middle of July, a rain made up of drops the size of spit wads spattered across everything. Each one landed and then bounced back up again, in a kind of check-mark trajectory. Everyone scurried for cover.

There was lightning and it flashed in the sky behind some newly planted trees that were meant to soften the new Times Square with another kind of green. Everyone seemed to be oohing.

Suddenly, the rain turned into hail.

Apocalypse, I heard a voice say with a German accent. But instead of fear, it was said with a kind of longing.

I noticed a familiar figure. Was that Kendo? It looked just like him, his loose hair covering his eyes like a cap with an overhanging fringe.

Ken! I shouted, the rest of it stuck in my throat. We were separated by the width of Broadway, a curtain of white fuzz and the scroll of slow traffic turning everything unreliable. He was standing next to a newsstand one moment, with the same look of wonder as everyone else, and then when he saw me, he turned immediately away. This made me consider that he *intended* to be where he was, that he was actually following me, and looked away because he'd been found out. But why?

Later that evening, I told Preciosa about the freak weather, putting myself in the center. She had watched everything from inside her apartment, too worried about her finances to have marveled. I may have exaggerated my telling to get a rise out of her. I probably turned everything into a small movie. Still, the tone was just what was needed for my segue into the next thing. I confessed everything that I had been involved in over the last few months: the homes I visited; the people who owned these homes; Shem, Suzy Yamada, Kendo; all the askew things that I sought to fix; and in the case of Cardie Kerchpoff, all the askew things that I was responsible for—without time to pause for breath in between. Yes, like a movie, breathless, running forward to meet the next thing. Me in the center. Then I added, Us, like an arm extended toward her. I wanted her involved. I knew it on the spot. A solution to her problems.

At first, she put up a weak protest. Something about being Filipinos and how would we be portraying our country to the rest of the world. This was a clear hem and haw. Preciosa had never lived her life as a sample citizen of anywhere. Though she still corresponded with people back home, she hadn't once been back since coming here. And not once did she entertain the idea of visiting. She calmly reviewed photographs sent along with the letters she received, photographs whose backgrounds she seemed to study harder than the relatives who were posed in front. This was how she gauged the passage of time, the places of her childhood turned foreign by development, by neglect, by the symbol-heavy defacings of various political movements. As far as she was concerned, this was all the visiting she needed. For her, as for me, everything from the past was burnt free, and to return would only be to satisfy a masochistic desire to be yanked back down to the level of a world we'd both been lifted from. Rescued. This, in essence, being the definition of immigration.

She went on some more: How could I? But I knew she needed the money. And so I merely waited for her outrage to play itself out, to give way to the clarity of pure exhaustion.

I did not tell her about my plans for Suzy Yamada, to make Suzy reconsider in my favor. A wake-up call, was all I said.

19

Two people gave me the evil eye. First was the El Dorado's doorman, a gaunt, elderly Latino with the narrowed eyes of a spy. You again, he seemed to be saying with his expression, as if surprised that Rowley hadn't disposed of me by now. His mouth only said, Third floor. But this came out with an unmasked disdain that even he was surprised by, turning him red. I know, I replied, giving no indication that I noticed.

The second person who evil-eyed me was, of course, the Swiss nurse. You again: this time she let the thought be articulated. And she wasn't afraid either.

How are you? I said, pushing back other, more natural words. I even bowed, hoping to shame her, but her mind was already made up.

She closed the door after me and, while still behind my back, asked, Mr. P know you coming to see him?

Yes, I replied. He asked me to come.

Well, this way. But be quiet.

We walked to the living room. All the curtains were open and I could see, very clearly, the treetops of Central Park, the sparkling kidney-shaped mirrors of a couple of lakes, and intermittently criss-crossing the scene, lanes of steady traffic, made ghostly and silent. The sky was like the rumpled hem of someone's skirt. Against it, Rowley's bald head made a distinct silhouette.

Mr. P, said the Swiss bitch.

Rowley, I said.

Ahh, said Rowley, who didn't move toward me. He let his hands fly to indicate the armchair facing him. Between the two was the heart-sinking sight of a tea set, sparklingly arranged.

The bitch left us alone.

Tea? Rowley asked.

Sure, I said, watching him pour.

I sat down. Rowley handed me tea with a trembling hand. Have you thought about my question, young man? he asked.

What question was that?

Your life. Already he regarded me with advance disappointment.

I want to continue doing what I do, I replied.

Helping people for good, he said, as if goading me to say some more until I tripped myself up.

That's right.

He sipped.

I mirrored him. My teeth were on edge.

I want to ask you something.

What question do you want answered, Rowley?

Not a question. I want to ask you a favor.

Me? I looked at him, thinking: What could it be?

As you know, I'm an old man.

Rowley, I said.

This was a conversation I'd had with him before: He was old. Not far from death's door. He wanted to talk to me before it was too late . . .

I'm not far from death's door. As you can well see.

Rowley, please.

And there are a few things I realize I would like done before I go. Things tied up. One of these things . . . I've been thinking . . . If this is a violation of, of . . . Have you ever used your skill to harm? he asked.

I thought: So it's come to this. Did he know what I could do to him: was that what the mention of being at death's door was all about—he wanted me to open it for him? Calmly, I said, What do you mean, Rowley?

Forget it. I knew it was wrong the minute I thought of it. But . . . What exactly do you mean by harm?

He looked at me. He turned his head to make sure we were alone. Let's go to the library, he said.

I followed his lead, leaving a full cup of tea on the living-room table. He wheeled himself into the library and shut the door behind us. Leather armchairs faced each other, separated by a long, low coffee table stacked with monographs and museum catalogues. I sat. Rowley faced me. His arms were folded on top of his legs. They looked like a single smooth stone.

What you do, William, it can cause harm as well as good?

When applied incorrectly, yes, harm can result.

And you've done that before? No, of course not. What am I saying? But that night, at Suzy's, when you said you wanted to be good— I thought, for a brief second, maybe— No. It's stupid. I apologize. Can you forgive me?

Forgive you for what, Rowley? What are you asking?

By now, I was standing above him, my height giving me an inquisitor's advantage. He wheeled himself to shelves by a wall. I followed.

Forgive you for what exactly, Rowley? Why are we in here? You can speak freely.

I suppose you've been in a million houses, you've seen every conceivable way of living. So what I have to say won't shock you. He took a breath. Last night in bed everything was so clear. You'd come into my life recently, as if . . . *planned*. As if fate had brought you here to help me.

And I have, I said.

That's not what I meant. What I mean is that I've had this longtime . . . yearning. For something to be righted before I die, before I join Adela again. Something, in fact, that is in Adela's name. And you came. Your timing was perfect. And you have gifts that could help me. And so I thought why not ask William.

Ask me then, Rowley.

I wanted for you to arrange someone's house in a way that would make them come to harm.

Rowley was clearly surprised by my simple and eager Who?

Suzy, he revealed.

Yamada?

He nodded.

I thought you'd made up with her.

We have.

I don't understand, I said.

She needs to come down in the world, he replied simply. In memory of Adela. The closer I come to death . . . he trailed off.

You want me to fix her house wrong?

No, the cowardly Rowley said. It was just . . . a thought. Nothing more. Please, what must you think of me now? A malignant old fool. He wheeled himself to a window, to look out at nothing. Viewed from behind, he became even more pathetic.

What he wanted me to do was already on my plate—whether I would get a chance to do it or not was the question and that depended entirely on Neil's work. This was not the problem. The problem was that to agree to his request essentially amounted to a confession. That I was something other than what I'd been advertising myself to be.

Either he was performing with the seamless skill of a master or he was shamefully innocent—either way he got what he wanted out of me: I would make a dying man happy. I'll do it, my voice rang out, louder than I intended.

Rowley turned around. Came over to me. He squeezed my hands warmly, the same way I saw him do with Suzy. You will be rewarded, he told me.

What do you mean? I asked, thinking about spiritual dividends.

I'll reward you.

I don't want anything, Rowley. I'm doing it for you.

Do you believe in my cause? he asked me.

I was silent.

Adela suffered, he told me. It drove her to her premature death. You have to believe me. Suzy must be held accountable. Her success came at the cost of my Adela's life. You won't be doing evil, William. You will be doing justice. Restoring it to the world. I thought I'd made peace with Suzy. All these years, seeing her, I'd tried my best to let my rancor die. But . . . Adela suffered so much. I want you to do this thing in her name. Would a photograph help?

What photograph?

If I gave you a photograph. For you to look at her, to see what Suzy was responsible for.

I believe you, Rowley.

But he was ahead of me, wheeling himself to his bedroom. When he came back, he had a photograph of his deceased wife in his hands. He gave it to me, using two hands turned into a cup, as if handing over an injured animal. I took it with great care, and because of this care, it gained a weight disproportionate to its physical properties. It was a composite. On the left side was the young, beautiful Adela, the blushing bride, with rouged lips and marcelled hair—the shine in her eyes so striking it could only have been a retoucher's addition. On the right was the ravaged, near-death Adela, with an emaciated monkey's face and five corrugated worry lines on her forehead like additional brows. It wasn't that this was the face of someone near death—and therefore natural—but that that death had caught its owner by surprise, with regret, a vast catalogue of ends left loose. It was the sad face of someone trying to master its own rot, struggling to no effect. The two faces were so unconnected I had to take Rowley's word that they were both Adela. When had he created this double panel and how long had he been keeping it? The intent of this picture was clear, singular: It was to stoke the fires of revenge, to make the spectator angry at the waste of the promise of that beautiful face. The before and after of a life ruined by a villain hidden in the wings.

The heaviness in my hands pushed me into a chair. Rowley looked at me, knowing no more words were needed.

Two people had it in for Suzy Yamada. Three, including Adela. It was as good as preordained.

20

The detective in those books Shem had given me had, by turning his inventory of facts and feelings a little to the left, a little to the right, letting the light fall differently on each, allowed a facet to surface that eventually set all the various components in their proper places. There were no ornate puzzle boxes designed to stump the reader, as in an Agatha Christie. No unnecessary curlicues meant to detain the eye while the writer's hand tricked behind the back.

But more than anything, the books corresponded to my view of the world. More than mystery itself, which was the initial attraction, and what kept me steadily reading, what lingered was a sense of sadness, of human beings mired in motives which fed on themselves and spiraled out of hand, ending inexorably in murder.

Everyone had to be accountable for their actions. A detective will come and ask you about everything in the end.

For a moment there was the clearest picture, a white light of full indictment. I realized that I had no core, that I merely went from one identity to another guided by nothing more than mimicry. As a child, I had imitated devoutness because there was the example of my family before me. And when that no longer served my needs, when I had slowly grown to accept—or rather when I stopped denying—my homosexuality, and found nothing in that faith to sustain or help me, I threw it aside and took the example of other people who had thrown it aside before me. People like an aunt who shocked the family by divorcing three husbands and having countless abortions. In other words, people who responded to Catholicism's censure by a conscious, showy flouting of its rules. In Los Angeles, I had followed men who skulked in parks, giving each other covert go-ahead signals with their eyes, thus learning one way homosexuals behaved: a conscious, if not exactly showy, flouting of the rules of Catholicism. In New York, I had fallen in step with the young, directionless, poor homosexuals who were my peers, and had supported myself the way I had seen them do, congregating at the Port Authority and places like the Port Authority where the smell of disinfectant and of urine mingled to form a boozy perfume that had the effect of turning every sordid action unserious, lightweight. And now, what was I doing? I was merely acting out the idea of villainy from past movie villains I had seen, molding myself according to a pattern that seemed—by its very age and durability—authentic, original. It was all there in the brain, like a card file, turning from one type to another, and then taking on the salient aspects of that type that I needed to become to be able to advance a station or two in life, or in some cases, to backslide.

21

It was a building I'd been to before—but only as part of a crowd, swallowed up, an extra. Today I walked there having been invited alone, and filled with the knowledge of this privileged status, I took my time, enjoying every minute. Encountering it from the outside, I noticed a new, sickly pallor in the paint job, a slouch to the facade, many curtains and blinds only partially drawn, giving to the windows a droopy-eyed look. It was as if the building had registered the insult directly.

The whole building has heard, said the doorman, who in his starched white uniform with the gold-braided epaulets looked like he was about to go off to command a ship. He was overjoyed to see me and shook my hands accordingly.

Preciosa stood beside me. Though her hips had healed, she was tapping the marble floors with her walking cane, an ornately carved thing with the head of some mythical beast for a handle—an instrument made to order for the performance she was about to give. Her hair was pulled back and then braided, and gave her an Incan look, the look of a priestess. Her eyes, correspondingly, were pulled to the sides, making her look not so much Chinese as . . . wealthy, her normally distant look magnified. Around her neck she wore a long necklace of multicolored beads looped around several times. They ticked while her walking cane tacked.

We went up. Neither of us looked at the other. Preciosa had needed only the briefest of prep times. She was so serious, in fact, that I found myself taking my cue from her.

As soon as I went in, I realized that Neil had been worth every fucking dollar. His efforts were so comprehensive, so uncalled for and yet so right, that I was straining for adjectives.

There was a mirror right in the hallway which he'd cracked. When I looked into it, there were seven of me staring back from different angles, as if about to start an argument with one another. This is so sad, Suzy Yamada said, standing at the doorway. Shockingly, she touched me, and the feel of those hands was like being exposed to a live current. I trembled inside, counting on the blithe housekeeper to make her appearance and earn me another diploma.

This is Walung, I said, introducing Preciosa.

Welcome, Suzy said, closing the door behind us.

Walung only grunted. She tapped in front of me, as if to prepare the way.

Show me everything, I told Suzy Yamada, whose namesake I had observed in not just one film, but two: *Throne of Blood*, as Shem recommended, and right beside it on a shelf at Lincoln Center, an added bonus—*The Lower Depths*. Both by Akira Kurosawa. Both showcasing a scheming, evil-eyed woman who shook her torso to communicate perpetual discontent, a movement to correspond with how the director used her—as the snake in the garden, the whisperer of naughty suggestions into Adam's ear. In *Throne of Blood*, she was set on usurping the king's throne for her husband, convincing him to kill the ruler so that she could become queen.

Yes, I have your number all right, Miss Isuzu Yamada, I thought as, having been touched by this Suzy Yamada a second time, I touched back. Because I was taller, my hands fell on her shoulder. I could feel her repulsion, but she walked silently ahead.

Walung was at the glass doors to the veranda, looking out at the breathtaking view of the city. Even with her back turned, I could tell what she was thinking. I'd warned her. But there are no words to adequately prepare someone who's been accustomed to shit all their life for an encounter with real, unsparing wealth.

Walung was the house cleanser, and would seek out the hiding places of evil spirits so she could perform the rites necessary to evacuate them. These spirits were responsible for the desecration that had happened while Suzy had been sunning herself in the Hamptons, in care of the blond couple, and while Kendo was bumming around with his father, who was divorced from Suzy.

Seeing Walung, Suzy asked, Is everything OK?

Again Walung only grunted.

Suzy looked at me, hoping I'd translate. But I, too, thickened things by keeping quiet.

The African totem was knocked onto the floor. There was a crack where the neck was. For insurance purposes and because I'd asked her to, she had left all the damage untouched.

This you should get rid of, I told Suzy, indicating the prone African figure, which looked defeated, impotent.

Yes, Master, she said.

In the kitchen, eggs had been taken out of the refrigerator and smashed against every surface. The cabinets, the sink, the stove, the dishwasher were filmed with the stuff, giving off a fetid stink. Several flies buzzed in a corner.

God, said Suzy, putting her hand to her mouth.

Have this cleaned, I said.

Thank you, replied Suzy, who was more than eager to move on.

The room where Rowley and I had conferred had suffered its special desecration. Books had been taken out of their shelves, torn in half, and then discarded on the floor. It seemed Neil had used this room to practice his shotput. Lamps and several glass knickknacks had been thrown around. The floor was littered with shards.

Who would do such a thing? I asked no one in particular, giving the line an exasperated, sympathetic spin.

Master, ventured Suzy, could it be that I'm being haunted?

By whom?

You see, she began, stammering. You see, someone I know just died.

Who? I asked, knowing very well the answer.

It's this man called Kuerten.

This woman, skinny as she was, was even skinnier ten years ago, when she had benefited from the spiritual as well as—it turned out—dietary rigor imposed by the guru Kuerten. I had managed to requisition a photograph from the Institute for the Advancement of Eastern Wisdom, and in it, Kuerten's disciples surrounded him with their newly thin bodies and their appreciative smiles. Suzy was in the front row, third from the right, and hers was among the biggest smiles, as if, by having subdued her flesh's appetite and reshaped her body according to the demands of her ambition, she had been freed to pursue her future. I had placed a phone call to the Institute saying that I was writing a *New York Times* article on Kuerten which included tributes from his current and former disciples, mentioning Suzy Yamada in particular because she had contributed the best quote. Sure enough, not only were they more than happy to confirm that Ms. Yamada had been among their favorite success stories, dropping nearly twenty-five pounds (and managing to keep it off! and look where she is today!), but that a picture would be in the mail for me soon. Sadly, they couldn't disclose why Ms. Yamada had parted ways with the guru Kuerten, except to echo Shem by saying that Ms. Yamada had achieved her full potential under the master and had fixed her sights on other goals.

Without Kuerten's concepts of Eastern pacifism, and specifically Buddhist karma, to weigh her down any longer, Suzy had been able to wrest Adela's company from Adela, a move that precipitated Suzy's spectacular New York rise. And yet, having achieved her goals, discontent and unhappiness still lingered, forcing her to have to seek out a master of Feng Shui, and now still another. And the extra weight she'd put on over the years, and for which she'd had to resort to Dexatrim to keep it down—could it have acted as a reminder of the price she'd had to pay for forsaking the guru Kuerten?

Inwardly I smiled, recalling her medicine cabinet.

Well, if it's true that his ghost is responsible, I said to Suzy, Walung will see to it that this will be his only visit.

Suzy closed her eyes, so grateful was she.

Her bedroom was where the most violent vandalism had taken

place. She stepped aside for me to take stock. How had Neil known? Wow, was all I thought as before me the chaotic overall impression broke down into distinct components: the ripped bedspread, the cracked vanity, the bathroom door torn off its hinges, and lamps and vases crashed to the floor. Behind each of these I could see Neil's gleeful figure, leaning in with his weight and sending them down, scattering everything in a pattern that was like a signature which only I could read. Had Neil left fingerprints? I asked Suzy. No, the police hadn't found any.

How did Neil get past the doorman? She said that that doorman had been fired for sleeping on the job.

Rearrange your bed, I ordered. Malignant, very malignant. I didn't even turn around to judge her response. Where to? she asked. Anyplace but here, I replied, before flitting off to the bathroom. There was a drip from a faucet. Water leaking from a broken faucet was like money being lost. The word "shui," after all, stood for water. But I told Suzy nothing. As I withheld this crucial bit of information, I thought of Rowley, who had helped to secure the gig by calling Suzy to put in a good word for me.

Downstairs, the priestess Walung was stuffing items into an oversized pocket stitched into her long black skirt—a color chosen for mystical purposes and to obscure the bulge of the loot we'd be reselling later, through an acquaintance of Preciosa's. I'd instructed her take anything that wouldn't be traced back to Suzy's place—things precious but not distinctive, not one of a kind. She whistled while she did this. Meanwhile, upstairs, detained by my disapproving overview, Suzy grew more and more sullen, like a delinquent student being read her deplorable habits.

She protested when I asked her to remove a beloved painting above her bed: But the Feng Shui master from before said—

What? I asked her. What did he say?

That it was a beneficial spot, that the color was right, that it would make my sleep more peaceful.

And is your sleep peaceful? I asked. (Seconal: check.)

She could only blink.

The painting in question was a Chinese scroll with carp whipping their tails beneath lily pads that were as wide as umbrellas.

Two quivering gray brushstrokes above the carp's heads created ripples in the water.

Carp are a symbol of good luck and of long life, she explained as a last defense.

Carp, I said, get big and fat and grow to a very old age doing only one thing, opening their big, fat mouths, and they are therefore a symbol of laziness and indolence and a life wasted. Is that what you plan to model your life on? Big? And fat? And a waste? Each time I pronounced the word "fat," I made sure to hold her eye with a meaningful look. (Dexatrim: check.)

She gulped but was still unable to overcome her native distrust. That was the thing about people who were themselves dishonest: they saw themselves as being microcosms of the larger world, justifying their ways as preemptive strikes: scam or be scammed. I don't believe you, I'm sorry, she said.

Why, Miss Yamada? I asked her. What school did this Feng Shui master go to?

She told me some silly Chinese name that sounded made up. In reply, I gave her another.

Mine, I told her, is the school more compatible with your house. With the way you live your life. The last phrase I italicized with a hidden meaning that I hoped she would catch.

What's that school again? she asked.

If you won't believe me, Miss Yamada, started the fussy housekeeper within me, the Filipina servant overtired from having to work too many jobs just to keep up, and who now let her frustrations override any fear of being fired. If you won't believe me, I don't see what the point of my being here is. With this, I made to leave. But not before playing my ace—a bit earlier than I had intended, but what the hell. I said to her: And what about your son?

She was shocked, but managed to stutter, What about him?

Did that earlier Feng Shui master, aside from not being able to prevent this sacrilege to your home, has he offered you the correction you were looking for in your son?

According to the *Physicians' Desk Reference*, Guanfacine was an "antihypertensive," as in hypertension, high blood pressure—the same thing that had laughably afflicted my mother when confronted with my spectacular waywardness. This was the route taken to my deduction, admittedly a gamble, but then there was also the picture of Kendo in *Metropolitan Home*—unhappy, disgusted, looking for trouble—as well as his obstreperousness at the party to seal me in my judgment.

And then she touched me. On the elbows. To detain me. I was halfway out the door and stopped in my tracks. I didn't turn around just yet but instead let a few seconds of suspense play out—would she ever see me again? Finally I turned, the arcing of my neck accomplished with an effortful, dramatic slowness.

Please, Master, Suzy said, bowing.

I sighed heavily and then bowed back, simultaneously thinking of Adela's before and after. I heard clinking from downstairs but Suzy gave no indication of being distracted.

I'll take that picture off the wall, she said.

Will you trust me? I asked, feeling like the priests of my childhood in Manila, those fucking fakers.

I couldn't hear her demure answer. Will you trust me? I repeated. It was all I could do not to put my hands on top of her bowed head, like a baptism, or an invocation of the Holy Spirit.

Yes, she said.

That picture should be taken down. Now.

She walked to the wall, her shoulders hunched, and taking off her shoes, put one foot, then the other, on the bed. As soon as she found her balance, she put both hands on the picture, and proceeded to remove it. It unlatched from a hook nailed to the wall. It was too heavy and she needed help to put it down but I didn't budge. Finally, she dropped the thing onto pillows. She waited for her blood pressure to normalize, the redness of her face to subside, before breathing a sigh of relief.

I went out onto the balcony adjoining her bedroom. I pointed at the rusted chairs. What is that? I asked.

Wrought iron, she replied.

Rust, I pointed out, is decay. Is things rotting. Why would you want such a thing in your home, even if it were outside and you could put a door between it and you? Why?

She, of course, had no answer.

Get rid of it, I told her. It was going to be my mantra with Suzy: Get rid of it. I would reserve the name of Pratung Song until the end. There, she could shop for all the replacements she would need to fill the vacuum I would soon transform her place into.

And this vanity, I said, pointing to the cracked mirror.

Yes, Master?

A woman and her vanity cannot be separated. (Estrogen: check.) But this time relocate it.

Where to, Master?

I pointed to the wall directly across from the bed, using the same trick I'd prescribed for Cardie Kerchpoff. Like that woman, Suzy Yamada would wake up in the morning to confront her face twisted by fitful sleep, and she would read into that old infant's countenance the cost of her rise in New York society: the tiredness, the deceitfulness, the hardness, the solitude. With any luck, one day she would wake up to see Adela's ravaged monkey face grafted onto hers, and she would understand completely the role I'd played in her life.

Where is your son's room? I asked next.

He won't let anyone in, she said, nervousness making her voice rise.

Why not?

He's locked it, she replied, not answering me.

Well, his door must be opened. Or you'll forever have a hole in the Feng Shui regardless of how well I arrange the rest of the house for you.

Yes, Master.

Call a locksmith now.

She did me one better. She phoned down to the doorman, who promptly came up. He kicked the door in with the heel of his boot, making the doorframe splinter.

Thank you, Suzy said, giving him a ten-dollar tip which made my mouth water.

Where is your son? I asked Suzy.

I don't know, she replied.

What kind of mother are you? I asked, tossing the judgment off.

Surprising me, Suzy began to cry quietly: Ever the achiever, she wanted, even in tragedy, to score an A plus. The hair was perfect,

none of her features disarrayed, as she continued her demure snif-
fles: a definite point of departure from her namesake, who would not
have been caught crying in the first place, and if she did, would not
have directed her grief inward. This pointed to the precision of my
bull's-eye. But what, in fact, was wrong with her son?

I went to the top of the stairs and, yelling, asked Walung how
everything was going. In reply, she sent up a loud grunt.

Everything's fine now, I said when I turned back. Walung has
cleansed your home.

She continued sniffling.

Please, Miss Yamada, I need your strength, I said, reaching out a
hand, which she took. Together we crossed the splintered threshold.

I told her to put incense at the four corners of her son's room. I
told her to tear down a poster for a movie which took up prime
space on the wall facing the bed. It was for a horror movie called
Suspiria, with the director's name in bold red above the title: Dario
Argento. There was an illustration of a long-haired woman with a
mouth like Munch's *The Shriek*, and blood coursing down the cleav-
age exposed by a purple nightgown with a plunging neckline. She
was made to look giant next to the haunted house which was presumably the cause of the shriek. The woman could've been Suzy,
and the miniature house Suzy's apartment, from which she would
soon be driven out by the spirits I was going to entice inside.

Suzy tore it down, making a diagonal rip through the poster.
Clearly, she was now more afraid of me than of her son. She came
back into the room with a garbage can and tossed the poster inside.
She looked at me expecting the garbage can to get more use. So I had
her throw away a few CDs.

There was a picture of Kendo with a man by his bed.

Who is this? I asked.

His father, replied Suzy. We're divorced. Should I throw that picture away? she asked with a hopeful rise in her voice.

Sensing this, I replied firmly, No.

Kendo looked neither like this man nor like Suzy.

Does your son see his father often? I asked Suzy.

Too often, came her lip-bitten answer.

What does he do?

He's a layabout. After a pause, she began an inventory of defects: He wasn't Japanese. He was Chinese. And right from the start, she should've known. Should've heeded her mother's warning that the gap between their cultures did not bode well. The Chinese were carefree people, too carefree. Messy, she said. While the Japanese believed in formalities. (She didn't even register the fact that I was Chinese, and that she could be offending me with her pat summary. This gave me a firsthand encounter with the traits relayed by Shem and Rowley. It also gave truth to the clichés about "brash" successful businessmen: "two-fisted," "gauche," "unthinking," "self-driven.") Her ex had since remarried. A black woman. They were perfect, she said. Both of them "downwardly mobile." Together they had two children. A boy, seven, and a girl, fourteen. It was to them that Kendo often went during the weekends. At least, she said, she had the comfort of knowing that he was with "ordinary" people and not the junkies and spoiled degenerates who were his peers and used to form his circle. These kids, she said, had been dispersed, sent to boarding schools abroad or to detox facilities by parents armed with the signed recommendations of Park Avenue shrinks. His group dissolved, Kendo didn't have the resources to assemble a new one. But left alone and without anything to focus his energies, he languished, turning his youth and beauty and privilege into a waste—which he displayed proudly in front of his mother, pointing the finger of blame her way.

I put down Kendo's picture of his father.

What was wrong with Kendo's life that he needed to throw away his days following me?

Twice more he'd shown up. First, outside my building—he was pretending to be buying sunglasses from a man who'd set up on the sidewalk. He tried a pair on and looked up with the eyes of a bug to check me coming out. Even when I let him know that he'd been found out, he kept staring. It was like a challenge. In the end, his persistence and his beauty defeated me, and I had to look away. Encouraged by this, he showed up again two days later. I was in my living room when a flash of light momentarily blinded me. I looked out, and there he was, surrounded by the swirl of Times Square, looking up at my window with binoculars. He'd found out where my apartment was, tracked me down. Perhaps, he knew everything I did, was doing. This, I thought, as I continued to orchestrate the destruction of his room, would let him know how dangerous I was: stop following me or else.

I had Suzy search out the shirt he was wearing at the party. Burn it, I told her, knowing it was probably one of his favorites.

Burn it? she asked. Clearly she knew how important the shirt was to her son.

In the fireplace.

I can't.

Will your will forever be subordinate to his? Do you know that your will, by being conditioned by this subservience, is demonstrating your weakness to malign spirits and encouraging them to enter your house, your life, and do whatever they please?

Suzy began to go down the stairs, shirt in hand.

Just to be safe, I made an announcement to Walung: We're coming down. And then made my footsteps ring as I followed Suzy.

Walung stood waiting for us by the glass doors like a statue. Only her head moved when she motioned for me to come near. Suzy looked at me. I went near and put my ear next to Walung's lips. She was done, she said. Her skirt was full to bursting. I looked down, careful not to brush up against her. For Suzy, I offered this translation of what Walung had to say: You should take down the bamboo poles. It'd been three weeks since the party and still there they were. There are evil spirits living in the bamboo, I said to Suzy. She hurried to the veranda, but I stopped her. First, burn the shirt.

She demonstrated her comic privilege by unsuccessfully trying to start a fire. By the time I was ready to help, I noticed that my hands were curled at my sides, gripped in anger, in an absolute and total lack of empathy or human understanding for where this woman came from, how she lived.

Douse the shirt in cooking oil, I told her. It was the only thing to do. No firewood or other kindling lay about anywhere.

After she did, I put a match to the shirt, and flung it into the fireplace. Immediately, I placed the screen over its mouth, and all three of us stood there and watched as the shirt was claimed by a line of black which edged furiously toward the center, eating all the red letters up. This ceremony—with the heat and the destruction—lent a momentary credibility to our make-believe purge and cleansing.

Afterward, she took down the bamboo poles. She rested them in a pile outside the front door, eager to get evil out of her apartment. But when she closed the door, there we still were, walking wherever we pleased.

Where are your maids' quarters? I asked, inspired by the return of the jingle in my brain: Filipinos make the best servants . . .

The servants don't live with us. They come in twice a week to clean. A sudden glint of suspicion emerged in her eyes.

What? I asked her.

I was thinking, she said, that maybe— No, they couldn't be involved.

No, they're definitely not, I said, and even though I had nothing to back this up, by this time Suzy was in the palm of my hand. What you must do, I told Suzy, is install a room to put the servants in. Your son keeps irregular hours. And you're away at work often. The house must not be left alone and unattended.

In my mind, I was doing this to improve the life of the Filipina maid, giving her these plush surroundings to live in. But by the time I realized that this would actually put her in twenty-four-hour servitude to Suzy, Suzy had already acquiesced, the deed done. To make up for it, I chose the best-looking room on the ground floor for the maid. This, I said to Suzy, opening the door to a guest bedroom, which had a view of the building's central courtyard.

But where would her guests sleep? she asked.

Why? Was it her only guest bedroom?

No, of course not, but it was the best.

Well then, I told her, it was what was needed for an occupant who would be there longer and more often than guests—and who would have to be compensated for being the "living guard" that would deter spirits from sneaking in to do harm.

I left her to consider what I said and flitted off to rearrange two mirrors which were already perfectly placed. I put them right next to the corners of walls, turning these walls incongruous and asymmetrical. Rounding each corner, Suzy and Kendo were sure to run into mirror versions of themselves, as I had on the streets, surprised, as if at a second, wholly new person. And these new people would serve as pincushions for their ire and everything that they normally saved themselves from—insults, anger, repulsion. In effect, they would be putting curses on themselves.

There was a room that was hard to get to, thrice locked and its door behind a metal garden screen that was a perfect camouflage. And because of this, it remained untouched by Neil.

Suzy opened the door with three small keys she kept inside the pocket of her tight pants. Everything was orderly, shelved—there were invoice forms; books filled with inventory; photographs of statues and other antiques she imported from the Orient—Japan, in particular—to show her clients; several books full of clients' names and pertinent information; and two Rolodexes of national and international contacts. Behind a blown-up black-and-white studio portrait of mother and son, taken a dozen years ago, there was a safe which she revealed with breathtaking trust. I told Suzy that Walung ought to see this.

Entering, Walung looked with eyes narrowed, as if to make out the things we with our mortal eyes couldn't. I wanted her to take stock so later we could discuss the feasability of returning for what was behind the vault. She understood immediately, and looking at me, shook her head No.

What is it? asked Suzy.

I motioned for her to keep quiet.

Walung answered with a grunt, louder than any she'd emitted before. She thrust her cane into the air and spun around several times. Scarily, I could hear a few items clicking underneath her skirt. To cover, she made her grunting even louder, and then started a rant in a foreign tongue. Suzy was clearly taken aback, looking on with a combination of horror and disgust. Walung was careful not to utter any Tagalog, lest the spell should be broken and I succumb to laughter.

When Walung stopped, I jumped in instinctively: The place is fortified, I said to Suzy.

Thank you, Suzy said to Walung, who again merely grunted. Then she left the two of us alone.

Suzy's home base of operations was arranged so perfectly—

everything in its proper, understandable place; within reach; with space to maneuver between each object—that anything I pointed out as needing correction would only make me seem inept, suspect.

This room is the only one that's correctly arranged, I finally told her, and doing so, supplied a reason as to why it was left undamaged. Suzy thanked me, and in a moment that caught me off guard, brushed her hand against a picture I hadn't taken notice of. It lay on her desk, surrounded by a frame of silver whorls. She took it up, offered it for me to look at. A young woman in traditional Japanese dress, with hair turned into two loaves of bread and a face made ghostly by white powder, looked at the camera with a pleading look, asking to be rescued.

It's my mother, she said in a whisper.

I let the moment linger, sensing the need for a tribute.

She continued, She was twenty-seven when she was widowed, and was not allowed to marry again because in the eyes of the culture, she was damaged goods. She had me and my brother to take care of. And she went about earning a living without complaining. When I was twelve, through some stroke of clairvoyance, my mother sent me to Canada to study. Two years later, my brother followed. And a few years after that, we came to this country for college. She worked as a laundry woman and as a caretaker of people's houses— an unusual job for a single woman, but she was able to convince her employers with her dedication and skill. She worked so hard, saving every cent, to be able to send me and my brother to school.

Is she still alive? I asked her.

In my heart she is, came her simple, true answer. And then she confessed, It's her I think about in my business, when I work.

She went on, How much this woman struggled to be able to keep the family above water. And all the time I never remembered her once uttering a single word of complaint. My brother, of course, being the younger, more sheltered one, didn't understand the bigness of her sacrifice. Men. They generally don't.

And where was her brother now?

Back in Japan. He owns a chain of department stores. He thrives there while I, of course, couldn't imagine myself having the same spirit of tolerance as my mother. I couldn't live there in the style to which I'd become accustomed here. To have the same freedoms, the same possibilities for success. As a woman. And so I married, had Kenny, and I stayed here. I was so in love, Master Chao. My relatives cautioned me about his being Chinese, but what did they know? They were sequestered in Japan, with no idea that the world had expanded. But then . . . She trailed off into a private world playing right in front of her, the past suddenly so palpable it made her eyes tear. I'm sorry, she said when she came to.

I didn't know what to make of this sudden human face. I heard myself say, encouraging, You were saying about your husband . . .

We were in love. Kenny—Kendo—sealed things between us. But then my husband started to complain about my working. Why did I have to work so hard, remove myself so often from the family? But the truth was, if I didn't work we'd starve. I had married a bohemian. At this word, she laughed. The laughter suggesting that other, more appropriate words had been passed over to help keep her venom in check. She looked at the blown-up picture of herself and Kendo to console herself. Between it and the small portrait of her mother lay her entire existence.

He believed, she continued, that we could survive on love alone.

Didn't he work? I asked.

Intermittent work, she replied. He freelanced, doing odd jobs for artist friends. The reason I know I was in love was that I was blind to his big defect. He was afraid of money. Like most young people, he was scared of aping his parents, of living well, becoming secure. Bourgeois, you know. The worst crime you could commit in the eyes of idealistic youth. I mean, look at Kendo. He loathes the way we live. But if he only knew. And also, my husband, I mean my ex-husband, Kendo's father, who didn't want to have to work too hard for money, also didn't want me to work. He couldn't stand the idea of being supported by a wife. The more I worked, the more his pride just continued to shrink. But I wasn't about to stop— She paused to pick out just the right word. I wasn't about to stop *succeeding* just for him. Between him and my mother, I knew which path was the right one for me to follow.

The speech seemed like it had come to a conclusive end, so I declared the tour of inspection over. We left the room, which Suzy locked in triplicate.

In the living room, while Walung and I waited in silence, Suzy went to get the payment.

Standing there, I remembered a final thing I had to do, a suggestion from Shem.

Here you are, she said, handing both of us small white envelopes.

Walung grunted.

Thank you so much, Suzy said to her.

Suzy came over to me. Once more she touched me. The prone African figure, which Walung had picked up and leaned against a wall, was staring at me with one eye.

Remember the incense in your son's room, I reminded Suzy.

I won't forget, Master.

It should burn for three days and three nights uninterrupted, otherwise you'd have to do it all over again. Saying this, of course, I knew Kendo would put them out, and the whole process would prolong comically.

And, I cautioned, watch out that the thing he puts up on the wall to replace the thing we took down— See to it that the new thing isn't evil.

I will, Master.

To reinforce everything, I told her, If there is any weakness that comes from the protection this new balance will begin to offer you, it will come from your son's room. He is, I feel, an unhappy boy, and unhappiness is the perfect accommodation for troublesome spirits.

Yes, Master.

And now—and here came Shem's little bit of business—that you have your home restored to a natural balance, I feel I'm sensing something very strong. Can you feel it too?

Walung, wanting no part of this, grunted to excuse herself.

I'll be right with you, I said as she strode to the foyer.

Feel what, Master?

I prolonged the suspense. I asked, Can't you feel it?

A vibration? she volunteered.

Love, I said.

Love?

The need for love.

She looked at me.

Yes, I echoed. The need for love, for the presence of a man, a protective presence, is so strong in here, particularly where we're standing—can't you feel it?—looking out at the wonderful view of this city, a view that emphasizes how lonely the people who live here truly are.

I waited for her to say something but she was too breathtaken.

I decreed, You need once more to introduce the head of a household into this house.

You mean my husband? she asked in a querulous voice.

No. A new man. A new love. Now is the time, I feel it so strongly.

You do?

Yes!

But I—

Close your eyes, I said, not allowing her to go on.

She did.

Now what do you see?

Nothing, she said, afraid of being scolded.

But I took that word and ran with it triumphantly. I said to her, And is it a *nothing* you feel you can live with for the rest of your life?

Bitch on heels, the men driven away. And once burned, her carapace even thicker, more impenetrable. In her medicine cabinet, no condoms, no birth control pills, no knickknacks betokening a love life. But still her romantic aspirations remained alive: her vanity fully stocked with makeup; estrogen to delay the onset of old-maidhood; and how many mirrors were in this place? Did Shem hope to be the man I was referring to in the abstract? Move in for the kill after I was done—an end to his estrangement from money?

Her closed lashes sponged tears.

Open your eyes, I told her.

Master . . . she said, wanting to confess but unable to find the words.

Can you feel it now? I asked.

I—I think so.

Open your heart.

It's so hard, she said.

But only then will you make room for love to enter. This line I stole directly from a beloved TV show hostess who uttered it frequently in show after show, regardless of the episode's topic. She was on a campaign to therapeutize the country, which for her consisted mainly of blaming men for everything that was wrong with the world and thugging her male guests into apologizing on camera to the women in their lives.

Open your heart, I repeated.

I'm trying.

Seeing her about to break into more tears, I stopped our session. Think on it. There's no need to rush into things, but think on my words.

I will. Thank you so much, Master.

She accompanied me to the foyer, where Walung waited, fingering the multicolored beads around her neck with an air of being disturbed.

Oh, by the way, I said to Suzy. And then I gave her the name of Pratung Song's shop, a place she could go to to refurbish her newly minimalist digs.

But, she replied, I own a business that sells these same things.

This stumped me. And then I said, But your business should not infiltrate your home. If you surround yourself with things that are not separate from your work, then you can never expect to be fully at rest. This will only send frenzied energy to vibrate around what should be a place of calm and tranquillity. Go to this place, I urged.

Why would I be encouraging her toward this establishment? Unless . . . Sharp businesswoman that she was, she gave a look of registering the fraud. But then, for fear of losing the peace that was promised in exchange for her full, unquestioning faith, she kept quiet. She told me, All right, Master, I will.

Suzy wanted to give me a hug but didn't want to embarrass herself in front of Walung. So, instead, she simply bowed.

I bowed back.

She bowed even more deeply, trying to win the contest of which nationality was truly the more formal.

I bowed even lower than she did.

She upped the ante.

This time there was no way I was going to outdo her. Already I could feel a strain—like tree roots bursting through concrete—starting on one end up my back and on the other down my neck to meet in the middle. The pressure making my spine curve, as befitting, well, a snake.

In *Throne of Blood*, Isuzu Yamada, after only the briefest of reigns as queen, had been killed alongside her husband.

We exchanged goodbyes and stepped out of her life. Behind Walung and me, the door closed with an imperceptible sound.

In the elevator, we counted our money—which turned out to be the lowest I'd ever been paid by any of my clients! Less than a thousand dollars! How much did you get? I asked Preciosa. Nine hundred, she said. Cheap bitch, I said aloud just as the doors opened. I was so pissed I didn't even acknowledge the obsequious doorman—who was wearing a Catholic medallion pinned to the pocket of his shirt and who obviously didn't let his Christianity interfere with his obeisance to me or to Preciosa, both of us with our articles of black clothing looking like representatives of the opposite camp.

With Preciosa, there was no relaxing of the mask after the show. I didn't get the feeling that she approved or disapproved, whether she had second thoughts, or what she made of Suzy, who, headlight-blinded by her own misfortunes, was unable to treat Preciosa with her, Suzy's, customary arrogance.

Even when Preciosa revealed a delicious tidbit, her face was hard to read.

When I asked her where the grunting had come from, she replied, Why? Wasn't it convincing?

No. On the contrary. It was just— I didn't know you were gonna do it.

She said, You asked me before what I did on stage.

At Lincoln Center in that play?

Well, that's what I did, I grunted. All night long, I just grunted. That was my performance. And, she continued, pulling her necklace up, I was wearing these. All I did today was give the exact same performance. Fuck, I even did my little spinning from the show. Spinning and speaking in tongues. She laughed, throwing her head back. And then she put on her regular face once more, and it was like a retraction of the small revelation she managed to let slip.

Primitives, I thought: A special encore performance for the New

York upper crust, in the form of Suzy Yamada. I looked at Preciosa, hoping for more revelations, but she would say no more.

The loot Preciosa took home. She would hand the items over to someone to sell and we would split the proceeds.

Later that night, I called Rowley P.

Rowley? It's William. It's done.

Really?

It's finished.

I'm so happy, William. You've made me very happy.

I just wanted you to know.

Thank you. You will be rewarded.

Rowley, I reminded him, I don't want anything.

I want to do this for you. Remember, William. Think hard: What do you want to do with your life? You will be able to accomplish a lot soon.

Five days later, this man was dead, having waited for just this moment before being able to peacefully retire. A day after that, I was walking into the offices of a man who identified himself as the executor of Rowley's will. In this will, Rowley left me his palatial apartment, and I could, said the lawyer, take possession immediately. Barring no obstacles, of course. Saying which, he pursed his lips as if to keep from elaborating on obstacles he knew would come.

There were diplomas framed above his head, spaced apart to suggest big eyes looking at me.

"Take possession": I thought, What a strange expression.

I had finally become like my victims. I now owned property.

PART 3

* * *

* 22 *

Brian Q did not get better. There were pustules around his genitals that were painful to the touch and would ooze blood and pus when too much pressure was applied. He was shamed beyond common sense and wouldn't go near a doctor, for fear that his business would be tainted. But he accomplished that feat by himself. Clients, unable to reach him, soon transferred their portfolios elsewhere. He was contemplating suicide. He let me know his status every day on my machine, begging for me to show up. The success of his hair convinced him that I was the man for the job. I did nothing to harm this man, doing everything by the book.

Word eventually got around about his "sickness." Perhaps he had competitors doing spy work, and as soon as he started crumbling, to ensure his total and complete defeat, they'd leaked word.

The girl, it turned out, wasn't named Norma. He'd tried to call her but discovered she'd given him a fake number. And then a few days later, drowning his sorrows in drink, he'd heard a most interesting conversation two barstools down—more or less the same pathetic scenario from a fat young man who'd brought home a "hot" girl from a party. She gave him the best head he'd had in a while. To commemorate the event, his wallet was freed of its contents and so was his closet, which he'd just stocked with new acquisitions from Saks. The boy didn't mention herpes but Brian Q was sure that that discovery would be made soon. It was too small a city to have more than one female crook with the same m.o. running around. It had to have been her—who introduced herself as Norma. She was a scammer. She showed up at Suzy's party with the intent to unload cash off some sucker. Herpes was only part of the bargain. Brian Q checked his apartment and found more than just the jeweled egg missing. He left me a long list: a painting worth thousands, a 24k gold picture frame that belonged to his grandmother, a first edition of *Winnie the Pooh*, etc., etc. None of these I had taken. How could he possibly replace all that? he asked.

One day, just to get it over with, I called him back. I left this message on his machine: The girl was sent to you by evil spirits to teach you a lesson, I'm convinced of it. Feng Shui cannot protect you against evil spirits if you yourself have welcomed them into your home, made them lie in your bed. The best chance for you would be to consult a witch doctor. This person will cleanse your house for you and cast away these spirits. But also, the good spirits can only help those who help themselves. Western science must not be discounted. First, you must get treatment from a doctor for your problems. Only then will you prove to the good spirits that it is their turn to be welcomed.

I left no suggestions on how to get in touch with a witch doctor. I didn't want Preciosa involved.

Lindsay S called and said he wanted to mail me something special. What is it? I asked. An article, he replied.

He said to give him my address and I would soon find out.

I reiterated my circumstances and said I hoped he would understand why I couldn't give him my address. Instead, I suggested we meet.

I went once more to his apartment. A net seemed to have been put over my renovations—that was how respectful he was being. He was doing well, he told me. Writing again. Reams. A career about to be revived. With him was a young man dressed in fine clothes that contradicted his street manner. He spoke in exaggerated Bronxese and moved like he had a chip on his shoulder, which made the hands at his sides hang heavy, balled to will himself upright. Assessing the two of them, I knew this was Lindsay's kept boy. Even if I weren't gay and hadn't been exposed to this kind of thing before, I would still have made the same assessment—that was how obvious they were behaving. They touched each other in front of a tiny picture of Lindsay's deceased wife, the woman who was, in effect, paying for the kept boy's pants, shirt, his gold necklace, his silver Bulova, the patent-leather loafers that seemed to be crippling his feet, turning them dainty with the caution required to keep everything neat.

Hello, I said to this boy, who smiled and revealed a goofy, likable face.

Hey there, he said, nodding his overgrown head in my direction.

Lindsay didn't bother to introduce anybody. Instead, he handed me an envelope. It's from *H*, he said.

H? I asked.

He laughed, this Lindsay, at my provincial ignorance. The women's magazine, he said.

Later, at a newsstand, I bought a copy of this magazine. The newsstand guy, an Indian man in his late forties, shrugged when I asked if he knew what the *H* stood for.

I called Devo, who wasn't home.

While waiting, I looked at the article and perused the magazine, which were two different issues.

The article wasn't exactly an article, but rather a listing, given the lofty title "The Register," in which the magazine pronounced on the "hottest trends and addresses" around "the world," by which it meant Paris, London, New York, and Los Angeles. There were lists for The Best Makeup, The Best Dog and Pet Care, The Best Nanny Agencies, The Best Hotels, The Best Resorts and Spas, The Best Restaurants, The Best Gift Trends, and in a section grouped pell-mell under the heading The Best of Good Living, there was my name, which Lindsay S had circled in red and then next to it placed an ecstatic exclamation point: "Master William Chao, the enfant terrible of the ancient Chinese art of harmonious living, Feng Shui." Beside it was my home number, the same number printed on my card.

And then from another section of the same magazine—a gossipy dozen pages penned by someone who signed herself The Duchess of New York—was a paragraph around which Lindsay S had drawn another red circle: *"And wouldn't you know it, dear ones, that the lives of several of our most illustrious citizens, among them the always beautiful and always* très chic *Suzy Yamada of Kendo Inc., have been vastly improved by the perfectly mannered, interesting-looking, and young-beyond-his-talents Feng Shui Master William Chao. Suzy told this bird how amazing the transformation of her life has been once Master Chao paid a visit to her gorgeous apartment, suggesting cosmetic changes that have eventually revealed their deep, profound implications. Among the benefits of this transformation, Suzy said, is that rare commodity that all you social butterflies would kill to have—hours and hours of gorgeous, uninterrupted sleep! And, indeed, Suzy's refreshed, youthful beauty was the talk of the party at the launch of the new Impudence! perfume at Barneys the other night. So for all you dear ones whose lives are too too beset with complications and stress, and believe, as I do, that there are more things that exist in this world than have ever been dreamed of by science or retail (!), the name of the magician again is Master William Chao!"*

Devo called.

Hey, man, I said. I'm reading this magazine called *H*.

What for?

It was just lying around, I lied.

So what's up?

What does *H* stand for?

That's what you wanted to find out?

What's it stand for?

Her, he replied, giving the word a faggy rendition. Or, as we on the Lower East Side call it, Ho.

A few days later, Neil called, saying he needed to talk to me. I didn't call him back.

The magazine *H* turned out to be a big hit at beauty salons and in doctors' waiting rooms. First Mrs. S called, and then Mrs. Y, then Mrs. T, and then another Mrs. S. All of them with the same trilly voice to say that they had just picked up the magazine and since they were already at the doctor's or at the beautician's—that is to say, fired up with the zeal for self-improvement—they decided to take the next logical step and call me.

So I came, wiped my feet on their carpets, and put fingerprints all over their belongings. They were four of a type, or maybe by this time everything was beginning to blur in my head. They weren't women who had tragedies they wanted operated on, or energies un-blocked, but instead—befitting their status as avid readers of *H*—were creatures who "lived and breathed" fashion and wanted to be "up" on the trends.

These people all had new *stuff*, lots and lots of it, piled around spanking new homes with a jumble-sale logic—the biggest things given positions of prominence and the smaller ones grouped in fours or fives around these bigger objects like satellites bowing and pay-ing tribute. Perhaps these larger objects represented them, and the smaller ones the rest of society, the arrangement a diorama encapsu-lating their hopes.

And not only did they have lots of servants; they also dressed them in designer duds and put gloves on their hands, as if afraid of contagion. And in the spirit of the return to calling things by their proper names, these servants were required to address the women of the household as Mrs. or, even more parodically, Mistress, and the husbands Master, while they themselves had to make do with You or Hey.

Speaking of the husbands, I didn't see any, paying my visits dur-ing workday hours. And as for children—the ones who had them al-ways made sure to sequester them from view when I visited.

These women wanted to find out all about Suzy Yamada, whom they'd been reading about for so many years, and photographs of whom they studied carefully to pick up on the latest trends. She had, after all, been named by *H* as one of the most stylish women of the nineties. Asian women, they all concluded, looking at me with the overdone eyes of raccoons or the jealously weary eyes of igua-nas, have the most beautiful skin in the world!

Their queries were disappointing because I was relying on them to fill me in on Suzy Yamada's condition—had the harm come to a boil? Surely, the peaceful Suzy Yamada of *H* was a thing of the past? But these women were only fans who glanced from afar, and who harbored the hope that soon, very soon, their husband's hard work—and their own, like hiring me, for example—would pay off and they would rise another stratum to find themselves in the same orbit as their idol. But before then, a lot of work had to be done. It was the work of refinement. And in its cause, they employed doctors (plastic surgeons, dietitians, exercise physiologists), beauticians, Feng Shui masters (plastic surgeons of the soul), personal shoppers at Bergdorf or Barneys, image consultants, and to rein in the things of nature that would otherwise impede their social progress: nannies for their children and mistresses for their husbands . . .

Of these women, my favorite was the second Mrs. S, who was "thirty-something," and was first the mistress and then, after a protracted battle of wills, the wife of a man who made his money raiding corporations. In the end, she had—she told me, laughing her infectious, vulgar laugh—"raided" him! Oh, it was the talk of society for ages! she said, referring to herself as the "barbarian at the gate." If she only knew, I thought.

Mrs. S had a wobbly neck that gave the lie to her professed age but two weeks later, on Fifth Avenue, had had it exchanged for something more fitting. Whereas before, she hid the disfiguring sight with chokers and pendulous necklaces that looked like fancy yokes, the entire thing was now proudly, nakedly thrust forward in display.

I congratulated her, and her soft, modulated reply—Can't talk too loud or I'll harm my throat!—continued to include an inventory of more things I would be amazed by in the next few months, things which were on their way out, like "fixtures" in a "hotel under new management and undergoing renovation."

The contents of Mrs. S's house were also constantly being rearranged. I was sure that after my touches had outlived their welcome, somebody else would come in to whip things around to keep her from getting bored.

And then, because professions like mine were too ephemeral for the meat-and-potatoes palate of American consumers, I received a few weeks later a call to say that I was being given the boost of yet another award from yet another women's fashion magazine. Apparently, one of the various Mrs.'s I'd visited had called to enthuse about my services.

These people were holding their ceremonies at the Plaza. Curiosity and boredom trumped trepidation, and so I arrived by limousine, which the magazine had arranged, making sure to be picked up outside a building on West End Avenue that I'd chosen for the occasion. The doorman of that building kept regarding me quizzically, not certain why I wasn't carrying the Chinese food he was sure I'd come to deliver. I was wearing a white shirt and black pants, which wasn't my waiter's outfit but instead a costlier version bought at Barneys to alleviate my nervousness. Speaking of Barneys, I could find no words to describe the singular pleasure of watching the plain-clothes security people—who seemed to have been trailing me all my life—stand by as I whipped out my new credit card to pay for everything. And as for the salespeople who made a show of their refusal to help as I looked, who stood there stonily, convinced that I was just an empty-walleted browser, well, were they sorry when the sales commission went instead to a young novice who'd had the smarts to recognize a purchaser when he saw one . . .

As I got out of the limo, there was a long stretch of red carpet that I had to pass, while on both sides the paparazzi made the exact sounds of their name: p's and z's electrifying the air. But as soon as I walked up, you could hear a mystified silence fall. Finally, a few photographers covered my presence—just in case. Behind me another limo pulled up, and this time the photographers went crazy. They repeatedly screamed some name that I was too zonked to hear. I took a deep breath and kept right on.

I imagined, to calm myself, Rowley close by, extending the protection that, along with the El Dorado apartment, was his posthumous bequest.

I went up to the third floor. Men in tuxedos and women in evening gowns converged all at once at the ballroom doors, rubbing against each other and making sounds like drinking glasses being strenuously dried. I thought to myself, You can still turn around. But just then, a magazine handler, spotting the nametag I had on, which had been handed by the limo driver, took my arm. I mumbled embarrassed thanks when we reached my seat.

The room was filled with about three dozen round tables, each seating a dozen people, and up front was a dais that looked like a holdover from a high school science fair, decorated with several prize ribbons and given a skirt made of shiny, blue-and-white-striped material. At the center of the dais was a podium with a microphone and at its foot was a riot of red flowers as if Christmas had arrived early. Above our heads was a constellation of pearly lights hanging off the tips of surprisingly simple chandeliers, gently swaying from the air conditioning. To make up for the minimalism of the chandeliers, the carpet beneath our feet was intricately whorled with grapevine designs and the backs of our chairs were used to glob on fluted and twirly things painted gold. Their legs ended in giant animal paws. At the center of the tables were floral arrangements with long blades of green drooping from all directions onto the tablecloth, like an upside-down wig. My big fear was that I would be recognized by people whose houses I'd done a number on—this seemed like an occasion they were born to infest, after all. But I didn't have to worry. There were real celebrities at some of the tables deflecting attention—boldface-type types frequently peppered on Page Six of the *Post*: actors from the movies and from television, record stars given the thumbs-up by MTV, and fashion models whose thinness seemed startling seen firsthand. And they all sat at their tables with the studied exhaustion of royalty, while all around them, faces were turning surreptitiously and not so surreptitiously in their direction like flowers feeding on a source of light. Throughout the evening, they kept being regarded in this way, and, in seeming response, the makeup on their faces, both men's and women's, progressively thickened and caked.

The food arrived, and a few minutes later the ceremonies were beginning. The magazine's cadre of bubbly young girls served as emcees. Of course, all the winners had been notified ahead of time, but still when some of their names were called, they made a show of being surprised. Best Debut Novel. Most Promising Male Star. Female Star. Best Kiss in a Movie. Most Influential Fashion Designer. The useless categories continued apace.

At the microphone, one word was repeated over and over. It was the word of the evening—had, in fact, been the word of the last two or three years—and no one would be left behind. Those hard-edged syllables—millen/: a foreign word picked up during the course of extensive reading, or perhaps in travels abroad;/nium: a chemical element pointing to fluency in heavy-duty areas like science and math—gave each speaker a momentary purchase on smartness. That, along with the glasses a lot of the TV actors and actresses, as well as the rappers, affected to wear.

I am so glad to be receiving this honor during the millennium, said a whiny-voiced teenage sensation (of what I didn't know, it was the only way he was introduced). He, along with every other recipient, made to transform that word into a baton passed specially to them to run with, making of the future an extended present tense, their dominance continuing. Undergirding their gratefulness was a fear that their success would turn out to be short-lived—that the m-word signaled a cutoff point where the present flopped over to present its ass for the future to kick.

Knowing that everyone was taking their cue from them, the celebrities obliged with high-wattage smiles and vigorous applauding which had the unfortunate effect of encouraging each person at the podium to launch into an impromptu novel.

They all held a laundry list of people to thank. And topping the list was, invariably, Jesus Christ or God. Even the black female rapper who won for Sexiest Album Cover was tearfully invoking the name of Her Savior, while behind her the winning photograph was projected for everyone to see: two shirtless, shaved-headed men were kneeling in front of her, flicking their tongues near her hot-pantsed crotch to suggest a pussy buffet about to begin. Thank you, Jesus Christ, she said, for letting me do what I do.

And then we were informed that there was a Latino music explosion underway, and drafted to illustrate this were two sons of the Savoy jukebox favorite Julio Iglesias, each of whom had had a hit record during the past year. I didn't catch their names and thought of them collectively as Spawn of Iglesias, and they sat at separate tables with their determinedly different "look," wanting to distance their images from one another, though to me, regardless of what each did with his hair, there was no escaping the similarity of their prematurely louche, Eurotrash fuckfaces, inherited directly from their father. And when one of them finally got up to perform, the other one looked away, or into his drink, or got suddenly animated with the person next to him whom he'd been ignoring all night.

Judging by the bilingual song one of the Spawn was lip-synching, I thought that if it indeed was typical of the so-called explosion of Latin music, then at least there was this to be grateful for: you couldn't understand half the crap being sung.

And then all of a sudden, as a respite from the "entertainment"-heavy first section, awards were being handed out to businessmen, most of whom had gotten rich on the Internet—a field that, despite the intimidation factor of new technology, struck me (after perusing these people's bios in the program, which included descriptions of their winning Web site businesses) as being a morass of idiocy being led by the idiots who were smart enough to recognize that since nobody else knew anything, they might as well, by passing themselves off as experts, profit from the whole fogbound endeavor; knowing also that the time to jump on things (pre-saturation and pre-one-hundred-percent-consumer-fluency) was shrinking.

I at once recognized, and didn't appreciate, the similarity with what I was doing. The similarity ended, however, with the money. The profits these people were making made mine look like the down payment on a shack.

Seated on my left was somebody's girlfriend, and on my right one of the magazine's staff writers, who, during a lull in the affairs, bent over to ask me, Does it really work?

Does what really work? I asked back.

You know, Feng Shui, she replied, in a tone to indicate that whatever I revealed would remain just between us girls despite the fact that she had a responsibility to the public as a journalist.

It's not a question of "works," I heard myself replying. It's a question of trying to create harmony, and from harmony will come the offshoot of peace, and from peace will come the offshoot of clarity. A chain reaction which, eventually, will lead you to the place where you wish to be. I was proud hearing myself come up with this on the spot. And as for the journalist, you could tell she was going to go far: her ears shut down when it became apparent that I was going to stick to my platitudes, and she gave all indications that they would only perk up hearing dirt or juice, or whatever newsroom term designated exploitable human frailty. For the rest of the evening, having sized me up, she left me alone, talking instead to some old geezer who looked so constipated I surmised he'd been dragged along by some chick he wanted to be a Boy Scout for.

When they called out my name, I considered for the briefest moment getting up and walking away, but the atmosphere of accomplishment suffusing the room had infected me, and now all I wanted was a plaque like everyone else. I realized that that was what I was here for, after all.

I got up, walked to the stage. Imagine that, just when I thought nothing would come of my life, here was proof otherwise. The sound of hands clapping, softer than before because obviously nobody recognized my name, but it was something. I almost stumbled on my way to the dais. Susan Sarandon, who looked pained in a tight-fitting backless thing and who was made vulgar by her look of instant rapport, handed me my award and gave me a kiss on the cheek. I took the plaque in my hand and managed to utter a sheepish "Thanks." Because all the other recipients had been so effusive, my monosyllable was greeted with more than its deserved applause.

All along, the entire evening had been meant to be viewed from where I was standing, solitary and hotly spotlit. I floated above them, yanked out of my dreamy impression of belonging. Seeing me, what would Shem say? Look at them, among whom I could now spot Pamela Anderson and Will Smith, surrounding me with their camaraderie and their perfect teeth. Why wouldn't they stop applauding? Were they waiting for me to say something else? Give them the gift of my Oriental wisdom, synopsize a fundamental tenet of Feng Shui as a departing "tip," making them laugh in an unctuous talk-show-host way that would not contradict what had been going on all night? Couldn't they see that my monkey act had reached its highest point of transparency? By now I was fully awake. And I recognized that each of them had started from far outside the prescribed circle of "it"-ness, aspiring to evenings like tonight. They had honed their acts until the right "look," and the "feel" for what the buyer wanted, was achieved, and having complied more spectacularly than the rest, were tonight being acknowledged, introduced to one another as members of a club.

I stepped down, headed to my seat, unable to look anyone in the eye. And they all wanted me to look back, as if delivering on-the-spot diagnoses on the states of their well-being.

Suddenly I realized that there were probably other masters of Feng Shui whom I'd beat out. I didn't know who they were but I was sure that they existed, and I was sure that they were—as I sat there, putting in my harmless two cents with the people at my table who had suddenly become interested in me, and pretending to enjoy food that had been parsed and simmered until it resembled wet thread—making calls to have my credentials checked.

Finally, the emcees were thanking everyone for a wonderful evening. And then, out of nowhere, the spidery hands of several matrons wanting to grab at my aura came into view. Sequins and fish spots and veins and the glitter of jewelry mixed into a horrifying pattern. I got up quickly, mumbled an excuse, and dashed out the door. It took some doing to get to the head of the pack. As soon as I did, I bounded down the steps and, ditching the limo, found myself on the subway.

On the table next to my bed was a card of a grinning orange tabby Shem had sent. Inside he'd scribbled: Who ate the canary?

Next to it were two Bill Hood books which I'd bought in the spirit of research: Why did Shem detest him so much? Certified classics, which implied that there would be a certain impermeability, but still! The words seemed conjoined by glue, squeezing out oxygen. Half the time I hadn't known what was going on, except a fuzzy sense that "big" things were being talked about. I'd been reminded of the Lincoln Center play Preciosa had taken me to, and had heard once more the thunderous applause greeting the end of the first act. An audience mistaking expensive words for erudition, confusing, as they consequently and beautifully did with me, stiffness with expertise.

It wouldn't be through his writing that I would understand this Bill Hood. So I'd consulted the jacket flap, where his picture looked back at me as if sizing up a prospective opponent. He had salt-and-pepper hair, a pear-shaped face, a longish hook nose, pockmarked skin, thin lips that suggested a stingy nature, and dim eyes that had the curved silhouette of an umbrella, sloping down on both sides. Those eyes made him seem antagonistic and sleepy at the same time.

And I could tell—even though it was a head shot—that the man was short. He was nobody you would look at twice on the street. Except that wrapped around the hand that was holding up his chin was a very expensive Rolex . . . I'd had a vision of Shem doing battle not with this man's physical being, which was trifling, but instead with the thing that was like King Kong towering over the Empire State— his accomplishment, the outsize reverence granted him by colleagues who had the influence to pronounce on such things and affect the climate of the culture. Colleagues who stood rungs above Shem in the writing world, with their boldface bylines and lengthier spaces in which to give their tiniest ideas free play, inflating the value of their own friends' work and pulling the plug on the new, the "foreign," with whom Shem had aligned himself. I'd thought, in perfect agreement with Shem: What a fucking stupid country to be living in! That they would erect statues to writers of sentences like these! Fuck, he was just cramming as much money into his fists as he could, trying to beat the ticking of a buzzer! Fifty-cent words one after the other. Meanwhile, his colleagues sat around applauding the vocabulary checklist he was marking off, paying back their motherfucking college tuitions!

Hadn't Shem been educating me? Hadn't he, by steering me toward Simenon, sharing his aversion to Chan Chuang Toledo Lin, talking and talking, been letting me in on what went on inside his brain? Already frayed, Shem's original story had begun to unravel even more. It didn't seem likely that he knew Bill Hood (because why hadn't I met him by now?), even though between them they shared a fondness for the same watches.

I couldn't sleep, disturbed by the scene at the Plaza, by the ease of everything. Waiting for me all this time was Rowley's place— well, that was the way I still thought of it: *his*. When would I "take possession?" The papers were made out to a guy named William Chao, and none of my forms of identification tallied with this man's name.

I got up and headed out. The night had gotten colder, with a wind whipping through the city. The taxi dropped me off on the deserted street, where the brightest thing was the open doorway of the El Dorado.

The Swiss Nazi had been given her leave and asked to turn in her key to the doorman. And this doorman, when he saw me walk into the lobby as a landlord, opened his mouth and kept it opened. He couldn't have predicted this turn of events. He tried to avoid my gaze and didn't say anything as he handed me the Swiss's keys. I didn't say anything either, counting on my trademark silence to dig the knife further in. But this victory was short-lived because immediately the doorman stuffed a huge stack of mail into my hands. The letters were addressed to "New Occupant" or to "William Chao." They came from contractors, interior designers, plumbing companies, furniture salesmen, property insurance people, the co-op board—there was even one from a Feng Shui guy! They made my shoulders drop, as if having the weight of stones. Most disheartening of all was an envelope signed: The P Family. Even before I'd stepped into Rowley's place, I'd finished this awful note. Rowley's family wanted to arrange a meeting, that was all it said.

I opened the door, walked in. Everything had been left as it was when I'd been here last. The curtains were opened, and in the dark windows I saw my disheartened reflection. I thought: This is not what a rich man is supposed to look like. I wouldn't be able to sleep here. Already, Rowley's family had invaded it in spirit. Exhausted, I sat down on the big armchair that was Rowley's throne. There I'd been, facing him, taking tea with my stories. And as for him, he was throwing away a million-dollar view to focus on my education, telling me the way one life was lived—a full life, to be sure, but studded with regrets he wanted me, in my own, to steer clear of. I fell asleep for a spell, and when I woke up, I felt a chill, as if somebody had opened a window. But nothing was amiss. I walked to the door, turned off the lights. I locked the door and didn't look back.

23

Can I come in? he asked, and breezed right in.

He sat himself down on more new cushions I'd gotten for the bench, patted them, and looked at me like the orange tabby card Shem had sent. Who ate the canary? It looked like Kendo had taken it out of my mouth and put it in his.

You enjoyed yourself in my room? he asked.

Your room was dirty. It had to be cleaned.

He stood up. Went to a bookcase, glanced at the titles. He took out the Agatha Christie I'd stolen from his mother. This looks familiar, he said, thumbing through. My mother gave this to you? So he *had* spotted me taking it that night. No, he answered his own question. You stole it.

It didn't occur to me to argue. I don't think she missed it, was all I said.

If you're supposed to be a fake, he asked, how come my mom's doing so well?

Finally I had my answer. Suzy was continuing to thrive.

What should I do? he asked aloud, phrasing the question in a teasing singsong. Should I . . . turn you in? Should I . . . blackmail you? Should I . . .

Is that why you came?

You hate my mother, right? he asked, sounding hopeful.

You're confusing me with you.

I mean, to scam her, you must like look down on her.

I'm not scamming, I said flatly.

Believe me, I know a scam when I see one, and right now I would say I'm seeing one.

But your mother's doing so well, I don't see where the scam is in that.

Tell that to the government. It's called fraud. He put the book back on the shelf. Walked to the windows. Nice view. My father lives just around the block.

Was that how he'd found me?

How much money you got? he asked, turning around. How much do you think your job's worth?

I don't know. I quit.

You're lying.

I hadn't quit—I was merely thinking about it. But again I told him that I had.

This time he believed me. How much you got saved up?

Enough.

Maybe I want half of enough.

OK, I said. My calm surprised me. The moment I'd been waiting for had finally come—the only surprise (and joke, joke being on me) was the unmasker's age. It really was time to quit if I had been found out by a kid. My exhaustion had finally caused me to slip up.

Still, pushed against a wall, I knew I could extricate myself. Once more, I was observing outside my skin, saying: Well, the guy's threatened, he'll have to do X, Y, Z. The concept of consequences didn't even occur to me, it was so otherworldly. Come into the kitchen, I told Kendo. In there was a cupboard with knives. Also, to get to it, we would have to round a corner. Anything was possible. The only difficulty lay afterward—how would I get rid of the body?

Why? What's in the kitchen?

My money.

You keep your money in the kitchen?

It's got good Feng Shui. Better than a bank.

You can't scam a scammer, he told me.

What's that supposed to mean? You're a scammer?

That's what I said.

I restrained myself from saying Duh because I wasn't sure that I'd really conceded to anything yet and therefore couldn't reveal my true person—of which Duh formed the central part. You might think you're a scammer, I told him, but you're not. This was one place where his looks turned into a disadvantage: Doris Day trying to play Barbara Stanwyck.

Where's your money? he asked.

I told you, it's in the kitchen. If you want it, you gotta come with me.

No, thanks, he said, with more than a clear understanding. This first beat of backing down began to spread slowly through his whole person. Pretty soon, he had both hands stuck into his pockets, defensively. I don't want your money, he said.

Excuse me?

It's not the money I want, he repeated.

So what is it?

How long you been doing this? he asked.

You want an interview? That's what you're here for? I've been doing this all my life. I trained. Like I told your mother.

Tell me something else, cause I'm not my mother.

Why do you hate her so much?

None of your fucking business! Who's Paulinha? he asked. That's you, isn't it?

Chao's my professional name, I conceded. And why not? I had told Lindsay S the same thing, after all.

Paulinha's not Chinese.

I didn't say I was Paulinha.

So why's that name on your mailbox?

Former tenant.

I asked around, he said.

Is that supposed to make your information reliable? You could've asked the wrong people.

He blinked, not noticing that I'd moved a step closer. Why do you want to know? I asked gently.

Cause, he said.

Cause what? Another step.

Just cause. I wanna be . . .

Yes? One more step and the motherfucker's neck could be wrung.

I want us to be— Suddenly he gave a start and was out the door before I had a chance to grab him. And then he turned around, peeking in the doorway to say farewell: I'll tell my mother everything and she'll send someone after your fucking fake hide!

With that, he was gone.

The next day, I had my phone disconnected. A few weeks before, I'd canceled my subscriptions to Condé Nast *House & Garden*, etc.

24

Feeling destructive, wanting someone to treat me like the fake that I was and at the same time looking for Kendo's stand-in, someone young and stupid on whom to test out scare tactics that were needed to save my ass, I went to a club. Also, and more truthfully, I was horny and wanted to see whether I still had "it." But the kind of new good looks I had just didn't cut it in the world I used to know. So I stood there, stranded, while around me people were bopping up and down or sliding from corner to corner to pick up on vibrations that they came expressly to places like this for, where one pretension rubbed up against another, and the money and the smiles and the cigarettes and the fingers tapping on the bar and the new-bought clothes and the drinks sloshing out of tiny glasses—these things were only doing the bidding of the dick. And the music—had I changed that much? It was house music—which was essentially disco given the sturdy backbone of a very audible bass beat. Above this hard thump coasted the melodic voice of a diva—just like in disco—singing about lost love, feeling hot and you better watch out, I'm coming into my own, can you feel the love in the house tonight! They'd been playing this music since the late eighties—when I'd turned twenty—and by now everything that had been fresh about it was being rendered by rote—the trademark diva growls and husky delivery in place; the obligatory rap solos serving as counterpoint; and certain surefire words repeated so often from song to song that they no longer seemed like words with any kind of meaning, like the way "God" sounded after you'd said it a million times in a row. The first of these words that I could remember was "party." Madonna's "Where's the Party?"—remixed and then played to death on club floors setting off a frenzy of copycatting: "Let's party tonight!"; "Are you ready to party!"; "Party in the house!"; "Party your ass off!" And then, let's not forget Prince's "1999," continuing in heavy rotation in light of the approaching turn of the century—no need for a remix, the original—more funk than house—was more than good enough: "We're gonna *party* like it's 1999!" It was as if, at the fever pitch of the AIDS epidemic, a call to life, averting the gaze from the pall of cumulative mortality, was being taken up—a kind of willed, fake triumph. Or a kind of distancing of one generation from its predecessors: "We're not the ones who're dying, so why take up the premature fashion of funeral black plus the aging weight of all that guilt?" After all, most of the ones who were dropping from AIDS had gotten it butt-fucking at the height of the free-love seventies. And then after "party," there was "free." Rozalla's "Everybody's Free" and En Vogue's "Free Your Mind," and beneath them, the horde of slogan-runners just cranked up the quantity. "Free": who was being liberated? Gays? Women? Adolescents just making the discovery of sex? Slaves to the nine-to-five? Myself? Was I now free? I looked around, noticing young men attired, or rather unattired, to be bought. Having money, I had graduated to the one who could do the buying. Free: it was just the same old shit. And really, the meaning didn't matter, it was only that the tail end of the word—stretched like taffy by the female singer—sounded great on the dance floor. Like the scene of an accident—eeeeeeeeeeeee! Inspiring a frenzy of pogoing and hand thrusting and torso writhing. And in this respect, it also sounded like electroshock—eeeeeeeeeeeee—"Let's go crazy!" "Get wild y'all!" "Screammmmmmmmm!"

Where's the party? Free. Crazy. Wild. A veritable roll call to amnesia. "Leave your troubles," said one song, "outside the dance floor." And then nearing the Judgment Day—with my twenties left behind like something thrown out a car window—there were the words "spirit," "soul," "light" to replace the foregoing words. From amnesia to awakening, exemplified by Madonna's "Ray of Light" album, called "electronica," which was essentially house music with the melodic flourishes of disco traded in for the synth atmospherics of goth (the better to carry quasi-religious lyrics), and with its bass beat trebled and then speeded up—like the heartbeat of some rat on crank—or slowed way down—crack for crank. Meditation, yoga, transcendentalism were once more, as in the seventies, the buzz-words. And you could tell, if Madonna—the head mall girl who approached everything as a trying on and taking off—had gotten hold of it, it was only a heartbeat away from dissemination among her disciples, whose idea of profound had been to capitalize and thicken the words SEX and POWER over and over in studiously squalid diary entries. But this time, instead of SEX and POWER, they'd be scribbling down HOPE and LIGHT, trading in black mascara for sparkles around the eyes—a look which made them appear to have smashed straight into a shower of stars. Near "heaven," as was their avowed goal. They were all here tonight, making me feel laughably square, with their pink and silvery-gray ensembles and their fluorescent wands which made circles in the air that I couldn't, not without the right drugs, appreciate. And you could tell, once these kids had gotten hold of the music, it would continue, just like house music before it, to get more and more popular, while its juice got more and more drained, until finally it became nothing more than a corpse of its original inspiration. Madonna, that undertaker of music.

The music at the club felt like a thousand needles stuck into your skin and on top of each needle was a current that was programmed to go in at intervals—boom, boom, *shoom!*—but really you didn't feel a thing, your heartbeat stayed just the same as it was when you first walked through those dark doors, above which you now realized blinked the red directive of Exit. Youth. Not youth. Exit. Stay. Good. Not good. Exit. Stay . . . Exit.

* 25 *

When I walked in, they were seated in a semicircle around a beautiful mahogany table that was so shiny their reflections doubled their unfriendly numbers. Their eyes were dulled as if they'd been staring at the door a long time before I showed up. I was wearing for the occasion what was by then my second skin of black and white. While they were all dressed in crisp, armorlike black, extending the observance of their father's death. The way they looked, they seemed the New Yorkers dressed in standard hip uniform, while I was the hick coming in for a job interview. There were four of them: the widow, who offset her severe black with creamy pearls; a daughter, who looked just like Rowley—a resemblance I was in no way to interpret as friendliness; and two sons, about my age, who looked just as Rowley had described his family: formless, without distinction. The boys sat inside their suits like tubs of butter melting under the heat. Next to the wife was the lawyer I'd visited, the executor of Rowley's will, who had announced Rowley's gift to me.

They were elegant and though unfriendly—trying to turn down the temperature of the room by their collective stares of sizing me up and suggesting that I'd been found wanting—were essentially harmless. All that fear, and for what?—was the caption I'd written underneath the picture—prematurely, as it turned out. Because if I had looked carefully, or just waited for the opening gambit, I would have realized that the black they wore was the same black of a jury who were out to convict, showing no leniency.

Hello, said the widow.

My condolences, I said, offering my hand, which no one took.

Please have a seat, Mr. Chao, said the lawyer.

That's not his name, said one of the boys, in a sulky tone. I was taken aback.

The widow hushed her errant son, who looked down as if to study the carpet. He kept his eyes down. The other son, however, renewed his accusing looks.

You have something we want, said the widow, not knowing, of course, that I'd come prepared to give the apartment back, making it look like the charitable impulse of a man used to so little.

Yes, I'm aware of that, I said. But before I could go into my preamble about not wanting anything, that the apartment rightly belonged to Rowley's family and not to me, the daughter spoke up. You could tell she'd been rehearsing all day just to get at the right pitch.

She said, We want it back and we want it back now.

Now, Miss P, cautioned the lawyer.

No buts, said the daughter. They were giving off the air of royalty in exile, persisting in their spoiled, rude behavior to prove to themselves that life was still as usual. The widow didn't discourage this one from speaking up. It was a matriarchy, with the two sons silenced, and the daughter elected the business manager, the one who would inherit everything after the mother passed away.

There's no need to be unfriendly, I said.

You cheated my father, said the other boy.

Again, the mother came back with a shushing sound. She said to me, I guess you know by now that we want the apartment back. The boy who'd just been silenced looked away.

You can have it back, I said, but my line had no triumphant ring to it, as I'd imagined. They knew that Chao wasn't my name. God knows they'd probably hired a detective. And who were they stashing behind that door at the far end of the room to bring out at the last minute to identify me as a Savoy degenerate?

Excuse me? asked the widow.

I'm prepared to give the apartment back. I never wanted it. It was as much a shock to me as I'm sure it was to you.

The daughter was trying to juggle conflicting thoughts inside her head. The prime one was this: Is this some kind of sick opening move in another con? The enormity of the effort was too much for her, so she gave an outward appearance of strengthening her dislike for me.

The lawyer was registering a look like he knew it would end like this. Again, he was careful to avoid looking at me.

Did the family have anything they wanted to hand over, in exchange for the forfeited apartment? Was there, for instance, an envelope filled with surveillance pictures? The mahogany table revealed their ghost counterparts but nothing else. And the door didn't seem likely to open—well, not now.

The lawyer said to me: Some papers have to be signed by you saying that you want to cede the property back to the family. He took out forms in duplicate, which he slid over. And then he gave me a silver pen with a click button at the top.

The lines with the red X marks, he indicated.

These people have so much, I thought, and they still want more. For a moment I considered what I could say to make them give up their efforts to get the apartment back. What had Rowley told me that I could use? Or could I bluff them, intimating possession of shameful family secrets? But did I want to live my whole life as Chao, stuck in a place—a palace, admittedly—difficult to dissolve when I had to make my escape? They were only depriving me of a weight around my neck, after all. The mail that had accosted me on my first visit as the new owner of the apartment—fixing me with its gaze of speculative interest—would transfer to them. Over the lines indicated I signed my name: William Chao. Just like that, everything was given away. And once more, I felt lighter.

When the lawyer took the papers back, one of the boys glanced over his shoulder, saying, What's that say?

William Chao, I said.

That's not your name! he repeated.

The mother said, Shut up. She knew not to push the matter further, having already gotten what they came here for. Besides, didn't the signature need to tally with the name stated in the will?

But it's not! persisted the son.

The mother wasn't above hitting her son in front of company. He jerked back, hand to his cheek. And instead of calming down, rushed out the door.

Alex, said the mother to the remaining boy, go look after your brother.

I ain't his nanny.

Are you going? asked the mother. Or do I have to make you?

Sulkily, the remaining boy left the room.

The widow looked at me and said, I don't know what kind of influence you had over my husband—

Ex-husband, I corrected.

A twitch played across her beautiful face as if it had been tickled by a feather.

I don't know what kind of influence you had over Rowley, she continued, but it must have been great.

Your ex-husband, I told her, asked for me.

To fix his house, she said.

It's called Feng Shui, I said.

Yes, Ilse told us everything, she revealed. Ilse was the Swiss goon.

What else did she say?

She spoke well of you, said the widow.

This floored me completely. She did?

She said you made Rowley's last weeks peaceful and calm. And he seemed to find you great company.

Your ex-husband was a wonderful man.

But old, said the widow. I didn't know what she was leading up to. And then, she said: Old enough to not be in his right mind. Easy to influence. That would have been our angle if you hadn't given the apartment back.

But he did, so there's nothing left to discuss, said the lawyer, who wanted any altercation avoided at all costs.

Like I said, I explained to them, wanting to play the part to the bitter end, I never wanted it. Your ex-husband put me into his will without my knowledge. I came to see him merely to carry out a service, and because he seemed to like having me around.

To do what? asked the daughter.

Talk, I said.

About what?

His life.

Did he talk about us?

Yes.

And what did he say? asked the mother.

He said that he was estranged from you.

Is that all he said? the daughter asked.

There were many things I wanted to say. For instance, I could throw back Rowley's adjectives at them: weak, spoiled, unworthy, insulated, perspectiveless. I could walk out with that air of triumph, like: I know all about you too, you're not the only one with a trump card. But I kept myself from saying anything. They had something over me, and as long as the transaction went smoothly, with the apartment back in their hands, I had a feeling that the mother would make sure that I was safe from unmasking. She seemed, despite everything else, to possess a code of honor. Though it was clear she disliked me, she was unable to fit me into any "type" and from that classification expound on my motives and my possible next move. In her eyes, a truce was the most desirable conclusion.

I told them: He said that he wanted to be close to you but that you made things impossible. I felt like a medium bringing back news from the dead. The daughter couldn't control herself and started sobbing. The mother comforted her, all the while refusing to stop looking at me. On her lips was a shade that was like chocolate, and if it weren't glossy I would never have been able to distinguish her mouth from the rest of her face. Without speech, she was perfect—a statue, an advertisement. Rowley was right: she had the gaze of a woman conditioned to regard the world as her enemy, unflinching, stoic, with a hint of challenge in the eyes. She and Rowley must have made a strange-looking couple: with his open, slightly mischievous face and hers that was like a window with the shades drawn.

Is that it? I asked the lawyer.

Thank you very much, Mr. Chao, he replied.

Will you be able to reach him if a court needs his sworn testimony? asked the mother.

About what? I asked.

If your signature needs backing up, she replied. To tell the court that you hadn't been coerced.

But I haven't, I said.

But in case the courts want to hear for themselves, she replied.

I don't think we have to fear that, said the lawyer. Everything's aboveboard.

What are you going to do with the apartment? I asked, as I stood up.

It's none of your business, said the daughter, who immediately resumed crying.

We don't know yet, Mr. Chao, the mother told me. Thankfully, she didn't put quotation marks around my name.

As I walked to the door, she stopped me. If we were to sell it, would you be interested in buying it? she asked.

I'm afraid you have me confused with somebody else. I don't have that kind of money. As if personally responsible for this state of affairs, the lawyer looked away in shame.

Outside, the two boys were waiting for me at the elevators. Their suits seemed more padded than before. They cornered me and the older one, putting his face right to mine, said, We know where you live. We can come get you anytime we want. We know people in Pittsburgh. They both turned their right hands into fists and hit them against open palms, over and over again.

We know people in Pittsburgh? Was he kidding? This was the funniest thing I'd heard in a while, but instead of laughing, I felt myself shake. The elevator opened not a moment too soon.

Before going home, I dawdled around several storefronts in Times Square. I picked up a pocketknife that flicked open with an impressive sound by a simple throw of my wrist. I did this several times, and then paid the black man, who took the money and kept his questions to himself.

26

Preciosa and I split the money, minus a commission for her friend who did the reselling of Suzy's goods. She came up to hand me the bills in an envelope and asked about my phone. I told her it was over, I was pulling the plug on the whole operation. How could she reach me, or I her, in case of an emergency? The way she asked made me feel as if she knew something was going to go wrong. I would get a new number from the phone company, I replied.

On my way to the phone company, I bumped into Shem, who was coming to see me. News had reached him—and if news had reached him, you knew that it had been circulating around a long time before that, given that he was a man continually out of the loop. What had I done? he asked.

It's over, I replied. You got what you wanted. I mentioned my work with Suzy—wasn't that the culmination of everything?

Hello, I said to the clerk at the phone company. I explained everything to him.

What do you need a new number for? he asked, adjusting his glasses behind a thick bulletproof panel that gave his face comic-book lines and whorls.

I'm being harassed, I told him, and at the same time I looked at Shem, to let Shem know that this was no line. Shem looked away.

OK, said the clerk, wondering who would want to harass a responsible-looking young man like me.

A minute later, he was back, and gave me papers to sign. In return, I handed over a check.

I couldn't tell Shem about Rowley and his leaving me his apartment. Couldn't say that that made me realize I had bumped up against a wall—that innocent people had been involved and had replied with a too easy, crippling generosity. Already, that amateur Kendo, with his Hercule Poirot aspirations, had found me out. And there had been Rowley's family too.

I'm tired. That's what I said to Shem.

Aren't you going to give me your new number?

What's the deal with Bill Hood really? I asked. By this time, we were out on the street and I'd stopped suddenly. I turned to look at him.

Shem blinked. That was all I needed to see.

What if Suzy wanted to reach you? he asked. We're not finished with her yet.

I've done my bit.

And if she needs touch-ups?

I was quiet.

How will I get hold of you?

I gave him my new number. There, I said, in the tone of somebody closing a door. But really, I was only giving him the key. Shem, I told him, you're not going to give it to anybody.

Scout's honor, he said.

I know about Bill Hood, I told him, bluffing.

He didn't flinch. What do you know?

It's OK, I said, giving my blessing. I've read his books.

Shem laughed.

While you're at it, I said, why don't you go after Paul Chan Chuang Toledo Lin? I've read his book too.

Lin, Shem reminded me, is already fucked.

This made me laugh.

B ack at Lincoln Center checking out movies. Barbara Stanwyck and Bette Davis. Movies Preciosa enjoyed so much she insisted on seeing them again. Two actresses Preciosa could've easily been next in line to. Stanwyck playing a cardsharp's daughter in *The Lady Eve*, and Davis a willful Southern girl in *Jezebel*. How had these two actresses sustained the energy to keep playing at badness? I myself was tired out from having to dupe all those people. At some point, it was no longer enough to hate them for their wealth. Or even for their crassness, their Neanderthal sophistication. Or their distance from common living. Something else had to be discovered, some new thing to despise. But instead, I discovered just the opposite, a trait to tie them to everyone else: A core of fuckedness, for which the outside trappings of being swathed and coddled were useless palliatives.

So for Preciosa, the tireless Barbara Stanwyck and Bette Davis, and perhaps through them, a dream scenario unspooling of what she could have been. And for myself, there was what? Wait! A title Jokey mentioned. A film he was in. I took it out.

Back home, there was Jokey dying from gunshot wounds to the chest, clutching himself in disbelief, while far away, an ambulance wailed like the lonely calling of a ship to the harbor. God, that made two deaths for Jokey. Was this a career pattern? Suddenly, his glamorous new career turned out not to be so glamorous after all.

27

Shem called.

Cardie Kerchpoff had been on a campaign to blame everyone for the dissolution of her marriage, calling up friends and perceived enemies alike to harangue them. The woman was tearing herself down. This kind of wild, irrational behavior, when it came time to plead for child custody, played perfectly into the hands of her husband's lawyer—boy, was that turning out to be an ugly battle!

Did I know the volume of calls that had been pouring in for my services, calls that somehow always ended up with Shem? Of course, he had to concede, my unreachability only fueled the furor.

There'd been *H*'s endorsement to persuade people. And then there was that stupid award which I kept in my bathroom, the one I'd accepted at the red-carpeted Plaza, where I'd been let in as a spy on a world only read about—making me realize that nothing could equal the imagined glory occasioned by gossip reports and by flashes caught on television. The real thing, in comparison, pushed you too close to sweaty stampedes and boring dinner talk and the sobering recognition of a social pecking order that seemed too vertiginous to transcend. This last thing, in particular, being the perfect antidote to fantasy.

Reading about me, the people wanted to get their share. All that Shem and I had talked about—these people's desire for inoculation, to be part of a growing circle of hipness, to help themselves acquire more—a volume that would serve as a shield against things given claws and teeth by millennial fever, things reinterpreted according to the specifics of each person's guilty conscience—all these were only being proven right one by one. There was no stopping the public's acquiescence to publicity.

Every day the papers were trumpeting a Greatest Cinematic Achievement in Ages! It only increased your anxiety knowing you were missing out on so much. So many great books to read, great bargains to be had, vacation spots to be visited. Enjoyment was turning into a virtual task. And a lifetime was becoming shorter and shorter. Was there any surprise that they'd be clamoring for the next hot commodity if that commodity happened to be peace of mind, tranquillity, silence—the silence of doing nothing, of no longer contributing to the general traffic?

And besides magazines with their awards and their trend-spotting one-upmanships and their embrace of the splashy generalization, the news was turning out to be my new best friend. The death of the guru Kuerten—only now was the necessity of that death beginning to be appreciated. That, plus a more highly celebrated mass suicide of a cult in Santa Rosa, California. People who wanted to commute their souls to the next plane before the frenzy of the times transformed everyone into beasts straight out of the pages of the Book of Revelation. These people had taken capsules of cyanide with their early evening tea, and then had lain down on blankets spread out on the back lawn of the compound. They died staring straight up at the vastness of an imminent embrace. The police on the scene had described it as the cleanest and one of the saddest sites they'd ever been called to. All these deaths had opened up a hole that needed to be filled. And filled not by more things aligned with death—which had always been the unfortunate flip side of new religions—but by *life*, a renewed commitment to it, by, yes, HOPE and LIGHT. Publishers were glutting the bookstore shelves with how-to Feng Shui textbooks, virtually giving the information away for free, and boy, was it moving. Proverbial hotcakes. And here we'd preceded the craze by a good six to eight months—enough time to be thought of as "established" by the magazines. The way Shem described everything, it was very simple, only cause and effect, connect the dots. And now, he asked, would I be ready to reap the rewards of all that hard work?

Yes, I thought, this man has a gift for seduction.

What should I tell all these people who keep calling? he asked.

Tell them, I replied, and against my better judgment, continued, that I'm on vacation and can't be reached.

All right, he said, sounding encouraged. After all, wasn't he a good persuader? Hadn't he persuaded me once before?

* 28 *

I'd been waiting for days for him to show up again. I had
the pocketknife. I was prepared. But he caught me by surprise by apologizing. He didn't know why he said the
things he did. He wouldn't divulge my secrets to anyone. Cross his
heart, hope to die. Would I go out with him to dinner? He would
pay. Earnestness and beauty. An irresistible combination.

We were separated by a door I had opened just wide enough to
be able to peek out. Preciosa came up the stairs. Seeing me stiffen,
and because Kendo suddenly took her presence in as being signifi-
cant, she passed my door with dulled eyes and went up another
flight.

Who is she? he asked, nosy as usual.

A downstairs neighbor. I don't know her. Nobody talks to each
other in this building.

Just then, of course, the cat woman had to come up and ask,
Have you seen Preciosa?

Kendo gave me a quizzical look.

I pushed back the redness from my skin. Who? I asked the cat woman.

Preciosa, she repeated. Hello, she said to Kendo, who nodded. Preciosa came up to see you.

Oh, I said. I haven't seen her.

That's strange, said the cat woman. Are you sure?

Uh-huh.

Well. Sorry to disturb you. I'll talk to you later. With that, she descended and disappeared.

I thought nobody talks to each other in this building, said Kendo, waiting to see how I would get out of this one.

It's just her. She talks to *everybody*, I said without a falter in my voice.

Who's Preciosa? he asked. That first lady who came up?

I told you. I don't know her. The one who just went down has cats. That's probably who she was talking about.

And this cat knows you?

Do you see a cat around here? I asked, putting a stop to that.

Will you please let me take you out to dinner? he asked again, smiling beautifully.

So there we sat. Red was the predominant color, just like at the Savoy. Tourists speedily consumed meals of sloppy pasta and greasy sandwiches before hoisting themselves out into the streets once more.

He said he admired me. Now who was scamming whom? He said that I shouldn't stop doing what I did. It was great. People like me—people who had been dealt the wrong hand by life but who sought to change that, regardless of method, regardless of who got hurt—were heroic to him. Of course, the extension of this logic was: Fuck his mother.

I chose my reply carefully. I said that his admiration was misplaced. That if I had a choice, did he think that I wouldn't trade places with him just like that?

He only shook his head. He couldn't understand the advantage he had over me, would, in fact, be willing to throw it all away, not having had to work for any of it.

He told me that he hated the schools he'd been sent to. In them, he was surrounded by boys who talked like perfect juniors of their cigar-chomping fathers. Out of their mouths came foreign and vaguely threatening words like futures, debentures, arbitrages, bonds. Clearly, school was simply a blind form to follow. They were in line to inherit lives that would make the things they were ostensibly in school to pick up unnecessary. They were boys to whom the future belonged, who could, in the time it would take to pick up a phone and punch a button, reorganize the world, move things around. They drove their fathers' high-speed trophy cars whenever backs were turned, and for them, yes, it was all about getting away *and* getting away with it, the top down, wind through their hair, massaging caution and all that sense of proportion shit out of their heads. And when among themselves they jived, the motifs also involved forward movement: "put the squeeze," "finger on the pulse," "move in for the kill," "pedal to the metal."

Ken himself had learned how to drive at sixteen. But he hadn't liked it. He found he couldn't go over fifty. Fifty-five, and his head would start to vibrate. It was as if, by slowing down, he refused to grant permission to something inside him that once let out would have to be fed constantly, as he had seen his peers and, closer at hand, his mother having to do.

Ken hated most of all that these boys, who were mostly white, saw him without question as being one of them. Asian. A stamp on the forehead that read: Most Likely Not to Trouble the Waters. And he wanted so badly to break free from it. Show all of them. Black people, he said with breezy authority, were lucky in that they had that revolt, that rebuke built into the way they looked, the way they spoke. Didn't I feel the same way? Wasn't that why I was scamming, to prove a point?

What did he think? That I aligned myself with "seedy" and not altogether savory things out of a need for recreation?

He only laughed.

After dinner, he mentioned a movie. There was this flick that purported to take up history's cycle where it had left off, which went something like this: First Asians had been wily, made mysterious by shadows falling on the planes of their flat faces; and then, after the hard work of revisionism that followed the civil rights movement, a curtain parted and out they came, fully lit and ready to be appreciated for their true dignified, stoic, and hardworking natures. And now, this new movie was upending the established morality by giving back to Asians the right to be "bad" once more.

"Bad" was proving to be Kendo's mantra, as "good" had been mine.

So Kendo took me. But you could tell even before he saw anything that he was already a customer: as he entered the theater, his eyes lit up like nothing I'd seen before, and during the movie, he guffawed even before the lame punch lines were finished. It was about Chinatown gangsters, peopled with extras from a Michael Jackson video. We're a nasty bunch of fuckers, aren't we? Kendo turned to ask me. On one side was his beauty, on the other his utter cluelessness, opposing forces on my shoulder saying alternately: befriend him; kill him.

Afterward, he was still unwilling to let me go. Could he talk to me some more? And this time, his admiration, edged with a clutchy desperation, came through clearly. I was touched and felt that perhaps I'd been wrong about him. He wouldn't harm me.

He wanted to discuss the movie. And he wanted me to tell about my life.

Why?

Cause I'm interested.

Why?

I told you. What you do, it's admirable.

We went to a bar called the Gutter Ball. Above the entrance were neon bowling pins that kept getting knocked down by a ball that came out of nowhere. The pins fell backward like drunken men, but a moment later, they were upright again, asking to be struck. Again the ball appeared, ready to oblige. This continued into eternity.

I ordered a light beer, and the boy had some vodka. I felt like playing the responsible elder, telling him to watch it, but decided against wasting my efforts.

He knew a lot of people. People like the ones we'd just seen in the movie. Not gangsters but . . . Heck, why not just come right out and say it, criminals. People on the other side of the law. Just like you, he said, giving me a friendly pat on the back.

He said he didn't know how he'd hit on the whole thing, but that as soon as he found himself in the middle of it, he knew it was what he should be doing. A calling, he said. Hanging out at an arcade not far from where his father lived, he started spotting scams left and right. Guys would rig the machines so that a quarter allowed you to play on and on. Also, they'd pickpocket dazed tourists to pay for their hobbies—besides the video games there was beer, skateboard magazines, sunglasses that would help conceal their age when they went to clubs, fake IDs that could be purchased in any shop that hawked useless tourist crap, and the nearby sex palaces of Times Square with their thousand winking come-ons. These were guys his age, who either lived parentless on the streets or had parents too exhausted to keep track of what they were doing. He befriended them. Took them out for meals, as we'd done earlier. In exchange, they offered up their stories. Just as, he was sure, I would do. Because most of them were black or Latino, it had taken him a while to be able to earn their trust. Like his schoolmates, these boys had read into his Asianness an automatic good citizenship. So to win them over, first, he had to dress down, putting slits in the expensive jeans his mother had taken care to buy from fancy department stores, and adulterating his shirts with paint or other disfiguring paraphernalia. And then, crossing over from simple empathy to full participation, he eventually agreed to lift the pockets of targeted passersby.

The first time was awful—he'd been caught, and his heart felt like it would bust out of his rib cage, but his feet on the other hand—oh man, block after block fell behind, and by the time he'd run out of breath, he'd found himself clear on the other side of town, having left even his comrades behind. The second time, however, things went smoother. He'd picked an old woman for a mark. The handbag dangled from frail hands like fruit ripe for the picking. He grabbed and then ran in crazy figure eights to shake off hapless passersby who were charging after him. That night, he and his buddies had a lot to celebrate. Three hundred dollars was gone in the space of a few hours, eaten up by so much McDonald's food and crappy Times Square merchandise that went kaput in a couple of days and ended up littering the streets. Three hundred dollars? I asked. I suggested that maybe that was the old woman's life savings.

He gave me a look to let me know that he knew better than to be taken in.

He picked up on the boys' stories, stashing away useful bits of information about how to run scams, about how to read people and see which was made of sucker material. He stored away the boys' personal histories in the event that one day he needed to pick a disguise for himself. It was like research for writing a book, except that the book he was working on was his own biography. He wanted to break free from the tyrannical hold of his mother, who saw in him he didn't know what, except that it felt like being suffocated. Did I know that she'd planned to send him to be brainwashed by that Kuerten guy, the same guy who years before had worked on her, and also, but unsuccessfully, on his father?

From the boys he'd moved on to more sophisticated operators—mainly, the people who lived in his father's building. To supplement their unemployment or Social Security checks, these people engaged in Welfare or food stamp scams, insurance fraud, faking Workers' Comp claims, being false parties at will contestations. He himself was getting smoother by now. That these people were willing to talk so openly in front of him—wasn't that a sign? He was like a magnet, more and more people just found themselves next to him, divulging truths that they hid from everyone else.

So what about you? he asked. He made a move with his hands like clearing the countertop to prepare for a long, juicy story—I was about to be inducted into the rogues' gallery, said this gesture.

What did he want to know?

Tell me about this thing you do. You go into people's houses, do some mumbo jumbo, right, they don't know the difference. How much do you make?

It's not mumbo jumbo, I said.

How much?

I studied. It's called Feng Shui.

Study? I've seen those books at the bookstore, man. I can plop down like twelve-fifty. I can study too.

What is it you want to know? I asked. You already know everything.

When did you start?

I looked at him. Six months ago, he was merely a photograph in a magazine. Today we sat next to each other, peers—well, almost; he with his sights set on grunging down (to be dirtied, throwing privilege away; to make fun; to undermine), me with my ingenue aspirations (to be cleaned up; to be taken seriously; ready to be overwhelmed by the powerful prevailing order), the two of us meeting somewhere in the middle. If I wanted to, I could reach right out and touch him. The distance I'd traveled, ending up next to the glamorous Kendo, ordinarily the length of a life, microwaved, made dizzying. Was that why I was swooning and couldn't look at him?

When did you start? I heard him repeat.

Six months ago.

How many people have you pulled this on?

Three dozen.

He made a whistling sound. Even in old age, he would be good-looking. And should his wish come true and he turn poor, he would still be a beauty.

I continued: It's like dominoes; you know, push the first one, the rest just follow.

A sucker born every minute, he said, in a self-congratulatory style of drawing a line and putting himself on the other side of it.

You said it, I agreed lamely.

Like my mom.

Your mom resisted, I told him.

Lucky for you somebody broke into our house, he said, winking at me.

What's that supposed to mean?

How much do you make? he asked.

None of your business.

No need to be so touchy, I don't want any of it. OK?

How do *you* get your money? I asked.

None of your business, he said, showing his own touchiness. But I could guess: his mom kept him on an allowance, and then when he reached a certain age, or should he marry, there would be a trust fund waiting for him. Petty theft to supplement the periodic sums Mom doled out. Money he saw himself as "earning" and which lifted him into the ranks of those he admired, who had to "work" for it, relying on skill and cunning rather than circumstance. "Colleagues" who turned the tables on people from his mother's circle whom he'd had the opportunity to study and despise his whole life.

Behind us was a man lining up his accomplishments for the evening on a rickety table: First he put up a row of seven empty beer bottles, and above that, he was now attempting to rest another five, going up like a pyramid. Of course, the entire thing crashed with a resounding whomp before he could even hoist the third tier into place. A waitress sighed heavily as she moved to confront the aftermath of this man's drunken lassitude.

Speaking of third tier, that's where Kendo classified me among his criminal acquaintances. Moving up, he said, flushed with pride. These were people with more elaborate plans than those previously encountered. Whose plans engendered bigger payoffs. Besides me, there was a woman he knew—well, in fact, he'd brought her to Suzy's party, the same night that I'd first showed up. She was the girlfriend of a topless bar dancer who lived next door to his father. Among the plans hatched by this woman: she picked up men in health clubs she joined only for a month, health clubs that weren't too hip but instead catered to the middle-aged, so that she could be sure that her looks, not entirely first rank, would stand out. Working out made these geezers so horny, and so comically, undeservedly vain, that they were virtually trailing her from one end of the gym to the other. She would welcome their advances, and then, after having sufficiently gained their trust, would enlist the help of some pal who was an expert at breaking and entering, and together they would fleece the guy of belongings that they could then turn around and unload for quick cash. Lately, said Kendo, she'd been striking out on her own, doing the quickie one-night-stand version. She went home with guys she met at business parties she crashed, had sex with them, and afterward made off with whatever she could. Money was always the best. Credit cards could easily be traced. Possessions were hard to carry out, but she knew an outfit that specialized in reselling to people out of state.

This girl has herpes, I said before Kendo could continue.

You know her? he asked, smiling.

You brought her to the party knowing that she had herpes and would pass it on?

She says she usually doesn't sleep with them. Just gives them blow jobs. With rubbers on. That's not part of her scam, OK? And if she sleeps with them—

This guy she went home with, this guy your mom knows, he got it from her.

Got what?

Herpes! I said. People turned to look, wondering what the joke was that led up to this emphatic punch line.

Well, it's his fault, said Kendo.

How is that his fault?

Well, Norma—

Excuse me? I asked.

What? he asked back, stopping.

Norma? I repeated.

That's her name.

Wow, I thought. So it was her name after all. What a brave girl. But what was I talking about? Who the fuck walked around using William while shaking the hands of future accusers? How, I asked Kendo, is catching herpes the fault of the guy?

Norma says she asks them to wear rubbers and put on, you know, gels and stuff, but there are guys who insist on putting it in her without anything, cause it feels better, and they *insist*, man, it's like you're a slut and you should be used to this by now, and hey I'm kinda an important guy and if you play your cards right this could be the start of a beautiful and profitable friendship, that's what they think, so she thinks, well, if they don't care about me, care that I might get pregnant, or might get what they've got, *if* they've got shit, well, she thinks, why should I care about them?

And that's why they deserve it?

Instead of arguing, he went on about his admiration for this Norma, who was trying to make enough money to get her girlfriend out of the life.

Impatient with his refusal to see things as they were, I asked, Why do you want to be bad? I knew the answer, of course—if his mother had been bad, he'd have wanted to be good—but I wanted him to confront it himself.

I just *told* you!

But why?

Because it sucks to be you know, like crippled by having to wear a uniform and all that shit!

A stamp on the forehead? I asked, hoping to use his very own imagery to discredit him.

Exactly! he said, missing my point.

I plowed on: So you wanna be like me? Do what I do?

Not exactly what you do, but you know . . . Have an option.

Like an adventure, I volunteered.

He knew where *that* line was leading to. He shouted, Hey, I'm not a kid!

You're not? I asked, with exaggerated disbelief.

I know the difference between right and wrong, he argued.

And what you're doing, you think that's right?

No, he said. It's wrong. That's why I'm doing it.

I confessed to him, I don't know why you want this so badly. I myself wanted to be good.

He gave me a look.

It's true, I repeated. I wanted to be good.

Oh, man! he said. That's exactly the kind of lecture I don't want to hear.

It's not a lecture.

You sound just like a goddamn Catholic.

Ex, I said. I'm lapsed.

Not so ex that you wouldn't want to convert me, he replied.

It's the other way around, I pointed out. You're trying to convert me. Or should I say, reconvert.

You? What are you talking about? You're way converted.

I quit, remember? I reminded him. (But I knew I would go back—I just didn't want him knowing about it, forever hanging on like an unwanted weight.)

You can't quit, Kendo said, looking me right in the eye.

It took me a moment to realize what he really meant. He meant that I couldn't quit *without his permission*; he wouldn't allow me to undo my negative heroism. Earlier in the evening, he'd said that he would keep my secret, telling nobody. But now it seemed that there was an unspoken clause to that promise. He wouldn't divulge my secret *if . . . ?* *If I behaved.* Obeying him.

I can't quit? I asked, trying to sound lighthearted.

You're the best. The best don't quit.

How about if I said I retire?

Not in your prime you can't, he said. He laughed and went back to his drink.

Had the scammer become the scamee?

29

The woman who greeted me at the door was Filipina. Oh, hello, she said, and then did a double take, having spotted me for a countryman. I made a mental note to myself: Get dark glasses. Come dis wey, she said. She was dressed in pink, like somebody about to usher me to get my hair shampooed. On her head was a headband that was an explosion of crinkles, and on her feet were orthopedic shoes that made squeaky sounds as she walked. The carpet was plush and gray and made me feel as if I was stepping on the back of a giant, well-groomed poodle. She guided me to a living room, where I sat on an uncomfortable antique sofa among classical statues of naked, athletic men set on low pedestals. Around their feet and across their shoulders billowed shrouds that were like extensions of their impressive musculature. I didn't have to wait long before the Dowager walked in. I stood up to greet her, but she made a motion to say that it was unnecessary. Another maid entered with a pitcher of iced tea and two long, tall glasses. We each took a glass and waited while the maid finished pouring us our shares.

I gave her my fake history about having had to flee my father's enemies in Hong Kong.

There was a momentary flash in the middle of this—like a preview of real life—when I heard myself say: Footprints had to be removed. I had to become this new person so wholly, so completely, that in the very likely instance that these people sent scouts to track me down, I would not be found in the places that someone like me, someone from my family, would be. I needed to reinvent myself so totally that I would become untraceable.

How had my father made enemies in Hong Kong? By his fantastic success, owing to Feng Shui. The business had become a magnet for extortionists and I had turned into a target of kidnappers. A sword had been made to hang over my head, his firstborn—whose death, if his enemies had been successful, would've had the symbolic power to topple the family business.

Sensing her desire for more, I embellished, leaning in to whisper in her ear: Also there was some trouble with the Hong Kong Mafia.

Now that she had this shameful secret to hold over me, she felt comfortable enough to reveal that her husband, her dead husband John, had had to do something similar. He fled Europe to escape creditors after the insurance firm that he'd founded had gone belly-up, and with the help of old family friends in America, took on a new identity, rebuilding his stock from the ground up. He became another person so totally that if you had known him in Europe and then had met him again in this country, you would hardly have been able to connect the two persons.

In light of this confession, the statues around us took on a new, menacing aspect, like guards or counselors whose burning looks for circumspection went unheeded by their mistress. But this woman didn't care. She was ninety. Besides, her husband and I were both refugees and it was the guards-down admission of one compatriot to another. Perhaps, she'd even asked me to come hear confession. There were some secrets that it was time to divulge for the sake of one's health, as her fellow matrons had done by hiring me—a group that the Dowager, by virtue of great old age (hence my naming her the Dowager), seemed to sit at the head of. Ninety, she had said over the phone, laughing as much at some unknown opponent whom she'd trumped by having outlived as at herself. Clearly, she knew the joke was now on her: she was too weak to eat much—which further weakened her—and though she made a point of refusing assistance as she moved from room to room, she was clearly helpless in the face of time's aggressive decimation—her breathing was ragged and her walk, though stiffly regal, was only slightly better than a newborn learning the process at the very beginning. Ninety, she repeated as we sipped our tea. And, of course, I took this to mean: between ninety-four and ninety-eight.

Confessing also felt deliciously forbidden—a trend that went through this woman's life again and again. It had been forbidden by her family to marry her husband because at that time he was without prospects, merely another struggler unable to give evidence that he could support someone like her, who came from old New York money. It had been forbidden to cut her hair, dress in jazzy clothes, in fact it had been forbidden her to go hear jazz in places like Harlem, around which a curtain of secrecy had for good reason been drawn. It had been forbidden her to decide not to have children. But she hadn't wanted children. She was, and still continued to be, a child. She didn't want to have her enjoyment of life curtailed by a mother's routine. And did she regret this decision, now in her old age, when her few contemporaries were being rewarded with the presence of great-grandchildren? Not one bit. Her youth had been gilded. And her old age, as befitting old age, was wretched. But for either, there could've been no alternatives to those that she'd chosen. And anyway, she saw all the beautiful artwork around us—the statues, for instance, some of them Rodins—as her children. Stepchildren, she clarified. Revealing that some had been gotten on the black market by her husband. Oh, but it was worth it to go through such methods just to be able to have beauty around you every day. What methods? I asked politely. Some of them were reputed to be Nazi loot, she revealed, smiling. She paused to tease out my sympathies. How would I react to the litmus test of that word—Nazi? I barely batted an eye. And so on she went. Oh, the Jews were this and the Jews were that. They complained far too much, even long after doors had been opened to let them in. Even after she'd had to find herself accepting them as co-members. They had so much money, and could enjoy life to the hilt, so why the hell did they feel the need to make things constantly ugly by invoking history? But, she revealed under her breath, as if there could've been spies among her staff who might rat her out should the time come, some of her best friends were Jews, and she loved these "girls" dearly.

She had on a Chanel suit with a matching hat, and covering dainty hands that she wrapped around the glass almost desperately were white gloves with a single pearl on each finger.

Her face was like cigarette smoke hardened into flesh, counterpointed by dashes of color put gamely, if not always carefully, on. Her lipstick broke through the contours of her thin, lined lips, as if she'd just had spaghetti. The beauty of it all was that she had a kind of ding-y, abstracted attitude that rendered everything moot—as if she were from outer space and had had to put on the required vestments just to establish a talking start.

Her cuteness, however, stopped right at the eyes, behind which sharp calculations, rubbing up against one another, gave off telltale sparks, glinting.

She said she wanted me to "fix up her place," but she didn't care to know about the particulars. She thought maybe I could do something about her rickety health. And if not, well, hey, she wasn't trying to fool anyone. God knows ninety was like having a foot and a half already in the grave.

While we toured the premises—seven bedrooms, two dining rooms, three living rooms, three studies, two kitchens, plus countless bathrooms—she would grasp my elbows for support. I was careful never to notice or to ask after her, taking the cue of household help I could spot skulking in the rococo scenery—people who stood by in the ever-increasing chance that she should topple to the floor and need to be rescued.

She had prized possessions as other people had dust in their households. The thing that stood out was a small Modigliani—no more than eight by six inches, with a gold frame larger than the actual painting itself—that hung above a toilet in one of the bathrooms. It had its own special light, and below it, sitting on the toilet tank cover, as if in the pagan tradition of propitiating deceased relatives, was an offering of fresh flowers in a vase. Pointing to the woman in the picture with the trademark elongated, sideways eyes, she turned to me and said, She looks just like you. Right, I thought, I'm keeping notes while people unselfconsciously take a crap in front of me.

By the way, where did her husband get his money? What business did he start? I asked, adding: I hope she didn't mind my asking.

You're a nosy young man, aren't you? she asked, in a tone of Now look here! But then she revealed her bluff with an approving aside: I like that in a young man. We shared a laugh over that.

I apologized for being so blunt. But I was curious. Aside from the Modigliani and the Rodins, there hung, in one of the kitchens, beside a refrigerator, a Matisse of flowers in a glass vase, drawn with a shaky line that made the whole thing seem to vibrate.

Oh, but that's not money, she begged to differ, that's *taste*.

Her husband, she said, had been in shipbuilding. That done, she quickly steered the conversation elsewhere, as if the revelation of the source of the wealth around us immediately marked down its value. You know Suzy Yamada? she asked, having probably been misled by the things she read, in which Suzy and I had become virtual bosom buddies.

Yes, I replied.

Had she brought the name up only to bunt it about like a prized object of gossip, something from high up brought down to her level, as those other women had done? No. She knew this woman, this Suzy Yamada, before she had *become* Suzy Yamada.

The Dowager said: *She came to me when she was just starting out in society, I think she had just—she's divorced isn't she?—yes, she'd just divorced her husband you see, a no-account from what I've heard— now who could've told me? maybe she did—anyway, so she was divorced, maybe she knew he wouldn't be the ticket to what she was looking for—I don't know, maybe I'm putting this all together after the fact, perfect twenty-twenty hindsight, seeing what she's become now, it's easy to suppose that's why the divorce happened. But anyway, she was so tough, this person, pushy, yes?, yes, pushy, and it's not something I would've thought was a Japanese trait, this pushy Japanese scrabbler, that's what I thought when I first saw her, what a hard scrabbler, I said to myself, my my what a little bitch, just asking for an audience with me, that's how she put it, an "audience," my God, made me sound like the Pope! I mean I have money—who are we kidding—but at no point did I ever entertain the idea that I could be royalty, so immediately when she talked to me in those tones my suspicions went up, but curiosity got the better of me and so I agreed to meet with her. So there I was, sitting in La Grenouille across from this woman who I've only met once or twice before at the kind of big parties where even an upstart like her could be invited. She was paying she let me know from the start, and I thought of course she better pay because I realized that I was allowing myself to be seen in public with her in La Grenouille of all places which was as good as an endorsement. So she opened her mouth—I remember this so clearly, like watching someone perform on a stage—even before the soup came, she reached her hands across the table and lay them on mine, and just as she was about to say a word I pulled my hands back, just like that by instinct, and I could tell that this offended her, and I was sorry, I mean I really didn't mean to send a message, I was repulsed by her easy intimacy, sure, but I didn't mean to communicate my repulsion. But it took her no time to regain her composure and when she did, she opened her mouth once again, to smile—she was determined to get back on that stage—and seeing as I'd been frank, she decided to do the same. She admitted that I could help her and that even if I didn't owe her anything yet—the nerve!—I didn't owe her anything yet she said, but she could be of use to me in the future, so why don't we trade favors, would I let her know who she should meet, who would be good to help promote her business—and this was before it was even her business . . . Ahhh, poor woman, this person who founded the company—*

Adela P, I said.

The Dowager drew a blank at the name, looking as if I'd interrupted for no good reason.

She resumed: *Well, I suppose I should've treated this girl with more seriousness but listen, considering how long I've lived, I've seen more than my share of climbers, and most of them don't know the first thing about getting anywhere, much less keeping once they've gotten, and this girl behaved no differently, believe me, so of course I wouldn't deign to help her, would you? And so when I heard that she'd gotten top rank in the company after a few years, and had moved into a coveted building on the West Side, and then got herself into a column in H—* *that god-awful newsletter of the nouveau riche!—all in the space of less* *than five years, my God, was I the one who was revealed to be the* *know-nothing!* She laughed, her laugh quickly turning into a pro- longed coughing fit like trying to spit out something that was block- ing her windpipe. When she was done, she looked at me, her spine ramrod straight, as if daring me to register the indignity of what had just happened, and seeing that I had nothing to say, she continued. *So all within the space of five years, it's like a fucking Joan Crawford* *movie.* Again, she laughed.

I thought: Not quite. It's more like an Isuzu Yamada movie. There was a new one to add to my list: Besides *The Lower Depths* and *Throne of Blood*, I'd discovered at the Lincoln Center library a film by Kenji Mizoguchi called *Sisters of the Gion*, about two geisha sis- ters, one virtuous and the other unheedful of propriety, who lived together in the "gay" quarters, struggling to be supported by pa- trons. Guess who played the sister unheedful of propriety? This sis- ter eventually chucked out a young, financially unstable boyfriend for his boss—a man who'd come to her in the first place to warn her off the younger man, whose work habits were being made erratic by his attentions to her.

The Dowager said to me about the Suzy Yamada of the Upper West Side, And now she's having a new love affair with a prestigious man. An older man. Her trophies just keep piling up. Still, announc- ing this, she seemed to be holding something back in reserve.

First the word "love" popped into my brain—the love of my planting, my prompting. And then the name of the prestigious man Suzy'd roped more than ever revealed my connection to everything, a connection mysterious and yet with a logic that was tempting to be prised from the facts that I already had in my hands. The name the Dowager mentioned was Bill Hood.

Yes, she said. The famous novelist. Frankly, I hear he's a spoiled little princeling. I wouldn't exactly call that a catch from a personal standpoint. But from a social one, well, hell, that's like tax refund day! At least it used to be. She cackled with pleasure.

Well, why shouldn't she have snagged him? continued the Dowa- ger. He's a Don Juan, has always been, my girlfriends have known more than a few young girls he's bedded and then thrown out like so much used goods. And she's a pretty little thing, isn't she, this Suzy Yamada. Is she still pretty? she turned to ask me.

Yes, she is.

And she asked for you. Is that right?

Yes. I paid her a visit.

Well, you must be good, then. Seeing as she finally got that elusive feather in her cap.

Elusive? I asked.

The Dowager obliged: She's tried to bag him before. She's thrown him countless book parties. Escorted him to functions all over the city. As if she thought being photographed in public together was like an announcement of an engagement. But he seemed to keep bypassing her, poor dear. Until you came along, of course.

I wouldn't say that, I said. But I felt directly responsible, having guided Suzy's hands, encouraging a renewal of her amorous efforts, as it were, courtesy of Shem.

Come, come, the Dowager admonished. Like they say in the tropics: It's not the heat that'll kill you, it's the *humility*! Again she cackled, like a bird making up for its smallness by cultivating an off-putting bark. So what, she asked, did Suzy want done to her house?

She wanted to have peace.

A piece of what? she asked. Oh God, she said, calming herself after another explosive bout of cackling, it's so wonderful to have fun at somebody else's expense, wouldn't you say?

I remained mute.

This seemed to work. It prompted her into a sober recitation of recent developments that she'd withheld until now, having finally run out of jokes about Suzy Yamada.

I had had no dirt on this woman, and felt that I could get by without any. I knew that she was old, and old people were generally easy to make afraid: mention "vibrations" relating to ill health, "messages" from the dearly departed, "time ticking away," and "the need to tie things up before it's too late," and you had them eating out of your hands. As it turned out, things were even easier than I'd expected. She'd wanted to keep a tight monopoly on the talking, and so, as I turned her belongings this way and that, I hadn't been required to provide the made-up rationales behind my maneuvers.

But what I couldn't have foreseen was that this woman, who I thought would be dithery and easy to make swoon, would be the one who would have a vast store of dirt and letting me in on it would make *me* swoon.

Bill Hood, according to the Dowager, had rebounded straight into Suzy's arms from a love affair that in its first heat had drawn much envy, more so for having been hoarded away from the laser eyes of press and the public. The breakup, however, had been anything but quiet. In fact, it had turned downright catastrophic—all that secretiveness had been for nothing because the press was now having a field day over the carcass of the affair! The woman, Bill Hood's ex, had a daughter from a previous marriage to some no-account—linking her in that sense to Suzy—and this kid was the cutest thing you could hope to see, with blond curls and a highly animated face—a look perfect to lend credence to her accusations: On the strength of the moppet's word, the woman had had no choice but to file a sexual molestation charge against the esteemed writer, effectively breaking off her two-year relationship with him. Child molester: the tag had then been taken up and echoed triumphantly in the press. And its taint—in a culture that needed a steady supply of fresh evidence to vindicate its campaign of watchfulness—had been difficult, if not downright impossible, to wash off. And here was the showbiz payoff, the thing that was seen as the cruelest retaliation against a man arrogant enough to want to partake of the benefits of celebrity without offering himself up as an exhibit in exchange—a photograph of the little girl at a deposition, her eyes black-barred and her hands spaced what seemed to be a foot apart to indicate just how big Bill Hood's "you know what" was—a judgment simultaneously saluting and condemning him. The photograph circulated for a week before it was revealed that it was a "recreation" based on transcripts leaked to the press, but the public's hunger tore straight through that flimsy distinction, making a hefty profit for its perpetrator, who'd been hired by *The National Enquirer.* It had been plastered across the pages of newspapers and magazines, and referred to on television as further evidence that the end of the world as we knew it was near; or taking the form of talk-show jokes with punch lines which involved some slipping in of the words *dick* and *bone*.

I realized that I'd stopped reading the *Post* as soon as I found my-self the subject of those girls' magazines.

I asked the Dowager the name of this woman, Bill Hood's ex and the girl's mother. Of course, I anticipated a match with the answers I already had in my head. The Dowager didn't know the woman's name. Was she a Jew? Yes, said the Dowager, she couldn't be sure but she was almost certain that the woman was Jewish. I thought of the fabled Jewish princess of Shem's story, his estranged ex-wife. And the child's name? Oh no, replied the Dowager, the daughter was too young to have her name revealed.

Was the child's name Beulah? I asked, persisting.

What?

Beu-lah, I repeated.

What kind of stupid name was that? she wondered.

It was Shem's kid's name. Shem who had coached his daughter to place both hands just so to indicate something, as I sat observing from the counter of a restaurant. Big. The gesture for big. Turned into claws, the gesture for scary. Or . . . Had Bill Hood scratched the girl too? Were those among the allegations? I asked the Dowager, who replied, Yes. She looked at me with an expression of amuse-ment. So, she remarked, she had been wasting her time telling me everything. It seemed I'd heard about the case too—even I with my reputed distance from real life had been tainted by the mudslinging of the national machinery.

Oh no, I thought, the machinery was strictly local: it was Shem who was the no-account married to, and then divorced from, the woman in question, who was not Bill Hood's daughter, as Shem had originally claimed, but instead Hood's lover. It was this same woman who by leaving Shem for Bill Hood had set off a chain reaction of re-venge. What was her name? Marianna! That was it! And between her and Shem was a daughter who had helped to carry out Daddy's plan perfectly: destroying the union between Shem's ex and Shem's rival. Everything was clear, and it made my head go light.

Like the daughter, I too had been chosen to be an instrument.

My part was supposed to end in Suzy Yamada's ruin—but how did she fit into this? That hadn't become clear. And now, Suzy was with Hood, the conjoining of Shem's enemies. Was *that* the revenge?

For the Dowager, the recitation was merely a detached way to look over the folly of those who formed her set, knowing so much more than they did and yet being unable to help or effect change— exactly like rehearsing for a posthumous life. And speaking of which, I once more felt connected to occult things, recognizing myself as the representative of shadowy people somehow connected with the dead or who were themselves dead, people with only half- clear plans who had picked me as their agent—Adela P, Rowley, Shem.

Did I already know everything? the Dowager asked, disap- pointed. She'd presumed that since I'd been on vacation I would need to be yanked back into the world, told what was what, and be- cause this was a role she delighted in taking with her friends, why not do the same with me?

Please go ahead, I implored, assuring her that I knew nothing, nothing at all.

The case against Bill Hood, continued the Dowager, had been dropped owing to an adroit move on Mr. Hood's part: He couldn't have chosen a better moment to be afflicted with cancer.

With no desire to involve her daughter any further, or to exces- sively punish a man she believed to have been served his just sen- tence, the ex-girlfriend dropped the charges. Thank goodness for her, only preliminary interviews with the child had been under- taken and the Public Prosecutor was only just about to be involved.

Still, the damage had been done: Bill Hood's world cracked: on one side a small core of steadfast fans, in whose eyes the brilliance of Hood's work still cast a blinding gleam; and on the other—visibly more crowded—the remainder of the public, headed by a vocal few who voiced their disgust in every conceivable pulpit, until the spec- tacular culmination was reached: a campaign to have Hood's books banned in high schools across several states met with resounding success. One moment planted firmly in the canon, the next—enact- ing their author's fate in the afterlife—burning atop a pyre. Shem's revenge was turning out to be on the entire culture for having paid obeisance to Hood instead of to Shem. A struggling writer's revenge for having been overlooked, consigned to drone work while his archrival held in one hand acclaim, and in the other, an income of six figures. Shem had exposed the culture as the laughable yo-yo it had always been, its exaltation of Bill Hood as nothing but a swooning acquiescence to ambition, to bigness, and its current shunning, nothing more than the expected response to seeing bigness cut down to size by scandal. An ex-husband's revenge for having been turned over for another. A father's for having been supplanted. Do you still love Daddy? he'd asked Beulah. If you want to prove it, you must help Daddy by doing one thing, but it can only be between you and Daddy, all right? . . .

Was the cancer real? I asked, and seeing the look on the Dowager's face, I knew I was only echoing her thoughts.

Apparently so, she replied.

So Bill Hood, broken and ill, was now with Suzy Yamada.

The thing that further mystified me was: How could Suzy Yamada, a woman well known for her tireless social climbing, stand calmly by while the world around her—whose good opinion she'd always courted assiduously—was tearing down her beloved and, by association, herself? Surely Bill Hood had become an unwanted weight around the neck? But maybe there was a kind of prestige to be had in being the nurse and companion of a great man in his dying days. Or even more preposterously, maybe the woman was in love.

The Dowager seemed to have read my mind. She said, I'm willing to bet Mr. Hood's days with Suzy Yamada are numbered. And I don't mean because of his illness. When she realized, said the Dowager, the complete intractability of social mores, and the hunger for the spectacle of punishment that attended the violation of these mores, a hunger the public would go to great lengths to satisfy—as soon as she realized there was no escape from these timeworn things, Suzy Yamada would drop Bill Hood like something hot to the touch.

Or—she offered an alternative scenario—Bill Hood might just rise to the occasion, turning the sad tatters of his recent life into a stirring defense of his own innocence. A work that might take the form, like his best, of a thinly veiled autobiographical novel. And if that were the case, Suzy's hospitality might pay off after all.

But the knowing tone of her voice put a healthy bet on the former possibility triumphing over the latter. It was the sad fact of a world of which she was one of the leading arbiters.

At last, the tale was over. I realized I had one hand to my heart, as if I was overcome. I took this hand down—the same hand that had officiated at Suzy's—to mark a piece of music coming to its end.

Her next appointment came in as I was being escorted out the door—a short black guy whom I'd seen playing the piano and singing standards to raise funds for public television. Oh, by the way, said the Dowager to this man, this is Master Chao, my Feng Shui man. But in her mouth it sounded like she was saying, This is my mystery insure man.

Had she even paid any attention to my renovations? It seemed she'd merely wanted to study the expression on my face as she narrated Suzy Yamada's defeat. Did she want me to go back to Suzy and tell Suzy that she, the Dowager, or more accurately, in light of her revelations, her proximity to the information at hand, the Empress, had taken pleasurable note of Suzy's recent misfortunes, intimating that Suzy, despite a superficial ascent, could still be stopped by powers wielded by the Dowager? Had I merely been called to serve as messenger between a ruler and an upstart? In which case, why reveal the chink in her own armor, the artwork bought on the black market—was it a frequent enough occurrence in her circle not to warrant concealment?

Hello, said the man, giving me a look I was used to by now—the look of sizing up a special case.

We shook hands.

He had a reputation for attracting capacity houses in venues with names like Carlyle, Algonquin, Oak Room, Rainbow Room—places with velvet interiors like the lining of a coffin, and music to match: soporific and tinkly like an airport bar send-off to passengers bound for the afterlife. It was said that he knew five hundred songs by memory and could play any standard in the existing repertory upon request. And how was his voice? It was growly from overuse, but not in any sense soulful. And it was neither melodic nor, for its unmelodiousness, particularly interesting. But everybody seemed to love him because loving him was like scoring points for "sophistication." The songs he sang conjured a return to civilized, mellower, certainly more elegant times—a respite from the confusing to-and-fro of city life, which, with its emphasis on youth and speed, its rewarding of both, had become a vulgarian's marketplace.

Well, if people were already so eager to applaud, why bother to get better, right?

After we exchanged handshakes, he left for the living room, where, presumably, he would be having iced tea with the Dowager—was that the only thing she imbibed?

This was the part where she was supposed to hand over the money, but instead she said: The check will be in the mail for you. I was too stunned to argue. Where would she mail this check? She didn't have my address. There was the Filipina maid again. She was spying on me from behind a corner. Would she say anything? That was the last thing I saw as the Dowager closed her door, and I realized that I'd just been scammed. Fucking piece of turd, I thought, though I didn't know whether I was referring to her or to myself. Still, hadn't her information been payment enough?

Barney from the Savoy, whose face I failed to register, passed me by on Forty-second and then made a one-eighty. Hey, you, he said.

It had taken me a moment to realize who he was. In broad daylight, he looked so much older and tireder. I had to push back an impulse to ask him, à la Chao, what was wrong, ready, of course, to rattle off an instant cure.

How are you? he asked.

I'm OK.

Looking respectable, he judged. Then relayed a piece of info he'd been holding on to for a while: That Indian guy you talked to at the bar, he began.

What Indian guy?

That Indian guy, he said. Young. About this tall. You know, one long eyebrow.

I don't know any Indian guy. You saw me talking to an Indian guy?

Yeah, he said.

Fuck, I thought. How was I going to get out of this one?

Well, continued Barney, he's been looking for you. He says to tell you he needs to talk. So call him.

You know his name? I asked.

Gurinder, he replied.

See, I don't know any Gurinder. So right there, that tells me you've got the wrong guy.

I *saw* you.

Wait, I said, miming thoughtfulness. Oh, *that* guy!

Yeah, said Barney, refusing to be fooled. That guy.

I don't know him, I said. He was a drug connection, you know. He wanted to talk. And I thought it'd be rude to just split. So I stayed for a bit. Really, I don't know him.

Well, he wants you to call.

I don't have his number, I said, lying.

Can't help you there, said Barney, who'd had enough of my show. Later, he said, walking away. He didn't make a comment about my not having shown up in a while. And I stood there, doing a weak wave of farewell.

I went back to work with renewed effort. There were still so many rich New Yorkers to be separated from their money—rich people who, I had to admit, were almost all white. This put me face to face with the enveloping extent of my racial grievance.

After the Dowager, I picked up a sheet Shem had filled with the names of prospective clients. The entire list could've been given a heading of Please Help, and again I saw many hands reaching out to try to grab a piece of me. I did a blind man's trick of pointing without looking. I phoned the woman whose name my finger had landed on. Her place was in midtown, on East Fifty-seventh.

But before my visit, I called up Shem's "professional source." This time, I met him face to face, behind Shem's back. I explained that this would be an ongoing procedure and that the relationship from now on would be between him and me, not between him and Shem. I made sure to emphasize its potential for profit.

We met in Grand Central, underneath a ceiling that had been newly restored to its former glory—but who could look up, what with the swiftness of the crowds and the reverberation of even the most unobtrusive step adding to my nervousness and confusion as I scanned the faces for a flicker of recognition? I had described myself to him, an Asian man in black jacket and pants, but was shocked to discover that I blended far too easily into the crowd: men and women, Asian and non-Asian, were dressed all in black, conflating auras of business success and prosperity with a palpably dreary sense of obligatory mourning: but for what? And then I remembered: Oh right, it's the end of the world. Still, perhaps tipped off by my not too subtle pantomime of I'm-Waldo-where-are-you?, the kid was able to spot me. That was what he turned out to be, a nerdy boy who looked fresh out of high school: a fact he would neither confirm nor deny. He had to keep pushing back thick-framed doofus glasses from a large nose, and was wearing a Charlie Brown T-shirt of alternating horizontal bands of yellow and black, matched with a pair of Dockers khakis. On his feet were dirty suede Pumas long past their original color, whatever that was. He had to train in from somewhere out of the city, he said. The suburbs. Did he still live with his parents? Again, he wouldn't answer, just smiling. Looking at his badly laundered pants, where dried-and-set stains could be observed near the hem and along the outer seams, I thought: No, he lives alone. Smile, he said, playing to potential observers by giving me an embrace. We're friends from school, he whispered into my ear.

Of course, I replied.

We disappeared into the noise and the frenetic scissoring of the crowd, and emerged a few moments later in a coffee shop on the other side of the station, seated across from one another. I wondered which bar Shem could've recruited Charlie Brown at, but we didn't talk about Shem. And he didn't ask me what I intended to use the information he was providing for. He showed the kind of behavior common to those whose primary interaction—and level of comfort—was with machinery. He dribbled coffee onto his chin. He didn't wipe. His gray Pumas pumped up and down on the floor, betraying both his nerves and his inability to deal in anything other than computer speed. He was unable to make small talk.

Before giving me the dirt on my new client, he explained how easy it was to break into someone's records. He talked with the pride of an expert. There was not even hacking involved in this case. He was simply able, by identifying himself as a pharmacist, in one case, and as somebody from the IRS in the other, to come up with this woman's prescription history and her bank records of the last nine months. He smiled at the ease with which he was able to penetrate the imagined wall of security governing all our lives. In other cases, he continued, educating me but with just enough to keep me dependent on him, hacking involved breaking through encryptions, hurdling past the need for passwords, etc.—but, he said, snapping his fingers, he'd devised programs that got him easily past those.

This woman, he said, handing over the fruits of his research, gets monthly transfusions of money from an outside source, which I finally identified as an ex-husband paying child support for two kids and alimony. As for her medical records, there's nothing that's out of the ordinary, except . . . Around this time a year ago, there were a lot of prescriptions for sleeping pills and painkillers—and not over-the-counter, mind you, but really strong, potentially-fatal-if-overdosed-on stuff. So, I thought, depression. But she hadn't been going to a shrink or anyone like that for close to a year. But suddenly I came upon a visit that she made to a surgeon coinciding with the temporary increase in those painkiller prescriptions, and this doctor is—are you ready?—a plastic surgeon. She had a nose job and a boob job.

Thank you, I said, sliding over a plain white envelope filled with five one-hundred-dollar bills.

He looked in and, satisfied, put the envelope into a back pants pocket. He got up and said, You know where to find me.

I reminded him, Shem doesn't know about this.

Who? he asked, smiling. He turned his back on me and I watched him walking away with bowlegs and no ass and a stooped posture that definitely betrayed his devotion to his computer.

Preparing for the woman on Fifty-seventh, I tried what was for me a bold move. Instead of a white shirt, I went in a blue one. My pants were still the same black. In the mirror, I looked like any other guy on the subway, on his way to the office. This was my dream, after all, I reminded myself: to resemble everyone else, and avoid being singled out for ridicule, the immigrant's fear of embarrassment enlarged out of all proportion. What I'd always believed was that the world, keying in to the frequency of unease and unbelonging that radiated so strongly in my heart, would do the only thing that was right and grant me my wish: Point at the sucker and laugh! So was this the revenge? The preemptive move of laughing first before anyone else laughed? But no, I wasn't laughing at myself. It was them I was laughing at, turning the tables on people I was more than convinced would be my tormentors if given the slightest chance. I was the one who was pointing. Look at their lives! Look at the tacky pieces of furniture and accessories given the patina of class by outrageous prices and hoodwinky brand names! Look at the expenditures, the easeful living that was like hacking off a limb and replacing it with a wheel that needed to be constantly greased.

The woman who lived on East Fifty-seventh had very tasteful, subdued decor. There was nothing that I could point to and laugh at. As it turned out, the laugh would be on me. She asked me to sit while she tied up other business in another room. But when she returned after an interval, it wasn't her at all, but instead, miraculously, someone who I thought belonged safely in the precincts of another, bypassed life—a woman whose voice still sometimes detonated inside my ears with the vehemence of childhood nightmares. At first, seeing this woman, I thought what an odd coincidence that I should be meeting her here, at the home of another client. And then, as she continued to walk toward me, her eyes burning, it slowly dawned on me that that had been the plan all along: that I'd been drawn in on the pretext of helping somebody else when all the while a trap was being set. I opened my mouth but could utter no sound. Instead, I took a long gulp of air, preparing for a monologue of recrimination. I saw my face transformed into a dartboard.

Cardie Kerchpoff didn't disappoint. Regarding me intensely, hatefully, with red-rimmed eyes that belied the fact that she had the advantage over me, she opened her mouth and out spewed the venom that she'd been waiting all these months to release.

Listen, you fuck! she said, finger thrust into the air with the frantic electricity that seemed to shoot straight down into her body from the fried red hair spiraling atop her sweating scalp.

My only response was to rear back on my seat.

I got a Feng Shui guy to come to my place, you fucking piece of shit! A *real* Feng Shui guy! And you know what he told me? He said that every fucking thing that you did—that's right, *you*! you little fake! you piece of shit!—everything that you did was wrong! Intentionally, harmfully wrong! You fucked me up! You little— She couldn't find the word that she was looking for and so gave a kick instead. That proved to be a weak punctuation, so she did it again.

Ow, I said. I had the presence of mind to stand up. Two pools of nervous sweat fanned out from my armpits. I knew it was because I'd deviated from my white-black armor that this was happening to me.

[handwritten margin note: Chao is superstitious]

You fuck! she said, putting her arms in front of her to strike. She got the side of my face. Fucking liar! Why?

The woman whose house we were in, peeking from a door that connected the living room to someplace small, like a secret chamber, saw that everything was going according to plan and promptly removed herself.

Why? boomed Cardie Kerchpoff—and this was her cue to break into tears. Her shoulders heaved and the sudden violence of the act, instead of giving her release, simply fueled her craziness. She screamed. Beat her chest. And then struck me again. This last thing took all the energy out of her, and she collapsed onto the couch. I quickly moved away, trying to find the front door. Seeing this cowardly act, she rushed to prevent my exit.

We looked at each other, two frightened things with a previously thin connection suddenly turned life or death. Here I was, confronted with the pathetic proof of the success of my revenge—a revenge which suddenly felt like it had nothing to do with me, but instead was something I'd walked in on at just the right moment, adding my own tiny pinch of ill will to something that was already preparing to boil over long before I'd showed up.

The woman was jittery, unable to successfully release her anger despite having found the target so close at hand. At one point, she raised a glass vase, ready to aim it at me, and then at the very last moment, recognizing her surroundings, she put the thing back down.

Why?! she repeated.

Why what? I asked, timidly. All the while I was trying to work the handle of the front door with my hands behind my back.

Why did you do that to me?

I'm sorry about your husband, I told her, as if this was the appropriate response.

This rendered her speechless. It was as if what I'd said was some kind of code marking my triumphant duping. Her sickly pale face could be seen giving in to a terror so big that she was forced to change tactics in the middle of everything. She quickly moved away, but didn't turn her back on me. The way she was acting, it occurred to me that she believed my very physical presence possessed the power to do harm and that, by courting my disfavor, she was only making ready for more bad luck. Oh God oh God, she muttered in a loop, disappearing. After a moment, I discovered her on the couch. She wouldn't look up at me, continuing to sob into her knees.

Do you have the key to the front door? I asked.

I kept repeating my question only to be greeted by her widow's wail. The corpse of the husband in question was not on the premises, but rather inside her imagination, a vision accompanied by the soundtrack of her contemporaries' malicious buzzing. That she'd been found wanting as a woman and had been replaced. This connected with the Indian nanny's criticism of her—a tale revealed at a very different meeting, when she'd still been on top of the world. I tried to remind myself that this was the same woman whose hatefulness had needed this very remedy. I had nothing to be guilty about. I was half wishing that she would reawaken and continue to spit out her awful words.

Seeing me towering over Cardie, the friend came in to intercede. This time I directed my question to her: Where's the key to the front door?

She didn't reply. She went to Cardie, and taking her up, made me see the face I thought I'd wanted to see. Unbecoming streaks went up and down her cheeks, and her forehead was wrinkled like an improperly dried garment. But it was her eyes—with that dead look of absolute, sobering hopelessness—that I immediately recognized. With those eyes, she could've fit right in at the Savoy.

Where's the key? I repeated.

Can I let him go now? the friend asked Cardie, who didn't reply.

I'm going to call the police, I threatened.

Are you? the friend asked with humbling flippancy.

What more do you want from me? I asked Cardie. Finally, I got her to look up at me. Why? she rasped out.

Unmoved, I repeated myself: I want to leave.

There was a thread of snot hanging from one nostril. She wiped it away. Beseeching. Baleful. I looked at her as I would at any object put in front of my eyes which was not the object I wanted to look at. It was clear that I was the victor. I'm going to lose my babies, she said. How can I go on?

Are you going to open the door? I asked the friend, who still did not move. Suddenly inflamed, I blurted out at Cardie Kerchpoff, You're an evil, selfish, backward woman and all that you've gotten is exactly what you deserve! You and your hateful little diatribe at dinner about how difficult it is to find good help! Disgusting! I said, though it felt neither cathartic nor triumphant—not as I'd imagined it would be in the daydreams I'd concocted during the first heat of my disdain.

Cardie put both hands to her ears. It was pathetic, my trying to put the screws to this woman who was already a discarded rag. There was no missing the white flag of surrender that flapped high above her head. Still, the friend standing there like a fucking statue, I was egged on. The sweat beneath my armpits was quickly drying. How much did you think you could fucking get away with, living the way you did, boasting about your station, did you think that you had this fucking free pass, the way you stepped on other people's rights and then made a joke about it to people of your own class, sharing your fucking privilege? Using your fucking privilege to look down on ordinary people? Did you think that Feng Shui could repair your ugly soul? Did you—

Get him out! screamed Cardie to the friend, who took out keys from her pockets to show me.

But no, I was on a roll now. I wanted to hurt this woman more than anything else in the world. The looks of her; the absolute defeat in her posture: childless, husbandless; the lack of character implied in such a willing surrender to her fate—everything needed to be underlined. You disgust me! I'm not fake! I shouted. You were only paying some other guy who would back up your arguments!

Looking for somebody else to blame. That's how you see the world! Well, the world is telling you you're wrong!

Get him outttt!

The friend said, You have to go.

I disregarded her. Under my feet grew a small platform, and I was just beginning to warm to the task. Your husband didn't leave you because of me! It was because of you! Take a good look at yourself! You're pathetic! Why blame me for what he did! He was cheating behind your back even before I came along! How convenient of you to blame me instead!

She wouldn't put up with it for another second and rushed out of the room.

You deserve everything you get! I screamed after her. A door could be heard slamming. I'm not responsible for you! I said. I did nothing wrong!

Please, said the friend, who touched me on the elbow.

I yanked my arm away. Gave her a look to say, *Now* you're opening the door.

She saw me to the entrance, and before being closed off, I asked her, still pushed along on the momentum of my righteous indignation: It wasn't a good idea to ask me here in the first place, was it?

I needed a drink. The only place I could think of was the Savoy. I didn't want to go but what choice did I have? The Savoy, after all, was like family, who only revealed their usefulness in dire circumstances like this. I rushed there like having been fired from a cannon. My hands were shaking. I knew that I needed to cram as many appointments as I could into my schedule—make as much money as I still could—before Cardie Kerchpoff, coming to her senses, started shrilling attention my way.

There it was—the grinning mouth of the Savoy. I could taste the backward slide in my mouth. Thank God Neil suddenly appeared out of nowhere to rescue me. Hey, man, he said. He steered me to an abandoned, boarded-up lot. To get in, we had to squeeze between two loose planks, from which bills of advertisement had been clawed off. I was so relieved not to be in the Savoy that it took me a while to realize how many shadows there were around us.

Why haven't you called me? asked Neil.

Call you? I stammered.

I've been trying to reach you.

Really? I didn't know, I lied.

You owe me, he said.

What do you mean?

The job I did for you.

Didn't I pay you? I asked.

Didn't I do a good job? he asked.

Of course. You did good.

OK. I need more money.

I paid you exactly what we agreed.

You're not one of those guys who likes seeing somebody else beg, are you? he asked, a threat in his voice.

I don't have money.

He laughed. You haven't even heard me say how much.

I don't have it.

Who do you think you're talking to? he asked, clapping me one.

Oh, I'm sorry, I sniggered back. Am I talking to Neil or to Gurinder?

I'm in trouble, man. Please. Buddy to buddy. All I need is a couple of thousand. You'll never hear from me again. Promise.

A couple of thousand?! I don't have that kind of money.

Are you sure? he asked airily, giving me time to reconsider.

What are you trying to say?

Because you know, he said, looking right at me with an expression like he'd run out of bullshit to toss back, I could just go up to that lady whose house you asked me to visit. And maybe she might have the money I need. In exchange for information about who wanted her house trashed.

My hand moved so quickly it was as if it wasn't connected to the rest of me. Before I knew it, there was the switchblade at Neil's cheek.

What's your problem? he asked, shaking.

What's yours?

I just told you.

Well, I replied, I ain't the solution.

Two thousand, man, he said, that's all I'm asking. It's nothing to you. He was sweating. Come on. Take that thing away.

I did, slowly. What do you need two thousand for?

To split New York.

Who's after you?

The feds, he said.

What the fuck did you do?

The tours. They think the things I made up are actually real, that the places I named are actually gonna be bombed. He laughed. They think I could rat out people.

What people?

You know, the *terrorists*. Fuck! Meanwhile the real terrorists are running around doing whatever they want.

I'll give you five hundred, I said.

Five hundred?!

No more, I said.

God, man! How'm I supposed to make a getaway with five hundred?

Take it or leave it.

You're the only one I know who can help! Don't you get it?

How about your cousins?

Are you joking?!

How about the tour people? I asked.

You're the only one, he said. I ain't fooling. Please. Two thousand, man.

I don't have that kind of money.

Who the fuck do you think you're kidding?! He spat on the ground.

I came to my senses. You know what? I asked him. I think you can come up with two thousand on your own.

Wait, wait, what're you saying?

I left him glowering in the middle of the vastly rubbled lot, the sky above us closing in to squeeze out any remaining light. I skipped the Savoy—and then I realized: Neil had saved me from going back. Surely that was worth something? So I retraced my steps. I would help him. But there was only the emptiness of the scene. What a strange sight, I realized—here was prime real estate untouched by developers. It had the aura of sacredness, of benevolence that attached to failed things. And a clearer definition of failure I couldn't think of. Torn down and neglected, shuttered from view, passed every day by thousands who had no idea of its existence. How could it remain the way it was, bearing witness to the New York of long ago—well, at least to the New York of last year, or at most two, three years ago? Surely, it was only a matter of time before redevelopment claimed it, and with it, right next door, the Savoy? Seen in this twilit way, I knew I had to pay the Savoy a visit, like final respects.

I walked in. There was a smattering of general laughter that seemed to have been waiting for some focus, which I immediately provided as I entered.

30

The cane was once more an ornament to hang on a wall. Showing me her improved condition, Preciosa even skipped up and down. We were at the fountain in Lincoln Center, the glass facade of the theater behind us. We had been celebrating the last of her physical therapy sessions, as well as her having cruised past money problems—all debts miraculously paid.

At a diner close to home, I ordered broiled Boston scrod. This item was listed on a page I wouldn't have even considered in my former life. The fish cost seventeen dollars—and it was the cheapest thing on that page! Sure, it came with soup plus a baked potato and a serving of vegetables, but these things were undistinguished and small-portioned.

Preciosa had vegetarian lasagna, which cost just a little less. We both knew we were eating beyond our means. But this was a celebration, after all.

The fish, when it came, was, thank God, a hefty thing. Still, it looked no different from the other, cheaper things I'd been used to:

fluffy white flesh with an outer layer charred brown by having been painted with grease and then stuffed into heat. It sat in the middle of a pool of butter and lemon juice. Each piece came off in discrete sections—so perfectly even and geometric as to seem made by hand. And the flesh, when you put it into your mouth and then started chewing, pushed right back. And suddenly, of course, I could taste the seventeen dollars, each bite richer than the last. And this was my favorite part: there were no bones!

What was Boston scrod? What did it look like as a thing swimming in water? My knowledge didn't extend beyond the fact that it was the cheapest item of seafood—well, the rainbow trout was the cheapest, but *that*, said the waiter, came with bones.

My connection to what I was putting inside my mouth was several steps removed from the original thing that it was. It was only "food": the sound of which conjured boxes, packets, playground things of bright plastic.

The early work of gutting and fileting that would render the fish unrecognizable from its original state had already been done. While I sat there with the stoic Preciosa, who looked like a beautiful cigar store Indian, somebody was cooking what I'd ordered. And soon it would be presented to me in a mound, as a shape nice on the eye. Biting into it, I would encounter it as texture—the fluffiness of it, the crispness of the outer skin—and as several flavors riding on the tip of peeling layers of flesh—I could taste lemon, pepper, the sweetness of onions only slightly caramelized, some kind of grease. It was something man-made just for my consumption. Words on a menu: Boston scrod, sixteen ninety-five; reading which, the brain began its tabulations of so much dry information—how many calories? rich in which nutrients? and did it suit my particular craving of the day? This was what it was to be alive. To focus the bulk of your thinking, your concern, your brain-picturing elsewhere: not to think of the fish as a fish, but as a conduit to pleasure, to comfort, to the filling of a need, like having punched a jukebox selection. Not to think of the man as a man, but rather as the conduit to things from heaven made available by the expenditure of cash. To think of him as like a lightning rod, one finger in the far reaches of the firmament, while his feet were plunked right down on the ground, inside your home, to conduct whatever electricity could be stolen from God straight to you. And I was just like the clients I made fun of, with no connection to anything except an overwhelming desire to be made comfortable—skin peeled, bones removed . . .

Did Preciosa ever think about going back to the Philippines? I asked. Only a beat later did I realize that my subtext was: Life here had spiraled out of control, and perhaps, the Philippines, that place of childhood simplicities, would be better.

Not until recently, Preciosa replied.

Why? What happened recently to make her change her tune?

Nothing, she replied. It was just that she was getting so much older, and it was getting harder and harder to keep up the fiction that she had something to gain by living in this country, that she could give something back, or could be made to feel productive—not that she'd ever been. She barely scraped by.

She must've come to America for some reason?

A faraway look came into her eyes. The story behind the look, however, whatever it was that was taking her back, would not be divulged.

Did she come here to fulfill dreams?

What dreams? she asked.

To be an actress?

Why did you come here? she asked me instead.

Followed my parents, I replied.

Why did they come?

They wanted a better life. This was how it always ended: at the wall conjured by those words, true though they were. What did those words really suggest except that the life being led was suddenly made intolerable by news of another life available elsewhere? News that revealed the first life for the unnecessary sacrifice that it was. The images of this good life, this better life that existed on the other side of a line suddenly drawn by knowledge, were at the same time fuzzy and vivid: It was the vividness of a foreground detail in a photograph, with the background turned out of focus and made, in effect, for lack of a better word, dreamlike. So we saw objects clearly, but had no idea of their true context, what was behind them. It was only that these foreground details that we kept our eyes on represented, for us—my family and me—luxury. The *idea* of luxury. That was the most important thing for us, who believed so strongly in the categorization "Third World."

What were these objects, these images? Wall-to-wall carpeting, for one. To walk on softness, coolness. On something manufactured to go nature one better, something that absorbed each step and cushioned it, like felt, or velvet. *That*, in our minds, was true wealth. (It would take me a long time to acquire a preference for wood floors. To see that as being out of the ordinary and, therefore, better.) The people in so many Hollywood movies seemed to go in and out of a series of carpeted rooms.

Mostly, though, I remember having been dazzled by brand names which wealthier school friends, when they invited me to their homes, would take out and make a show of: General Electric, Sunbeam, Hoover, Proctor-Silex, Pfizer, Zenith. They were all a shorthand for beauty, for quality, things that wouldn't break—as our appliances often did. That, for the longest time, had been my family's going definition of a better life: to own things that took a while to malfunction.

And, of course, look at me today: what did those names signify except an earlier, younger, stupider self transcended, an existence I'd have to reach so far back in memory for that it automatically achieves a mythic, a hallucinatory quality—perhaps it never even happened at all.

In the bathroom at the Port Authority, there had been a hyperactive automatic hand dryer which was a Proctor-Silex. I remembered laughing to myself when I saw it, like a secret joke between two different versions of myself, both of whom recognized the words "Proctor-Silex" finally for their true, their hidden meaning, which was: as a shorthand for all the changes that are bound to happen in the process from wanting to get there to finally getting there, the process from dreaming the dream to eventually getting it—or some would say, killing it.

31

I had to buy new shoes. The soles of the Florsheims had worn out mysteriously quickly. I hadn't even had them for a full year. I'd been told that I was a foot-dragger, but surely eight months of intermittent foot-dragging wasn't sufficient to wear down those shoes? And what did I have to drag my feet about—hadn't my life changed enough to require another set of steps? Still, there they were, soles that looked like paper. The new ones I got somewhere else. I could afford to do better now—soles that would not only withstand the ball-and-chain tendencies of my feet but would be soft and pliant enough to double as sneakers: I needed to be able to dash free in an instant from the people who were already after me. That Cardie Kerchpoff had yet to show up was only because she was still waterlogged with grief. The moment sobriety came, oh you can bet she would emerge with wings on her back and wheels for feet. Oh, she would love to burn me. The red hair on her head was there for some reason, after all.

Because of my new shoes, I kept staring down as I walked. And when I looked back up, it was like confronting a new place, a city which shared in the newness of my new shoes. And the sky! This wasn't a town known for its light, for anything above your head that wasn't man-made. But today, all that didn't matter. The gray of the buildings didn't seem too gray, and the blue in the sky was just enough to set off the sun, the clouds, the yellow and orange of the sidewalk trees—announcing winter just around the corner.

It was in this spirit that I once more laid eyes on Brian Q, who at first I didn't recognize, because the last time I'd seen him, he was crying—and now, here he was, the walking embodiment of the passage of seasons. He was smiling. He was the same roly-poly guy with the bookish, old-making glasses, his goatee stuck to his knobby chin like a starting gesture of transformation that the rest of his face refused to heed. He had on a caramel coat that was unbuttoned to reveal a light blue shirt and loose-fitting khakis. On his feet were brown shoes that looked new. Two pairs of new feet facing each other: here we were, brought together by fate to tie up unfinished business. Nervously, I stopped him.

Oh my God, he said. Master, I didn't even see you.

And the thought that entered my mind was: I could've just walked on.

But then you're the one with the eyes, he continued. You see everything.

I didn't know how to take this, so I remained mute.

Well, he said but couldn't go on, as stuck for words as I was.

How are you, Brian? I finally asked, dreading the reply I was sure he would, despite his jovial exterior, give.

I'm fine, Master. I was just— I was on my way to— Listen, he said. He took me by the elbow. I had no choice but to follow. Where would we go? But it was only to a bench in front of a large outdoor sculpture that was two blobs of white joined together by a thick black cylinder, like a barbell the size of a house. We sat down. Office workers with the look of momentary surprise on their faces—being reminded that sunlight and fresh air existed—surrounded us. Some were talking to one another. Others smoking. They all looked like people I, Chao, could help. But nobody saw me.

Master, began Brian Q.

Please, Brian, it's William.

But he persisted in calling me Master, as if he knew better. Master—

I preempted this man whose story I knew entirely too much of. No more talk about herpes. So I said, as if he'd already finished: I'm sorry, Brian.

He was perplexed. For what, Master? he asked.

For what happened to you. I'm so sorry.

No, no, don't apologize. All that's behind me.

I'm so glad to hear it, I told him, though I was skeptical. I couldn't help stealing a glance at his crotch.

In fact . . . he started.

I could already tell what he was going to say: I've gone back to the only thing I know. I've jumped into my work with renewed energy. And the money I've since made—wow!—it's enough to correct the glitches and then some!

But Brian Q did something that was a first. Of the people I'd met as Chao, he was the only one who did this. He *surprised* me. Everyone else behaved more or less according to type, according to the idea of them that was the popular idea, the—well, the census profile. Just as, in their eyes, I did. I guess we were all carrying out a polite campaign to keep things as they were. Not trouble the waters. To say that these things had been graphed out by people who'd preceded us, and we were, by following form, by not rebelling, only doing the simpler, the smarter thing: What we thought of as society was founded on obedience to these tenets, after all. But Brian Q put me to shame.

I've founded this organization, Master, he told me.

An organization? I asked.

It's a charity group that collects donations for AIDS patients in Manhattan. People can give money or clothes or food. We solicit. And then we warehouse, and then distribute. We have corporate sponsors, the entire basement of a new building in midtown where the work is done. We have trucks. The whole nine yards. So that's what I do every Wednesday. In fact, today! He laughed.

I smiled at him, dumbfounded.

Not that I'm needed. He laughed again. I mean the place practically runs itself. I just make an appearance every now and then. You know, the guy the charity's named for. A—what do you call that?

Figurehead, I said.

Right. Figurehead. Well, I didn't want to call it after myself, but then my mother said, Why should you be embarrassed about doing good in *this* world? He smiled. And taking my hands in his and rubbing them warmly, as if cued by my sudden shaking, said: I have you to thank for this.

I didn't know what to say. His charity, which had sprung up out of nowhere, made me ashamed. I was the one who was supposed to provide the surprises, but here I sat with a buzz inside my head. The guy had big hands, almost twice the size of mine. Soon my hands were getting overwarm, so I slid them out of his grasp. And then when the buzz subsided, I formulated my first credible thought: He's doing this for a tax write-off. And then I thought: You're a Catholic, why should you be taken aback by this pattern of sin and then repent—repentance taking the form of a pendulum swing to the farthest side? Give it time, the pendulum would swing right back.

After my, you know, my problem—his voice lowered conspiratorially—my life just went to pieces. I didn't know what to do. I know I must've come across as a crazy man to you then. I'm sorry.

Please don't apologize, I said.

No. I'm sure I must've frightened you away. That's why you didn't come. I mean you came, but those other calls after that—I—I was at the bottom, Master. You have to believe me.

Did you, uh, did you— I didn't even have the strength to mention it.

The witch doctor? Yes, I did.

And did it help?

He replied, I knew you were just telling me to do something just so I could do it and finally relax. But I did it. And you know what, Master? You were right. I had to do it.

But you didn't believe? I asked.

I knew that it was a, a symbol, you know—action had to be taken, and I took it. But the thing itself, I'm sorry, Master. I believed in *you*, don't get me wrong. But this, this thing . . . But afterward,

I felt so much peace, I couldn't tell you. And in this peace, I realized . . . Oh God!

What? Was he late? But no, it was only to emphasize the bigness of his epiphany that he said it.

I realized that I needed to do something, that being so close to nothing for the first time in my life had made me understand how fortunate I've always been, and that maybe one of the reasons my life had always felt so screwed up—you know, the hair, the girls, or girl in this case, my deadend work—was because I was always taking and never giving back. And that was my realization—I had to give back. That was the lesson I was being taught. I had to find some way to give back. I mean, I could have chosen to see it either as a lesson or as a midlife crisis. So I chose the first. He laughed. *But I didn't know what to do for the longest time. What was the solution to my problems? Why had they happened to me? One day I decided to devote a whole day to meditating. I unplugged the phone, pulled the shades down, didn't eat, didn't do anything but* focus. *In my mind, I kept running the same word over and over. I thought: herpes, herpes, herpes. Like if I said it enough times it would lead me to where I needed to go, right? After all, it'd happened to me. All I needed to do was figure out its meaning. Didn't you yourself say so? "Things happen to you for a reason." OK, so herpes. What was herpes? Then I thought: Sex. Sexual. Illness. Shame. Abandonment. AIDS. And that was it! I'd made the connection. I had to do this thing. It took me two weeks tops, by then we were accredited as a legitimate charity, all I had to do was find the right people to help. And getting them was easier than I'd imagined. I spoke to friends, and they spoke to their friends. And pretty soon there we all were. All looking for the same outlet. And we were like a, a family. And this is what we do every Wednesday—today!* He smiled.

Think of it. The basic ingredient: a vain-with-nothing-to-be-vain-about, spoiled young banker, wanting to extend his uneventful bachelorhood by holding on to his hair. His character? Something built on not having to encounter much resistance, hardship. What happens when he meets up with debilitating herpes (getting lucky only to get unlucky)? From comedy to tragedy, right? End of story, right? Write him off: the clown stumbles, leave him with his ass on the ground. The surprise, the shame-making (to me) surprise of it all was that though this was indeed the path taken, there would jut out from it a new branch, a way up, out: That a man who'd never exhibited any of the resources to become a hero would, indeed, turn heroic. He could've become bitter and watchful, just like me. But he didn't. Instead, he went so far beyond.

I shook Brian Q's hands as he took his leave. He couldn't wait to get to where he was going, it was clear from his strides. The cuffs of his pants hitched up with each bouncy step to reveal pink socks above his shiny brown patent-leather loafers. I looked at him and recognized that life was long, and it curved. Once again, there had been a contest, and I'd been left in the dust.

I passed Suzy Yamada's building. Screwing up my courage, I decided to do the unthinkable.

Are you expected, sir? asked the doorman when I walked in. He was a new guy and didn't recognize me.

No, just passing by.

I'll call Miss Yamada. It'll only be a second. He picked up a phone on the wall and punched white buttons. Hello? said a voice that didn't sound like either Suzy or Kendo.

If there were any people who were my peers in these scenarios, they were the doormen whose faces were the first things that greeted me upon my entrance. They were the ones to whom I first flashed my brand-new look, practicing: something like tightening the skull underneath my skin so that every single emotion required an effort. The smile that I gave them, for example, was a tight little number and was as much to put a distance between us as to acknowledge their friendly greetings.

Taking my cue from Shem, I realized that they would lose all respect for you unless you acted in accordance with your status: which was with a certain aloofness, squinting, as if their very presence depended on you for verification. The way Rowley P's doorman—whom I'd tried to befriend—treated me was only proof.

Assessing myself against these men, who were almost always Latino or black, I did not think in terms of duping or of putting on a show or of getting the better of them. They were, after all, the way I had been, minus the ambition, and I understood their situation completely: the desperation of the job hunt that made the landing of a job—any job—grotesquely happy-making; the struggle to make ends meet; the livelihoods dependent on subsuming their satisfactions and ideas beneath those of others; the belief, drummed into them by the repetitive tasks they had to perform daily, that they deserved no better. I thought of myself as having started at the same line, but somehow rescued by being the owner in greater quantity of the following traits: initiative, discontent, pessimism, clarity, duplicity, obstreperousness, not obsequiousness.

Miss Yamada would love to see you, announced the doorman, and indeed, when I went up, she was waiting at the door with a smile—the same smile I was flashing her, two tight little numbers confronting each other. She gave me a hug, and then took my coat and hung it.

What brings you here? she asked, with a look to say that I was intruding on her day.

Who's that? I could hear Kendo ask. And then when he saw me, he froze.

I gave him a look. Did it register?

Hello, Kendo, I said.

It's Ken, he replied automatically.

I'm sorry. Ken.

Oh, pay no attention to him, William. Here. Have a seat.

We were back on the couch, but this time as equals—well, almost.

Kendo was hovering over us. Don't you have somewhere you're supposed to go? Suzy asked him.

Ahhh— Yeah, he replied, looking at me.

Oh, I said. Where are you going?

See a friend, he replied, raising both eyebrows. Clearly, the boy wasn't skilled at improvisation. The befuddled look on his face kept growing until everything turned comically curvy. Fuck, I thought, I'm so in love!

Well, have a good time, Suzy said.

But he continued to stand there.

What! asked Suzy.

Nothing, he said. I have to go to my room. And finally he disappeared.

How are things going? I asked her as soon as we were alone.

Very well, she replied. Does he appear strange to you? she asked.

Kendo? I mean, Ken?

Oh forget it. Kendo's acting strange—what else is new?

How has he been acting?

He's no longer grouchy. He's actually been very nice to me. Today must be an off day. Saying so, she smiled meaningfully to acknowledge the success of my work.

And everything else is fine? I asked, taking a quick inventory: Everything cracked had been replaced with a twin, and so the apartment looked exactly as I'd remembered it. Except for the African totem—the spot remained vacant where it had stood. Where were the decorations from Pratung Song's shop?

An improvement I'd instigated appeared, as if to make up for the lack of the rest. In walked the maid to hand us glasses of iced tea. Thank you, Teresa, Suzy said to her. It was not the Filipina, but instead the white girl. She left the tray on a side table and disappeared.

Teresa lives with us now, said Suzy. Clearly Suzy had chosen the older, uglier girl to keep Kendo looking elsewhere.

On a table which held a bare candelabra, I spotted a framed photograph which hadn't been there before. In it, Suzy Yamada stood in front, while from behind, putting his thick arms like massive branches around her in a gesture part affection and part using Suzy as a shield, was the short, imposing Bill Hood. On either of his wrists there was no watch—the watch he and Shem favored, a gold Rolex. He'd taken it off because it was a reminder of his former life, his former love, Marianna. It was a gift from her. Of course. She'd given one to Shem when they were together. And in his turn, Bill Hood had received his. Up until I saw this picture, I hadn't understood.

I suppose you want to see the apartment, see for yourself how everything looks.

Yes, I said.

She smiled, got up. I followed. The kitchen was sparkling new. Teresa, seeing us, stopped what she was doing and stood at attention, as if she too was being inspected. Next was the room where

Rowley P. and I had conferenced. New books lined the shelves. Lamps and vases had been replaced by sturdier, nonglass versions. When we went up to Kendo's room, the door was, once more, locked. Suzy knocked. Kendo confronted us. What! he said, in a mean whisper. He was looking at me the whole time, like I'd broken a contract—and maybe I had.

William would just like to come see the room.

What for?

I'm sorry, it's all right, I said, making to leave.

Kendo, said Suzy.

It's Ken!

Let us in.

The boy stood aside as his mother held the door open for me. She followed behind. The poster on the wall was a painting—a thin slash of color like a suppurating wound was squashed in on both sides by thicker, heavier blocks of like but different-shaded color, the whole thing forming a kind of imperfect square.

Aside from that, it was just another boy's room. The curtains were drawn, turning the room secretive and hivelike. Clothes lay everywhere. There were headphones lying atop his jumbled pillows. And the sheets were bunched up in a corner at the foot of the bed. Thin, unused-looking books fell haphazardly on the low book-shelves.

OK? Kendo asked, cueing us to leave.

Thank you very much, I said.

You're welcome, he said, looking down at his feet.

In Suzy's bedroom, the carp painting had not been replaced. The bed had been transferred, pushed against an adjacent wall, and the vanity placed directly across from it. I heard the tap leaking in the bathroom. And outside on the balcony, the wrought-iron chairs were gone. In their place stood tall wooden chairs with hemp can-ing, like large dogs with ears pricked at attention. And because Suzy'd been in charge, everything of course looked perfect, premed-itated—as if this was what she'd intended the room to look like from the start. On a bedside table was another black-and-white of Suzy with her new man. This time he was smiling, and the smile gave his face a drunken quality. Perhaps he *was* drunk. God knows, with his recent turmoil he needed to be.

So that's it, said Suzy, when we found ourselves back downstairs.

I could see the walls with the crooked mirrors, which weren't there anymore. Instead, she'd moved them to the center, where they'd originally been. She saw what I was looking at, and gave me an innocent look of challenge. I moved them, so what? said this look.

And yourself? I asked her. Is everything all right with you?

Where was the tragedy in her life which was supposed to have been effected? Even her child molester boyfriend didn't seem to be dampening the dewy look in those eyes.

Yes, William. Thank you for your encouragement.

I pretended not to know what she was talking about.

What you said about love. It was true. Thank you.

Oh, I said. So who is he?

His name is William. Just like you.

William, I said.

William Hood, she continued, expecting the name to ring bells. And when I remained stoic, she said, He's a writer.

Her disappointment grew, until it turned into anger. He's very famous, she said.

What does he write?

Literature, she replied, huffing.

I decided to play some more. Is he good? I asked Suzy Yamada.

She looked at me openmouthed, as if she couldn't believe what she was hearing. Finally, she brought herself to utter: He's a master.

Like me? I asked.

I'm sorry, I have to go back to work now. There was a look that flashed in her eyes as if she was reconsidering the value of having a famous boyfriend who was turning out not to be that famous after all. Perhaps after my visit, she would dump him.

Well, thank you for showing me around. I bowed.

She bowed. There was no contest.

Kendo was watching me take my leave.

Where are you going? Suzy asked, as he brushed past her toward me.

I told you. To see a friend.

Who is this friend? she asked him.

He's *my* friend.

Well, does this person have a name?

William, Kendo said, looking right at me.

My God, there seem to be a lot of Williams going around these days, aren't there? she asked, laughing.

Well, that's his name, sulked Kendo.

What does this William do? Suzy asked.

Is he a master? I asked Kendo.

What? Kendo replied, shocked.

Just a joke, I hastened to explain. There seem to be a lot of masters going around these days as well. I said this looking at Suzy, who continued to seethe.

I don't have time for jokes, Kendo said, and turned his back on us.

Well, have a good time, Suzy told him. And be careful.

Kendo grunted.

Thank you again, I said to Suzy.

Oh, William, she said.

I had already stepped outside the doorway, but she gave no indication that she wanted me back in. In fact, she pulled the door closed behind her, as if there was some listener inside the apartment. There's something I meant to ask you, she said. I don't even know if I should mention it but . . .

Kendo was gone.

Walung, she began.

What? I was out of it for a moment, thinking she'd spoken Tagalog, having discovered my true identity. *Walo*, she seemed to have said. The number eight? What significance did that have? Eight what? Or did she say *wala*: nothing? It still made no sense.

The priestess you brought, she said.

Of course, of course, I hastened to correct myself. It was just the way you pronounced it, for a minute—

How well do you know her? Are you friends?

My first instinct was to protect Preciosa. Somebody recommended her to me, I said. A colleague.

I've been missing some things, she confided.

What do you mean missing?

Things have been stolen.

But of course, I said. You were broken into.

No. After that, she said. I had to itemize my losses for the insurance company and so I know what was left after the break-in.

How soon after?

After you came to visit. With Walung.

Are you sure?

Well, I don't know who else could've taken these things.

Could it have been Kendo? I asked.

Suzy looked at me for a second with a flash of fear across her features. But then she decided not to play along. No, it wasn't Kendo.

How can you be sure?

I've been watching him like a hawk, she said.

How about the maid?

I've searched her room and found nothing.

What things are we talking about?

A gold candlestick, she said.

I thought: Eight-fifty.

A Lalique vase.

Lalique? Fuck! All we got was twelve dollars!

An English paperweight.

Rejected. Had to throw it in a trash can.

A gold-plated letter opener.

Five bucks.

An antique jade Chinese snuffbox.

The thing broke and we had to chuck it.

Two miniature porcelain birds with jeweled eyes.

The jewels turned out to be costume, worthless.

An antique cigarette holder inlaid with mother-of-pearl.

Finally we got somewhere: Twenty dollars.

A commemorative silver coin from the U.S. Treasury.

Surprisingly, this item fetched twenty-five dollars.

Several silver rings.

Jackpot, I thought: Fifty bucks apiece. For a one-fifty total. Tsk-tsk-tsk, I said aloud sympathetically to Suzy Yamada. These were things accumulated during a lifetime, each holding a tie to some cherished occasion. So many cherished occasions suddenly stolen from her. I nodded my head. Touched her. Said, I'm sure it wasn't

Walung. It's what you owe us, you cheap bitch, I said to myself. Nine hundred dollars! Shame on you!

But— she began.

I was only too eager to cut her off. Please, Miss Yamada, I said— the return to formal name a clue to my feelings—I'm sure it wasn't her. And if it was—if— Do you realize how difficult it would be to— I would have to trace her through this colleague of mine. And even then I can't guarantee that we'll find her. That's the nature of the profession. The best that I could accomplish would be to spread the word, warn other people about her. But it's not something I feel comfortable doing. Because she's good at what she does. It would be unfortunate to deprive the world of her gifts.

All I want, she told me, are my things back.

You want to confront her? I asked.

Not confront, she said. Just, just ask.

All right, I said. I'll try to arrange a meeting. But you have to be very sure. A hundred percent. Now are you?

Yes, she replied.

Without a shadow of a doubt?

Yes, William. I wouldn't be telling you otherwise.

All right. But be prepared, I warned. The damage we might do to Walung's career would surely require some reprisal on her part.

But nobody has to know, she said.

Well, her feelings might be wounded.

Suzy gulped.

And I continued: You have to ask yourself, Is it worth it?

She remained quiet.

Do you want me to proceed?

Ahh—

Do you want to hear my advice?

Sure, she said, looking with eyes grown gigantic.

My advice would be to call up the insurance company and say that there are items you just discovered had to be added to the list of things stolen by the thief.

And let Walung get away with it? she asked.

The way I see it, the occult should not be tampered with. Especially if the person calling up these spirits is herself deeply flawed and cannot restrain the dark side of herself from contaminating her work. Of course, I was also speaking about myself. And I hoped Suzy understood perfectly.

Suzy had nothing more to say.

All right? I asked.

She closed the door.

On the streets, Kendo emerged out of a doorway.

What's the deal? he asked.

We don't know each other, I said, moving away from him.

What?

Your mother could be watching from up there, I whispered.

Understanding, he took the opposite path, only to reconnect minutes later at the Seventy-ninth Street subway station, a few blocks away.

I'm sorry, I told him. I was just passing by and I wanted to see for myself.

We're late for my father's.

And indeed, when we entered, there they were—his father, his father's black wife, and their two beautiful children, a teenage girl and a boy barely seven—gathered around a rickety card table, on which were arranged platters individually heaped with orange triangles and brown squares and green strips. They'd been waiting for ten minutes.

I'm sorry, Kendo said to his father.

His father didn't reply, but it was clear from the look on this man's face that he'd enlarged on our being late to mean that his hopes for his son were far too big for what the boy was—in the first place, it was his son who'd begged his father to throw the dinner, an occasion to introduce his new friend to the family. I hated myself for making him late, and sat down hesitantly on a chair indicated by the wife, who smiled weakly at me, sensing the discomfort between father and son.

I'm really sorry, I said.

Please don't apologize, the father told me, in a tone that said he knew it wasn't my fault at all.

Hey, Kenny Rogers, said the teenage girl, who was clearly thrilled by her half brother's presence but who didn't want to get on the wrong side of the old man.

Whatsup? Kendo asked.

Hi, Kenny, said the young boy, in a girl's piping voice that was like a blast from my own past. Like him too, I'd been very skinny and easily abashed. The boy looked down at his plate as if expecting food to just appear on it. Or maybe he was trying to avoid my eyes.

Whatsup Tyrone, said Ken.

I don't know, came the little boy's reply. He continued to keep his head down. His feet hung a few inches from the floor and he swung them back and forth, making a sound that nobody seemed to notice.

The father sighed deeply. This sigh took the place of all the words he knew better to say. And then he started cutting into the brown squares—pork chops. He took his share and told the girl to pass the plate to her mother.

The orange triangles were yams, and the green strips were bok choy. The wife told me this. I smiled. After everyone had their share—myself and Kendo last, as punishment for our tardiness—and had a few mouthfuls in them, the atmosphere seemed to relax.

So—William, is it William? asked the Chinese father, who could've been mine. This man and most of the older Asian men I saw on the streets could've been my father in that they all shared the same look of silent defeat, like having just been handed a bill of divorce. Or, as was the case with my father, like an insurance salesman unable to convince strangers of the value of what he had to offer—a man formed by being on the receiving end of a steady string of noes. They all looked like they'd imploded some time ago but then had had too many errands left to run and so just continued going.

Kendo's father was in his late fifties but he looked, in that odd way that some ethnic men did, younger than his years and at the same time more hollowed out. He was chewing noisily while he looked at me, waiting for my reply.

Yes, I answered.

William what? asked his wife. She had curly hair cropped close to the scalp. There were patches of shocking white amidst the black. She had on two pairs of earrings. One was two green frogs and the other two blue-black flies. Throughout dinner, the frogs kept trying to catch the flies, and the flies kept trying to evade the frogs.

Paulinha, said Kendo. I looked at him.

William Paulinha, echoed the father.

Uh-huh, I said.

What is that? What is Paulinha? asked the wife. Her hands ended in fingers that were scaly from too much laundry or dishwashing. Her nails were ragged.

The girl and boy looked at me eagerly to hear what I would turn out to be. Filipino, I said.

Oh really, said the wife. One of my co-workers is Filipino.

Lula works at the post office, Kendo explained.

Where in the Philippines is she from? I asked, but Lula didn't know.

William's from Manila, Kendo offered.

Manila, mouthed the father.

That's the capital, continued Kendo.

Is that far? the boy asked no one in particular.

Very far, said Kendo.

Wow, the boy said. He looked at me and smiled shyly, as if suddenly the distance I'd had to travel to get here had revealed me as his favorite kind of creature, a space alien. I reciprocated. There was a chip at the bottom of one of his front teeth.

What happened to your tooth? I asked him.

But he only looked down at his plate once more.

Baseball, the girl said. So how do you know Kenny? she asked me.

Oh, I said, looking at Ken.

We were both waiting in line at a movie, Ken said matter-of-factly.

Are you still throwing your money away watching that junk? asked the father.

They're not junk, Dad, said the girl.

The father raised the fork he happened to have in his hands and pointed it at Kendo. You, he said, should be old enough to realize that whatever you do they copy. On the word "they," he pointed the fork toward his two younger children.

Ben, said his wife Lula. It's called entertainment.

What you should be doing, said Ben to Ken, is reading. My God, this is your youth. This is your time. You shouldn't be throwing it away! This sounded strange coming from someone who'd been de-

scribed to me as unambitious, irresponsible, as "downwardly mobile." Suzy Yamada might've been lying, after all.

I'm not throwing it away, Ken said, unable to look at his father.
Instead, he looked to Lula with a plea for assistance.

I thought this was going to be a nice family meal, she said.

What movie did you guys see? the boy wanted to know.

SuperPigeon, I said.

Kendo looked dismayed. *SuperPigeon* wasn't cool, and more than
anything, what he was in his siblings' eyes was cool. At the same
time, his face registered an awareness that I wasn't joking: I'd indeed
seen *SuperPigeon*—and so what kind of nihilist role model did that
make me?

You said you didn't go see *SuperPigeon*! the boy accused Kendo. I
wanted to go and you said you didn't want to go see it!

I didn't, said Kendo. I fell asleep. He gave me the evil eye.

Did you like it? the girl asked me.

Like what? *SuperPigeon?*

Uh-huh.

Lula looked up with interest. After my reply points would be either added or subtracted.

Yeah, I said, with enough trepidation to suggest that I did so by
a narrow margin.

Hmmm, Lula said, and looked back down at her plate to spear
some yams.

The father didn't appear to hear. He seemed like the kind of man
who heard only what he wanted to.

Was it cool? asked the boy.

It was, I replied.

Is it like a two-times movie? he asked.

A what?

Like, do you like it so much that you gonna see it again, like two
times?

Sure, I said, giving myself away. There it was, the naked truth:
I'd loved *SuperPigeon*. And from that, it was only a short step to:
high school dropout, with gutter tastes.

You wanna see it with me? asked the boy. He spoke so softly I
was amazed I understood what he was saying.

Sure, I told him.

You have school, Lula told him.

I wasn't talking school day. Like weekend. OK? the boy said.

Is it still playing? his sister asked.

Yeah, he answered. At the three-dollar movie place. He looked to me and asked, So you'll take me, right?

Sure, I replied. I looked at his mother and father, who both pretended not to hear. How many other derelicts had Kendo brought home, and how many in their turn had befriended the little boy, promising things they never had the intention of following through on?

The boy gave a little cheer, hitting the table with his elbows. This caused one of the legs to buckle. A plate had to be moved while Ken futzed with the leg, readjusting.

Later, after dinner, I was led to the living room by Ken, who was himself following his father. Lula had been left to wash the dishes and clear the table. We passed the girl's room, where a lonely guitar sat on a worn-looking bed. On the floor was an open, battered guitar case, and not a single window could be seen. There was a bathroom whose chipped floor tiles were in need of serious mopping. I realized that the entire apartment shared in the same provisional, makeshift quality of the dining room, at the center of which sat that grease-streaked table with the unreliable spider legs. In the living room, furniture looked like it had been accumulated one piece at a time and then simply left next to one another over the years. The couch, the armchair next to it, the low table holding the TV, the bookshelves with their dingy fake wood, milk crates on which were stacked plastic pots of climbing ivy with nothing to climb on, and what seemed like a hundred floor lamps with moldy shades—nothing matched. A single bulb casting dim, yellowish light stuck out from the stucco ceiling, and it gave to the assorted furnishings not just a worn but a *timeworn* quality, a particular feeling of being excavated from a time capsule. These were things, I thought, that would not look out of place with a cordon placed around them—things not to be used, but rather to be considered at a distance for their oddness, their wrongness. So when Kendo's father sat on an armchair, making a small dust cloud rise in the air, I felt a moment of shock. Seeing everything, I'm sure Suzy Yamada would have felt the same way. She'd run screaming, indignation plastered on her refined, unlined face. And seen in this light, of course, things made sense, like stray sentences circling around their unifying thesis, which was this: a repudiation of the way Suzy lived her life. That was why Kendo sought out this haven as often as he did.

He sat on the no longer white couch with its faint pattern of green flowers. I sat beside him.

Good meal, said the father.

It was wonderful, thank you very much, I replied right on cue.

Oh, that's Lula, you have to thank her, he said. How are you, Ken? he asked, saying the words like a formality.

OK.

How's your mother?

She's herself.

You getting along with your stepfather?

He's not my stepfather yet.

Tell your mother I said hi.

She doesn't care. Why should you?

The father looked at me and asked, Are you married?

No, sir.

Sir, repeated Kendo, ready to laugh. I didn't understand: Hadn't he claimed to love his father?

You have a girlfriend? the father asked me.

I looked at Kendo. No, sir, I said to the father.

What do you do? he asked.

Me? I replied, stalling.

Kendo looked at me and began, William—

Let William talk for himself.

I'm a writer, I mumbled, embarrassed.

What do you write?

Fiction.

Yeah, Kendo chimed in. He makes things up.

Instead of published, the father asked me if I'd been "printed."

Uh, no.

So how do you make your living while you write?

Odd jobs.

Odd jobs, he repeated thoughtfully.

A little of this, a little of that. Like I clerk.

Clerk. That's good work, he said, nodding his head.

And I used to messenger.

Tell me, he said. What you write— He paused.

It's good, lied Ken.

You've read it? asked the father.

Yeah. And he can write. Kendo looked at me, giving me a small smile as he declared with all outward sincerity, You really can.

What you write, his father asked, is it sad, or is it happy?

I hemmed and hawed. It's sort of both.

Both? he asked, and then appeared to be thinking about what the combination would be like.

The dust on the books haphazardly stacked on the bookshelves was so thick it must've been a while since anyone had cracked anything open. Not that anything looked worth reading. There were several self-help volumes with exclamation points at the end of their jingle-catchy titles—things about repairing the rift between men and women; how to break free of financial binds forever; the ten commandments of self-actualization; interpretation of dreams as a key to solving unhappiness, which seemed like the Feng Shui of a previous generation. That they sat in this house with its air of being shored up by dust and cobwebs only testified to their fraudulence. There were also several vaguely weepy, brunet women who looked like the same woman plastered across cover after cover. These novels had titles like perfume names, using a common store of words like dreams, love, water, light, endlessly mixing and matching to form combinations that were different enough to be distinguishable from one another and yet were really the same thing. These were the fictional counterparts of the self-help volumes, both selling uplift like a formula. I attributed them to Lula. There were also books about dinosaurs, spaceships, undersea creatures, zoo animals—books which, having been outgrown by the young boy, were left to languish.

How old are you? he asked me.

I'm thirty.

Crucial time.

You say that about every age, Kendo said. You say that about my age.

It's true, replied the father. Between twenty and thirty, well actually between eighteen and thirty-five, it's a crucial time for a young man in this country.

He put his feet up on a milk crate, drummed his hands on his insubstantial belly. For the first time I was recognizing that he had a body. He had on a white undershirt that he didn't fill. His entire presence had the quality of being a remnant of something more substantial. A beaten man. Though, according to Suzy Yamada, it was he who had beaten himself. It was he who, having single-mindedly cultivated fun in his youth, now found himself with no resources to ease the sting of responsibilities that had since caught up with him.

Possessed by the spirit of curiosity, knowing that I would probably never return to this place—the same spirit that had made me ask the boy about his chipped tooth—I asked, How much do you weigh? The sound of those words was surprising and rude. But the father merely laughed, as if, more than anything, it showed me to be a lovable person.

I know, he said, patting his stomach. I eat so much, but I can't put anything on. If I were a girl, he continued, I'd be rich. I'd be a, a— He looked at Ken. What is that name for girls when they're . . . they put clothes on and they walk and smile or usually not smile—

Supermodels, said Ken.

I could be a supermodel, he said, laughing.

Lula came in with coffee for the three of us. When she leaned in to pour milk into my cup, I saw that she had the angular beauty of deprivation, of asceticism.

She shook my hand, said how nice it was to have met me, and excused herself to go to bed. She'd had a hard day at work and needed to get up early. Husband and wife exchanged no greeting.

There was more small talk, talk that seemed to be hiding more important things which, when father and son came close to them, made both suddenly hesitant and shy, retreating as if expectant of defeat.

You should do what William does, the father said at one point.

Ken and I looked at each other. He asked, And what's that, Dad?

Write. Or something like that. Be— Have— Do something. Something extra. And work to support it.

What do you like doing? I asked, suddenly taking up his father's post.

What? He couldn't believe himself.

Do you like art? You like writing? You like music?

Shut up, he said.

I didn't believe that this boy had the talent for trickery. I didn't believe that that would be his life, despite his ardent convictions. And I wanted him to confront the alternatives—before it was too late.

The father came to my assistance. You're good at music, he offered.

No I'm not, Ken said.

You help your sister out, the father continued.

That's her, Ken replied. She's the one with the talent. I just listen and then give her my comments.

The father, having come to yet another wall, kept quiet. Was this how it had been between me and my father? I didn't remember the old man being interested in my life, except to din into me that I was not, regardless of what I took up, to embarrass the family—never to become the subject of bad news that would reach relatives left behind in the Philippines. Having already equated in their fervent Catholic hearts our trip Statesward with a descent into hell, they ought not to be provided living proof of the validity of those fears. He never asked me about my day, nor I him. Never asked about my interests, or my ambitions, having assumed that I would be just like him—not necessarily sell insurance but something along the same lines. Was this how it was for most fathers and sons?

I'm gonna go see Kendra, Ken said, rising. Wanna come? This was my cue to leave.

I rose. It was nice talking to you, I said to the father, who nodded. A weight seemed to lift from his whole body as soon as I got up. I was the guest, and they were, in their own way, trying to impress me for the sake of Kendo, as if performing for a visiting dignitary. And yet, the apartment hadn't really been tidied. Nothing had been done to make it festive or presentable. Or, maybe sadly, it had, and this was all that they could manage. I didn't doubt their fondness for Kendo, or Lula's sadness, or Ben the father's there-and-not-there quality, a sense of him being a stranded proxy of his former self— though what that youthful self was I had no way of knowing, as there were no pictures on any surface, unlike at Suzy Yamada's, with her penchant for commemoration. I didn't doubt that they'd been genuine in their talk, their welcoming of me as Kendo's guest, but my presence was nonetheless a big inhibitor.

I followed Ken to his half sister's room. As soon as we entered, she closed the door behind us, but it wasn't because she had secrets to reveal. She wanted to play Kendo something on the guitar, and she didn't want to disturb her mother, who was asleep next door.

From the bed, she moved notebooks whose narrow lines were crowded with tight handwriting, clearing a space for Ken and me to sit.

This is new, she said to introduce a number, as she sat on the bed propping the guitar up on folded legs. Kendo looked at me, to signal the arrival of a treat. She began to pluck the strings and then, softly, she started singing. It was something she'd written herself. Words were missing here and there which she filled in with an mmm until she could think up suitable replacements. Her voice was pretty. It was modeled, as far as I could tell, partly after Mariah Carey, partly after Phoebe Snow. Still young and without a life of her own other than what she saw around her and absorbed, she interwove her twin inspirations and the resulting synthesis became her own, her thing to offer to mark her out in the marketplace. But she was still years from joining that marketplace. Her strumming was sometimes off, and sometimes her delivery, when it was most nakedly herself and not inflected with her role models' particular dictions, was weak. But there were some lines on which everything would all come together and for a brief moment it was like looking into the future of this girl. Mostly, these lines on which she came through had to do with love, lines that made Kendo wince. But the girl sang them with winning simplicity, believing. When it was over, we both applauded, and the girl beamed like this was the thing she'd been looking forward to—the approval of her half brother, the beautiful, rich, chic Kendo Yamada See, who, having been singled out by fate, had the power to extend this sense of distinction to the things he touched, the things he looked on with favor. You really liked it? she asked, not even looking my way.

Of course, Kendra, Kendo replied. You know you're good. Right, William?

Yeah, it's wonderful, I said, adding my voice to the chorus.

Thanks, she said, resting the guitar on the floor against the bed.

So when did you write this?

Two weeks ago.

You played it for Dad?

You know him. He just grunts. Talk to them, Ken.

Please, they don't listen to me. Lula looks at me like I'm a flunky.

But that's what you are, I said. Every opportunity to skewer this fortunate kid I took, because they didn't come too often. Kendra looked at me with a mixture of defensiveness and admiration—how could I talk to Prince Kendo like that?

I'm sorry if I'm not as good in business as you are, Kendo replied with a meaningfulness that piqued his half sister's curiosity. But she was too self-conscious to ask in my presence.

There were pictures Kendra had clipped from magazines and taped to the walls, which were painted a shade of pink that must've been her own doing—it was the only room in the apartment that showed some care, filled with the hopeful spirit of its occupant. The way she'd closed the door when we walked in, filled with something close to relief, began to make sense.

On a table pushed against a wall opposite the bed was a computer of a model several years old. Its dusty screen and dustier keyboard told of infrequent use. A ragged backpack had been thrown carelessly near the leg of a chair. In contrast, the guitar case showed that much pains had been taken to prettify it—just as on her walls, pictures had been pasted together to form a decorative collage: ten thousand eyes belonging to the celebrities of her dreams stared out at us, as if acquainting this girl with her future of standing in front of an audience.

When I noticed the two of them again, it was a scene that was classic Kendo: He'd been trying to help Kendra with the song, filling in the blanks. A lot of his suggestions had not only been approved but met with a grateful kiss from the young girl, whose bountiful curly hair shook and made a noise like leaves falling. It was only in the last suggestion that Kendo was meeting with rolled eyes and vociferous noes. The line in question, already complete, was: Time may pass but I'll still love you. Kendo had suggested that instead of love,

Kendra should use the word "hate": Time may pass but I'll still *hate* you. At which, the adoring sister turned resolute, replying: Have you been listening to the song at all? It's about love! Love fits! I ain't taking it out.

In the end, Kendra won. When we left, to tease her half brother, she strummed the guitar and sang: Time may pass but I'll still LOVE you!

The young boy was asleep. Kendo closed the door to his room. Lula, too, was sleeping. In the living room, Kendo's father quickly popped open tired eyes. We're going, said Kendo. Thanks for having us.

Glad to have you, he said, trying to focus his eyes.

Thank you so much, Mr. See, I said. I offered my hand. An embarrassing moment passed when it hung there, untaken. I realized that he didn't see, and moved closer in. Finally, he shook it limply. He struggled to get up out of the comfortable chair, where he probably would've spent the night if we hadn't awakened him.

It's OK, said Kendo. You don't have to see us to the door.

The father sank back down. You going back home? he asked Kendo.

You sound just like Mom, Kendo said mockingly.

Are you?

Of course.

You behaving, aren't you?

Dad, I'm twenty-three.

His dad looked at Ken and said meaningfully, Kendo, bad rhymes with sad. I hope you know that.

Don't go profound on me, Dad, Kendo replied.

Just be good.

Dad, good rhymes with wood. I hope you know that. With that line, he ushered us both out the door, laughing.

Bye, sir, I said.

Once outside, Kendo dragged me two doors down, and before he knocked, he gave me a look to let me know that the evening was about to take a more interesting turn.

32

The stripper was sad-eyed and big-bellied. It'd been three weeks since Norma had left her, but she still thought about Norma a lot in the daytime, just before she went to sleep after her hard night's exertions. But of course, she said, it was Norma's prerogative to leave. It was always the younger one's prerogative to go, to look for a better offer elsewhere. And Norma was the younger one by five years. The stripper made herself sound ancient, but really she was only thirty-three. Kendo and I sat there, not daring to ask the burning question. But it was as if she'd received our message telepathically, because she answered, without looking at either of us: She found somebody else. Some guy who lives in New Jersey.

She lives in New Jersey? asked Kendo.

Yes, she whispered, closing her eyes as if trying to picture her lover living in this new place.

Well, said Kendo, she's got her punishment right there.

The stripper smiled. She was clearly very fond of this boy. Her

name was Maricelle. She was Dominican, with black skin that
glowed as if freshly oiled. This gave to the muscles of her legs a
beautiful definition. She had a mole above her thin and very red
lips. This mole had a mind of its own, refusing to move when she
opened and closed her mouth to talk. Or perhaps the sadness of
what the stripper had to say made her mouth move too slackly to
even induce the mole to bop along. But this time, hearing Kendo's
line of consolation, it rose like the mercury edge of a thermometer,
warmed up by its owner's smile.

Judging from first the See family's dwelling, and now this
woman's—which was gray and rained on—I could see the same kind
of hovel multiplied into infinity and stacked one above the other to
form this building whose tall exterior, when you encountered it
walking up the street, made your spirits sink. To catch up with the
work of renovation inching its way closer to this block—which was
a stone's throw from where I lived—someone had thought it appropriate to slap a new coat of paint on the building from top to bottom. Unfortunately, it was a shade of red that was so iridescent that
even up close the paint job looked undried. And anyway, nobody
seeing this new color would've been fooled. There was something in-
definably cursed about the place that no renovation short of demoli-
tion could reverse. So, I thought looking at it, this is Kendo's ideal.
What a stupid kid—on whom so much has been wasted. In the corridor, before we entered, I smelled at least ten different kitchens,
and could guess that the people inside could smell them too and
were trying to devise schemes to escape and be forever rid of the af-
front of those long-clinging odors that weren't their own.

The stripper excused herself to prepare for the night's work.
First, she went into the bedroom to put on her dancer's outfit—a
string bikini gussied up with sequins that were silver all over, except for two red rings where the nipples were. Kendo made her
show us, taking a strange pride like some demented master of ceremonies. Tell William what you do, the rubbing-in-their-faces thing,
he said to her.

Oh, you know, she obliged, looking at me, I spray some beer
here—she indicated her crotch—and so when I go dancing and
when you know I'm putting it in their faces because that's what
they like they get a smell of their favorite thing and that's why I'm

their favorite dancer that's why my tips you know I have to make most my money from tips so that's why of eight nine dancers in the whole place my tips are the best because I give the guys exactly what they like.

Beer and pussy, said Kendo. Two for one!

Beer in pussy, laughed the Dominican Maricelle. I put it like perfume in bottle to spray and I just spray every time I get a break and go backstage. But nobody no other dancer knows. Because I don't want nobody to make copy of it OK? Because that's my how do you say that? She looked at Kendo.

Copyright, I replied.

That's my that's right copy-*right*! She laughed as she put on jeans and a ratty T-shirt over her outfit. And then she sat down to tie up sneakers. Seeing her head bent over her feet, I realized that she must do exactly what I used to—aside from dancing she "entertained" her customers. What was the going rate nowadays? It'd been a while since I'd "entertained," and my offices being a bathroom stall, I'd of course had to charge much less than the normal fee, though I'd tried to make up in industry and effort and versatility for what I lacked in atmosphere.

I stopped looking at the top of her head and moved to a bookcase. On one of the shelves was a picture of Maricelle with her arm around the long-nosed girl at Suzy Yamada's party, Norma, whom Ken had invited with a desire to intersect both his worlds, black with sterling silver. She was uglier in this photograph than she'd been in real life—and perhaps, when I'd seen her having cornered Brian Q with his ludicrous imitation of Don Juan, she'd already left the person who she was in this photograph behind. Like me, she'd been on an upward trajectory—so upward, in fact, that in a few months she would leave behind this gray, dank hovel and go live in New Jersey, which, despite what Kendo and Maricelle thought, I saw as someplace green and uncramped.

Speaking of Brian Q, there was something on the bookshelf, not far from the picture, that I couldn't stop looking at. *Winnie the Pooh*. Hadn't Brian Q told me that he was missing a copy of *Winnie the Pooh*? A first edition? Wasn't that one of the items this Norma had pocketed? I took it out, cracked it open. There, I found what I was looking for—at the back of the title page were the words "first edition"! My heart was thumping. Why hadn't Norma taken this with her? Or dumped it somewhere—she was sure to fetch a tidy sum for a prized volume like this, with its yellowed, leaflike pages. I had a jacket on. I could sneak it inside. My thoughts were rushing. They were like Lego blocks, each piece put next to the other without design, and when I finally stood back to confront the thing formed, I was shocked by its strange rightness.

Brian Q, with his belly that was growing and a receding hairline temporarily stayed, the perfect comic figure, which was how so many people—myself and Norma the primary ones—had seen him. Brian Q, with his four-figure suit which he believed to have been invested with powers of transformation—not! Brian Q, a photograph of him fresh from college, aligned with geek buddies each with his own particular misery abandoned for just one shining moment under the blinding sun—and now that innocent, happy picture was the cause of his torment, his particular misery compounded by middle age, by the steady realization that his life was hollow, and that if something didn't happen soon he would be condemned to live out his days cursed with solitude. A fear that drove him into the arms of Norma the spider, who spun him around and then afterward, when he was dazed, made off with his precious belongings, leaving him what? Herpes. A lingering souvenir that burned and humbled. And what had this silly, bumbling man done after all that, untrained by experience for anything but collapse? He'd reached out to others. Forgotten about himself temporarily. A man of action. Was this what I'd meant when I'd said I wanted to be good?

Realizing this, I knew I had to return Brian Q's childhood book to him. He'd earned it, after all. It would be not just something restored to its proper place, but more important, coming from me, a tribute, a thing to quiet my deep shame. This shame—which at no time as Chao had ever surfaced, had ever been coaxed into the light by any of these people, who for me were personifying truths about the world as I'd already learned from the *New York Post*, and yes, from Agatha Christie, and now, from Georges Simenon—needed this very thing to be erased, absolved, dissolved. I would take *Winnie the Pooh* and bring it back to Brian Q. I would say to him . . . what? That . . . Yes? That I'd been walking around and saw this book in the window of a used-book store. And having remembered his inventory, I decided to buy this book to replace the one he'd lost. And he would, turning to an inside page with a telltale mark that only he would know about, say that it was the very same book! How about that! I had reunited him with a prized possession he thought he would never see again, something carried over from his beloved, trouble-free childhood and having lost which had begun a period of ill luck for him. And now, the return of this beautiful object was surely a sign—with his charity work, he was on the right track, good fortune would be once more his. He'd gone from inheriting luck to having worked hard for it, having deserved it! Saying all that, he would smile, give me a hug, recognizing me once more as the provider of miracles in his life.

As soon as Maricelle left us on the streets, Kendo looked at me and let me know what he saw. A regular klepto, aren't you? he asked.

There was no use putting on an act. He'd seen me. He seemed to keep seeing me. So what? I asked.

Well, the so what was that the evening lengthened a little bit more. It suddenly struck Kendo's fancy to devise a test for me on the spot. Hearing him order me—there was no other word for it—I knew he would be a lingering problem in the future. I woke up from the dream of our developing friendship (duh!) and thought of putting a stop to him right there and then—push him in front of an oncoming car. But with me there was sometimes a long tunnel between thought and action.

This was what he said to me on the streets: See that stack of fruit over there? He was pointing to a pyramid display outside a deli, manned by a hawkeyed Puerto Rican kid.

What about it? I asked.

I want you to steal something from it for me.

What?!

You heard me, he said. His tone of voice was all business. He had something over me and for the first time he was taking advantage of it. And there was nothing I could do. Having confessed everything, having been expertly seduced into it, I was now under his powers. And he knew I knew as much because, even though I was sufficiently angered to stand there frozen, I wasn't moving away. That was how bound up with him I'd become.

If you don't, he cautioned, I'll call the cops.

Now there it was: everything made clear enough for a retard. Saying it, he didn't smile.

As Chao, I had controlled things, Shem only a teacher. When I quit, Shem had pleaded, knowing power was in my hands. But now, Chao had found another Chao, and if he wasn't careful would be out-Chao-ed.

I looked at the Puerto Rican kid and took a deep breath. I would have to outrun him, that was all there was to it.

But before I could go, Kendo decided to make the game even more interesting. He said, No, scratch that. I want you to go inside and grab me some beer instead.

What? I repeated myself like a dumbfuck.

Grab some beer.

That meant that the proprietor inside would have enough time to shrill to the Puerto Rican guy, who would then be waiting for me at the sidewalk with something in his hand, or maybe just his hand— which, even from a distance, looked powerful enough. But what could I do? I looked at Kendo's unflinching stare, his handsomeness turned into an insult.

I could hear my heart beating so loudly I was surprised the Korean grocer didn't look up as I walked right past him to where the cold drinks were. There was a six-pack that I took up without even looking. There were ten steps between me and the outside. In the middle sat the grocer, who, sensing me approaching with merchandise, looked up. In that one instant, I was like a spring sprung. The man began shouting, but by the time I was on the sidewalk, the young Puerto Rican kid still didn't understand what was going on. This gave me a minute's advantage, which I took as if grabbing a baton and pumping furiously ahead. Two blocks. Three. Four. The kid had begun the chase but he was proving not to be fast enough. When I stopped at my building, there was Kendo waiting for me.

Seeing the beer, he laughed. He just laughed. And then he said, You passed the test. You're really one of us now.

I thought: Today beer, tomorrow what?

PART 4

* * *

⋆ 33 ⋆

Shem's revenge, the sheer left-fieldness of it, deserved applause. Even if—as I realized at this late date—I was being groomed to be his dupe, the only one the trail would eventually lead to. That was what he'd come to the Savoy to find. Somebody smart enough to understand his plan, but not so smart as to think through all its possible ramifications. And I was just the man for the job. I was at the very bottom, after all, when he'd recruited me. What did I have to lose? From the Savoy, everything else was a step up. Or, using Kendo's terminology, several tiers up.

The evening with Kendo seemed to have awakened me, made me realize the spot I was in. Like that boy, everything beautiful I'd come close to had a core of danger that would burn me if I didn't act first. I knew I had to kill Kendo. But how? Or, at the very least, I had to completely disappear from his life.

And as for Shem—how could he make sure that I wouldn't, by a simple opening of my mouth—my language turned profane and up-to-the-minute to forever eradicate Chao from the face of the earth—

involve him irrevocably in this whole mess? And where would his revenge be then? That daughter of his would then be made to retract her claims. And hooray for Bill Hood, Jewish martyr and writer extraordinaire! Newly aglow with an aura of saintliness, of extra suffering, his books would live forever!

Maybe . . . If I were Agatha Christie, and Shem merely a character I'd made up, what would I make him do to protect his own interests? I would . . . have Shem send someone to dispose of me.

But not if I was nowhere to be found. Not if, ahead of the game, I managed to get myself into hiding before he set the dogs loose. There was no way that, having endured the indignity of poverty for so long, I would—having just discovered seventeen-dollar Boston scrod, cushions to soften an impossible bench, a whole series of books I couldn't wait to own, and perhaps one day smooth wood floors of my own to walk on—give up my lease on this life. I would claw out the eyes of the man sent to deprive me of my chance at the good life. I would never just fold up and die. I would never die. Fuck Brian Q's library with those books full of effete, wilting heroes, their chests turned tubercular by despair, by enough free time to turn privilege into convolution: Life is hard, life is pointless, life is a goal none of us truly achieve. In these books, no matter what each was about, suicide seemed an adjunct thesis. Well, fuck that! Not for me! I would scream and kick: Life is precious, life is so fucking precious! Now, with money, I understood what that line truly meant.

Money. What I'd had I'd spent freely—books, movies, meals in restaurants, clothes. I was drunk on showing off. On showing up the people whose job it was to keep their eyes on my hands as I walked from department to department. At the penultimate moment, I would pull out my plastic and walk like a grand marshal of a parade to the cashier, making sure my hands were visible at all times—in one hand, all the goods I meant to have; in the other, the most potent sign of my new station in life, a piece of plastic held like a weapon. Before I knew it, not much was left of what I'd saved. Well, like they say, a fool and his money are soon parted.

At my highest point, I had fifty-seven thousand five hundred dollars stashed in the bank. This was from everything: my consultation fees (of which Shem took ten percent; and which varied from client to client, each paying according to his or her own discretion, though it was subtly hinted by either Shem or me that the base hovered at a thousand dollars; though a handful, like Rowley P, went way past that figure), my side business with Pratung Song (who paid me in cash, leaving no paper trail), and the money from the pawnshops. In six months, I'd spent more than half that amount. On what, exactly? What did I have to show for all that? Well, as it turned out, not much. A few new outfits, which were more or less the same outfit—black and white, representing unequal halves of my soul. Shoes. Haircuts. Cushions. New books. An expanding waistline. A completely unmemorable day would go by and then at night, counting the change in my pocket, I realized a hundred dollars had vanished. It was all from living in this fucking city, in which the civic spirit was best accessed through shopping—thought of that way, my inevitable departure didn't seem too tragic.

Now, with nothing but escape on my mind, it became imperative for me to rebuild my bank account. I would ask for as much as they would let me get away with, then disappear, go underground. Of course, I would take Preciosa with me.

And so, back to work with a renewed zeal in my performance: Chao adrenalized by fear.

There was a woman in the East Village who ran a photo gallery in SoHo—one of the oldest and most prestigious in the country. Business was going well, better than ever before, except during the art boom of the mid- to late eighties, a high that would be impossible to duplicate. There was an influx of European money. Europe was the Japan of the late nineties. Their economy was bustling, and they were looking to unload their hard-earned money to partake of the stolid chicness of things American. They were interested in the new photographers whom this woman had the good luck to represent. (Later, she would refute that term: Good luck, hah! she said, revealing that the careers of her stable had been choreographed with such precision it would put the MGM musicals of the fifties to shame. Glitzy openings. The cultivating of celebrity clientele. Or of celebrity spouses or mates: the men, in particular, didn't have to be encouraged to squire models around the city, be photographed doing this. Their names dropped in all the young, hip magazines. And, of

course, the gallery owner's genius stroke of licensing these images
for advertisements and book covers, sometimes before the pictures
were even shot, like portraits made on commission—practically giving them away to these licensees, knowing that the dividends would
come years down the road after the photographs had "traveled" a
bit, having pounded the pavement of the collective pop consciousness and achieved something of an iconic status. Of course, this was
always a gamble—there might instead attach to the pictures a patina
of ordinariness, having been connected to everyday commerce, or
worse, of cheesiness.)

Among these "hot" photographers, there was one who had recently killed himself at thirty-five. A heroin overdose. This simple
fact immediately tripled the going rate of his pictures: shots of
naked young waifs who confronted the camera like dimwits being
asked to read an eye chart, their big eyes about to break into tears
from the pressure of having to stand there and be made to be visible.
The tone of the pictures read very clearly: Victim! And as expected,
mouthwatering controversy had been generated—feminists on one
side and freedom-of-expression-ists on the other, throwing popcorn
at each other—and this controversy succeeded in giving to the pictures what the photographer—despite the nakedness—had no talent
to do: a gloss of the forbidden, a sexiness of being "of its moment,"
and so the hip and moneyed of Europe came to New York to pay
their respects. In Europe, this guy—named Mauricio G—was practically a god in the pantheon. Very soon after, the Americans, sniffing
at the Europeans' butts, came calling, and by then the prices for the
pictures had happily quadrupled.

I'd gleaned some of this, inferred the rest, from my visit to this
woman's gallery, which, however, was a misleading preview of the
real deal: her apartment in the East Village turned out to be as fastidiously gaudy as her gallery, according to the interior design dic-
tum of the moment, had been fastidiously barren.

You walked along an unprepossessing street and entered the
smallish door of an unimposing three-story red-brick ivy-choked
building surrounded on all sides by dilapidated storefronts and low
brownstones, and once inside you realized what a clever decoy the
neighborhood was. Everywhere I looked there were the twin colors

red and gold. An explosion of cushions covered in sari material sat
on canopy beds, on teak benches and daybeds; mosquito netting
cascaded from above to cover these pieces of furniture, turning them
fairy-tale gauzy, the indolent air of summer and of outdoor living
preserved through this bleak, gray season; lanterns hung from various points in the broken-mirror-encrusted ceiling; tile-mosaic tables;
jeweled screens and curtains; diamond patterns on every conceivable surface; and yes, in the thick of winter, Technicolor-green dwarf
palms hunched languidly like spoiled, overfed children in a tropical
greenhouse with its own climate control. Walking in, I began to
sweat. Perhaps I imagined it, but I could even hear the wild cawings
of birds unseen overhead. On the walls of her bedroom were faux-
primitive renderings of dark-skinned men and women going at each
other in a variety of positions.

An overall atmosphere of being in a select, foreign country had
been successfully cultivated, and there was no denying that you'd
entered a place owned by someone privileged enough to will it into
existence. But why? Did she have any kind of ties to or romantic as-
sociations with Morocco, for example, or was it just because at the
front door the tumultuous clatter of urban America needed to be
held back?

She was dressed in her most conservative Wasp outfit of cream
blouse inside a dress suit of dim gray, pearls around her neck, and
sex-starved librarian's glasses above her unhumorous nose. I half expected her to undo her pinned-up hair, shake it loose, and take off
those glasses so she could better bat her eyes to reveal what she had
had to restrain at work, her true nature as a voluptuary, hence the
cultivated humidity of her home. But she continued pointing and
reciting in a businesslike, let's-be-done-with-it manner, exactly as
she had in the gallery. Her voice was being squeezed out of her big
horn, sending her glasses jumping up, and for the first time I'd
found a voice to go up against Cardie Kerchpoff's high-pitched emergency tone in the freak-show exhibit in my head.

She rubbed her forehead. She'd been having bad dreams for a
year now. A lot of these dreams had to do with death. Her death.
She was being hit by cars and by New York city buses night after
night. Sometimes even dragged along the road, her beautifully man-

icured suits too thin to provide adequate padding against scrapes and gashes. She was falling down a ladder into a deep, black chasm, so deep that her shouts for help spiraled upward without ever reaching the surface. Her hair was being set on fire, and she would run screaming in search of water, which she'd never find, and by then, she'd be awake, her forehead soaked. Now, she'd read up and had discovered that when you dreamed about death, it wasn't necessarily death that was being foretold, but instead the opposite: birth. Death, in other words, usually meant some phase of your life coming to an end, and a new one about to be inaugurated. Death in dreams, then, could be said to augur positive things. A new business, perhaps. Or a new lover. Or a move to a new city. Was this true? she asked.

No, I said in the bluntest tone I could find.

She gulped. The look on her face said: What could my art world cachet do for me now?

I would embroider out of all bounds of the books I'd read. Aware that everything might soon come to an end, myself be discovered, I turned reckless, enjoying myself. I told her that death might not mean death in the Western interpretation, but for the Chinese death meant exactly that: it was a warning, a chance given to the dreamer to clean up her act before it was too late.

This woman, who had said that she wanted help with her weight as well, who for years had yo-yoed precipitously in one direction and then the other, looked at me with the stricken look of having lost her appetite forever. There, I'd as good as offered my dietitian's services. Wouldn't that be worth a hike in my fee?

I continued: But in these dreams, you are only being given a glimpse into what will eventually befall all of us. That you have been given such insight only means that you have been handed an opportunity to come to terms with your life, rearrange everything so that your accounts are settled in your favor, the list of credits out-totaling the debits. In fact, encoded in the dreams themselves are no indications as to when your death will arrive, only that it will. So it doesn't mean that death is just around the corner.

What could she do? She looked at me. Was there something wrong she was doing that could be set right?

I turned my face into a mirror, deflecting the question back at her: What do you think? I asked.

Well . . . she considered, before coming up with a worrisome idea: Mauricio was her number one seller, particularly since he'd killed himself. The tragedy of a young life cut short had transferred to the neutral, undistinguished pictures and pushed them past a flimsy line of good or bad and directly into legend. Perhaps selling work like that was not good karma, she said, and in hearing these thoughts articulated for the first time believed immediately.

Perfect, I thought: she'd come up with her own punishment. I nodded to confirm her worst fears.

What should I do? she asked, dreading the obvious, which of course I would not contradict.

Again, I asked, koan-like: What do you think?

I think . . . I should . . .

Think from your heart, I encouraged, turning my voice mellow.

I should . . . She stopped. And then finally gave in: I should give up Mauricio's work, she replied, the recognition of what she'd said dawning on her only after the last word had been spoken. Her face slackened, dropped, and she felt a sudden weight on her chest that made her have to sit. Give up money? Was she crazy? She looked at me but I was no help. She excused herself to go get some water. When she returned, she caught me fingering a silver ornament on her mantelpiece, but she didn't think anything of it. All right, she told me. I'll do it. I'll give up Mauricio's work. To whom should I give Mauricio's work?

I shrugged.

But whoever I give it to, doesn't it mean that that curse would pass along to this person?

I replied: The important thing is that the works are no longer with you.

Suddenly this loss wasn't so bad after all. It was turning out to offer lucrative possibilities. She considered the enemies she wanted to transfer this load of bad luck to. She gave a sly smile.

And then, just to increase the comic value of my visit, I told her that she should build an altar, and on this altar should put any sculptures of . . . of frogs (green!) that she could find because . . .

frogs were good-luck totems symbolizing long life and fertility. In her case perhaps not the fertility of producing children, but rather that whatever new endeavors she undertook would be successful. To make up for the loss of Mauricio G's work.

Of course, I had chosen the word "fertility" knowing that she hadn't been able to have children and had tried to adopt but had, for some reason or other, been denied by the agencies.

But, she said, perking up at my accidental clairvoyance, she wanted children, she'd always wanted them.

Well then, good, I replied, then an altar of frogs is exactly what you need to build.

Where should she place this all-important altar? she asked.

Location didn't matter. It simply had to be a place that was well lit and that she would pass by every day, and the sight of it would act as a reminder of the fuse of her life burning shorter and shorter.

She gave me two thousand dollars inside a plain white envelope, literally shooing me out.

I went to the Savoy. It was the middle of the afternoon, and there was nobody there I recognized, except Barney. I ordered beer after beer. A guy in a business suit was seated with a girl who might actually have been a girl. Barney looked at me as if about to begin a conversation, only to look away again. He put glass after glass in an orderly line behind the counter, and when that was done, wiped the spigot of each bottle, and then rearranged them so that the labels faced out perfectly squarely. This care and ceremony was a revelation, and it occurred to me that I might've—in the manner of Chao—infected this man whom I'd never known to care about his surroundings.

I looked at him, wondering how I was going to get him to talk to me. I came on a mission, after all.

And then in came the black guy who was a regular, the writer. He couldn't have walked in at a more perfect time. A writer—what a perfect plant for my story! He dawdled at the bar, while Barney began the motions of fixing him his usual—poured from one potent-looking bottle after another. Jesus Christ, how soon did he want his memory obliterated? It wasn't even five. Come to think of it, maybe he wouldn't be such a useful witness after all.

He retired to his corner, where the shadows concealed him. Once more, he was at his observation post, anticipating the staggering-in of his "material" from all around the city and from New Jersey, and he began to get settled, shifting in his seat until he found just the right dip in the worn leather and taking a first sip from his killer drink.

I can't stand this cold, I said to Barney.

What? he asked.

I said I can't stand this cold.

It hasn't even gotten that cold, he replied.

Where's someplace warm? I asked. I got myself some money. Give me suggestions on where to go.

Hell, replied Barney. I hear that's warm.

How about Florida? I asked, naming someplace I'd never been to and had no intention of ever visiting. Yeah, I said aloud, I like the sound of that. That's where I'll go. I'll go to Florida. They got a Disneyland there, don't they?

The trail for me would lead to the Savoy, and when asked, Barney would tell the investigators exactly what I wanted him to: He would say to them, That guy mentioned something about Florida . . .

I made sure to engage Barney's eyes as I put an inordinately big tip on the counter. And what I had to say I did slowly, like someone instructing an idiot. I said: Next time you see me I'll have a tan. I'll send you a postcard from Florida.

Next on Shem's list was the guy who had just bought the building in the West Village, two blocks from the cobbled alleys of the meatpacking plants where, at night, transvestite prostitutes displayed themselves and conducted business. These "girls" could be spotted disappearing into empty meat trucks conveniently parked in dark shadows and left open, unattended. He loved the "flavor" this gave to his digs, he told me.

Near the bank of floor-to-ceiling windows on the top floor he'd placed a telescope to get a better view of the nightly action. And as if this weren't enough, on the two bottom shelves of his entertain-

:enter sat a large collection of porn from all over the world
.ccording to some order of predilection. In this unit also stood
screen TV.

He didn't have to show me any of this; it was only that he wanted
to make sure that everything potentially counterproductive to my
task was brought to light. About the porn and his telescope, I politely refrained from making any comment. Seeing me turn away, he
marked me out for an abashed, sexless man. I anticipated his observation, secretly laughing to myself. And then, I realized he was exactly right: When was the last time I'd had sex? Every aspect of the
role had bled over into my real life.

Thank God the core of my black, black heart remained intact, ra-
diating invigorating, bilious hate to sustain me. This hate was what
made me get out of bed in the morning. I hated Shem for putting me
in my predicament, and yet at the same time knew that I was in-
debted to him. Even as I was living it, I was looking back on this period of my life as my prime. My clients fueled this hate effortlessly,
they couldn't help themselves. I took the subway to and from work
and everyone I saw now became a walking argument to end the human race.

I didn't know what the man with the telescope and the porn did
for a living. Even after ransacking his "files," there was no occupa-
tion to be found or any kink from which to extrapolate much of anything else. His income-tax returns of the last three years listed him
as "self-employed" and were for amounts that certainly didn't match
up with his new residence. Perhaps here was a man who'd had his
own files cleaned out, intending to do something in the near future
for which his past would stand in the way. What was the scam here?
I couldn't figure it out.

He was young. Perhaps about to become an up-and-coming
celebrity of the type that fitted incompatible nouns together to form
a new meta-creature vertebraed by slashes or hyphens: These people
were so anxious not to miss the shortest trip to fame that they kept
all bases covered in the event that luck and circumstance should
prove to be their old, reliably intractable selves. The one thing I
knew was that his place smelled like glue. In the half hour I'd been
looking at things, I was starting to get a buzz. All rooms were pre-

sented to me. In none of them could I find a clue to the smell or to his livelihood. There were guitars, violins, framed lithographs, artists' materials like paintbrushes and unstretched canvases, a word processor, stacks of books—tools of various professions but none of which looked like they got much use, only assembled together like things to consider in a game of multiple choice: which to take up for the day? And except for the telescope and the porn, his personality was similarly impermeable. There was no personality at all, and therefore nothing to eradicate. Rote mumbo jumbo flowed freely from my lips. All the while, I was relishing the thought of the look on this boy's face when the revelation of fraud was made in the press: one impostor having been gotten the jump on by another.

Before I disappeared from the West Village guy's life once and for all, I reconsidered my silence and decided to punish him by forcing him to readjust the only clues of personality in his home. The porn, I told him, was fine for now, but I was afraid that it had the potential for attracting malign spirits. He took this to mean that he needed to conceal it from view—perhaps a new, unobtrusive storage place was the answer? But I set him wise: He had to dispose of the porn. Human nature being what it is, I knew he wouldn't heed my directions, and that from now on, whatever small thing went wrong in his life, whatever ripple of trouble manifested itself, he would look on it as the price to be paid for being led on a leash by his body, its urges, for having kept his beloved tape collection against my orders. He would forever have to tally things according to that equation, the same way I'd used the cost of a McDonald's hamburger to relate the worth of everything else purchased. In other words, I was bequeathing him the gift of my Catholic upbringing: the nasty war between desire and responsibility. As soon as the metal entrance slid closed behind me, I counted my money: fifteen hundred dollars!

Pratung Song I had left behind, wordlessly. What would he make of my disappearance? And when led to him by a few sharp-minded clients who would suddenly be gifted with retroactive wisdom, what would the cops be able to glean? Could I trust him to keep his mouth shut? No. Confronted by the sternness of the police, this immigrant man would be more than happy to volunteer information about me, seeing the act as a way to declare to the world his loyalties—in other words, as another form of naturalization. But what could he say? Did he know where I lived? Did he know my real name? Did he know where I left for?

And where would that place be?

Didn't Preciosa mention thinking about the Philippines? Is that where she would go if she left New York? Did she have any other alternatives?—returning to the Philippines, after all, seemed like an admission of defeat. Could you imagine the glee of relatives who would point you out in family gatherings, then launch into a story about going to live in the fabled United States only to crawl back with your tail between your legs—kicked out, in effect?

Though it had been common in our relationship to go without seeing each other for days, weeks even, I sensed in Preciosa's recent absence an avoidance, as if, having gotten herself out of debt, she no longer wanted the shameful reminder of our fraud which my presence would have the power to trigger—I felt as if conveniently assimilated into the long list of shadowy jobs and involvements Preciosa had once intimated, pushed behind and out of sight. Hadn't she once spoken of having been associated with "undesirable elements"? Was that how I myself would now be classified in her stories to others? An undesirable element? Had I, after all, misjudged her lapsed Catholicism as a sure sign of fellow feeling, an innate understanding that the endeavor we undertook together was with one eye turned to check for God's displeasure?

I knocked on her door with trepidation, but there she was, seemingly in one of her light moods. The apartment looked newly cleaned, and Divina Valencia sat fat and lazy inside her bowl.

And more surprisingly, this woman, who had never said much about her life, who retreated like a turtle inside its shell anytime anything was broached, was finally willing to talk. Without prompting, she told me about her history in New York and before that. Shock and puzzlement made me miss her first few lines.

When she was very young, a naive girl from the provinces coming to Manila for the first time to work as a maid in a wealthy Chinese household, she came under the spell of a sweet-talking older boy and was waylaid into prostitution. I looked at her fingers, which were working overtime drumming out beats on a table she seemed to have specially cleaned for the occasion, playing it as an instrument. Later, of course, I would realize that I was the final burden that she had to be relieved of, that she launched into this long-anticipated story as a way to "explain" herself, and that she was doing it to a quick-ticking clock inside her heart, counting out the precious minutes before she could clear out.

But she wasn't at the brothel for very long, Preciosa hastened to add. The audacity of her escape—feigning illness in the middle of the night, only to jump out of the ambulance and run to her freedom—my God, it prepared her for New York! Because New York, or rather America, was, without knowing it, what she'd been working toward! Filled with cunning now, and the residual bitterness of having been duped, she put an ad in a publication intended to unite old white Americans with potential brides from the Third World, young girls filled with the talent for pliancy which in American girls had long gone out of fashion. These men were looking for a servant, a nurse, a companion, and, whenever and wherever they wanted, an imaginative and responsive whore. A large number of these men had been soldiers enlisted in Vietnam and it seemed that what they wanted and what these girls could provide was a reinstatement of their carefree, powerful youth.

She said that the letters poured in. The ones she deemed promising—about a dozen—she responded to. Within a month, all of them were writing to see if they could come to the Philippines and meet her. She knew they wanted to find out if she looked like her picture. They wanted their money's worth and were coming to inspect the goods beforehand. Estranged from her family ever since her days of prostitution, she had to pay a group of strangers to act as her family, put all of them up at a reasonably dilapidated house just a stone's throw away from a squatter area: she wanted to be seen as a traditional girl, a girl close to her impoverished family, for whom marriage to an American—regardless of how fat and ugly, and most of them were—represented an upswing in life. These guys saw indebtedness as an aphrodisiac—why, these girls could be made to do just about anything, knowing that they owed everything to the men. Preciosa had instructed the woman who played her mother to act tough, implacable, as if the daughter she had the power to surrender

[margin note:] preciosa's mask

to any of these men was a precious and rare commodity. The gambit worked. The cumulative picture Preciosa assembled plus the persuasive fact of her beauty were more than the men could withstand. Impatient, they were as good as issuing ultimatums. Choose, they said. The man Preciosa chose was the oldest. Looking at him, she said to reassure herself: He doesn't have that long to live. The skin on his face was shrunken, holding fast to the skull for fear of falling off. And his dentures were like a mousetrap—they practically jutted out of his quivering mouth every time he talked, snapping with each consonant. But he was gallant, tipping his hat to her and to her fake mother every time he wanted to underline an important point. Such as that he was well off, having invested his army pension wisely, and could therefore support Preciosa in a way that even most Americans would concede was luxurious, never mind somebody from a down-at-heel country such as the Philippines. That he said what he said about the Philippines somehow seemed to vouch for his honesty, his honor. Every other suitor had painted the country in such far-fetched, pastel terms more suitable for a brochure—using words like paradise (Yeah right, she thought: paradise of TB and malnutrition!) and heaven—that by the time this old geezer came along, speaking in his plainspoken, countrified way, her ears pricked up.

But he lived in *Texas*—the very sound of which put her on guard. In her mind, she saw guns, chains, a million cactus sentries put up around the house she would live in. But she kept repeating to herself: This man doesn't have long to live. And besides, an American passport would be hers forever. For her that was the bargain being made. Sure, the women in the brothel had told stories of other women who'd been married to these *kanos*, in essence agreeing to a life of voluntary servitude. The abuse and torture inflicted on these new wives made the tellers grateful for their own, lighter version of hell. Why, some of those women, thinking that they would live in America forever, ended up missing. Their families never heard from them again. They were feared dead. That was the price paid for disobeying these men whose power needed the girls for an audience.

So Preciosa's strongest memory of arriving in this country was of a tight chest. She held her breath all the way from the airport to her new home, fearing for the trade she'd made. All those stories worked their black magic in the first few months of her life here. She didn't want to leave the house, an act her new husband misinterpreted as a kind of affection, of loyalty. Surprisingly, he turned out to be a kind man, as kind as his advertised self, but she was waiting every day for the kindness to be dropped, when he could relax in front of her with a whip crack in the voice and a gun stashed near at hand to reinforce the orders his kind had historically grown used to issuing to her kind. She found herself growing more tender than she could've predicted. Imagine, having to look at that frog face with its wrinkly, perpetually sweaty skin dotted with all those carbuncles—and imagine having to kiss it! This was no fairy tale: having been kissed, the frog would still remain a frog. But there were days, believe it or not, when she didn't mind having to do just such a thing. He was so old that even being alive was for him a kind of virility, a sign that he'd surpassed what was expected of a regular man in this country. He still had sexual appetites. And to gratify them, Preciosa all the while thought of the dark blue cover of her new passport, thought of the Philippines as of a dilapidated building on the wrong side of town passed by without a second glance from a dark-windowed, air-conditioned car. She had transcended something, and it was now at her back. Even if the sex was disgusting, it was still sex in Texas, U.S.A. And even if Texas was dry and boring and filled with big things that sat there like impediments to the view, it was still attached to the rest of the U.S., which was merely waiting for her husband to up and die before it opened its doors to her. And she found this out about her husband: not to gratify his sexual wishes made him stronger, more vital. And conversely, when she gave in, his already weak heart grew weaker. In a year and a half, the frog was dead. Afterward, there was the minor inconvenience of a family skirmish involving the man's will—he'd left everything to Preciosa. The family came in to contest, but surprising them, Preciosa took only a small sum—enough to start a new life elsewhere—and tossed the rest right back to them.

New York she'd heard about from a friend she'd run into in Texas. Like Preciosa, this woman had married her way into the States, leaving the provinces of the Philippines to live in arid, smoky San Antonio. And after the brave (and unheard-of) move of divorcing her gun-toting, Klan-affiliated husband (and managing somehow not to be killed), this woman had left for New York.

The first few years, Preciosa had simply followed the pattern established by this woman. Whatever jobs this woman had taken in New York, testing the waters, Preciosa took eventually.

There was her stint accosting customers at Saks with a perfume bottle. While doing that, she'd been spotted and invited to model for a painter. Nothing came of that, however, because the painter had merely been a wealthy man indulging fantasies of an artistic life, and his canvases were so evidently bad that not even his bankroll could persuade a gallery to display them in public. She'd danced in a modern dance company, and not particularly gifted, had had to drop out soon after. By this time, her woman friend had decided to go back to the Philippines, having been outrun by the pace of this country, turned ragged. In the short time this woman friend had been here, her beauty—which had been her only contribution—had been used up, and thus erased, she would only be as good as all the other Filipinas she saw in the city: frumpy nannies, matronly aides pushing wheelchair-bound wards on the streets, and nurses with the faces of servile dogs—people she felt personally ashamed for. To become like them, in her opinion, was a fate worse than death. At least, back home, the exchange rate would make the hard-earned dollars she'd saved a virtual fortune, and with it she could, say, start a business, or buy herself a few homes, wealth nullifying the fact of her spent beauty. She'd be going back in triumph, the neighbors ogling her like a newly minted celebrity. The last Preciosa heard, she had bought several shopping centers in Manila, and was exporting tacky arts and crafts goods to America.

There was the acting job at Lincoln Center—how Preciosa got that was how people in this city got anything: through connections. A friend she knew during her modern dance days had introduced her to the casting director. She went to audition, and because the play didn't require great acting skills and what the playwright and director were looking for was only the right "look," something that would put the stamp of authenticity on the whole thinly imagined enterprise, she had of course knocked them dead. But the excitement for her didn't last long. She'd been told what the play was about and what was expected of her—the partial nudity and all that. And she was game. She knew that she wasn't talented enough to expect otherwise. But not until after a few Filipino friends came to see the performance and she saw their faces did she realize that what she'd perceived as a triumph was the farthest thing from it. And this time, the trade she'd made of her dignity was visible for all to see— there was no finessing her way around that, no trying to blur the shameful aspect of the thing by rationalizing that the audience could hold the complex idea in their heads that she might be the character in the play and yet at the same time was outside it, merely an actress. Because they couldn't see. For them, she was as good as what the title of the damn thing had promised them: a primitive! From then on, she'd gone onstage every night with a deep, burning shame. And when required, during her penultimate scene, to swivel around and mouth all that native gibberish in a fit of being possessed by a pagan demon, anger had surged inside her and turned her performance even fiercer. The audience and her co-actors on stage had to rear back, so convincing had she become, possessed by a desire to undo everything that everyone was willing into shape: this ridiculous story intentionally turning back the hands of time so that she could be returned to the pages of a history book, all her English unlearned, her beautiful blue-black American passport handed back. In her mind, she was being returned to the Philippines, thereby doing away with the need for an actual trip.

Afterward, she looked for other work as an actress, seeing herself weighted with something that had to be erased, overcome. But she couldn't find anything. Her looks could never be put in front of the words the characters she was up for had to speak. The writers and directors responsible couldn't see her embodying any of that. Again and again, she was told that she was better suited to silence. Roles as an extra. But how could these roles ever erase the embarrassment of *Primitives*? The period of her life that followed was the lowest. Depressed and demoralized, without a reason to get up in the morning, she'd let herself languish until one day it was made clear to her that she owed four months' rent.

What did she do? She laughed. She said she went to a loan shark—and seeing her, this man had broken her string of bad luck, saying that she was just the type he was looking for. On the spot he cast her for the part of his mistress. That was how she'd managed to borrow against what she needed for her hip operation. The man, now her former lover, had cut her some slack, extending the period in which she was supposed to pay him back.

This man was a character straight out of the seventies, wearing flashy, multicolored suits that seemed like such a loud, stereotypical declaration of badness that for a moment you considered just the opposite: why would a man truly criminal dress in the avowed fashion of criminals unless he really wasn't one, unless he was someone who only wanted to adopt the "look," like dressing up after having seen a movie? But if you thought that, you'd be making a big mistake. This man had killed a few people who owed him money. He had boys who did the job for him, were glad to do it, in fact lived for just such a thing. They had no other talents in life, but once they had a debtor cornered, cowering and sweating, they smiled with the fullness of the knowledge that this was what they were born to do. She'd seen them rough up a few people when they bodyguarded for their boss, her ex-lover. And it was their faces she saw once again when she had to default on her payments. Lucky for her I'd suggested what I did. She thanked me for it. But now she was back on her feet and would leave my world behind.

Just before I left, I looked her in the eye, and asked, Is there something wrong, Preciosa?

Instead of replying, she asked, You didn't betray me, did you?

Betray you? What do you mean? Who would I betray you to?

You didn't, right?

Of course not.

I had more money to collect, and couldn't dwell on Preciosa's cloudy portentousness. The list Shem provided was far from depleted. Christmas was approaching, and people were growing more anxious about acquiring peace in their lives. And after Christmas, there was New Year's Eve, a dreaded countdown to what many believed would be the end of the world. Everybody was trying not to think about it, but this turning of the head sideways was proving to be a great strain on the neck.

In Murray Hill, a neighborhood of old residential buildings relatively unattacked by commercialization, I walked up to a short, comparatively new building that stood out against its neighbors because of a coat of new, disturbingly Floridian orange—the color worn to ward off hunters in the forest.

The woman who lived there had a popular cable show in which she shared useful bits of homemaking advice, both practical and decorative. To improve and prettify your surroundings was, according to her, tantamount to elevating your consciousness and well-being, which seemed to me a perfect (and judging from her popularity, profitable) paraphrase of Feng Shui. That she chose this hideous, afraid-to-be-shot-at building to live in, if her philosophy was to be believed, spoke volumes about her spirit, which she corroborated soon enough upon greeting me at her front door.

She asked me to take off my shoes so that I wouldn't dirty her newly waxed floor. This directive was to be repeated over and over. Anything I touched she would immediately have to take up and reset on the desks, the shelves, the tables, even if I hadn't moved them in the slightest. My hands on the couch, on the picture frames, as soon as they left, would be replaced by hers vigorously dusting away. She made me feel like I was leaking sawdust all over her chintzy, semiprecious belongings.

What school did I say I came from?

The North River School, I replied, having vaguely recalled the phrase from one of the many books I'd scoured.

The what? she asked.

I repeated myself.

There's no such thing, she said, with a note of triumph in her voice. I know all the schools. There are—

I stopped her before she could enumerate. Are you an expert?

I trained, she replied.

The man you trained with, what is his name?

She gave me some chop suey name that wouldn't even pass the grade in a Charlie Chan movie. Hah! I said.

What? she asked, genuinely alarmed that perhaps I had the dirt on this guy, that perhaps she had the misfortune to walk straight into the most legendary dropout of the Feng Shui schools, her accreditation as an expert in these matters about to be revoked.

He's nobody.

He's the most respected Feng Shui expert in China.

In China, hah! Is that why you had to ask for me?

I asked you here because I'm doing a segment on my show and having heard so much about you, I wanted to find out for myself.

But you had China's foremost expert at hand, I said condescendingly. Why didn't you ask him? Or yourself, if, as you said, you've already learned from the best.

She stammered. I heard so much about you.

Whatever it is you've learned isn't compatible in this country. Things have to be modified. Everyone knows that.

There is no such school as the North River School.

I thought: Get yourself out now. To her I said: That's where my knowledge comes from. You've asked my clients? I'm sure none of them are complaining. And then I remembered Cardie Kerchpoff, and my throat went dry.

She was stone-faced.

Finally, she conceded: They all swear by you. She rattled off names: Lindsay S, Mrs. S, Brian Q, a few minor society matriarchs whom I thought of as a chorus of dim brown birds, and, most shocking of all, Suzy Yamada. She too had given her endorsement.

But the cable-show hostess, who saw herself as nothing if not a reliable font for information—which, having been gathered from certified experts in various fields, she relayed to her viewers with a confident, no-time-for-doubt briskness, but with the added genius of simplification and homeyness, all technicalese defanged—stuck with her original idea: between the expert in China (who had the motherland's imprimatur) and the avowed expert in New York (whose advantage was celebrity), she stuck with the former, her original source.

Eventually I conceded defeat. Losing my confidence, I stopped holding her accusatory gaze. I went to the door, opened it, but before leaving turned to her. I offered this gift, controlling the anger in my voice: You will die within the year, I said. Thinking of her building, it occurred to me to specify: You will be shot by a hunter. And there is nothing you can do about it.

I saw that she became afraid, not knowing to distinguish between a prophecy and a threat, and that was the last I saw of her. It made me feel momentarily better, though I knew that it was only a reprieve before real defeat: I was losing my touch.

Real trouble came very shortly on the heels of that, but first there was one more sucker to—as per the writing in some of my favorite books—"play like a violin."

This sucker was a theater director who, having had no time to unpack since a recent move, invited me to inspect his new, ghostly digs in the West Village. The daisy chain of involvement clicked like a clasp closing when I found out that he knew Lindsay S, my very first client. And now, to end my life as Chao, this sucker would be my last.

It was Lindsay who'd referred him to me. All his life, this man, Peter L, had been fighting not to succumb to a susceptibility to superstition that he'd inherited from his Southern family, in particular his beloved grandmother, from whom he'd also inherited a high, whiny voice like a blender awhir, and a tendency to whip his head and torso around very quickly as he spoke. But with his great good luck mounting over the years, he'd found himself becoming more superstitious. He wore medallions that he believed transferred good energy to his endeavors. Hung garlic at the top of doorframes to ward off evil spirits. Saw a clairvoyant monthly to chart his plans. He knew that he'd gotten more expansive with each success, and with this expansiveness had rubbed a lot of people the wrong way, people who would like to see him step wrong, step off that golden ladder of success—and he was doing everything in his power to guard against that. I was extra bulwarking.

This man had two off-Broadway hits waiting to transfer to Broadway at the very same time that he already had two musicals on Broadway—he was a virtual hit factory, beloved by his backers, and by the critics, who, gushing, guaranteed him a servile, eager-to-be-hoodwinked audience. How did I know this? The man, wanting me to know who I was dealing with, had sent me a press packet of review after euphoric review, most of them rife with claims about his being the big hope of the American musical theater—the one true indigenous art form of this country.

He also gave me tickets to see both of his Broadway musicals. The first was about a bunch of people who were so happy that they felt compelled to screech songs at the top of their lungs given the slightest excuse. And strangely enough, so was the second one. Two happy, happy shows, filled with actors exuding tireless, determined cheer, their smiles like wax decorations applied on top of their real faces. But this had been the tradition of their tribe from the very beginning, all those people with their exclamation points and their teeth—which, I suppose, was what the critics found indigenously American. Not that these were vehicles compatible with the exploration of deep thoughts, but talk about simplicity! This director had a simplemindedness that made me think he was deprived in childhood of everything but the basic eight-color Crayola set—simple blacks and whites were his forte.

His idea of directing seemed to be: Let the shit fly as fast as you can and make sure to fade the lights down before any of it lands. The actors looked like they were hooked up to an electroshock machine offstage which would instantaneously jolt them if their joie de vivre went below a set level. They looked like they were going to be punished if they didn't meet a certain quota of decibel violation. (And to further aid this, the director had staged everything downstage, right up against the audience's noses, as if their entire comprehension of the pieces would be jeopardized should they even miss the slightest ooh-wah or doo-da-dee-dee.) Their cheer was industrious and aided by the timing of hucksters selling dubious property. Both evenings were traffic-jammy with too much. Suddenly the word Technicolor seemed a suitable anagram for the word Punishment. The audience both nights cheered thunderously at the end, making me feel as if I'd walked in from Mars and had missed the turnstile where they handed out an instruction manual to explain the customs of my new home.

This man was the least humble of anyone I'd met. Ironically, he was part black and part Native American (a jackpot, guilt-inducing combination!), but that was precisely why he thought his achievements possessed an exponential sense of victory—because he had double color to overcome. In my presence, he'd trotted out the same tired-sounding rhetoric of having to be "ten times better than a white counterpart" to succeed at the level he had. Even if true, this

was only one in a long series of excuses and explanations he was offering all afternoon—and the defensiveness which underscored
these pronouncements undercut the picture of himself as an unqual-
ified success that he was trying to paint.

This man gave off a sense of having had to be his own agent all
life long, of having had to talk himself up in front of others to convince them (and himself) of his worthiness, thereby setting himself
up for the next gig. There were phrases he tossed which I'd already
read from the press releases he sent. Phrases like "the dearth of color
in this country," like "the responsibilities of art and of artists to the
society in which they live," like "the soulfulness of civics." The echo
chamber of being in his presence induced a splitting headache. I
suppose this was one way to view his success—as a capitulation, a
surrender to his buzzy, bizzy act. People would be so eager to escape
his lack of doubt about anything that they would agree to anything
he asked.

There was nothing to move in his white apartment. Everything
was white—the ceiling, the walls, the rough plank-board flooring.
And light filtering in through two south-facing windows in the
front room gave to the white box a churchlike, sepulchral glow.
Yeah, I thought, a church for self-worship.

He wanted me to plan the layout of his home for him.

I told him everything he wanted to hear. This behavior didn't de-
viate from the treatment he'd grown used to, the treatment which he
in fact expected of his minions—the backers, the critics, his actors,
the public. They were so eager to be collaborators in the startling
game of success he found himself being the ringmaster of that they
said yes at the drop of a hat, in effect buttering their own bread.
This man doled out livelihoods to people he thought could be seen
to extend his work. He did this by linking a central element in the
work of the various actors, writers, set and costume designers, com-
posers, and choreographers that he hired to his very own political,
moral, religious, artistic concerns of the moment, giving interviews
in which he cast these people's accomplishments in the shadow of
his own greater, overarching brilliance. He parceled every small bit
of generosity out in front of a crowd, making sure to interpret the
action for them so that there would be no doubt that what he was

doing was a siring of artistic progeny, bequeathing his much-needed artistic legacy to New York, the cultural center of the world at the turning of the new century.

This man would, like the photo gallery owner before him, be the one responsible for planning out his own misfortune, and I would only stand at the side and be a compliant, nodding facilitator.

The front room, of course, looked like a front room, and we both agreed it would remain so. Next to it would be the library. And beside it the dining room. The kitchen would be two rooms with a joint wall knocked down.

This man, proclaiming he knew so much, didn't know much at all. The room he chose for the library had a window which faced a busy street, and between the dining room and the kitchen was a narrow entryway that seemed too narrow and cumbersome to constantly traverse, especially if, as he said, he wanted to throw many large parties as soon as he was settled in.

In the middle of our session his cell phone rang. As he listened, his face registered surprise. Suzy, he said into the receiver. He got my undivided attention. Oh yes, he said. Master Chao is here. Oh? Oh?

When he was done, he said that Suzy wanted to come by. Would I be willing to wait?

What did Suzy want with me?

She said there was something wrong that she couldn't tell me over the phone, something that's been troubling her life recently that she wanted to talk to you about.

So, I thought, Rowley's revenge, Shem's revenge had arrived. What would it be? My curiosity overpowered any apprehension I might have had.

There was nowhere to sit, and no tea or coffee to be had while waiting. This gave Peter L the perfect opportunity to continue educating me about the hardships of being a colored man in the American theater in the late twentieth century. He wanted to be more than just an envoy of his peoples, he said, and so was actively looking for shows that had nothing to do with the black or the Native American experience, nothing to do with slavery or racism or the reservations or suffering. Which was why joy was such a big deal with him, a veritable "issue." Speaking of which, what did I think of the musicals?

Very entertaining, I replied.

He was smart enough to know that my compliment had been selected to cover something unsavory in my essential attitude. Perhaps it was also the way I'd said the word. The word "entertaining" having been picked at the very last moment like a curtain suddenly drawn to obscure things.

But did this stop him? No. He went on and on.

Inside his head, this man seemed to have built himself a house whose walls were pasted together from his press releases, and he lived every day enclosed, entombed within the narrow confines of the role he'd been cast in. Every palaver, every written corroboration of his self-worth (and extending from that, the inferiority of everyone who'd preceded him historically and, even more so, the inferiority of all of his peers—a word he wouldn't even deign to use because he viewed himself as essentially peerless), he believed in fervently. And just like that piano player I encountered at the Dowager's, this man, blinded to his own faults, had no reason to improve. Why improve? Every single sneeze or yawn could be palmed off as the act of a bravura showman—perhaps his having been a colored man wasn't a hindrance after all, but rather a boost, seeing that so many people, eager to apologize for history's wrongdoing to the black and the Native American races, conspired to crown this man—chosen for no other reason than that he was close at hand: a literal two birds by which one stone would provide the easy solution—as the king of what had been essentially a white American enterprise—the musical—thereby forcing the twentieth century to a close with the homiletic sight of the banner of "the brotherhood of man" flying sturdily and high above the American horizon.

Finally, he excused himself to go upstairs, check on things. He was gone for an inordinately long time. Even when I heard a knock on the door, he didn't appear. I went to let Suzy in.

Kendo was standing there. He looked like he'd been running a marathon. The words that came out of his mouth made me understand perfectly. My mother knows everything. She's coming because she knows everything.

* 34 *

But of course, all this time, I'd forgotten about Neil, or
Gurinder—I didn't know which name he'd used to introduce himself to Suzy. He'd gone to see the Isuzu Yamada
of the Upper West Side, and she, like a queen receiving word from a
spy, had closed her eyes with the satisfaction of being vindicated in
her suspicions. People were after her, she'd always known.

But then after Suzy had heard, after she'd paid Neil a token reward and shooed him away from their home, there passed for Suzy a
moment of disbelief, of great indecision. Suzy, just like me, just like
Hamlet (to be or not to be, etc.: I knew more than Shem thought I
knew) before her, would take a while to turn thought into action.
Perhaps, knowing that she'd been personally responsible for several
people's unhappiness, she wasn't content to just be handed my
name. Surely, other people were behind my appearance on the
scene? And just who were these people? She wouldn't be content
until she got to the true puppet masters—until the names matched
up with the ones she had in her mind, enemies known to her, filled

with motives which, having provided them herself, she understood completely. Would she know to end up at Shem? Shem who didn't fuck her, whose connection to her was no different than that of just about everyone I encountered: a gazer from a distance.

Suzy needed one more thing, one more visible proof of the truthfulness of this Indian man's assertions. Once she got it, then she would know exactly what was to be done.

Then one day not long after Neil's visit, she received it. The streets brought her face to face once more with someone she'd met before, someone, in fact, she'd been trying to set her sights on again.

It was Preciosa, who, though no longer hobbled by a cane, still could not walk away fast enough to escape.

Suzy'd stopped her. Kendo was with his mother. Of course he recognized Preciosa immediately from having seen her outside my door, but didn't know that she was also the priestess Walung, the woman who'd been drafted to help inside their house and whose voluminous black skirts had hidden objects stolen from the mantelpiece, from various tables and pedestals. This Walung's invocation of the spirits was an act that had been thought up by none other than Max Brill Carlton, a performance replayed solely for Suzy's benefit.

Hello, Suzy had said to Preciosa. In Suzy's eyes Preciosa was still Walung. Nothing suspicious had yet emerged.

It was Preciosa who had started fidgeting, unable to look Suzy in the eyes. And what's worse, she had turned voluble. The woman who, as the haughty primitive, hadn't even deigned to speak, merely grunting, and doing it in such a way as to suggest that she refused to be lowered to the level of such a common tongue, had begun to talk a clear and casual English. Hello, how are you? she'd asked the pair. This shocked Suzy Yamada.

But not until Kendo spoke, offering his own two cents after Preciosa had left, did Suzy *know* once and for all. Eager to be of help, he'd told his mother that he'd seen Preciosa before. Where? his mother wanted to know. And not wanting to jeopardize me, he put Preciosa in a building other than mine. He told Suzy that Preciosa lived in . . . the same building as his father. He didn't realize what this would mean. And hearing, Suzy had her incontrovertible proof. Everyone who lived in that building was in some way malformed.

Most of them had criminal records. And the others, well, they were just waiting to be caught. Kendo's father, for example. God knows what he was involved in now. And that unsavory wife of his. The two of them, plus those two poor children who would be sure to perpetuate the trend. How could they not? Even if the parents had straightened out, the children still couldn't escape daily contact with all those crooked tenants, people like Preciosa who, either through osmosis or by active recruitment, would pass on their legacies the way rats passed on fleas.

Suzy knew then that if Preciosa lived in that hellish building, then there was no doubt that she wasn't Walung. That she had no powers. That she had indeed stolen from her. And that I was exactly who Neil claimed.

And so now the search was on for me. But not so she could exact punishment. No, Kendo assured me. She wanted to see what my price was. She wanted me to reveal the name of the one who had sent me, who was masterminding her public humiliation. A humiliation which revealed, as if suddenly lit by lightning, Bill Hood as exactly what he was—a stone around her neck.

We went to Preciosa's apartment. No one answered the door. Kendo proved his criminal apprenticeship by opening the door with a credit card. I was shocked, thinking it only a fiction from the movies.

The shabby couch with the unraveling piece of knitting thrown to cover the worn-out cushions. Divina Valencia blowing bubbles inside her bowl, her eyes just as big as mine. The kitchen cabinets revealed a full stack of dishes. The drawers pulled out with individual squeaks, and every single fork, spoon, chopstick, knife that sat there looked shiny, placed inside each cubbyhole with care. Inside the refrigerator sat a single container of soy sauce and some cellophane-wrapped pink meat that hadn't been touched. Cans of soup, of tuna, of beans sat neatly on a bare shelf above the rack holding pots and pans. Nothing sat inside the sparkling sink. The place had been recently cleaned, awaiting the return of its owner, who, for all we knew, had just gone out to replenish her fridge.

But inside the bathroom, the medicine cabinet was bare. And in her small bedroom with the bed that had recently been refitted with a tougher mattress in accordance with doctor's orders, the closet pulled open to reveal a whole rack of clothes hangers. Only two pairs of worn-looking shoes sat on the floor. No suitcases or bags could be found.

Kendo admitted to having visited Preciosa after he left his mother, the same way he'd visited me, wanting to draw out a story, expecting friendship in the same way that he'd established with all his shady acquaintances. But Kendo, as he did with me, conducted the interview with the air of the blackmailer, a cocky kid for whom the acquisition of knowledge made him puff out his chest and speak in the tones of holding back a threat.

And so, Preciosa had confessed everything to him.

Kendo now realized that she must have begun packing as soon as he'd left her.

Afterward, she told me everything that she'd never been able to tell before. It was her way of saying goodbye, and she was sure that, looking back on her telling, I would understand.

Kendo apologized. If only he hadn't told his mother that he'd seen Preciosa before, and if only he hadn't said that thing about her living in his father's building. He didn't mean for any of this to happen. He knew that he himself had fucked up the beautiful arrangement we had. Still, he said, trying to reassure himself, his mother didn't know that he knew me.

Empty, Preciosa's apartment seemed holy, its remnants somehow awakened, anxiously awaiting their owner's return because only she knew their special value, their meaning, and without her they would be lost, returned to being mere *things*. The most surprising aspect about the apartment's dereliction was how unsurprising it all was: that even while Preciosa had lived there, it had already had an air of vacancy, of transiency about it, an air that I now realized was a transfer from its owner, who, even before she had revealed the story of her peripatetic life, had already had the look of someone who would make of her present address a somewhere else, another in a long line of somewhere elses like the country she'd just vacated to get here, on and on as if carrying out the directive of some deficiency encoded into her genes, a hunger, some basic discontent. This, being one more definition of immigrant—torn between the competing pulls of the fiction of the promised land, on the one hand, and the fiction of the sustaining mother country, on the other. The empty couch, the old dining-room table brought from the Philippines and which could easily fetch a mint for some enterprising interior decorator, the dusty curtains framing the beehive view of a sooty, billboard-choked building across the street, even Divina Valencia, whom Preciosa had bought on a sudden celebratory whim—all these things were now revealed to be more meaningful in the wake of Preciosa's abandonment. Seeing them, I once more remembered Preciosa's lesson: We could just walk away. She herself had followed it, demonstrating how easy it could be, how natural to our lives as eternal immigrants: just walk away, turning our backs on the consequences. And after all now, when I die, it would not be Preciosa who would come to claim me, make sure I was given the proper rites. But then I remembered: I did not intend to die.

I went to the bank. Withdrew all my money in various denominations, stuffed everything into separate white envelopes. At home, I packed neatly folded clothes into a medium-sized tote, and put the envelopes of money in between the layers. I zippered the tote, stashed it in a closet. In this same closet I noticed a cashmere blanket I had bought but had never used because I'd been afraid of ruining it. It had cost me seven hundred dollars, and looking at it now, I remembered having once laughed at people for whom such purchases were commonplace. I'd bought it as a visible reminder to myself that I'd crossed a line into a new station in life, as an encouragement, a joke (a seven-hundred-dollar joke), and now I was pulling past that station and heading for an unknown place.

I tore up Shem's card, his Feng Shui pamphlet, and tossed them and my interior design magazines into the trash. I took the garbage bag and, going out of the building, threw it into a Dumpster behind a pizza joint two blocks down.

Fortunately, just like Kendo's father's family, I owned no pictures of myself, and therefore was saved from having to burn them. There had been no special occasions I'd wanted memorialized—no graduation, no promotion, no family gatherings. Everything I'd lived through would never be gone, of course, it would continue to take residence inside my brain, be dislodged by drink, or pot, to haunt my weighted sleep, or blur the useless day, but otherwise it'd just sit there, collecting dust, making its presence known over the years only through my head tipping lower and lower with its collective weight. Or sometimes I would actually be brave enough and take certain memories out to look at. And depending on the disposition or temperature of that particular period of reflection, these reclaimed instances would seem either triumphant events of gaining wisdom or under-the-skin-sad events of losing some essential thing that would never be recoverable—innocence, vitality, faith . . .

There was the neighbor woman downstairs to take care of. Three cats stood between us, and they took turns rubbing up against my pant leg. The last cat, however, could sense my knees shaking, and so immediately sprang clear to the other side, and from that moment on, refused to relax its brilliant, accusing stare. Don't pay any attention to him, laughed the cat woman. He's just playing with you.

I filled her in. Told her that Preciosa had returned to the Philippines. Her mother was seriously ill, and she'd gone back to take care of her family. She wasn't sure when she would be coming back. And she wanted me to tell the woman goodbye for her. And as for myself, first, I would be going to Florida to get away from the cold, and then I would be joining Preciosa in the Philippines. But only for a month or two, perhaps spend the first few months of the new year there, but I'd be coming back soon after.

Finally I went to see Shem. The time had come for that. The doorman announced my presence on the intercom. There was an involved discussion between him and Shem before the doorman, with a quizzical look on his face, directed me to the elevators.

Shem had this same look on his face when I came up. How did I know where to find him when he hadn't told me? He stood aside as I entered but didn't say anything.

He thought it only proper to start with polite formalities. In his very own home, he would indulge in the things that he laughed at in the homes of others. But when he said those nice, starched words, I brushed them aside. Suzy knows, were my first words.

The expression that flickered briefly on his face was a miffed one of having to adjust to the too early arrival of a train.

The white couch I sat on had been placed perpendicular to three windows that looked down on West End. But we were so high up and everything so quiet that for all I knew we could be anywhere but New York. Across the street was a building the exact same height, with the same Art Deco columns and trims—seemingly built by competing contractors to face each other like giants in a standoff. Facing me, Shem sat on an armchair upholstered to match his couch. Between us was a newspaper opened to the obituaries. How does Suzy know? Shem asked me.

I explained everything, mentioning Kendo, how he'd found me out and how I'd had to let him in on our plans. I didn't have any choice, I said.

He knows everything?

Yes, I lied. I meant for Shem to think that Kendo knew all about him as well. I meant for Shem to take care of this Kendo because I wanted it out of my hands.

Later, I would imagine an alternate version of my visit: My chest fake-puffed with the unshakable confidence of holding something over Shem. Not sitting, but instead pacing to and fro, looking over his apartment as Chao, infusing comments about the way his place looked, the way his furniture was arrayed with an irony of How do you like the taste of your own medicine?

But I just sat there, looking at that man's face the whole time. He'd just shaved, and the cleanness of his sharp jawline was accentuated by the perfectly turned-out and stiff collar of a pink long-sleeved shirt with a polo player stitched on a breast pocket. The polo player was frozen in the position of being about to hit a ball, his stick up in the air. And I waited for Shem to finish off that move, to actually hit the ball straight back to me, but he was very quiet, though not in a fearful sense at all.

He asked me if I wanted something to drink. I told him I was fine. The politeness was like a little joke. Our conspiracy, having started at the otherworldly Savoy, was being tied up in this den of bourgeois respectability, complete with doorman to make sure that nobody unsavory came in. It was a station he'd claimed to have disavowed a long time ago. But here he was, white linen-upholstered couch, bookshelves stacked with volumes that helped an observer to fill in its owner's accomplishments, or to make up for the gap between what he hadn't been able to accomplish and what—given the extent of his learning—he still could. On the wall just above one of the bookshelves were two framed pieces of paper. Citations, or diplomas, I didn't get close enough to read. There was a mahogany clock with a shiny silver pendulum swinging behind me, flanking one side of a door that led to an undisclosed room. The few objects on the coffee table between us, on the mantel by the windows, on the bookshelves revealed Shem to be a scrupulous, proud, discerning owner.

He was a Jew who directed his animosity toward other Jews with a vindictiveness that verged on a calling. Bill Hood, the top Jew, was usurping the position that rightly belonged to him, to Shem. And he wanted, in a way that was devised on the spot, piecemeal, a plan that was so far-fetched nobody would believe there had been a plan—as if thought up by Agatha Christie for an entertainment that would jazz but would not bear up under scrutiny—he'd wanted, using this plan, to move from the sidelines into the center. He belonged in the center by virtue of his talents, of what he had to offer. Until, of course, he ran straight into the wall of Bill Hood and was denied. Whatever intrigue happened between the two I couldn't be sure, but it occurred to me that in the relationship between the Dowager and Suzy Yamada there might exist a parallel: one master using his considerable powers to block the entry and rise of a young man he viewed, perhaps justifiably, as an upstart and a troublemaker. And Shem had watched helplessly, as first this journal, and then that publisher, had rejected his writings. Watched the gap widen between where he stood and where Bill Hood stood, not only esteemed but wealthy, embraced by the critics, on the one hand, and the dazzling social scene on the other, firmly entrenched in the order of things. But with his plan, Shem would reverse everything, turn the tenets of this social order against itself, offer to these people the very things they cherished but inverting their value so that the hollowness of their code, of their hierarchies was revealed.

That was it, I realized, looking at his acquisitions rendered suddenly distinct with their revealed meaning: These things weren't native to Shem. They were things which, because he hadn't grown up with them, he'd dreamed of acquiring one day. He didn't come from the same place as these people. He came from *below* them, and aspired to their status. His carefully arrayed, polished belongings smacked of nothing less than custodianship, unease. While for those for whom such things were commonplace, for Max Brill Carlton, for example, the basic attitude was one of indifference, casualness.

Shem's marriage to Marianna had been an ascension, after all, not the union of equals. He'd married her hoping it was the first step in his social rise—only to fail by being chucked out because of an infidelity. But who was this mysterious woman?

In the uncomfortable, vaguely threatening silence that covered the space between us, I volunteered another statement about our relationship. I said to Shem: Bill Hood is now with Suzy Yamada.

When he didn't reply, I continued: That part I don't understand. But the rest, everything else, I know about, Shem.

What do you know?

I told him about Marianna and Bill Hood—lovers, not father and daughter. And her daughter, the blond, affable Beulah, affable enough to be coached to manufacture claims against Hood. Very smart for Shem to have chosen such accusations that bypassed logic and went straight to the nerve center of the culture. And how about Feng Shui? Had he first encountered it in *Metropolitan Home*, in that short article about Suzy Yamada? And was that how the two had become inseparable in his head, because when he encountered them, they were already together, a unit?

Shem's reaction was one of elegant sobriety, and it made me see the essential absurdity of my claims. But if everything was absurd anyway, why stop short for fear of embarrassing myself, why not extend my claims further? At least it might get a laugh out of him, any reaction other than the one he had of looking at me as if there was a microscope between us.

Suzy might've been the unofficial queen of her set, and therefore was the right target for our plans, but surely there were other queens of other, slightly more or less elevated sets to choose from? So what other reason could Shem have for singling her out? Perhaps, Suzy had indeed been Shem's lover. The moment I said it, it began to take on the ring of truth. I'd disregarded it for having been too obvious, too neat—but hell, why fight it now, at this late hour, when there was nothing else to take its place?

Perhaps he'd fucked her as a bid for advancement, hoping to transfer to Suzy's world, the next step up, precipitating his own divorce from Marianna only to find Suzy having closed her doors to him as well—well, Shem, other than raw ambition, had nothing to offer this Suzy who herself was looking to latch on to someone who would elevate her to the next level. Ironically, immediately after Marianna had divorced Shem, he saw Marianna being taken up by his other nemesis, Bill Hood. And seen in this light, her value had become more obvious than ever before. How could Shem have let Marianna go just like that? Now he was between two locked doors, and this was when the idea of revenge came to him.

A revenge capped by the union of his two nemeses: Bill Hood with Suzy Yamada. We knew how Bill Hood had been trounced. But what was this Suzy's comeuppance? She surely wasn't behaving like someone comeupped, but rather as a prizewinner, despite the tainted reputation of her boyfriend. The Dowager had told me that reprisals in her circle came swiftly, and surely if they hadn't already descended on Suzy, they would never descend? Or perhaps, and more frighteningly, this was a new Suzy nobody could've predicted —a Suzy in love, a Suzy who, newly awakened, would sacrifice every little thing scavenged over the years for the man she'd always loved.

Shem didn't even blink when he heard. What was he thinking now? "Do you suck cock?": "Not anymore." How could that boy whose essential qualities were stupidity and hunger—besides being the right Oriental—how could that boy be sitting here now, having first discovered where this Shem lived and now having discovered the rest?

Catching me looking at the open newspaper before me, he closed it, making it rustle with a decisive sound of ending things. It was as if even from such a harmless everyday object I would find a clue from which to embroider some more on his schemes. Shem uncrossed his legs. He wouldn't say anything.

What's going to happen? I asked, expecting him to remain silent, which was exactly what he did. It put the onus on me.

I got up. Shem remained seated.

This was the man who had, by offering me a part in his plan, improved my life. What this plan required—a fundamental contempt for my fellow men, gleefulness at watching harm befall others, and, most of all, a vivid understanding of what it felt like to have been overlooked, cast aside, rendered unimportant, invisible, only to be scoffed at when seen—all these things were already in me before I'd even met him. They'd only been waiting for his appearance, for his stories, his indoctrination that had the powerful effect of linking action to thought, to inchoate feeling. He was like a hand turning the flame underneath my heart. Could he see that I wouldn't do anything to harm him, unless he decided to harm me first? I had no way to articulate the vast undercurrent of emotion of that moment, as if I was swimming just below a wide black net, pushed down. I was at the door, behind Shem, who didn't turn around. Finally, sadly, I closed the door on him.

Looking back on it, I realized I had, in my own way, puffed my chest out for Shem, limning my words with the suggestion of danger. By calmly recapping everything, holding his gaze as I did so, I had, in essence, been telling him: If this boy has the brains to gather as much as he has without your help and without any incentive other than curiosity, imagine what he could do when his life was threatened. There was, of course, the added unknown of the criminal acquaintances I was sure to have picked up in my history of being the right Oriental—all of them ready to act in reprisal for me.

I hurried home. I would get my things, all that I'd stuffed into the tote, and I would scram. Where to? It was a week to Christmas, and while everyone, buff with padding, clutched themselves closer in, I was sweating, red-faced. I would call the only person I could think of, the only friend I had left—Devo—before Kendo realized what was what. More than Suzy, or even Shem, I was afraid of this boy whose attachment to me, though having started as doglike, was now closer to that of a master, the one holding the leash who would, if given the slightest chance, determine what direction I would take, what my next moves would be, all guided by nothing more than whatever brought him the greatest, the most perverse pleasure.

Fear spread through me as I entered the apartment—my last time. All the time that I'd been living here, this place had been nothing less than a sentence passed by God the Punisher, while in another part of town not so far away another group of people lived in a completely opposite way that repudiated the very idea of sacrifice, of making do that this place, this container of my "soul in repose" perfectly embodied. That was the exchange I'd made with all those wealthy owners I'd duped: I gave them a taste of my class disdain. And they in turn infected me with a lingering sense of discontent about the way I myself lived—a sense I'd never had until meeting them because after all there'd been that lifetime's jackpot of having been lifted to America from the Philippines, and I'd been content to make do with even the slummiest version of America available to me because in my mind even an American slum existed several notches above the wealthiest Filipino residence.

I took the tote from the closet, rushed out the door. I would call Devo from a pay phone. Tracing the last call made on my phone, nobody would be able to find out anything. A killer, the *Post* had reported, had been apprehended by just that method: He'd placed a call from the home of his victim to his very own home, where, rushing in afterward, the police found him sitting up in bed, naked and defenseless.

There was a figure standing outside the building, looking lost as if she'd come to the wrong part of town. The traffic had turned on headlights, making globes of spectral light skid across my vision. One of these balls went across the face of the woman who I found was blocking my way. Apparently, she could see me very clearly. Hello, Master Chao, she said, with an elation that suggested that she realized she'd arrived in the nick of time. I recognized her as the nosy reporter who'd sat next to me at the awards ceremony at the Plaza.

Hello, I said, gulping.

Or should I say William Paulinha? she asked, continuing to smile and at the same time giving this smile a visibly new meaning.

Who?

Mr. Paulinha—

That's not my name, I said, making to move her out of the way.

How would you think the public would react if they realized that they'd been swindled? she asked.

I knew I couldn't kill her with so many witnesses around. I don't know what you mean, I told her.

We have sources who know about your past, who claim that you were a male hustler. Would you like to comment on that?

I don't understand.

You weren't a male hustler?

A what?

Male. Hustler. A prostitute. Were you or weren't you?

A prostitute? I asked, opening my mouth wide in shock. My God! Of course not.

We have sources, she continued, as if that was the definitive proof of my guilt.

Who are these people? I asked, simultaneously providing my own answer: In my mind, I saw a gallery of people with fingers outstretched, aimed at me: Barney, Shem (could he have worked this fast?), and the rotund figures of businessman after businessman with saliva dripping down their lips and all their flies undone.

She said, both to herself and to me, Our sources are very reliable.

Who are they?

We can't disclose that information.

Of course not, I said, trying to summon a laugh, but she cut me short.

And your last name is Paulinha, not Chao. You're not Chinese.

Don't I look Chinese? I asked, seeing the hands of a giant clock refusing to hold still any longer.

Actually, you don't, she said proudly, as if the first point had been conceded to her.

Well, what does a Chinese person look like? I challenged her, knowing that she could not be obnoxious enough to detail one set of features as the determining factor of Chineseness. I have to go, I told her.

Again she stepped in my way. The art of Feng Shui is an ancient Chinese art which you claim to know—

Of course I do. Don't be stupid.

—and claiming to know it has brought you a lot of money, hasn't it? It's allowed you to quit hustling altogether.

I told you, I said, reddening, I am not a hustler. I pronounced this last word like a hand swatting away a fly.

Well, not anymore. She laughed. Why did you decide to pull this stunt on the citizens of New York? she asked, making me sound like Kuerten, a man traveling a circuit to hawk and hoodwink.

Even the buildings looked like they would be interested in my answer, squeezing in closer. My resolve failed me. Get the fuck out of my way, bitch, I finally said, giving her a forceful shove.

She laughed, knowing that I'd as much as signed my confession. Surely, those words could not be Chao's, the man whose eloquent monosyllable at the awards ceremony had been commented upon by more than a few guests, set up as a model of breeding, of elegant distinction.

I put her behind me, and suddenly she was screaming for attention. Help! Thief! Help I've been mugged! Someone please help! Help! Help me please!!! Hearing those words was all I needed. I sprinted, remembering Kendo's story of trying to elude captors after having snatched an old lady's purse. He'd weaved, bobbed, he said. I decided to do the same thing, at the same time not believing that I was copying Kendo, of all people. Judging from the faces of several pedestrians, who were frowning and regarding my running as a prankster's attention-getting stunt, there was no one behind me. I managed to get as far west as I could before stopping, and by then I was panting.

Please be there, I prayed as I picked up a pay phone to dial.

Hearing Devo on the other end, it was all I could do to keep from crying.

I'll be there soon, I told him without elaborating.

I didn't know what Devo could do for me. He was, if anything, more resourceless than I. But what choice did I have?

To the subway—no, too many people. As for a cab, well, it was rush hour. There was a cap inside my tote which I took out and put on, securing it tightly around my head and making sure that the brim cast a shadow over my eyes. I checked myself in a storefront mirror. Perfect: Eyeless Man, resembling everyone else. And then, before I could turn and go, I remembered something that stopped me. Something I'd left undone, left inside the apartment. Shit! I had to go back. There was no way I could leave that thing just lying there. I'd made such a big deal about acquiring it and so had no choice but to follow through.

I walked slowly back. Resigned. With each step, undoing the victory of my earlier sprint. The glare of Forty-second Street was like a series of taunts, onning and offing. A tired-looking Santa Claus stood with a big bag of loot to parcel out to children, each of whom seemed to be thrusting at least ten arms toward the poor man with his crooked Broadway smile. They were all standing underneath giant Mickey and Minnie, who, looking down, seemed to be sanctifying their eager appetites. Parents stood attentively by like customers making sure to get exactly what they'd paid for. Last season's fashion innovation had been to affix phosphorescent strips to the backs and collars and arms of jackets, while this season's was to color the entire jackets in those phosphorescent, iridescent shades, and together they made Times Square look like a glimmering, hallucinatory stream straight from purgatory, hard and effortful to go across. Surely, the reporter was gone by now? The entrance to the building revealed nothing. I held my breath, knowing she could've wormed her way in, and then I opened the doors, first the main entrance, and then the one at the end of the vestibule. Still nobody. I climbed the stairs, my head bowed low to avoid the cat woman, to evade the reporter if she— But then, I realized, I could kill her now. There would be no witnesses. Thinking this made me stiffen with pleasure, and I took my hands out of my pockets. In one was the switchblade, which I flicked open, making a noise for the reporter to hear. But there was nobody waiting for me in the apartment. There was only the thing that I'd come back for. Brian Q's *Winnie the Pooh* book, all ready to be mailed, sitting on one of my bookshelves. I took it up and left, pounding the steps back down. I couldn't leave it behind, this book that had suddenly meant more than I could explain. The police, finding it, would certainly put it on a list that would be made available to my clients. And seeing the list, Brian Q would think that I'd stolen the book from him. And I didn't want this man to think that of me. Of course, I realized that that would be the least of what he would think. But still. The book was rightfully his, not just in the sense of ownership, but a sense of having deserved, having earned it by his personal transformation—a prize for having won the contest of goodness. And he would have it. I would see to it.

I dropped the package into a mailbox.

Free! At last I was free. My ties to this city severed completely.

At the next block, however, motioning for a taxi, I hailed some-one else's attention. And then it became clear why I had to go back to reclaim Brian Q's package. Because otherwise I would have missed this appointment for my final judgment, the thing that would for-ever determine me in my path, irrevocable.

Neil came over to me, opening his jacket, just a quick flicker, ex-pertly learned from shows on television and from movies such as the one Kendo had taken me to—where gangsters had cautioned their captives not to act foolishly by flashing guns just underneath their jackets.

I had no idea where we were going. It was only that Neil was be-hind me. The crowds were so thick that there was no way I could rear forward without having him right on top of me. And as for the traffic, everyone just sat there, passengers staring out at the pedes-trians, and vice versa. It seemed I was the only person on the streets without my hands full. My single tote bag looked sorry next to everyone else's armfuls of packages, never mind that I had forty thousand dollars in mine.

We passed the Savoy and headed toward the alley at the back. We had to wait for the crowds to thin out. Standing out on the street, looking helplessly at Neil, I finally began to feel the cold.

I can give you the money you asked for, I said to him.

It's too late, he told me, sounding as sorry as I was. Someone else made an offer.

Who? What offer?

The lady whose house I trashed.

What? I asked, dumbfounded.

Actually I made the offer, he said, smirking. And she agreed.

Finally, we snuck into the lot he'd taken me to before. He pushed right behind me.

What offer? I asked.

He patted my pockets. He found what he was looking for, taking out the switchblade. He flicked it awkwardly, then tried a few more times. When he thought he had achieved the required expertise, making the thing come out like an extension of his fingers, he announced, She's paying me to kill you. The "you" timed perfectly with the blade pointing my way.

I reared back, and at the same time, connected to me by an oversensitive cord, he reared forward, guarding. We were separated by the length of an arm. We looked at one another. He could just extend his hand and the knife would go easily into me.

There was a tattered camouflage sleeping bag by the far wall, and next to it a blackened copper pot resting on top of burned-out kindling. Scum oozed over the edge of the pot, dried a wintry gray. Neil saw this at the same time as I did, and seeing, knew that he had only a few minutes to do his job before the man to whom everything belonged came back.

I'll pay you more, I found myself saying.

I'm a man of my word, he said. I already promised.

I'll pay you more, I repeated, knowing that he was far from a man of honor.

He tested the space between us with the knife, and I jumped back. He shook his head, as if he was greatly disappointed by what I'd done.

Please, I begged. Ten thousand, I said.

He laughed. Surely your life's worth more.

The winter air was so crystalline I could smell alcohol coming right through the walls from next door. Suddenly that smell seemed the most beautiful thing in the world and I regretted that I didn't get drunk more often when I still had the chance to.

How much do you want? I asked him. The man who owned the sleeping bag was my only chance. I stretched everything hoping for his entrance.

Forget it, Neil replied.

How much? I persisted.

After I'm done with you, I can finally disappear.

Where are you going? I asked, making my voice extra friendly.

Out on the West Coast, he declared. This easy reply chilled me. That he could divulge this information in such an offhand tone made me realize that he didn't intend for me to live to tell.

I'm sorry, he said, moving closer.

I moved back. He kept coming toward me. Pretty soon, there'd be no more place to retreat to.

There was another fragrance hanging in the air. A heady, swoony smell of someone just out of a bath, and now about to lay himself to rest on a soft bed, toweled dry by thick white cotton sheets. A scent of luxury. Smelling it, I believed my end was here. What I'd been working toward in this endeavor. It was so easy. All I would have to do was stop struggling and accept. Lie down. No more tired, tortuous living in the company of people who made the idea of people seem wrong and ugly and laughable. No more having to make my daily calculations of either this one for dinner or that, but never both, because even now I couldn't afford it. No more having to be burdened with the shame of being my parents' child, my country's citizen, the stooge of my undying, forever victorious faith. No more . . . Suddenly, there was the memory of Jokey dying two times, having given up each time without a fight, without the least bit of struggle, as if the surrender of life to whoever wanted to claim it was already a foregone conclusion, exactly what a plot engineered to serve the greater good demanded, and realizing, I snapped back and tried one last seduction on Neil, whose one long eyebrow was like that of a wolf, but whose hands, I noticed, looked fuzzy from shaking, like newborn things. Had he killed anyone before? He seemed like an amateur. Twin plumes of frosted breath came out of both our red noses. The sky bled its last light. And now for every move each of us made—him going forward, forcing me to gradually retreat, closer and closer in to the wall that connected us to the Savoy—corresponding shadows made us seem even twitchier, two greenhorns playing out a game of adult revenge and murder. I said to Neil, Listen. How is she going to know that you've done the job? Either way, she'll only have your word for it, right? So why not take money from both sides? No one'll be the wiser. She's not going to know I lived. I promise.

No? he asked, though I knew he wasn't considering my option but just bouncing back words to fill in the space until his deed was done.

He twitched to one side, making me counter to the other, but it was just a fake-out. He laughed.

She's not going to know, I promised.

How? he asked.

Again I could smell that smell, that taunt from God. Because, I replied, like you I'm leaving New York for good.

Neil, with his supposedly improved sense of smell, couldn't make out the odor that was getting stronger and stronger by the minute, and so I recognized it as a portent intended only for me. Was that what death was, a great beckoning toward luxury, toward beautiful sheets on a soft bed that would cushion my fall and allow me to lay my troubles down along its perimeters, finally get them off my shoulders?

He thrust forward. I put my tote in front of me, and he scratched it, making the vinyl rip with a fearful sound. The knife caught for a moment, and then released, the force making Neil's wrist do an extra, ungraceful turn in the air. Frustrated athlete. Fictional terrorist. First-time murderer. The graduation made perfect sense, though, of course, the last role did not need me to fulfill it. But who else could it be? I'd as good as spat in his face the last time we were together, here, in this very same lot. I rushed to a corner, knowing I had no more moves left. Who would discover my body, and how would they react? With pleasure? With curiosity? Or would they start, then scream, or sob? Or would I, even in death, be passed over? Concrete poured over my remains to serve as a foundation for one more building that would be yet another pair of hands thrust sky-ward in a gesture of prayer—"Please, God, more money." Thinking of this made me hot with anger. Fuck! No way was I going to be in-volved in prayer! I growled, I swear to God I did, just like a rabid dog, scrunching my torso forward in a gesture that referred to the funny theatrics of professional wrestling. It was so ludicrous it worked, making Neil stand back.

I'll fucking kill you! I shouted.

But just then, before I could make good on this promise, who should come in, and wearing white no less, but Kendo, from whom I finally recognized the smell was emanating, the smell of luxury, of money, of everything he wanted to give up, but which clung to him, his skin, like fate's tag. It wasn't death at all, it was just Kendo, my buddy. And he was true to his word, having followed Neil or me, and now intending to put his theories, his wayward sympathies to the test. Rubble scrunched under his feet, making Neil turn.

At first Neil couldn't make him out.

Given this second's reprieve, I rushed as far away as I could.

And then Neil's face turned up as if the smell had finally penetrated his dumbfuck nose. Clearly, he recognized Kendo. But what was Kendo doing here?

Ken spoke up. You don't have to do this anymore, he said to Neil, firmly, softly, with the throwaway confidence that he brought to every single endeavor, from the most ordinary to the most dramatic. I spoke to my mother. And she said you don't have to do this thing anymore.

Was he telling the truth? It didn't matter.

Did you hear me? continued Kendo. It's over. You have the money. You can keep it. It's fine. My mother told me to tell you she's changed her mind. But you can *keep the money*. Deal's over. OK?

Neil tried to overcome the look of Duh! on his face: I made a promise, he uttered.

My mother—Kendo repeated, as if having been programmed to loop the same line over and over.

Let's go, I said, interrupting Kendo.

Kendo looked at the tote in my hands. And then looked at me, an understanding in his eyes. A moment later, I recognized that this twinkle in the boy's eyes had been misread by Neil: The boy was celebrating the premature victory of his lie.

Neil came forward, having received his answer.

Kendo was not afraid. He just stood there, returning Neil's gaze, looking right at him to let him know that he was not playing a trick.

I. Promised. That was what Neil said with a rocklike tone of making sure he followed through on this promise.

I know you did, Kendo floated casually, even managing a chuckle. I know you did, he repeated, a lulling trick in his voice. In the dark, with his white jacket and cream pants on, he was virtually shining. And when he showed his teeth, it was like a flashing crown. No, he wasn't death, he was life itself. I know you did but that promise is no longer valid. Don't you understand? I'm here to tell you my mother is taking it back.

You're lying.

Cross my heart, replied Kendo, and he did. And hope to die.

You followed me, said Neil, as if this was a point against Kendo.

My God, exclaimed the exasperated boy, what part of what I'm saying isn't clear to you? Of course I followed you. My mother asked me to. She wanted you to know—

Why isn't she here then?

Kendo looked at me and tried to instigate a silent joke between us. Looking back at Neil, he laughed. Can you see my mother in a fucking dump like this?

The man whose home this lot had become still hadn't shown up from his scavenging trip. The hole in the boards from which I'd come in was right behind me, only a few steps away. I could've easily slipped out. But I didn't want to leave Kendo with Neil. He'd come all this way to rescue me, his role model, the most criminal of his criminal acquaintances. It was very clear to me now. The first leg of this risky adventure was all his, the last leg depended on me.

OK? asked Kendo.

I. Promised. My death was far more important to him than I'd realized. Like some last rite he had to perform to keep the furies, those officers in dark blue, away from him, to buy him time to disappear. My death, for him, a virtual talisman which he meant to have, which he must have.

I know. But why don't you talk to my mom again? OK? Can we arrange that? She'll tell you exactly what I just told you. Come on. You don't want to make a mistake, do you?

Kendo, let's go, I said.

Hold on, he replied, so confident of himself.

Stuttered Neil: You're. You're. It's a trick.

It's not. Kendo opened both hands to show how empty they were, how defenseless he was. Then looked at me: Go.

No, I said.

He's not going anywhere, said Neil.

You're not going to kill me, Neil, I said to him.

Neil made a gesture with the knife to disagree, slashing the air. Unfortunately, all he did was make it catch on his own jacket. Trying to disentangle it, he caused something from his inside pocket to fall. When it hit the ground, it made a hollow, plasticky sound. Neil's embarrassed face completed the picture. The gun, lying there on the ground, was a cheapshit, cracked in two and useless. And this was a man whom the cops were trying to track down, whom they believed was a dangerous terrorist?

Come on, I said. Let's get out of here.

Neil got the knife free and thrust it in the air, missing Kendo by just this much. I want him, Neil told the boy.

What for? Kendo asked. You don't have to do this. Listen. Are you that eager to kill someone? Asking this last question, Kendo suddenly realized what the stakes were, realized that Neil was indeed hungry for my blood and would not be dissuaded from his quest.

Ken, I said. Let's go. The dumbass ain't gonna kill no one tonight.

Oh yes, I will.

Kendo, who moved through the world with the freedom from incident befitting someone of privilege, mistook this blessing for the protection of dark forces he believed saw him as a true acolyte. He took slow, cocksure steps as only a twenty-three-year-old can. All those things he had told me about—his travels in the world of "crime," his induction into that world, his apprenticeship, his disavowal of his entire life's legacy—were about to be tested in those short steps. Of course he would win. Hadn't he always?

Kendo, I said, reaching to yank him back, but he was too far ahead of me.

Neil saw the panic in my face and again misinterpreted it: not panic for Kendo, but panic for *him* instead, for Neil. Why was I afraid for Neil? Surely because Kendo's approach was not innocent? Kendo meant to harm, right, there was something in his hands that Neil couldn't see? Afraid of being hurt first, Neil struck. He put the knife in Kendo's chest. It went in with surprising ease, past the white, insubstantial jacket. A little wet farting sound sealed the knife's entry. I couldn't see Kendo's face. But Neil's was a horror show. He was quivering. Kendo's hands had gone instinctively to the knife in his chest, and Neil, seeing how empty those hands were, how weaponless, began to realize what he'd done. He started shaking. He looked up at me.

Oh God, I said, and I realized my words were mere sounds. They were like the hiss of a radiator or the rumble below our feet of an incoming train signaling the uninterrupted boredom of life continuing apace.

Kendo turned around to look at me. His knees, buckled, stayed like that while he tried to stay upright.

I stood frozen.

Bubbles formed and broke on his lips. His eyebrows were pushed together, though his eyes were gentle, undyingly romantic and mellow, and his hands, bunched together around the knife, could've been carrying a bouquet instead. A sound escaped from his mouth, a series of words jumbled together into one long whistle of shock.

Neil, recovering, put his hands on the knife's handle, intending to pull it out and use it on me. Before I realized what I was doing, I was at him, the tote coming down on his head again and again. All that money was like a cement block. His hands slipped from the knife, the motion pushing Kendo finally to the ground. Kendo's head made a ghastly sound.

Neil also fell, then tried to get up. I was kicking him by now, pure animal moves that someone ought to have been laughing at, but for Neil and myself all the humor of life would be exhausted for a long time. I stopped kicking, breathing loudly. He moved slowly away from me, defeat in his limbs, with each move testing to see what I would do, but I remained still, and then quickly he scrabbled on all fours until, finding a spot far enough away from me, he got up. And then he snuck underneath the opening in the boards, disappearing into the New York light. He'd left his gun lying there on the ground—it would trace back to him, unless someone else decided to take it. And the knife, which had slipped out of Kendo, lay close by. I took it up, brought it over to Kendo, from whom I could hear fitful breaths getting weaker and weaker. Now he had to pull in three breaths for every one just to get enough air, and all of it seemed to be leaking as quickly as it'd come in right out of the wound in his chest. He was anticipating some gesture of comfort from me. I realized that this was the solution to my problem, the loose end that Kendo represented. I went over. I brought the knife and, using the edge of his jacket, wiped it clean of my fingerprints, and when he realized that that was why I'd approached, his eyes filmed with sadness and with venom.

His jacket was daubed with patches of dark red that the cold air kept fresh, shining with an obscene vitality. I knelt down. Looked at him. He didn't even have the strength to turn his eyes at me. I didn't say a word. What could I say? It was all over for him. By not acting, not rushing to get help, I had acted, making my decision, the quickness of which shocked me but didn't really shock me. He knew it too, the knowledge continuing to push his eyebrows together. He'd saved my life, exactly what he came here to do. But not the way he'd intended. Not to exchange his life for mine. I was keeping him company, that was all there was to be done.

Isuzu Yamada had sent someone to kill me but had instead sacrificed her own son. The rightness of it came directly from that name: *Isuzu Yamada*. Reality extending from the geometric perfection of the Japanese movies I'd studied, in which she'd been the star, the black, shining star whose vitality provided a counterpoint to the hero's drab goodness, but for which she was always, invariably, punished. And I also realized: Suzy, who'd been unaffected by my disastrous rearranging, had in fact been powerful enough—being the owner of a gigantic will—to have transcended it, had finally succumbed. She'd lost the game. And when I looked down at Kendo, his wastefulness given the fitting crown of a wound in his chest, his blood finally coagulating around the tear in his coat and on his hands, I realized that I was in fact looking at the successful revenge of Rowley P and of Shem. It had arrived, at last. All that time checking for the payoff of my handiwork I had been inspecting the wrong things. Here was the big thing Suzy Yamada was to be deprived of to pay for what she had stolen from others. The biggest thing. He lay there. He was dead. Eyes opened, confronting the joke he'd played on himself.

All those years reading about corpses in my novels and in the *Post* hadn't prepared me for the sheer stupidity of death, its complete lack of meaning, or how, as I'd expected, assessing backward from this final point, the life that had preceded it would be made to make sense, reordered and given a shape that was as meaningful, as satisfying as any story in books.

And what were those sentences: *The corpse was blue.* Or, *It just lay there, cold as night.* Or, *Days later they found a maggot-infested corpse in a Dumpster by the pier.* Or, *Last night an unidentified body of a woman was found along the West Side Highway.* Or, *The victim's body was fully clothed and its hands were bound from behind with a thin electric cord.* Or, *The face had decomposed beyond identification.*

And many adjectives, many possibilities: *shocking, tragic, horrible, peaceful, pitiful, stench-filled, anonymous, mutilated, stiff, violated, forlorn, oblivious.* I knew I would no longer read any of those words in the same way, that behind them from now on would be the weight, the heft of Kendo's body lying there, his beautiful hair violated by the dusty, germy ground and one hand as if trying to scratch an itch where the wound—looking like one of his countless designs intended to mutilate the perfection of his mother's shirts—puckered. In his eyes was a too late wish that he'd found some other hobby instead, and on his lips a curse for me that he didn't have the breath to finish. His eyes were staring not at me, and not at anything in particular, but were like twin dice that had rolled to a stop and had come up with a numerical total neither big nor small, unmomentous. For a moment, I saw the Kendo of my first sighting, and except for a few crucial differences, he looked exactly the same as on that first night: sprawled on his bed, in the dark of what turned out to be his room, his sanctuary, too tired to put up a fight with his mother's boring party to which I'd been invited, too tired to continue making a show of his discontent, the Kendo that was most nakedly himself, a simple boy without the vitalizing aspect of hate, of revolt, of a theatrical disgust. I was the sole witness to that scene and was the privileged first for this. This same Kendo had wanted to die, pointing out the new painting in his room, the one that had replaced the *Suspiria* poster—the blocks of color with something suppurating in the middle. A Mark Rothko lithograph, he'd said. Did you know that he killed himself? he'd asked, smiling to let me know what he thought of such things. He saw it as heroic, as the biggest fuck-you gesture there was, and yearned one day to join the illustrious company of famous suicides. And just like me before him, he'd declaimed: I can't wait to die.

He lay there frozen in a posture of one last attempt at clinging on, one hand around the wound as if to close it, and the other one, lying on top of the ground to connect himself with this earth, touching it, holding on, refusing to be pulled away. Suddenly, as if animated by electricity, that hand was moving, making me jump up. I caught my breath. Stared. He didn't open his lips. Didn't look at me. He was just clawing the pavement. He kept repeating that motion over and over, raking, making pebbles rise and fall between his fingers. Please, said that gesture. He was beseeching me to reconsider, to laugh and reveal my stoniness as a joke, and go for help. Finally, knowing by the look that I gave him that there was no way I would do such a thing, he died.

35

After I told him everything, except what happened to Kendo, he surprised me by breaking into tears.

What are you doing? I asked.

I don't want you dead, he said.

Don't be silly, I told him.

No, it's just— To think of it— It'd be a pity, to lose you—just when my life was getting really good and I could be a better friend.

Shut up, Devo. You were always a friend.

That's nothing, he said. That was just hanging out. Now we can do more.

Like what?

I don't know. More. I don't want you dead.

Oh please, I'm not going to die, I told him.

Good. And then he started crying again. Was he high on something?

Devo—I said, before he cut in.

I love you. You're my buddy.

And I said very quickly before anything else got said, And if I were to die, no big deal. I'm always saying I can't wait to, anyway.

Shut up, he said.

But I suppose that's the way with some of us, we can only stand emotion if it's filtered through a protective layer of nonchalance or a kind of jokiness that passes for wit between friends.

The next day we got into his car, a four-wheel-drive he'd had for a few years but which I'd never known about. We were heading to his country retreat, a small cottage in upstate New York that he'd gotten a few months ago, to help escape the pressures of city life. What pressures? Wasn't he just a layabout, occasionally employed and frequently bombed? This house was another thing I was hearing about for the first time.

As it turned out, he'd been setting some money aside all this time just to be able to buy himself a place in the country. He tried to make light of it, explaining it away as being no different from what all his contemporaries were doing, part of the upholstery of urban fag life—drugs, designer duds, parties, tans, gym physiques, vacation shares in Miami, country houses just a couple of hours from Manhattan to escape the collective headache and "pressure" of all of the above. What I wanted to know was how he'd come by the industry and the thrift required to get himself enough money for the down payment. That was what I found stunning, that someone like Devo, without any history in those departments, could suddenly, at the very last minute, reveal his convenient ownership. I guess whatever virtues existed in human nature would continue to throw me for a loop . . .

On the drive with him, I assumed Preciosa's role—volunteering everything except a fistful of information I regarded as the important things and was determined to keep secret, safeguarding. Like I said, I didn't tell him about Kendo, that whole side of the story culminating in the boy's murder. It was the last thing I wanted to think about. I didn't tell him about Neil. I didn't tell him about having been found out by the nosy girl reporter. All I said was that someone was after me, having discovered my game. I'd told him about Shem long ago, so this time I didn't bother. But, I said, just in case something should happen to me I want you to give this information to the police. I wrote Shem's name and address on a ripped-off sheet of paper and handed it to Devo. Who is this? he asked. The police will know, I replied.

Snow, miraculously, had begun to fall and, combined with nighttime, made the driving slow. I imagined Kendo's body being steadily covered in blankets of the stuff, concealing. Snow falling on his girlish lashes, trying to tease them open. Falling on his white, smooth cheeks. On that skin that hadn't been carved into by experience, by need. Or maybe he was safe from the downpour, having been discovered and brought to a morgue, where he lay on a stainless-steel gurney. A twisted sound rose up from my throat. I had to put my head to one side away from Devo. What's the matter? he asked. I made like I'd been coughing, brushing his question aside. Suddenly, I was crying. He let it pass.

Later, we had a good laugh over the gullibility of the people whose existence was supposedly beyond our reach. His was an overdramatic laugh that didn't have much conviction in it but was intended to keep me company. Feng Shui means wind water, I began.

What? What does it mean? he asked.

Pay attention. Feng means water. Or, wait wait wait. It means wind. Feng means wind.

How do you say that?

Fung.

Fong.

Fung. Ung. Ung.

Ung ung.

No. Fung. Ffff.

We laughed.

What's the other one? he asked, with his American tone of pure skepticism.

It's Shui.

What?!

Shhh.

Shhh.

Weee.

Weee.

Shweee.

Shweee.

That means water. Shui means water. So together they make wind water.

Wind water? he asked. What the fuck does that mean?

Life currents, I explained. It's all about getting the right currents to flow inside your house so that your endeavors and your ambitions have the proper support to thrive.

He gave me a look. You're not shitting me now, right?

No, I said. That part's all in the handbook. And then I explained what else the handbook had said.

At the end, he said, whistling, Wow, and they bought all that shit from you?

For some of them, like this fucking bitch, the way I did her house was like to invite bad luck into it so that her life could crumble.

Again he whistled. Like what did you do?

Like for example you're not supposed to have a mirror facing your bed.

Why not?

I explained it for him.

He took a moment to consider, and then said, That's kind of poetic.

Mmm-hmm, I replied. Poetic justice.

What the hell did this woman do to deserve this?

Believe me, she deserved it. A nasty fucking piece of goods.

And then he asked me, Can you do the cottage?

What do you mean? What cottage?

Mine. My cottage. The one I'm taking you to. You'll have a few days there. No one'll disturb you.

Do what exactly? I asked, though I knew the answer.

Like do the Feng, the, what do you call that?

You're joking, I said.

No. You said you know how to do it, didn't you?

You're joking, I repeated. Listen, Devo, what do you think I'm trying to get away from in the first place?

Well, he countered, who's saving your life?

After a sulky silence, I agreed.

Good luck and all that, right?

Whatever, I said.

Come on. When I was young, he explained, I didn't need luck. I had youth. I had optimism. But now—

Now you have a cottage. You have a four-wheel-drive. Listen, Devo. Your initiative is more than enough luck. Really. And I'm not just saying that. My God, I can't believe what you've done with your life. I'm so impressed! I really am!

And I am with you too, he said, patting me gently on the hand.

Don't shit me.

Really, he said.

He stated in a clean, simple way the same thing I hadn't realized I'd always felt until I was in the thick of it: how we shared a common hatred for those who did better than us, for whom New York seemed to have been exclusively built. Immediately, all those forgotten occasions returned to memory: staring at the padlocked facades of houses on the Upper East Side; having been stared at every time we went into a fancy shop to admire the goods; recognizing the equations in movies between poverty and integrity, poverty and honor, poverty and earthiness as nothing more than a false consolation for having lost out on the real goods.

If you want to know the truth, I said, I don't want to have anything to do with this shit anymore. I don't want to think about it, I don't want to invoke the spirits or shit like that anymore. I want it to be over. A complete break. A clean start.

But that's fine. Afterward. After you do it for me. Then make a break. Think of it as a way to balance out the bad that you've done. To guarantee your own safety. Square it with the gods. Right? Think about that.

There are no gods in this thing, I reminded him, remembering the one God of my one faith, who I hoped had witnessed Kendo's death, cringing at my participation, or lack thereof, who I hoped took notice, though in the end I doubted anyone had. Not that I wanted to be caught. Punishment was the furthest thing from my mind.

Spirits then. OK? You'll love this place, he said. It's a fixer-upper but it's got great potential. And it's quiet, that's the main thing. The nearest neighbor is a dozen miles down the road.

Sounds great, I said, watching the gray of the concrete and the radioactive glow of the streetlamps along the side of the road replaced by the skeletal outlines of tall trees that were just as sad, marking time and the travel of people on the road in their own primeval style, objects of warning imparting some lesson that the night and the snow made even more compelling—a lesson that seemed to have something to do with the cost of things that ostensibly, though we were putting them to our backs, would still have to be charged at some juncture up ahead. The wiry prongs of the treetops were fringed with aureoles of fuzzy, funny light, as if they were hooked up to some current in the air, conductors, and it occurred to me that what the trees resembled were petrified bolts of lightning, aimed down at us and just missing.

In the daylight the next day they looked only like trees, thin poles that seemed to be holding up the entire gray sky, a sky whose only source of light seemed to be what was being reflected back by the thick, clumpy snow on the ground.

Devo went back to the city. He would return in five days, he said. My fate was up to him entirely. For all I knew, the next time I saw him he'd be flanked by cops drawing guns, the entire scene colored by the underwater blue of revolving police car lights.

I "did" his house for him.

At night I slept on the cushioned daybed right by the windows, stiff as a fork inside a cupboard, ready to bolt up at the slightest noise. Which I did repeatedly. The woods at night was a scene created to unravel my last nerve. Cries that I later deduced were animals calling to each other, and the sound of twigs broken underfoot, which I also later ascribed to them, made me see the gang of accusers crouched outside the tiny cottage, having made the trek from New York all the while petting their pitchforks and medievally carved sharp instruments waiting to come face to face with the man who had, mirrorlike, revealed them as the buffoons that they were, the man who in himself had incarnated every single millennial fear that they'd nurtured, wishing for these things to come true, be proven right, so that they could finally face their guilty consciences squarely and be purged of the fear that was the price exacted by a life of such drive, such forward momentum.

In the daylight, finding myself still alive and therefore needing to get out of bed, I took a walk in the outlying areas. There was a water pump at the back for my bath and for the drinking water. The place was heated by a wood-burning contraption. There was no television. No phone. No electricity. A fixer-upper, indeed. I took out my money, recounted it. Forty thousand dollars. I took five thousand of that and, both as a gift for Devo and, should he not find it, as an insurance policy for myself, stuffed it underneath the daybed mattress.

They say that silence encourages reflection. But reflection inevitably pointed to Kendo. I'd been a sucker for his beauty, something untouched by understanding and because of which was allowed to fester into glamour. Now, he was in the company of the thieves and skank celebrities whose predilections had as good as turned them into compass needles pointing toward death. He'd followed, believing that he would be exempt from having to pay the same price. As for myself, never having been a hero, I'd developed no resources to see me through. At the same time as I was entertaining this thought, I recognized that I had lived through one brush with death and could just as easily live through many others.

In my case, instead of reflection, all the quiet of the country did was to make my newly fat ass even fatter. I ate as much of Devo's canned goods as I could stand. And by the time he came back, fresh with news of terrorists running amok in New York City (hearing which, I had to keep from laughing), I could tell that he was restraining himself from commenting on my new love handles—he looked with a look like his eyes were airbrushing instruments trying to magically eradicate these awful things. Clearly he was thinking that if gaining weight was a corollary of being a criminal, then thank goodness he himself was turning over a new leaf.

I'd decided I would hide out in California. I could extend my thirty-five thousand dollars to last about nine months, probably longer. Nine months—more than enough time to be reborn. I would play dead for nine months, and afterward, like Jesus Christ before me, be resurrected, come out of hiding to adopt the new situation that someone like me—in the very likely event that scouts had been sent to track me down—would not seem likely to inhabit. What that would be I didn't know, but in my mind all I saw were my hands turning over the pages of a book to a new chapter, a blank page. "Good"? That was a thing of the past. More than ever, I was clear about that. I'd been a boy. I'd been afraid. Only the strong survive: that small bit of fortune cookie wisdom was now my new motto. And I was strong. Another thing that comforted me was the knowledge that all around the world, there were people just like me, rebounders, scrappers, *survivors*. People who cheated and schemed, and who, having found that the schemes had run their course, retreated. Some of us, it was true, capitulated to the moral blackmail of religion and politics. But I didn't care about any of that. I'd been hurt. I'd been cast aside. Passed over (Shem's joke to me: I've been passed over so many times it's enough to make me twice Jewish). Looked at askance. Rebuked. Now I had gotten what I'd been hungering for all those dark, basement days—enjoyment, impunity, an equal footing—and I had gotten it by force, by wrong, by a clear-eyed assessment of the world *as it was*, and not a fairy-tale pining for what could never be, except as a conscious retreat into the imagination of a child, of childhood. Well, Pratung Song was right: Fuck childhood! Fuck everyone! Now it was clear to me what my time with Shem had been all about: I'd been going to school. And California was where I was determined to go to continue being able to learn. It was also the cold that put me in mind of this place, and seeing myself wearing only the same ratty T-shirt (not white) and jeans (not black), day in and day out, had confirmed me in my decision.

Where will you go? asked my only friend in the world, Devo, as he let me out at the Port Authority, where I would take a bus to evade my responsibilities.

I took a breath and heard myself say to him: Florida.

A young girl with a frightening android look which only in religion could be construed as a positive—reclaimed as devotion, as worshipfulness—singled me out among the many pedestrians minding their own business. She thrust a small pamphlet into my hands. I took it and moved on. On the sidewalks in my neighborhood, a corps of converters had appeared and their numbers were steadily increasing. They always had a gleam in their eyes when stopping pedestrians to chat about the forthcoming end of the world. More than anyone else, they yearned for its arrival, when everything shabby about their existence would be turned to gold as a reward for their committed, lip-bitten disavowal of material goods, of comfort, of common sense. According to them, just before the world exploded in a divine fury of simultaneous hellfire and ice, there would be a single moment of grace, called the Rapture, when those who'd kept the faith would suddenly appear to cling to a giant skirt of light that would lift higher and higher, propelling them out of harm's way, while below, those of us who remained, who were left behind, watching helplessly, and, it was hoped, enviously, would be standing like pins knowing all we could do was wait for God's big bowling ball of retribution and hatred to strike us all down. Kaboom! these street preachers would sometimes say to end their fevered narration, and the pedestrians—who seemed to me to already be of the faith, or why else would they stop for such a lengthy speech?—would shudder appropriately, making signs of the cross over their faces and chests.

The pamphlet had a pale green cover. On it were the words: How to Know God.

I put it inside my pocket.

Inside the Port Authority, everyone looked worried. There were two cops patrolling the premises on the top floor. They kept a lazy eye on the crowd washing through, thumbs clutching their belts cowboy-style. I passed them with my tote. They didn't see me. On the second level, there were another two, and again I wasn't spotted.

Newspaper kiosks had the *New York Post* out on display but I didn't go near. Reading about Kendo's death, there would no longer be tantalizing questions, but instead, definite, hateful knowledge. I said to myself in progression: You did not know this boy. You do not know this boy. *What boy?*

I went to a ticket booth, asked about getting to L.A. A big woman in her mid-forties whose blond hair kept coming down over her eyes said that there would be a series of stops, and that I would have to change buses at each stop. First in Philadelphia, then Pittsburgh, then Cincinnati, and on and on. Would I like to buy the whole block of tickets now?

I asked her for the first five, giving myself a chance to change my mind.

I tried not to think about the rest rooms—where, not very long ago, I lived another kind of life—as I passed them on the way to where the buses embarked. But there were noises inside that made me stop. Noises that sounded routine, but still I wanted to satisfy my curiosity, check the stalls, the sink, the mirrors to see what had changed, as if by looking at them I could get a clearer picture of the distance I'd traveled. At the last minute I turned my back and walked away from the open doorway, out of which a grandfather, adjusting his fly, was hobbling, carrying a ragged plastic bag that clanked with what sounded like cutlery.

There weren't very many of us on that bus to Philadelphia. A lot of young people, perhaps students, who, looking at me, could barely summon up the interest to wonder about my life, perhaps having already filled in the blanks and moved on: What unspecial person could I possibly be? A tourist? Another new immigrant? One more college student, just like them? None of those roles merited closer inspection.

Leaving New York City, the bus seemed to be taking a route to point out one more time various places of significance that I would be leaving behind for good: the Savoy, behind which I'd left Kendo; my building, on which hung the defunct sign Peep Corner, and with two apartments, mine and Preciosa's, newly vacant (was Divina Valencia dead by now?); Kendo's father's building—where lived the young boy who would be expecting me to show up soon and take him to the movies; the Times Square station for the 1 and 9, the 2 and 3, the first two of which would shoot straight up to Suzy Yamada's, or to Shem's—each person with a distinctly different reaction to the news.

Finally we were on the highway.

I took out the pamphlet and flipped to a page. The heading said: The Evil of Being Away from God. Underneath it, random quotes from the Bible were grouped to illustrate this theme. I read one:

The Lord is with you while you are with Him. If you seek Him, He will be found by you; but if you forsake Him, He will forsake you.

—2 Chronicles 15:2

Then another:

But the transgressors shall be destroyed altogether; the future of the wicked shall be cut off.

—Psalms 37:38

Yet another said:

You believe that there is one God. You do well. Even the demons believe—and tremble! But do you want to know, O foolish man, that faith without works is dead? . . . But be doers of the word, and not hearers only, deceiving yourselves.

—James 2:19–20; 1:22

And finally:

Who may stand in His holy place? He who has clean hands and a pure heart.

—Psalms 24:3–4

I threw the pamphlet down, stomped it with my foot.

Most of my fellow passengers had faces disfigured by overlarge hats and caps, and by Halloween glasses, a disfigurement they appeared to have devised in protest against the holiday cheer that was uniting the world and making them, with their willful refusal to participate, seem malformed—or were we simply a busful of escapees trying to conceal our faces? And though most of them got out at the Philadelphia station, more people with the same faces got on at the other stops.

Somewhere in the middle of the trip, the New Year came. We were traveling on a highway made ghostly by the seasonal desertion. The bus driver, a rotund fellow with the broken blood vessels of drink on his thick nose, tried to instigate some merriment, turning up the radio that was tuned in to the Times Square countdown. But none of the passengers could be persuaded into going along with his singsong counting, and so finally, he gave up. I had, after all, found my compatriots.

A lot of the new people had beaming smiles on their faces, put there by the latest paperback novels that they read with an intensity like vengefully shutting out the onset of a new year which was new only in name.

Days whisked by. The sun and the dark took turns in the sky, the former pulling the curtain up on the touristy particulars of a landscape that I was encountering for the first time in my life, and the latter, in competition, turning these things scrolling outside my window even stranger by taking away the certainty and the definition the daytime provided. Still, they made me feel nothing, lacking an aspirational quality which the New York cityscape had, an implicit challenge to measure up that every building, every storefront, every armor-clad New Yorker walking the long, unending streets possessed.

In the bathroom at the back, I discovered a dictionary someone had left behind. Who would leave such a thing in the bathroom of a bus? I took it back to my seat and scanned the pages absentmindedly. I looked up the words obsequious, obstreperous, ostentatious, oracular, not because I wanted to know what they meant, but only to kill time. And then I suddenly remembered a word I'd wanted to know the meaning of.

Scrod. The dictionary entry read: *"A young fish, as a codfish, or haddock, esp. one split and prepared for cooking."*

I had to look up haddock. It said: *"An edible gadoid fish* (Melanogrammus aeglefinus) *found off the coasts of Europe and North America."*

What was gadoid? The dictionary had this to say: *"Of or like the family (Gadidae, order Gadiformes) of bony fishes including hake, burbot, and cod."*

So I had to go all the way back to cod. Looking it up, I discovered three definitions. The first one: *"Any of various gadoid fishes of northern seas, important as a source of cod-liver oil and food, esp. any of a genus* (Gadus) *with firm flesh and soft fins, found off the coast of Newfoundland and Norway."* The second: *"(Archaic) a bag/ (Dialect) pod, husk/ (Obscene) the scrotum."* That made me chuckle.

But it was the third that made my heart beat fast, like having come to an X marks the spot. It read: *"(British slang) noun 1. mock, sham 2. a parody or satire verb 1. to fool, hoax, trick, etc. 2. to tease."*

Finally the bus pulled into an underground lot and braked to a stop. I got off, my first time in Los Angeles since I'd left my family. It was a grimy city of sunshine where the residents had the blank faces of people leading improvised, part-hopeful and part-given-up lives—which was exactly the state I was in.

The tote next to my chest shuddered and shook as, pulling in the first deep breath of my entire trip, I began to cough. Nobody else seemed to mind the dirty air.

PART 5

* * *

* 36 *

The *New York Post* had a headline that read: Shanghaied! A picture of me which no longer looked like me became even more unreliable broken down into distinct Benday dots. It was the picture some photographer had taken outside the Plaza as I walked up to the awards ceremony. Fuck, I'm ugly! I thought.

Inside, the reporter from the girls' magazine issued an "exclusive!" that claimed that William Paulinha used to be a male hustler and his role as the stooge-maker of upper-crust New York simply extended from this scummy involvement of his youth. Of course the story had its hold on the public imagination and was greeted with the appropriate sounds of horror and regret from the friends and acquaintances of those duped—a horror and regret underlined by a superior sense that they themselves would never have been so foolish as to have believed the young man's claims without having checked them out beforehand, especially in this day and age when even religious leaders were branching out into charlatanism. But a competing article from *New York* magazine trumped that claim a few days later, the public duly moving on, and the girl reporter, incensed, finally revealed who her source for the Chao story had been and what her power over this source was: in an article for a muckraking weekly, she "outed" the hot young actor Martin Roces—Jokey.

Jokey had been picked among the stars to watch in the next millennium by the same girls' magazine which had picked on me. Brought up to the next level of visibility, rumors had mysteriously sprouted and began to attach to him. The reporter, with her native, lucrative distrust of everyone and everything, felt it only her duty to check these out. Her diligence had paid off. Armed with eyewitness evidence from a few sour former colleagues of Jokey's, she'd gone to him, hoping to broker an exclusive. And that boy, finding himself cornered, offered her another, juicier story as a way out of his bind. Master Chao, claimed Jokey, was a fraud. He used to be a gutter-level male hustler. Just as Jokey had been, which was how Jokey knew. And between him and me, the girl reporter knew which stone would make the bigger ripple. But, of course, when that story was made suddenly worthless by the competing, and more vivid, claims of *New York* magazine, she awakened, realizing that what was at stake was her professional reputation.

Ironically enough, now that he was an acknowledged homosexual (and a rehabilitated hustler, at that), Jokey's stock rose even more. He was suddenly being offered lead gay parts in independent movies and was being taken up by the new leaders of the gay organizations and charities—happy, hip homosexuals whose m.o. for societal acceptance and whose primary idea of a civic contribution seemed to be to groom themselves to within an inch of their lives—making of themselves more perfect versions of the human male specimen than had been endowed by nature—and to submerge their fundamental, unassimilable difference under a patina of sexless, neutered, harmless "humanity," having learned the fundamental showbiz lesson that if audiences became helpless at the warm, gooey sight of puppies and children, then it was only a matter of locating the inner puppy and inner child in each homosexual (i.e., the heroine's best friend; the lead actor's touching, elderly science teacher;

the quiet, dignified object of a town's derision, the link between whose oppression and sainthood being made more ex- than implicit) to sell the country on their heartwarming validity. For this, Jokey— a young, good-looking, on-the-verge actor made instantly ubiquitous by scandal and forced into contrition by his own ambition (and the guidance of a savvy management team)—was perfect.

And together, these homosexuals' smiles were plastered across the "on the town" pages of various magazines and were indeed like what the conservatives had always accused them of being—recruitment images for the gay life. Looking at them, with their perfect physiques, their up-to-the-minute haircuts brilliantined and combed back or fastidiously tousled, all manner and attitude bespeaking a lack of intimacy with pain or aging, why wouldn't you want to be just like them?

New York magazine had *the* article to beat about my story. It was one that wallowed in the lives of the rich people scammed. On the one hand, it had the finger-wagging tone of: Now it's time to pay the piper, reasoning that people who had accumulated wealth by pulling the wool over others' eyes had it coded into their karma that their wealth would be relieved from them by the methods they themselves used; while on the other hand, it kept sticking that very same finger into its mouth to pull out a whistle of envy and appreciation: the writer was trying to spin the readers into a delirium by giving an inventory of the trappings of wealth: salaries of a house staff; prices of various furnishings ("a ten-thousand-dollar couch, fifteen-thousand-dollar dinner table" etc.), art to decorate the walls, parties ("twelve hundred dollars per guest, minimum of a dozen guests for an 'intimate' evening"); the fees for interior designers, publicity wranglers, beauty experts; and every other line a chichi brand name because, well, that seemed to be the editorial policy of the magazine—so many brand names, in fact, that it was like having your neck whipped while you passed billboard after billboard on a freeway. I bet this was met with a great deal of applause by New Yorkers who participated daily in the put-them-up-and-then-tear-them-down game that made them feel better about their own crummy lives: people given the false consolation that implicit in bigger lives was the ongoing risk of bigger punishment (but by whom, exactly?).

In the article, the person who was supposed to be me was reviled and yet at the same time spoken about from a distance as if from a fear of being too close to black magic. Around this guy swirled smoke and a sense of: He has the potential to fuck you up. A posthumous vibration. Who wrote this article? Shem C. And everything that I'd thought about him was finally confirmed: He'd been both contemptuous and envious of the social set he'd set his sights on. The article was a clear revelation of a schizoid personality. And in it, as with his leaks to the *Post*, he had given me another fictional name: William Paul—a half-Filipino, half-white young man torn apart by having no foothold in either world.

The article began: *I first met William Paul when he insinuated himself into my company at a party for the Hong Kong tycoon ———. It was an uncharacteristically cool day and the rich and beautiful who crowded the penthouse with its gorgeous terrace overlooking the harbor were attired in the season's Hermès scarves, Chanel sweaters, and Zegna sports jackets. The Hong Kong stock market was up that day, and you could see it in the pampered, pleased faces gathered. And besides the stock market, another thing seemed to be a staple of conversation, a thing that was, in fact, being touted as directly responsible for the stock market's health: Feng Shui . . . Seduced by his easy and quiet confidence into writing an article about his burgeoning Feng Shui practice, I interviewed William Paul one day over drinks at the ——— Social Club in Kowloon. Mr. Paul revealed himself to be of mixed parentage, a fact that would make poetic sense when I realized later the magnitude of his "split" character. This character wanted to belong to the "white" world—a world he saw reproduced in magazines and in the movies, where servants took care of the little difficulties in life; as for the larger difficulties, money would be the salve to smooth them over. And he knew by instinct that the "yellow" or Asian part of him was a hindrance. His whiteness, courtesy of his father, was not in a quantity large enough to satisfy him, which was to say* full *whiteness,* full *belonging. He could never fully fit into that world to which he so desperately aspired. And ironically, when it came to the Asian world in which he also had a precarious foothold, it was this same "white" part in him that put him outside the circle of the Chinese with whom he grew up. In their eyes, he was considered a "gwai-lo," or foreign devil, and was taunted mercilessly. Because of this formative childhood hurt he swore to align himself with his "white" part, casting out his Asian heritage. He shortened his name from Paulinha to Paul, perfected his English by going to school in California, where he soon assumed the speech of characters in movies, of Hollywood. And yet, years later, irony of ironies, what allowed him entrée into the "white" world was to adopt a highly exaggerated version of the self that he had killed a long time ago: the Hong Kong Oriental.*

Reading this, I thought Shem C might as well have affixed his signature at the bottom to designate a signed confession about himself. Not about being racially mixed, but rather that part about aspiring to be part of a world which, when he realized it wouldn't have him, he swore to avenge himself on, turning cold and bitter.

"With Suzy, things usually are very simple. She wants to move ahead. That's all that there is to her. For us to give her the complex motivation that we think her success and demeanor deserve is definitely to confuse her with someone else." Shem's words could be turned perfectly on himself.

Just like Inspector Maigret of the Georges Simenon books that Shem had admired (with the fervent admiration of seeing himself reflected in their pages, I now realized), Shem had come from humble beginnings. And just like that fictional character, he had risen from those humble beginnings to assume the cherished role of an explainer, an unlocker of secrets, an expert, a celebrity (finally!), accorded the respect and the resentment appropriate to all those roles.

In the article, he'd cited *Hud*, the Paul Newman movie, as my favorite: the story of a young man and his strut. This lie was so left field it left me scratching my head for days. And then I just simply enjoyed the fact that detectives from all over, plus those that I'd scammed, would be scouring every frame of this movie—which I hadn't even seen, much less loved!—for clues to my character, my motives. Later it occurred to me that Hud was Duh spelled backward and that it was just possible that Shem, hoping that I would read the article, was sending me a wink from his side and wishing me well.

Suzy Yamada, who didn't know of my friendship with her son and who didn't know that I'd been there when he'd died, had been too distraught to contribute a quote to the article. But everyone else obliged. There was Brian Q, shaking his head in sadness, saying that he was sorry to have made my acquaintance, sorry to have been made a believer. Nothing was said about the book that I'd saved and sent to him. A book that I'd risked my safety for. There was the Dowager, who, forgetting that she had escaped without having to pay me a cent, said: "Oh, I could tell by the way he asked me about the precious art in my home that he was not altogether who he claimed to be. Because, after all, how can someone who was truly of the spirit look at my Matisse, say, or the Modigliani which I have in a bathroom, with the same look of acquisitiveness and expertise as . . . well, as me!" I could hear her triumphant cackling complementing her words. Cardie Kerchpoff, invigorated by her advance rightness and by the fact that suddenly her having been a victim softened the public perception of her, said: "I was right all along! I didn't deserve all the horrible things that have been happening to me! It was only that I, along with so many of my unfortunate, my do-gooding peers who only wanted to try out the wisdom of all that the world, regardless of cultural origin, had to offer, were made the butt of a joke of a cruel, destructive, evil man! He must be arrested at once so that all our souls, which we had entrusted to him in a liberal gesture of joining hands with the rest of the world, can be restored to their former states of peace." Then there was the gallery owner who lived in the East Village, who volunteered her theory to help muddy the scenario: deducing backward to the man she had unloaded Mauricio G's work on (which she was suing to get back), she had the police check him out, convinced that it was he who had hired Chao to persuade her to make the unfortunate transaction. Unable to find anything, the police had to release this man, who brought a suit of his own, charging the woman with defamation of character and wrongful accusation.

There was no word from Rowley P's family. And others were simply too embarrassed to want to be identified, much less quoted.

Surprisingly, Lindsay S came to my defense. He said that what I'd given to people during the time of my masquerade must not be discounted altogether, especially if, as many of my clients had claimed, they'd benefited from my handiwork. The new discovery of what I'd perpetrated ought not to reverse those benefits made possible by my touch, my applications, benefits that had allowed him, for example, to start work on a new suite of poems, which was about to be published. In his words of support I could spot the homosexual's tendency to project himself into the place of someone publicly vilified, hoping one day for someone to come to his defense when the likely occasion arose for his own vilification, but still I was grateful.

The round robin of Master Chao's progress through society, passed from one supposedly sophisticated client to another, never traced back to the introductory point of Shem. He rerouted the whole chain to point away from himself. But still, I was surprised that nobody decided to do any fact-checking.

The New York Times Magazine, in a how-to Feng Shui article that was half jokey and half earnest, asked an authentic Master to look in on the renovations I had suggested in the homes of three clients and to tally the things I had done wrong against what the proper procedures ought to be. In the left-hand column were all my mistakes, and in the right the remedies. Even the things that I thought I had executed properly were revealed to have been off.

And then, I discovered that two people were rushing out books about me to the printers, trying to beat each other: One was Max Brill Carlton, and the other, Paul Chan Chuang Toledo Lin. I half expected Bill Hood to join this list, in a book to be edited by the famed monologuist Cardie Kerchpoff. But he was on his deathbed, separated from the grief-stricken Suzy Yamada, a queen without a king and an heir.

This was how the race played out: Shem C slipped in under the wire, under the radar, and came out with his book first, beating everyone. It was an expanded version of the *New York* article, which was to say that it was gossipy, breathlessly firsthand, and was written in simple, direct sentences that were crammed with information and propelled the reader forward. It was, admittedly, hard to beat.

Max Carlton, wishing to return to the good graces of the critics who had crowed over *Primitives*, decided to go back to his former hamfisted, dumbed-down style, using me as the inspiration for a novel in which he expounded on "five-alarm themes" like affirmative action, immigration, who can you trust in this day and age?, the nature of expertise—all of which turned out to be the wrong "five-alarm themes." While Paul Lin tried to fit me into his patented, pet theme: Orientalism. But having already chewed over the novelty of that topic in his previous book and without the writing gift to improve upon the blatant journalistic facts of the case, he merely elicited yawns from the critics and from the book-buying public. Finally, he decided to out himself, giving himself new things to write about, but unfortunately this move was met with boos from his staunchest (Asian) supporters, for whom his sudden homosexuality was an impugning of their masculinity that they wanted promoted to the world and for which they believed they'd found the perfect spokesman in Lin.

So many things were said about me in these competing accounts. So many theories proffered, some of which, though untrue, had a density of thought that would have, if I hadn't been involved myself, struck me as highly likely. Still, nobody touched on the simple truth at the very heart of the matter, which was: How could it have been fraud if I myself believed—sealed in my belief by the death of Kendo, which had been effected by taking the faith and warping it for disastrous ends: Feng Shui to harm your life?

37

I bought a narrow-ruled notebook with light green margin-
less pages. I bought a blue ballpoint pen, nothing too nice
because I didn't want to have to take too much care. I
would just try to write the first thing that came to mind, not pausing over my handwriting or anything like that, or I would force
whatever puny inspiration there was back into hiding. Just nice,
simple sentences like those that I'd admired in the Simenons. I began:

This was my life.

*Every morning when I woke up, New York City announced itself
outside my window, and hearing it my face would immediately contort:
my first look of the day a ghoul mask. A million souls taking the
headachy subway. I felt myself there, with those people on the subway,
my ghoul face the real, undisguised look behind their placid, numbed
demeanors. I imagined myself next to them, getting on, getting off, hear
the tap dance of impatient feet, hear the shift in sound when those feet
turn from subway car to platform, and then onto the steps leading up to*

the light of another business day, pushing past the revolving doors of buildings so tall we all become ants, feet going into elevators, unsteady fingers pressing the buttons for up, or in some instances down, and already low shoulders further drooping when confronted with the doors they will go through, rooms of confinement for the next eight or so hours, to carry out menial tasks, as I had been doing. In a flash I made that trip as I woke up each morning. I never forgot, not to have to work was a gift, to be free, to be enslaved only in memory: and remembering this, remembering everything, the ghoul mask would slowly dissolve: a look of gratefulness would be the next and lasting look of my day.

This is my life.

My name is William Narciso Paulinha. I am Filipino. Not Chinese. I used to say yes to everything. Are you Puerto Rican? Why not? Dominican? Of course. Brazilian? Not only that, the boy from Ipanema to boot. Usually, these things didn't matter. Small lies, useful for ending unwanted conversations two lines in. Why bother to backtrack and tell your whole life story to a complete stranger? The pace of the city was fast, and the faster choice was what was needed. Drop them, and go forward . . .

38

I t was the tenth month. I marked another numeral off the calendar in my brain. I opened the curtains, peeked out to discover another day suffused with the same kind of light that, unless parceled out, would soon become like punishment. The man who was sent to track me down, kill me, that man who I was certain existed, and did his spy work with the patience of an immigrant, conditioned by laws that only he understood, could not be seen outside. I would go out again, catch another movie, spend my day under that vast awning of sky that made you feel like you were one floor below heaven, with some escalator ready to take you up unseen, hidden behind clouds. These same clouds also seemed to house all the dead looking down on me: Rowley, reunited with Adela; Kendo . . . whom I mustn't think of; Preciosa, who might as well have been dead . . . I would walk the streets with the face I've always had, but turned askew by a new, ugly haircut, and by overzealous washing each morning as if trying to return to a virgin status that had deserted me long ago. And without my forty-dollar pomade, my hair had returned to its original strawlike texture, sticking out in all directions, and this established for me the inarguable truth of something I'd always taken for false advertisement: that the rich, having the money to spend on themselves, were more attractive than the rest of us. Walking the malls of L.A., I felt that I was truly a changed person. It was only a matter of time before I began not looking Chinese, or even Filipino. I didn't know how it happened. Living in the sun, I turned darker by the day. Most times, people mistook me for John Wayne Indian. Sure, I told them. What tribe? they'd ask. And I would pick out the obvious brand names: Navajo, Cherokee, Cree—names I'd heard from the movies . . . I liked California. It was full of people like me, ghosts with histories receding daily. Next door to me lived a certified dope dealer, and next door to him, an ex–champion surfer with straggly blond hair and a bloated belly as if he was about to deliver any day. They had breakfast, lunch, and dinner at the 7-Eleven, and some days I joined them. They drank several six-packs a day, but I didn't. In the evenings, they would sit around talking in the courtyard that was nothing more than dry gravel and garbage. They would plop their butts on folding chairs and stare in front of them, ostensibly at the horizon, but there was really no horizon to speak of, just a lot of lights winking half-assedly like tired whores. I would hear them drone on into the night, bragging about the events that had destroyed and then condemned them to live out the rest of their lives in this apartment complex with strips of wood peeling off the ceiling and walls, and, everywhere you looked, lizards—green and brown and a no-color that made you think of corpse skin. There were so many of them, how did they fix on this place? These creatures were connected in some intangible way to the peeling wood and to the surfer's straggly hair and to the spiral of circumstances being narrated outside my window every night and pretty soon everything jumbled together into a kind of design that seemed like mysticism, something you couldn't take apart and analyze, but just had to go with—this was one thing I realized California did to your head. God felt so near, nearer than at any time in my life.

One day, I saved the surfer's dog from being run over, and when he found out, he turned full of exclamatory thanks, which was surprising, considering that I'd seen him kick this thing more than once and also go for days neglecting to feed it. It had to scavenge for itself in trash bins around the neighborhood, earning the neighbors' unceasing ire. Come to think of it, the dog was probably trying to commit suicide by going into the middle of the street. The surfer, not content with his effusive thanks, got down on his knees. He kissed his dog repeatedly, showily, saying that it was the only valuable thing left in a life that had run itself ragged but still refused to relinquish its breath. And then to top everything off, he broke down and cried. What kind of life was this that would bring a man down to his knees in front of a stranger and make him savor and at the same time torture a beloved companion? Too full of my own story, I didn't ask him to elaborate on his. And at night, when he was offering clues outside my window, I merely used it as a backdrop to my dead, dreamless sleep, like the buzz of an appliance used to eat up the stillness.

The surfer tried to stuff a trophy from his former life into my hands. Take this, man, he said. I refused. After all, a dog was so easy to love. It wasn't even bravery, natural instinct simply took over. At the same time, I resolved never to be caught doing good again. I didn't want to be good, I wasn't good, what was "good"?

He thrust the trophy in my face. It's got real gold, dude, he said, all you gotta do is scrape it off and sell it. I still refused.

All right, he said, pausing as if to collect thoughts that I knew would never come.

Finally, he let me go with a promise that I would collect on his debt. All I had to do was tell him what I needed and he'd be more than happy to oblige. He gave the dog a wet smack on the lips, but even the dog knew not to be fooled, licking the smack off with the quick flick of a tongue. As I was leaving, it followed me with its eyes and I swear the look in them was asking, Why did you even save me?

My shit had returned to solid blocks of dark brown, unchanged day after day. No more loose, runny, privileged Rich People Shit for me. My diet the same things I'd eaten when I'd previously lived in Los Angeles, cheap, starchy things usually a few days away from the printed expiration dates on the cans and containers.

I looked in the phone book for a listing of my family, but there was nothing, which left me with three possibilities, all of them equally unlikely: they'd gone back to the Philippines—unlikely because they detested the life back there; or they'd moved to another city, another state—they were the opposite of vagabonds and were in fact still exhausted from that lifetime trip to the States; or they'd just decided to pay the extra fifty cents a month to have the phone company take their number off the listing—they were just too damned cheap and unsophisticated for this to even enter their thinking. But what if there had been those miraculous seven digits? Would I have strung them together in my head, bouncing them around like balls for days, making sure the sound they made bouncing around was right before I called? Would I actually have called? And then what? Hung up? Or told them who was on the other end, trying to pick up from where he'd left off, giving them the satisfaction of a biblical parable fitted to their lives like a personal thumbs-up from God—the return of the prodigal son?

Most days, I walked around, sunglassed, looking into shop-windows and taking in the displays with the deep curiosity of a museumgoer. But it was only that I was made numb and that I couldn't, no matter how hard I tried, put a single thought together and so blinked blindly at objects on the off chance that they would reveal things to me. It was the perfect frame of mind to view movies in. I went daily, sometimes staking out a picture I liked again and again, so that the ticket vendors and the staff at the multiplexes came to regard me with a courtesy that made me realize I was now being looked at as an eccentric, as among those who might harbor criminal tendencies, as, for example, people who tried to shoot public figures—sociopaths who were discovered to listen to the same song or read the same book over and over again.

One movie I saw, about a bank heist gone wrong, stood out from the rest. In it, the perpetrators were each eventually touched by the finger of death. Each of these death scenes—most of them quick, but for the head perps slow and set up—made the audience gulp, relaxing tensed shoulders. You could tell that the audience wanted these people, these bank robbers dead. They'd done wrong and didn't have the saving grace of being name stars, and so deserved to die. And the movie was delivering in spades. From that, I could tell that it was going to be a hit.

The last person to die was—Jokey, who had risen enough in the last year to have his screen deaths postponed until the finale, therefore assuring him more screen time, but who still had not risen to the level of being thought of as life material.

Perhaps one day they would make a movie of my life and then they could cast him as Chao, and finally, he would be able to play the kind of part that had always eluded him: someone who lives, who, in that way, I suppose, triumphs.

Or would they, in the movies, kill me?

But apart from seeing Jokey again, my life remained an uninflected one of stalking around unbothered, until finally one day a thought succeeded in forming itself: that what had been a lifelong irritant—that I walked around the world unseen, as if invisible—had now become a strange and beautiful blessing, freeing me to live my life all over again, as if the previous one had only been a rough draft, a vague outline to be crossed over, exceeded, to be transcended, as if that life was the earthly life and this one, the California one, with myself benumbed and calm and floating inside the bubble of mall after white mall—places that were like hospitals with their piped-in music and blanching light—as if this life, finally, was the heavenly one.